Antonia's lips were entirely too near for reasonableness. He kissed them. And met a response so intense that it took his breath away and destroyed the last vestiges of his common sense.

After their first start of surprise her widened eyes had closed, her fingers had sent his hat toppling to entangle with his hair, and she had simply surrendered to the wonderful, heady glow that overpowered her. She would never have dreamed that the mere touch of his lips, the teasing of tongues, could turn the balance of nature topsy-turvy. All she really knew was that she wanted the moment to last forever— and this man to love her.

Both notions were ridiculous, of course. . . .

—*from* SCANDAL BROTH

By Marian Devon
Published by Fawcett Books:

GEORGIANA
MISS ARMSTEAD WEARS BLACK GLOVES
MISS ROMNEY FLIES TOO HIGH
M'LADY RIDES FOR A FALL
SCANDAL BROTH
SIR SHAM
A QUESTION OF CLASS
ESCAPADE
FORTUNES OF THE HEART
MISS OSBORNE MISBEHAVES
LADY HARRIET TAKES CHARGE
MISTLETOE AND FOLLY
A SEASON FOR SCANDAL
A HEART ON HIS SLEEVE
AN UNCIVIL SERVANT
DEFIANT MISTRESS
THE WIDOW OF BATH
THE ROGUE'S LADY
DECK THE HALLS
MISS KENDAL SETS HER CAP
ON THE WAY TO GRETNA GREEN

SCANDAL BROTH

♥

A QUESTION OF CLASS

Marian Devon

FAWCETT CREST • NEW YORK

A Fawcett Crest Book
Published by The Ballantine Publishing Group
Scandal Broth copyright © 1987 by Marian Pope Rettke
A Question of Class copyright © 1988 by Marian Pope Rettke

http://www.randomhouse.com

Library of Congress Catalog Card Number: 97-90962

ISBN 0-449-00209-8

Manufactured in the United States of America

First Edition: March 1998

10 9 8 7 6 5 4 3 2 1

Contents

Scandal Broth   1

A Question of Class   163

Scandal
Broth

Chapter
One

THE QUILL SCRATCHED RAPIDLY, FALTERED, STOPPED. MISS Antonia Thorpe brushed her nose absently with the goose feather and eyed her composition, quite unaware that she herself was under surveillance. "March 5, 1815," she read.

Dear Papa,
I arrived yesterday. Your concern was wasted. I proved an excellent sailor, not queasy once. Had the channel been rough, however, the story might have been quite different.

Oh, dear. Enough of that. Papa wouldn't be pleased to pay for an extra sheet, and he hated trying to read a crossed letter. She must bring him quickly up-to-date. Antonia sighed, dipped her pen in the inkwell, and tried again.

The Hall is even more grand than you described it. And everyone has been

Once more the quill's scratching ceased. This time the young composer tried blowing upon the feather for inspiration. None came. And she could not possibly write what was foremost in her mind—that she didn't like Uncle Edwin above half, found her Cousin Rosamond insipid, and England too bleak for words.

The pen made another journey to the inkwell, then hovered

indecisively above the paper. "Oh, botheration!" Antonia glared indignantly at the spreading inkblot.

"It seems I'm interrupting you, Miss Thorpe."

The voice that jerked her head up was deep, aristocratic, and tinged with irony. A gentleman wearing creamy buckskins and a superbly cut dark blue riding coat was standing in the open doorway watching her. "Of course, if my timing is inconvenient," he continued, managing to sound gentlemanly and faintly sarcastic at the same time, "we can always cancel this interview."

His actions, however, belied such flexibility. For the young man stepped inside, closing the door behind him. As he crossed the room to loom over her writing table, Antonia grew faintly alarmed. She looked up at him warily, feeling more at sea than at any moment during her recent voyage. What she saw was a man of twenty-eight who looked slightly older, who was rather above the average height and well above the average handsome. But most of all, and for reasons of his own, he was also above the average hostile.

Antonia, not normally so easy to intimidate, swallowed hard before inquiring, "You wished to speak to me, sir?" Her voice sounded tremulous to her own ears.

The gentleman abandoned any desire he might still have had to bridle his disgust. "Frankly, Miss Thorpe, I find your excessive missishness a bore. Keeping me dangling in the doorway with your faked preoccupation was too coy by half. We both know why I'm here. So under the circumstances it seems ludicrous to indulge in these charades. Ours is a business arrangement, purely and simply, and to view it otherwise is a hypocrisy I, for one, find intolerable."

"I can assure you, sir, that indulging in charades is the furthest thing from my mind." Antonia tried to make her tone placating while she glanced furtively around the room for a handy weapon. But the library did not lend itself to self-defense. What a pity her uncle had no taste for weaponry. True, there were some weighty tomes upon the shelves that lined the paneled walls, but getting to them could pose a problem. The brass poker by the Adam fireplace looked substantial enough to be effective but was also too far removed for practicality. The inkwell seemed less adequate but was at hand.

The deranged gentleman, Antonia concluded, was made more dangerous by lacking the physical prerequisites for a bedlamite. The deep blue eyes showed no tendency to roll; his gaze, in fact, threatened to impale her to her chair. Not only did his raven hair lack the required wisps of straw, it also was meticulously arranged, à la Titus, or she missed her guess. A square-cut jaw and high cheekbones were bound to give a deceptive look of character even to a maniac, she supposed. But despite all appearances to the contrary, there could be no doubt about it, the man confronting her was stark-raving mad. Her only resource was to humor him till she could summon help. She felt her way carefully.

"You spoke of a business arrangement we should discuss. I fear the matter has slipped my mind. Momentarily. But if you'll refresh my memory, I'm sure we can arrive at an understanding." To further demonstrate her desire to please, Antonia stretched the muscles of her face in a manner calculated to produce a smile. The effort evidently went awry. At least it failed to elicit the appropriate response. For instead of beaming back, the gentleman's countenance grew even more thunderous.

"See here, Miss Thorpe. I only arrived home yesterday. And"—he looked pointedly at the ormolu clock on the mantelpiece—"I have a great deal to do before leaving for London in the morning. I was given to understand that everything had been arranged by our respective parents and all I had to do was put in an appearance here. Now, if this directness doesn't coincide with your romantic notions, well then, I'm sorry. But I'm damned if I'm going down on one knee to you. Let's at least begin our liaison with honesty, if nothing else."

His blue eyes had narrowed during this impassioned speech. Antonia's had grown saucer-sized. She had ceased to be concerned about his mental state; it was her own that now concerned her. Surely she was imagining this whole scene. "Are you *offering* for me, sir?" she choked.

He swore. Not quite underneath his breath, if indeed that had ever been his intent. "Miss Thorpe, you might as well know

now that I am not a patient man. Just why you've chosen to be so coy about all this escapes me, but I'd be much obliged if you'd drop the pose. My father informs me that every detail—including your compliance, I might add—has been worked out between your father and himself. Furthermore, since you do stand to profit more from the arrangement than I do, though it's hardly gallant of me to say so, it does seem the outside of enough for me to be expected to jump through hoops. Frankly, Miss Thorpe, despite all my celebrated failings, it seems to me that you are to be congratulated on this match. Young ladies of your dubious background do not often get the opportunity to become baronesses."

"Are you calling me a cit, sir?" Antonia might be confused on every other point, but she did know an insult when she heard it. Her apprehension was rapidly turning into anger, overriding all her instinct regarding the proper kid-glove handling of bedlamites. She rose to her feet and glared across the table. "I don't know who you think you are, sir, to cast aspersions on my background. What's more, I don't believe for one moment that my father would arrange my marriage without consulting me. My father simply could not—" She suddenly faltered while her righteous indignation sputtered and went out. She stared up at the stranger, suddenly appalled. "At least I don't th-think he would," she stammered. "Of course, I didn't really see why he insisted that I come here. In fact, I'll grant you that it made very little sense to me at the time. But I never dreamed . . . Oh, how could he!" She sank down into her seat. "Of all the shabby, despicable—"

"Well, I may owe you an apology, Miss Thorpe," the gentleman said grudgingly. "Unless you're a better actress than Mrs. Siddons, it seems you really didn't know our marriage has been arranged. I agree that your father's conduct leaves a lot to be desired, but let's not allow that fact to divert us from the purpose of this meeting. For even if my offer does catch you unawares, I can't believe that you seriously object to it."

Antonia, who had been running through her father's professed reasons for packing her off to England—reasons that had seemed lame at the time and now appeared devious—

returned her full attention to her arrogant intended. "If you can't believe that I seriously object to marrying you, well, then, sir, I can only say that you show a serious want of imagination."

"I beg your pardon?"

"Am I not plain enough? I don't care what sort of arrangements my father may have made behind my back, I wouldn't marry you if you were the last—" She snapped her teeth shut on the cliché. The situation called for something fresh and new. But it was not forthcoming.

"Are you refusing me, Miss Thorpe?" His lip curled in disbelief.

"How could I possibly be? You haven't actually offered for me, have you?"

"So, we're back to that again." His jaw tightened. "Very well, then. If you must make me perform, so be it. Only I won't go down on one knee, by God. Well, this is it. Pray pay attention. Miss Thorpe"—his voice was as insulting as the exaggerated gesture with which he placed a hand upon his heart—"will you do me the honor of becoming my wife?"

"No."

"No?" His eyebrows rose. "Don't play games, Miss Thorpe. My father only requires that I ask, you know."

"Well, you just did so. Now please leave."

Relief warred with disbelief upon his face. "I trust you don't intend to change your mind the moment I walk out of here. For, let me warn you, I shall consider this your final word."

"Well, not quite my *final* word." Antonia surprised herself by discovering a need to prolong his agony. She had found it rather galling to have her answer taken in the spirit of a gallows reprieve. So now she gleefully watched the hope fade from his eyes and the hauteur return.

"So, it is not your final word?"

"Oh, dear me, no. My final word is that I find your attitude insulting and your arrogance insufferable. And I can feel nothing but deep pity for the poor female who does agree to be your baroness. For I would not marry you, sir," she finished triumphantly, "if you were next in line for king!"

The speech, intended to be crushing, fell far wide of the

mark. For the gentleman gave her a bow that was only halfway mocking and flashed a smile that came close to taking her breath away. "Well, then, Miss Thorpe, may I say that you have my admiration—to say nothing of my gratitude. For I never expected you to have the courage to defy your father. Nor did he, I'll wager!

"Well, now, pray forgive me for wasting so much of your time. And, if I'm not being premature again, allow me to wish you and your curate happy. Good day, Miss Thorpe." His step was light as he crossed the room and shut the library door with a firm click of the latch behind him.

Antonia sat rooted in her chair and stared at the closed door. "My curate?" she whispered faintly. "Wish me happy with a *curate*? Dear heavens, I was right in the first place. The poor gentleman is raving mad!"

Miss Thorpe did not long remain the only person to harbor misgivings about the Honorable Fitzhugh Denholm's mental stability. Her uncle, Sir Edwin Thorpe, who had been lurking in an antechamber off the hall in order to be the first to congratulate his distinguished visitor and welcome him into the family, could only gape incredulously after Mr. Denholm's terse announcement. "B-but that's impossible!" he blurted. "She can't have refused your offer. She wouldn't! Oh, you must be mistaken."

"I assure you, sir, that I am not." Mr. Denholm made very little effort to hide his distaste for the rotund, encroaching little man gaping up at him. "Miss Thorpe refused me in no uncertain terms."

He was thwarted in his attempt to walk on past Sir Edwin by that gentleman's convulsive clutch upon his sleeve. "Oh, well, now. You mustn't refine too much on that, sir. Why, it don't mean a thing." Sir Edwin tried without much success for jocularity. "A man of the world like yourself must know what women are."

"I'm man of the world enough to realize that no member of my sex knows what women are." He shook off the restraining hand. "Now, if you'll excuse me."

"Why, the chit just don't wish to appear overanxious, that's all." Sir Edwin interposed himself between the exit and his guest. "The ladies like to be coaxed, don't you know. Why, it's practically a rule with 'em not to accept a gentleman's first offer. Ain't considered good ton. Oh, but she means to have you, all right. You'll see."

"That I will not." Sir Edwin recoiled under the icy stare. "I have complied with my father's wishes and offered for Miss Thorpe. She in her turn has refused me. The matter is at an end."

A powdered footman, struggling to keep his face impassive, leaped for the door. But, as he afterward related in the servants' hall, "His nibs almost beat me to it and opened it himself—he was that anxious to be gone! Couldn't wait to see the last of Sir Edwin or I'm a Frenchy! And may God strike me blind if this ain't the very gospel, just before I went to shut the door behind him, I heard that starchy gentry cove go off whistling. Merry as a gig he was."

Chapter Two

"ROSAMOND!"
Regardless of whatever damage his nervous system might have been suffering, Sir Edwin had found tongue. His bellow preceded him down the hall and reverberated within the library where Antonia was trying to resume her composition. "So, there you are!" he thundered from the doorway as she raised her head. "Oh, blast it, no. It's you!"

Is there something about that threshold that turns English

gentleman into instant boors? Antonia wondered as she struggled not to take offense. And once again she was struck by the evenhanded treatment fate had accorded to two brothers. Her father had got the looks and charm; her uncle the estate and the business acumen. The only thing the two Thorpes had in common was that both had married delicate females who'd died young. Sir Edwin now looked ready to follow suit from a fit of apoplexy. "Is something wrong, Uncle?" she inquired with sympathy.

"Wrong? Wrong? I should say something's wrong!" Sir Edwin swelled with indignation while his niece watched in alarm, expecting his waistcoat buttons to become projectiles at any moment. "Things are as wrong as they possibly can be, miss. I would never have believed that my own flesh and blood could make a mockery of all me dreams. Rosamond!" he shouted again. "Where is that girl?"

Antonia glanced upward at the crystal chandelier, fearful the glass had cracked. "I rather think Rosamond's gone for a walk, sir. At least, as I was coming downstairs to write Papa, I saw her leave her room wearing a cloak and pattens."

"Going outside! Going for a walk! Running away from home, most likely! Afraid to face me, b'gad, and well she should be. Of all the wretched, ungrateful girls! To fling away her chances with no concern for what it might do to her father! Oh, my God!" Suddenly in need of support, Sir Edwin clutched the edge of the writing table and stared down at his niece. His mouth was working soundlessly, like a beached cod's.

Antonia, on her part, resolved never to sit in that particular spot again. One more encounter like the two endured this morning and she'd swim back to Belgium. Her uncle, after several swallows and a huge gulp of air, managed to croak, "Just how long have you been sitting here?"

"Since about ten-thirty."

"And Rosamond went outdoors, you say, just as you were coming down the stairs?"

"Yes, sir, so I assume."

Sir Edwin just did manage to totter to the nearest wing chair before collapsing. "Then, it was you he talked to." His voice had sunk to whisper level, and his eyes were glazed.

Should she ring for the butler? Antonia wondered. Her uncle appeared to need a restorative, at the very least. But just as she half rose, intending to walk to the bellpull, the scales dropped from her uncle's eyes and he glared at her through a red haze of fury. "Is that what happened, miss?" he spit.

This sudden alteration of mood wiped the bellpull from her mind. Her uncle's latest start demanded full attention. By some freak of nature, had the entire male population of Kent gone queer in the attic this morning? "Is what what happened, sir?" she asked aloud, groping for reality.

"Did the Honorable Fitzhugh Denholm come in here while you were sitting there?" A trembling finger pointed accusingly.

"Well, someone certainly did come in. But he hadn't the civility to introduce himself. Now that I think on it, he did say he'd be a baron someday, so I suppose that could make him an Honorable now. I never could keep track of—"

"Will you stop blathering!" Sir Edwin was on his feet again, his mien choleric. "Just tell me what Mr. Denholm said!"

"Well, I'll try. But it won't be easy. He took me entirely by surprise. And was quite incoherent."

"Damn it, girl! What exactly did he say?"

"I'm doing my best to remember." Antonia had had a tiring morning. Respect for her elders was wearing thin. She glared back at her uncle in kind. "It's not easy to reconstruct the interview, for the gentleman was obviously raving mad—or next door to it. He actually seemed to be offering for me. Said his father and mine had worked the whole thing out—which I'll not believe Papa would do without first telling me. Besides, the gentleman was absolutely furious at the notion. Nasty and insulting. Obviously a bedlamite. For, if that was his idea of a proper marriage offer, I'd hate to be around when he challenged someone to a duel. Still, under normal quarrelsome circumstances perhaps he'd be the soul of amiability."

"You nincompoop!" Sir Edwin regained his roar. "Do you realize what you've done? Oh, don't bother looking at me with those big innocent eyes—of course you do! Oh, I knew I never

11

should have agreed to let Adrian foist you off onto me. Bad blood! That's what I told him when he married, and by gad, I've been proved right. Bad blood! Will show up in the third generation every time. A viper in my bosom. That's what your father's sent me—a viper!"

"Uncle Edwin!" Antonia's voice shook with rage. "How dare you speak to me in such a fashion? There's nothing at all the matter with my blood. Not unless I've inherited some taint from you that I don't know of. For you must be dicked in the nob, sir, to fly up into the boughs this way. Will you please calm down and try to tell me sensibly just what it is you think I've done?"

"Done? Done?" To match another sudden mood swing, Sir Edwin's voice rang hollow. "You know perfectly well, young woman, what you've done. And if this is your warped idea of a prank—well, all I can say is that your father at his worst, which was certainly bad enough for a more feckless fellow—" He pulled himself up short. "Your father at his worst would not have stooped so low. Bad blood—"

"Uncle Edwin, don't you dare start up about my blood again. Just tell me, calmly, what this is all about. *What am I supposed to have done?*"

"You've pretended to be Rosamond; that's what you've done. You've pretended to be me gel and ruined her life."

"I've done no such thing. Of all the sap-skulled notions. Why ever would I? Oh, my goodness—" Stunned disbelief overrode her anger. "Surely you don't mean—" A gurgle of laughter inadvertently escaped before her good sense could act as censor. "Are you trying to say that that odious man actually thought he was offering for Rosamond? Oh, but that's too absurd."

"Absurd, you say. What's absurd is to pretend you didn't know it. You—you—viper!"

"Uncle, you are making it most difficult for me to maintain my composure. Of course I didn't know it. In the first place, I thought the man was mad. And in the second, he called me 'Miss Thorpe,' which is my name. Even you must admit I've as much right to it as Rosamond. More perhaps. I've had it four

12

months longer. And I certainly never dreamed that a man would offer a serious proposal of marriage to a woman he doesn't even know. Can't recognize. Who *would* think it?"

"Of course he knows her," Sir Edwin blustered. "He saw her grow up. Our estates march together. It's just that he's been out of the country for the past eight years and would expect to find her changed. And I suppose you two do look a bit alike." This notion did not seem to please him. "So, it was a perfectly normal mistake for the Honorable Fitzhugh Denholm to make. What was not normal was for you to allow him to continue under such a misapprehension. I call that low, miss."

"Oh, do you, sir?" They were at daggers drawn now and no mistake. Neither the avuncular tie nor the gray hairs that ringed his shiny pate could put a damper on her anger. "Well, I won't waste my breath any longer trying to convince you of my innocence. But if you insist on putting the worst possible interpretation on my encounter with the future baron, let me give you this to chew on, Uncle. Just what would you be saying to me if I had accepted his nibs's so-called proposal? There, I thought that might overset you. Well, now, sir, if you continue to treat me in this high-handed fashion, I might just send word to the Honorable Lunatic that I've changed my mind and will marry him after all."

"Oh, my God!" Sir Edwin, poleaxed, collapsed back down upon his chair, groping for a handkerchief to blot the beads of perspiration that had erupted on his forehead. And his niece, recognizing the perfect exit line once she'd uttered it, went sweeping from the room with her head held high.

This lofty attitude made vision difficult. Antonia collided with her cousin, who'd been kneeling by the keyhole. "Shhh!" Rosamond put a finger to her lips warningly, then grabbed Antonia's hand. She pulled her cousin upstairs and into her bedchamber, where she quickly locked the door and leaned against it. "We must talk," she whispered with a conspiratorial air.

"No, we mustn't." Antonia spoke at normal volume and ignored her cousin's "Shhh!" "At least, we aren't going to talk till you've ordered tea. And something to go with it, when it comes to that. I've already had two too many interviews this morning, and something tells me I'm not going to like this one above half either. Why didn't you go to the library as you were supposed to? No, don't answer yet. I certainly don't blame you for wishing to avoid that odious Mr. What's-his-name. But why did you allow me to walk straight into the lions' den, for heaven's sake? No, don't answer that question either. For heaven's sake, Rosamond, ring for tea!"

Antonia ignored her cousin's fidgeting and ate her way stolidly through a huge slice of nuns' cake and a ginger nut, washed down by two cups of China tea. Rosamond, jumping up every few seconds from the Grecian couch the cousins shared to listen at the door for footsteps or to cross the floor to peer out between damask curtains, refused all food and found little time for tea.

"For goodness sake, do sit down, Rosamond. You'll wear the carpet out. Try a ginger nut. They're quite delicious."

"Oh, how can you eat at a time like this?" Her cousin moaned reproachfully while plopping down again upon the couch.

"Easily. I need the fortification." Antonia touched her lips daintily with the linen napkin before replacing it upon the tray. "All right now. This should sustain me through your explanation. What sort of mare's nest have I stumbled into?"

Rosamond's story came tumbling out amid much hand-wringing and some few tears. Lord Worth, the county's most awesome aristocrat, she explained, had commanded his scapegrace son to return to England and reclaim his character by marrying his highly respectable young neighbor. "L-lord Worth thinks I'm the perfect choice for Denholm, don't you see, not only because our estates march together and Papa's rich, but also because no hint of scandal has ever been associated with the Thorpe name. And though the Denholm family is well above our touch in the normal way of things, Lord Worth says I more than make up for that by being so—so very—"

"Dull?" Her cousin hazarded a guess.

"Retiring. You see, no one would ever have heard of me, and we could marry and live quietly and raise a family." She paused to shudder. "And soon, so Lord Worth thinks, everyone would completely forget about Mr. Denholm's lurid past. But I don't believe that for a moment, Antonia. At least, I know I shall never be able to look at him without recalling it."

"My goodness." Antonia stared at her cousin with alarm. "What has he done?"

"What hasn't he done?" the other replied darkly.

"I've no notion. But I'd advise you to start naming the deeds, not the omissions, before I scream."

"Well, for the worst—at least, I hope it was the worst, for Papa wouldn't tell me very much and I had to pry the story out of one of the maids, who keeps company with a Denholm footman—he was caught, well, you know, in 'flagrante delicto' "—she was quite proud of the highsounding phrase—"with this married woman. And then the husband called him out. And they fought a duel, and the husband almost died. And he and the woman had to run away to Venice." She paused for breath.

"And where's the woman now?"

"I'm not through." Rosamond gave her cousin an injured look. Antonia did not seem sufficiently impressed by this lurid history. But then, what could you expect from a soldier's daughter who had been reared abroad? "There's worse to come. This all happened years ago, you see, seven or eight anyhow, when the Honorable Fitzhugh was twenty. Anyway, the scandal had all but died down, and Lord Worth was thinking of fetching him home again. His lordship didn't wish to disinherit Mr. Denholm, who's an only child, you see. But then Lord Lytton—it was Lady Lytton Mr. Denholm had run away with—fell in love and wished to marry again. So he tried to get a parliamentary divorce, which fanned the whole scandal back to life again just when it was dying down. And then what do you suppose?"

"I haven't the faintest notion." Antonia's head was developing a tendency to spin.

"They found out that the Lytton marriage had never been valid in the first place. For Lady Lytton was already married to someone else. She'd been very young, and it was a secret marriage. He was a sailor and the thing didn't take right from the start, so they both just chose to forget all about it."

"How very convenient," Antonia murmured.

"Well, no, not really. For the bigamy came to light in the divorce proceedings."

"Well, at least it solved Lord—who did you say?—Lytton's problem."

"Well, yes, in a way. But it rather made a laughingstock of both him and Mr. Denholm. All that fighting over a woman's honor who hadn't ever had any. And to make things even more complicated, the sailor suddenly inherited a title and a fortune that he had formerly been only third in line for. Or fourth, perhaps. I've forgotten which. But at any rate, he was definitely a long shot. Well, when this happened, Lady Lytton, as she'd been called, suddenly remembered he was the one she'd loved all along and went back to him."

"Poor Mr. Denholm," Antonia remarked with a total absence of sincerity. "Sounds as though he got his just deserts. But at least there's no light-o'-love now to prevent his picking up his old life again. The prodigal returns, and all of that." (She almost compared Rosamond to the fatted calf but fortunately thought better of it.) "And his father's probably right. Folk will soon forget his history. So I expect," she opined shrewdly, "that there's more to your aversion, Rosamond, than just Mr. Denholm's past."

The other Miss Thorpe was deeply shocked. "More! My heavens, Antonia, isn't the fact that he's a rake, a libertine, a here-and-thereian enough?"

"Well, I suppose so," the other agreed doubtfully. "Though, personally, I'd prefer his reputation above his odious arrogance. Still, they go together, I daresay."

"Well, I certainly could never marry a man like that," Rosamond said virtuously, then added with her chin quivering, "Oh, Antonia, do you think Papa will force me to?"

Privately Antonia believed her uncle capable of any sort of despicable behavior. But this was not time to be candid with her cousin, who was clearly terrified of the inevitable interview with her irate parent. Rosamond's fit of quakes might well prove terminal. "Well, at least Uncle Edwin's giving himself time to calm down," she remarked heartily, "and when he does, he'll doubtlessly think twice about forcing you into a marriage that you find so distasteful. You did acquaint him with your feelings, I collect."

"Well, I tried to. But you know Papa."

Again Antonia thought it kinder not to comment.

"I got no further than telling him of the attachment between Mr. Hollingsworth and myself when he went flying off into the boughs and there was no reasoning with him."

"Mr. Hollingsworth?" Antonia's eyebrows rose. "Ah-ha! I rather thought there might be more to this than the rakish Mr. Denholm's reputation."

Her cousin looked offended. "I can assure you, that is quite enough. Who would wish to marry such a man?"

"According to him, no end of females. And if he's as rich as you say and has a title in his future, I expect he was right in that much at least. Oh, by the by, is your Mr. Hollingsworth a curate?"

Her cousin looked astonished. "How ever did you know?"

"It stands to reason. No, no, I was only funning. As a matter of fact, Mr. Denholm mentioned that among his ravings."

"Oh, my heavens! Then, Mr. Denholm knows about Cecil. How awful!"

"Why awful? If you ask me, Mr. Denholm is your greatest ally in this matter. For he seems no more anxious for the match than you are. Less, if anything. Really I can't think what possessed the man to make his offer. He didn't strike me as the type to be forced into a marriage against his will. But it obviously was the case. For I tell you, Rosamond, he looked at me as if I were an insect. Anyhow, your troubles are over, for, believe me, Mr. Denholm has washed his hands of the whole affair."

"But that's absurd. He hasn't even seen me. It's you he's washed his hands of."

Antonia stared at her cousin, not believing at first that she was serious. "Oh, come now. He thought he *was* offering for

17

you. And obviously he hated the necessity. Do you really think the sight of you would have changed all that?"

The question hung unanswered. Rosamond assumed a look of modesty while Antonia tried to assess her cousin from a male point of view.

It was easy enough to see how the case of mistaken identity could have happened. There was a strong family resemblance between the cousins. Both had fair hair, for instance. But Rosamond's was flaxen, Antonia's of a slightly darker hue. Rosamond's lovely blue eyes were ingenuous; her cousin's, as vivid in their color, had the disconcerting habit of seeing far too much. Rosamond's figure was smaller, softer; her mouth was "rosebud" as opposed to "generous." And if Antonia considered her cousin a trifle vapid, she was of the opinion that most gentlemen would find her otherwise. "Perhaps you're right," she conceded grudgingly. "Mr. Denholm probably would have reacted differently to you. But now tell me about your Mr. Hollingsworth."

Mr. Hollingsworth and Rosamond, it seemed, had been meeting regularly in the lane, quite by accident, ever since he'd come to assist the local vicar six months before. The curate was handsome, sensitive, and very much in love. He was not, however, so Antonia gathered, of the required mettle to beard her ogre of an uncle in his den, let alone stand up against the power of Lord Worth. Mr. Hollingsworth was, in fact, prepared to play the martyr and lose his love.

Antonia fought hard to hide her contempt for such spineless resignation. It was easy to see from the love light in her eyes that Rosamond considered the Reverend Mr. Hollingsworth the perfect beau ideal.

"You could always elope," she offered; then seeing the shocked look on her cousin's face, "Well, perhaps not," she retracted.

"Mr. Hollingsworth is a *curate*." Surely, Rosamond's tone implied, even a cousin reared in foreign parts should see the incompatibility of that particular vocation and an elopement. Her eyes brimmed with tears. "Oh, what shall I do, Antonia? Papa will get his way. I know it. He always does."

"Not if you stand up to him, he won't. He can hardly drag you to the altar, Rosamond. You simply must not allow him to rule your life to such a degree."

The only effect this stouthearted assertion had upon her cousin was to cause the tears to well over and cascade. Still, the exhortation to the troops was not entirely wasted. For Antonia recognized the promptings of her inner voice for what they really were. Let Rosamond quail and quake if that was her nature. But she for one, by Jupiter, was not going to remain in Kent much longer beneath her Uncle Edwin's autocratic thumb!

Chapter Three

WHEN THE LONDON COACH DEPARTED FROM THE VILlage inn the next morning, Antonia was on it. Leaving the Hall undetected had been no problem. Sir Edwin had been closeted in the library with his only child since breakfast-time, dictating her future. Antonia had simply put on her dove-colored lutestring pelisse with its matching bonnet, picked up her portmanteau, and trudged off down the avenue unobserved, her breath fogging in the crisp morning air. She'd left a note for her uncle with the inn landlord to be delivered after the coach's departure.

The Honorable Fitzhugh Denholm had not escaped his ancestral seat quite so smoothly. The interview after his return from Thorpe Hall had been stormy, with his incensed parent accusing him of deliberately antagonizing Miss Thorpe. "It was all arranged," Lord Worth, distinguished-looking and still handsome despite his years and habitual expression of discontent, paced up and down the library while his son watched stonily from a stance before the fireplace. "Sir Edwin and I had come to a perfect understanding."

"So you said. Unfortunately, no one seemed to have consulted Miss Thorpe's feelings. Believe me, sir, the young lady was adamant."

"You can't have behaved properly."

"If you're implying that I did not go down upon one knee and declare my undying love, then you're right. Hypocrisy is not my style, sir."

"No, that's the one vice you seem to lack." The parent spoke bitterly while the son's jaw tightened.

"Even if I had played the part of the smitten suitor," Denholm replied, just managing to rein in his temper, "I don't think it would have made any difference. In spite of what Sir Edwin may have led you to believe, Miss Thorpe strikes me as a young lady who makes up her own mind. She does not wish to marry me."

"Well, sir"—Lord Worth stopped his pacing to face his son accusingly—"yours has been a spectacular achievement. You have brought the proud name of Denholm so low that even the daughter of a jumped-up squire—my God, the man's barely more than a cit—refuses to share it. And who can blame her? None of us will ever outlive the scandal you've brought down upon our heads."

"None of us? I can assure you, sir, that I for one do not intend to remain as encumbered by my history as you appear to be. I'm sorry that my indiscretions have caused you humiliation. Too sorry, in fact, since remorse made me override my better judgment and offer for a girl whose acceptance would have made us both miserable. Thank God, she, at least, seemed to have some common sense in operation. Be that as it may, when you're cataloging my list of sins, do acknowledge the fact that I tried to please you—and with my usual lack of success, I might add. Now I intend to follow my own inclinations and go to London."

"To London! You can't be serious! Your appearance can only serve to revive all the old scandal."

"Then, let it. I assure you, sir, I'll be no more than a nine-day wonder before the gossipmongers find other wares to sell. And even if I have a longer run"—he shrugged indifferently—"I certainly do not intend to rusticate for the rest of my life in order to avoid being the subject of their drawing-room tittle-tattle."

"It's too much, I suppose, to expect the sort of conduct due your name."

"Not at all, sir." The Honorable Fitzhugh Denholm smiled crookedly. "As you took pains to point out when you summoned me back home, my chief duty is to produce an heir—legitimate, of course—to carry on that name. And since I've exhausted the only matrimonial prospects the neighborhood has to offer, I'm forced to look elsewhere for a bride. What better place to search than the marriage marts of London?"

After this painful session, Denholm's intent had been to leave early the next morning and avoid a further confrontation with his father. In this he was successful. He was not quite early enough, though, to avoid his mother's tearful farewell. Lady Worth's unspoken reproaches were far harder to bear than his father's haranguing. Therefore Mr. Denholm was in the blackest of black moods when he tooled his curricle into the yard of the Cock and Magpie.

But even had his disposition been sunnier, he probably would have paid little heed to the public coach just pulling out upon the highway with an overload of passengers jammed inside and the leftovers perched precariously on the top. Nor did Miss Antonia Thorpe, squeezed between a farmer's wife and a drawing master suffering a bad cold, bother to glance out at the "bang-up-to-the-nines rig" the latter had mentioned with a touch of envy in his denasalized voice.

She was far too busy having second thoughts about the rashness of the decision she had come to. What Papa would say about her flight from the Hall didn't bear thinking on. Nor could she be totally sure that her grandmother would welcome with open arms a grandchild she'd never yet clapped eyes on.

The letters that arrived from Mrs. Blakeney once a year along with some handmade remembrance for her birthday had always been warm, affectionate. Of course, Grandmother would be glad to see her, Antonia stoutly assured herself. Whatever had caused the rift between her closest relatives, it certainly had had nothing to do with her.

Major Thorpe had always refused to discuss his deceased wife's mother. But somehow Antonia had formed the impression that it had been her grandmother who had severed the relationship. For it was apparent from those annual letters that Mrs. Blakeney was a nabob. Major Thorpe had evidently married well above his touch. And the scandal of her only child's elopement with the second son of an undistinguished family had obviously been too much for Mrs. Blakeney's pride to bear. But she'll be happy to see me, I know she will. Antonia squelched her nagging doubts. Blood's thicker than water, they always say.

And ale more satisfying. Mr. Denholm was reviving himself with a pewter tankard when a hand clapped convivially on his back splashed some of its contents upon the oaken bar. "My word, Fitz, it really is you! Thought for a minute there I was seeing ghosts."

Denholm turned to look into the round, beaming face of Lord Thayer Edgemon, a crony from his schooldays. "Thay— you old son of a—what the devil are you doing here?"

Lord Thayer, it seemed, was also on his way to London. And after a brief résumé of each other's activities during the past eight years, the old friends strolled out into the inn yard together, where they stood for a moment, each admiring the other's cattle.

"You *used* to be a famous whip, Fitz," Lord Thayer observed casually, smoothing the soft leather of his driving gloves. "I expect wallowing in the fleshpots of Italy changed all that, though."

"You think so? And I was wondering if the Whip Club hasn't lowered its standards disgracefully since I've been away." Denholm's eyes flashed wickedly as he drank in the ankle-length drab-colored coat with the enormous mother-of-pearl buttons and three tiers of pockets that marked his friend's membership in the elite driving club. "Care to try me?"

"Thought you'd never ask." Lord Thayer grinned.

And so it followed that two sporty curricles went tooling down the King's Highway in the London direction at a fast and furious pace.

The coachman saw them coming, neck and neck, just before he reached a sharp bend in the road. Quite losing his head, he cracked his long whip out over the backs of his four horses and took the curve too fast. Lord Thayer gained the lead and swept on past him. Mr. Denholm, cursing, pulled up his pair as the stagecoach rocked precariously, then slowly tilted sideways into the ditch, coming to rest against a steep bank prickly with hoarfrost.

The coachman, knowing where his interests lay, looked to his horses. It was left to Mr. Denholm to disgorge the passengers from the angled coach. He had at last succeeded in heaving a shrieking, overweight matron into a sitting position and had then tugged her along the seat and up and out the door, when, panting from the exertion, he turned back to assist the others and met fully the enraged gaze of Miss Thorpe. "My God, it's you!" he ejaculated.

"I might have known" was the tight-lipped reply. "You seem to have become my personal nemesis."

"What the devil are you doing here?" He lifted her from the coach, even in his preoccupation thankful for her lightness.

"I *was* traveling to London," she began bitterly, "until two irresponsible ninnyhammers decided to turn the highway into a racecourse."

"Now, look here. If that cow-handed coachman—" he began until the driver in question, along with the irate passengers, closed in around him and made Miss Thorpe's comments the highlight of his day.

Some time had elapsed, and his purse was considerably lighter, the contents having greased palms all around, before the Honorable Fitzhugh Denholm climbed back into his curricle, envying the callousness that had enabled his friend to go barreling along, oblivious of disaster. He was just about to crack his own whip when his eyes were pulled back, against his will, to the stranded group of passengers. Miss Thorpe, looking very young and quite forlorn, stood at its edge. A slimy-looking character, a thatch-gallows if he'd ever seen one, was edging toward her. Cursing once more underneath his breath, Denholm dismounted. As he approached, the slimy one slithered away.

"Surely you aren't traveling alone," he said abruptly.

"Surely I am. Being new to this country, I was unaware of its hazards. No one told me of the maniacs upon the road."

Denholm chose to rise above her conversational level. "Where are you going?" he asked with resignation.

Her opinion of his mental faculties had been poor from their earliest acquaintance. It had now reached bottom. "To London," she replied carefully, distinctly. "This is the *London* coach you've just overturned."

"*Where* in London?" His patience was on short leash.

"Oh. Grosvenor Square."

"Come on. I'll take you."

"But I can't go with you."

"Don't be tiresome. If you wish to stay in this company, it's all one with me." He nodded toward the probable cut-purse who averted his ferret eyes. "Just hang on to your reticule."

Denholm, in the act of climbing into his curricle, heard rapid footsteps. With a notable lack of enthusiasm he jumped down to help Miss Thorpe up onto the red-leather seat, then took his place and sprang the horses.

They rode in stony silence for a while, the curricle moving briskly. She stole covert glances at his face. He was frowning in concentration. Something she'd said kept niggling at his mind. "What did you mean back there about being new to this country?" he finally asked.

Antonia gave a scornful laugh. "You still haven't the slightest notion who I am, now, have you?"

"Of course, I know who you are." He looked her up and down as though in confirmation. She found it rankled that he seemed unimpressed by what he saw. "You're Miss Thorpe of Thorpe Hall."

"I—you dolt—am Miss Thorpe of Brussels. That's in Belgium, in case you'd care to know."

He gave her glare for glare. "What the devil are you raving on about, Miss Thorpe? I knew you in leading strings."

"It's news to me if you ever did. If you actually even bothered, which I seriously doubt, to look down your nose at a neighbor's child, well, then, you saw my Cousin Rosamond. So now you know, you loose screw. You proposed to the wrong woman!"

Chapter Four

"I DID WHAT?"

"You heard me right." Antonia was suddenly enjoying herself. Riding in this fine equipage, breathing deep of the crisp, country air, was certainly preferable to the crowded, stuffy coach. What's more, she'd finally managed to plant a leveler. The starchy Mr. Denholm was reeling from the shock. His eyes were glazing over. "That offer of marriage you flung in my teeth was evidently intended for my cousin Rosamond. I am *Antonia* Thorpe."

"Then, why the devil couldn't you have said so?"

"Why the dev—that is to say, why should I have introduced myself? Never in my wildest imagination did it occur to me that a man would offer for a lady's hand without even knowing who she was. I took you for a bedlamite. As a matter of fact, I'm still not convinced—"

"How the deuce was I supposed to guess you were a ringer?

Old Thorpe has only one daughter—who, so he said, was waiting for me in the library. I had the vaguest recollection of a fairhaired little moppet with big blue eyes. You fit the description. The two of you must look a great deal alike."

"Not that much. Actually, my cousin is a nonpareil."

"Fishing?" He sneered.

"No." Her color heightened. "Trying to make you feel regretful, I suppose."

"Well, you'll not do that. Your cousin could be the reincarnation of Venus for all I care. I still wouldn't—Oh, my God!" The full implication of his position had just hit him. "Then, I haven't been rejected. Well, it seems I've left in the nick of time. When my father learns of my mistake, it will be bellows to mend with me." His jaw set grimly.

Miss Thorpe was scornful. "It is beyond me why a man of your age—not even to say of your reputation"—she quailed a bit under the look he shot her but stuck to her guns—"should allow himself to be pushed into a marriage that obviously disgusts him. But let me assure you that my cousin desires the match even less. Though I don't think for a minute," she confided in a rush of candor, "that Rosamond will have the backbone to stand up against my Uncle Edwin. But it does seem odd that you should be so spineless."

"It might be just as well, Miss Thorpe"—he slowed down his team to rest it—"if you refrained from speculating about matters that are none of your affair."

"None of my affair!" she blazed. "How dare you say so? You made it my affair when you offered for me. Now Uncle blames me for the whole ridiculous situation. Just how he thought I was supposed to know you were coming to offer marriage to my cousin when I'd only just arrived the evening before and had never even heard of you, let alone of your intentions, defies all reason. It was Rosamond he should have rung his peal over instead of me. She not only ran away like a scared rabbit, afraid to face you, but she saw me walk into the library and didn't lift a finger to warn me away. But did my uncle raise his voice to her? Oh, no! *I* was the one responsible for ruining my cousin's prospects." She glared at a weather-cock atop a stone barn that they were passing.

The Honorable Fitzhugh Denholm studied her thoughtfully, a look of comprehension dawning in his eyes. "I'm not usually such a slow-top, Miss Thorpe. But I have had a great deal to occupy me—a rejected proposal, a row with my father, a reunion with an old friend, the race, the wreck; is it any wonder that I've become dull-witted? But a young lady traveling alone, with no baggage to speak of—break it to me gently, Miss Thorpe, for my nerves aren't at their best. Are you or are you not running away?"

"I would not call it that," she answered stiffly.

"Then, let me phrase it differently. Does Sir Edwin know you've gone?"

"He will when the note I wrote at the Cock and Magpie is delivered."

"I see. Well, well, well. It's true, then. Miss Thorpe of Brussels is running away. That note should send your uncle flying up into the boughs. But it won't be a circumstance compared to the news that you've run away with me."

"Run away with you? Whatever are you raving on about? No one in his right mind would think a thing like that."

"Your uncle's bound to. You've just said that he already suspects you of deliberately intercepting his daughter's proposal. Now here we are, tooling off to London together. My God, I can already feel the noose tightening."

"Well, loosen it," she snapped. "I'm no jellyfish like Rosamond to be forced into a marriage. Nor is my own father the toadeater Uncle Edwin is. He would never be so blinded by a title that he'd not care who bore it."

"I think I've just been insulted, but never mind. Your words still bring relief. Now tell me, who is it you plan to visit at Grosvenor Square? You do have someone waiting for you there with open arms?"

"Of course." There was more conviction in her voice than she was feeling. "I'm going to stay with my grandmother in her town house."

"I can't tell you how gratified I am to hear it," he murmured

27

as he looked with narrowed eyes at the road ahead. "Damn and blast!" They were coming to a posting house, and he'd spied a familiar vehicle in its yard. "Thayer's waiting for me," he said by way of explanation for his outburst. "Wants me to pay up now, no doubt. Well, he'll have to whistle for his winnings. It took all my blunt to grease the coachman."

"You actually wagered on that race? That's disgusting. How could you?"

"Oh, easily enough. It was money in the bank till your coachman lost his head and landed in the ditch." He turned his team into the inn yard.

"Oh, indeed?" Her tone was scathing. "It did not escape my notice that you were behind."

"Only temporarily, m'dear." He grinned suddenly, an act that changed his whole countenance and caused her to look at him curiously.

Lord Thayer was emerging from the inn, wiping his lips fastidiously with a snowy handkerchief as Denholm reined in beside his curricle. His lordship's eyebrows threatened to unseat the jaunty beaver he was wearing as he strolled toward them. "Wondered what kept you, Fitz," he remarked affably. "Might've known. See you ain't lost any of your old touch. Who else could go to the rescue of a coachload of cits and come up with a gorgeous bit o' muslin. Oh, I say!" He was pulled up short by the warning look on his old friend's face.

"I can see, Thayer," Denholm groaned, "that you haven't lost the knack of putting your boots in your mouth. Miss Thorpe, allow me to present Lord Thayer Edgemon. Miss Thorpe, Thayer, is the niece of my neighbor, Sir Edwin Thorpe. She had the misfortune to be a passenger on the coach that you forced in the ditch with your cow-handed driving."

"Oh, I say, Fitz." His lordship was stung by the accusation. "Don't call me 'cow-handed.' That coachman had all the room in the world to let me pass." Suddenly recollecting his manners, he turned quite pink. "Honored to make your acquaintance, ma'am. Pay no attention to what I said. Should have thought. It's just that Fitz here is noted for . . . that is, he used to be—" He grew more flustered.

"Your apologies are about as graceful as your driving, Thayer. Which, by the by, hasn't improved at all during the time I've been away. I was right. They must let anything into the Whip Club nowadays." He chose to ignore Miss Thorpe's face and kept his attention upon Lord Thayer.

"You've got no cause to be insulting," the other blustered. "Beat you, didn't I?"

"Technically, yes. But actually, without leaving all that mayhem in your wake, which of course you knew I'd have to stop for, you couldn't have done it in a million years."

"Fustian!"

"Oh?" Mr. Denholm's eyebrows now outdid his friend's for altitude. "Are you just blow, Thayer? Or would you like to put the matter to the test? We're about—what—five miles from the next crossroads? Would you care to make it double or nothing for the one who reaches it first?"

"What about her?" His lordship nodded toward the passenger. "Miss Thorpe, that is to say."

"Oh, she don't weigh much. And I'm sure she's game. Aren't you, Miss Thorpe?"

She was opening her mouth to assert that indeed she was not about to be a party to another disgraceful race on a public highway when he quelled her with a look. "See, the lady doesn't object, Thayer. So how about it; are you game?"

"Don't see why I should have to beat you twice," the other grumbled. Then his sense of fair play, egged on by a conscience troubled over ignoring the plight of the passengers in the coach, came to the fore. "Still, if you ain't convinced. Double or nothing? Hmmm. Oh, but I say, I've had a chance to rest me cattle and you ain't. Don't want you coming up with any fresh excuse, Fitz, when I beat you a second time."

Denholm was about to waive this objection when prudence intervened. Though he was confident of beating his old friend, he was not nearly as unimpressed with the other's skill as he'd implied. He already had the handicap of a female passenger. No need in making matters any worse. "You've got a point there, Thayer, and it's damned sporting of you to bring it up. What do you say we engage a private parlor and build up our strength with a nuncheon while the horses rest? I've had no breakfast, and I'll bet a monkey Miss Thorpe left without hers as well. Am I right?" he inquired politely.

Antonia nodded, while wondering just how much further dining with these two pinks of the ton in a public inn unchaperoned would sink her reputation. Oh, well. One thing was certain: It was impossible that she could meet anyone she knew. "You goaded him into this race," she hissed as her traveling companion helped her down and they followed his lordship into the inn.

"Had to." He grinned, speaking low. "Pockets to let. Unless you've a hundred pounds stuffed in that reticule you'd care to lend me. No? I thought not. I've little other choice then but to win my money back. It's play and pay, you know."

"No, I don't know. But I'm convinced that Uncle Edwin owes me a debt of gratitude for saving his daughter from a gamester."

"Thorpe knows well enough what I am" was the cynical reply. "You'd be amazed at the number of shortcomings these encroaching types will tolerate."

Though she'd tried to convince herself that it didn't matter, Antonia felt considerable relief to find the public parlor empty as they passed through it to reach the smaller one Lord Thayer had bespoken. But when they emerged, almost an hour later, after a sumptuous repast of wine-roasted gammon and dressed lamb followed by orange cream, she was not so fortunate. A half-dozen travelers, in from the cold, were huddled near a parsimonious fire. And one tall, handsome fellow with a profusion of dark curly hair and side whiskers was wearing the uniform of the Third Dragoon Guards.

He was holding his hands near the feeble flames, too intent upon rubbing some circulation back into them to pay attention to the threesome crossing the room, though others in the group did look curiously at the two young swells and their pretty companion. Antonia felt her face grow hot as she met the bold stare of one male member of the party. She quickly averted her gaze, which then rested upon the guardsman. Mr. Denholm heard her gasp of dismay and quickly stepped up to shield her.

30

His action came too late. "Tonia!" the military man exclaimed in a carrying voice. "Tonia Thorpe! Is it really you?" He started toward them eagerly but was halted in his tracks by a haughty stare leveled through a quizzing glass. Mr. Denholm spoke with icy politeness. "I rather think, sir, there has been some mistake. Lord Thayer, will you escort my sister to our carriage? She is, I fear, unaccustomed to the overfamiliarity that one encounters in public travel."

The soldier's face turned red. "I beg pardon, sir." He bowed stiffly to Mr. Denholm, but his puzzled eyes continued to follow Miss Thorpe's retreating back. "It's just that your *sister*"— he emphasized the word—"bears an amazing resemblance to a young lady whom I knew in Belgium. I fear I momentarily forgot myself. You collect how it is in a strange place. One is always imagining he sees acquaintances. A natural reaction to loneliness, perhaps? I trust I did not embarrass your *sister*, sir. Pray convey my apologies. I meant no offense."

"I'm sure none was taken. This is not the first time my sister has been mistaken for someone else." With a curt bow, Mr. Denholm followed his companions out of the parlor. The soldier, frowning thoughtfully, strolled over to the window that faced the courtyard.

"Friend of yours?" Mr. Denholm inquired politely as he climbed into the driver's seat next to Miss Thorpe and picked up the reins.

"I know him. He's in Papa's regiment," she answered miserably. "Do you suppose he believed that I'm your sister?"

"He did if he's a gentleman," was the brief reply.

Miss Thorpe gave Mr. Denholm a hostile look. It was quite obvious that the upcoming curricle race weighed more heavily on his mind than her reputation.

Chapter Five

"WHAT HAPPENS NOW?"

"Why, we run the wheels off Thayer's rig." They were maneuvering their way through the crowded yard toward Lord Thayer, who was holding his team with some difficulty out on the highway. "Think you can hang on?"

"I'm the last thing you should concern yourself with. My own prayers are for all vehicles and pedestrians unlucky enough to be abroad today."

"Just the same, brace yourself," Mr. Denholm instructed as he pulled his team parallel with Edgemon's.

Antonia looked dubious. The lightweight, open, two-wheeled vehicle was built for speed, not passenger accommodation. "Brace myself how?"

"Plant your feet against the rest. And if necessary hang on to me. But for God's sake don't get in the way. Ready, Thayer?"

"Go!" the other yelled. His long whip snaked out over his horses' heads with a pistol-like explosion. His grays responded with a burst of speed that was quickly accelerated by an echoing whipcrack and the sound of the other high-strung pair being sprung behind them.

"Catch me if you can, Fitz!" Lord Thayer called over his shoulder.

"Intend to, old boy!" Mr. Denholm whooped as Miss Thorpe screeched "Oh, no!" beside him. "My bonnet! My bonnet has blown off!" She'd loosened the strings during their nuncheon and neglected to make them fast again. "Oh, stop, do!" She tugged at the driver's arm. "I must go get my bonnet."

"Are you daft?" He shook off her arm, which had caused him to jerk the reins. His whip cracked once more to urge his team on and shorten the distance between the two vehicles. This accomplished, Denholm steadied his cattle down, content to follow six yards or so behind Lord Thayer's rig. Only then did he give Miss Thorpe his full attention. "I told you not to interfere with my driving," he growled.

"But I've lost my hat, you wigeon!"

"The devil with your hat!"

"I can't go into London without my hat! Surely you must know that! It's the only one I have!"

"Then, here, take mine!" He removed the jaunty beaver from his own black locks and clapped it firmly on her head. It came to rest just above her eyebrows. "Now, then, you have a hat. May I return my attention to the race? Two hundred pounds will buy any number of dowdy bonnets."

"Oh, will it?" she sputtered, unjamming the beaver from her head and with a quick, deft wrist flick sending it sailing. Antonia watched with satisfaction as the breeze caught the curly-brimmed hat, lofted it like a kite, then left it to come to rest finally on the lower branches of a tree. Mr. Denholm, too, had watched the flight. He now turned a baleful eye back on his companion. "Feel better?"

"Some," she admitted.

"Then, can we get on with this race?"

"You can try. Though you obviously haven't a prayer." Lord Thayer was urging on his horses and the gap between the curricles was lengthening.

"No? Just watch me." The whip exploded in the air. Unleashed, the team put on an awesome burst of speed. Mindful of the driving arm this time, Miss Thorpe clutched the third one down of Mr. Denholm's five-caped greatcoat and hung on for all that she was worth. Both curricles were flying now. Antonia had never known such speed. The wind tore through her hair and stung her eyes. It was fearsome—terrifying—exhilarating—glorious!

The driver spared a thought for his passenger as he rapidly closed the gap between his rig and his opponent's. "Are you all right?"

"Oh, yes."

The tone of voice surprised him, and he glanced down to see that her eyes were shining with excitement. "Oh, famous! We're catching him!" she crowed. "Can you go faster?"

"Hang on for the curve." He grinned and threw a protective arm around her as they increased their speed and took the bend of the road upon one wheel. "How are you doing?" he yelled in a manner almost comradelike as they straightened out on a long stretch of highway with nothing in sight but the other speeding vehicle.

"Don't worry about me!" she whooped back. "Just catch him!"

"All right, then. Here goes!" He gave a shout as the whip cracked once more. His cattle responded. Lord Thayer looked back over his shoulder to assess the threat and plied his own whip desperately. But it was soon obvious that his team was spent. They did spring forward for a moment but quickly flagged. Thayer was cursing and whipping for all he was worth when the other rig came tearing round him with Mr. Denholm, hatless, handling the ribbons with consummate skill while Miss Thorpe, in the same bareheaded state, shouted huzzahs of encouragement.

Lord Thayer, knowing he was well and truly beaten, slowed down his weary team to a humane walk while the rival curricle took another curve with only the slightest reduction of its speed and headed down the homestretch to the crossroads.

"Oh, we've won! We've won! We've won!" Antonia chortled, bouncing up and down on the red leather seat in her exuberance. "I never thought we stood a chance, and we've beaten him to a standstill. Oh, you really are a none-such! I'd no idea what a curricle race would be like. I tell you, it was famous!" She looked up at the grinning Mr. Denholm with glowing eyes. Finding her enthusiasm irresistible, he enfolded her into his arms before he realized what he was up to, crushed her against his greatcoat, and indulged in a victory kiss that began platoni-

34

cally enough but soon heated up into a great deal more than he'd bargained for.

"Oh, my goodness," Miss Thorpe gasped when he'd finally released her. Her cheeks were now flushed from more cause than just the cold. Completely flustered, she reached up to straighten the bonnet that wasn't there. "Oh, dear heavens!" The full realization of the depths to which she'd sunk now hit her.

Denholm, the thrill of victory now overridden by the strong desire to kick himself, watched her expressive face change from bewilderment to mortification. "I'm sorry," he said abruptly. "I should not have done that. Put it down to the exhilaration of the race. And, pray, do not refine upon it."

"Oh, I won't." Her voice was so earnest that he looked at her sharply as he picked up the reins and flicked them lightly. She caught the look and elaborated. "I have not forgotten, except there for just a bit perhaps, that you are a rake."

His smile was a bit grim. "You do believe in plain speaking, don't you, Miss Thorpe?"

"Oh, is it wrong for me to use the term? Then, I beg pardon. But I was led to believe that gentlemen were rather proud of that sort of reputation. Should I rather have said 'I know you are a devil with the ladies, sir'?"

"You rather should keep quiet," he growled, and gave his full attention to his driving.

Antonia had no trouble complying with that directive, for they were approaching the metropolis, and she was caught up in the sights and sounds and smells of London. Aware of her wide-eyed absorption and disdainful of the rude remarks of other drivers forced to maneuver around him, Denholm pulled his pair to a halt on Westminster Bridge.

"Oh, perhaps you shouldn't stop here." The driver of a heavily loaded cart had just cursed them roundly.

He shrugged and quoted: " 'Dull would he be of soul who could pass by a sight so touching in its majesty.' "

"Why, that's Wordsworth." Antonia looked up at him in astonishment. "I would not have thought—" She faltered suddenly.

"That a rake would read poetry? We can't be whoring all the time."

"Well . . ." She tried to pretend she hadn't heard him and rose precariously to her feet to drink in the view. "It's certainly all there, the things he spoke of: 'ships, towers, domes, theaters, and temples.' " She wished Denholm to know that he was not the only literate person in the curricle. "But I wouldn't call the prospect 'bright and glittering.' And"—she wrinkled up her nose—"it certainly isn't smokeless. Oh, my goodness!" she gasped, and sat down suddenly as a phaeton sped round them too close for comfort, and their team jerked nervously. "And it certainly is not 'calm.' "

"No. Of course, Wordsworth was here at sunrise. And since I've no desire to imitate his example, I'll take his word for the conditions." He clucked at his team and continued the trek across the bridge.

Antonia turned toward him impulsively. "Thank you for stopping, though. I'll always remember this when I read the poem."

The sweetness of her smile totally disarmed him. "You're welcome," he murmured, feeling suddenly like a very callow youth.

Antonia's few moments of carefree tourism proved to be short-lived. As journey's end grew near, she gave no more than a passing glance to the sights her driver pointed out. Carlton House and St. James's Park might have been everyday occurrences in her life. The truth was, her apprehension was growing at an alarming rate. When her guide at last announced, "Here's Grosvenor Square," he noted that his passenger had turned quite pale.

"It's elegant, isn't it?" she offered a bit unsteadily.

"None more so." Denholm frowned as he pulled the horses to a standstill and stared at the imposing house just beyond the iron fencing. "Are you sure you have the direction right?"

"Of course."

"Then, we're here. But I could have sworn—well, never mind." He jumped lightly from the curricle, looped his reins around a hitching post, then came round and helped her down.

Miss Thorpe was staring apprehensively at the magnificent facade and smoothing her hair nervously. "Oh, you're quite past
praying for," some imp prompted him to say mischievously.
"Your grandmother will just have to recall you from better
days."

"But she's never seen me before," Miss Thorpe confided as
they ascended the three marble steps together. "I do wish I
were at least wearing my bonnet." Then it occurred to her that
Mr. Denholm's presence could prove more awkward than her
bonnet's absence. "You needn't wait," she said dismissively. "I
do thank you for bringing me here, but it's not necessary for
you to stay."

"If I were sure of that, I'd be off in a flash." His face was a
study in martyrdom as he reached in front of her and gave the
knocker four demanding whacks.

It was Miss Thorpe alone, however, who came into view
when the door opened a grudging crack. A slightly stooped, august, though ancient, butler looked Antonia up and down. His
disapproving gaze then came to rest, or so she fancied, upon
her unclad head. "Yes?" he inquired frostily.

"Is this Mrs. Blakeney's residence?" she asked shakily,
quite overset.

"This is Lady Thirkell's residence" was the frigid reply as
the butler prepared to reclose the door. He was diverted from
this intent not by the heart-wrenching groan from the young female but by a strong hand on the knob that pulled it from his
grasp. He found himself craning his neck to look up sideways
at a young gentleman who made his own efforts at imperiousness seem pitifully second-rate.

"Perhaps you may know whether a Mrs. Blakeney lives
elsewhere in this neighborhood. The young lady here was
given this address."

"Would it be Mrs. *Claire* Blakeney that the young lady
wishes to see?" The butler appeared to have had a revelation. "Whereas this is by no means her residence, that particular Mrs. Blakeney does, in a manner of speaking, reside
here. What I mean to say is, Mrs. Blakeney is her ladyship's
companion."

If it had not been for Mr. Denholm's firm grip attaching itself at just that moment to her elbow, Miss Thorpe might have seated herself suddenly upon the marble stoop, which had developed a curious tendency to pitch and yaw. Mr. Denholm's in-charge voice was also proving to be an added stabilizer. "You do tend to make some odd distinctions," he said to the majordomo. "Suppose you move aside and let us in. Then go tell Mrs. Blakeney her granddaughter's here."

Though, as Morton afterward informed his underlings below-stairs, there was something decidedly havey-cavey about the girl; well, he hadn't been in service all these years without knowing a gentleman when he saw one, even if the aforesaid gentleman did have the effrontery to show up upon her ladyship's doorstep without a hat. Cloaking his curiosity in the habitual dignity requisite to his calling, Morton opened the door wide and ushered the peculiar pair inside.

Chapter Six

A WIDE EXPANSE OF HALL WAS ENCIRCLED BY ASCENDING branches of a marble staircase that ended in a gallery running across the entire back width of the room. An imposing figure in black bombazine stood squarely in the center of the gallery staring down at them. "This will not do. Stay where you are," she commanded in a deep, imperious voice that the visitors automatically obeyed.

The surveillance continued for several seconds. Then the elderly lady turned, crossed the gallery, and headed down the staircase.

"Oh, God, why me?" Mr. Denholm groaned underneath his breath and leaned weakly against the door. With mesmerized fascination he and Antonia watched the regal, slow descent. The white-haired, white-capped old lady used an ebony, silver-mounted cane to assist her progress. But in no way did she exude dependence. She held herself rigidly upright. Her height would have been impressive for a man. For a female octogenarian, the effect was intimidating. As were the hawklike nose and the sharp black eyes that did not appear to require the quizzing glass that she now untangled from the mass of jewelry on her bosom and employed as she stumped her way across the hallway toward them. Antonia felt a profound relief that her companion was the object of this stare. The old lady's progress came to a halt squarely in front of Mr. Denholm. She faced him, eye to eye.

"It is you. Thought so," she declared. "Well, this will not do, Fitzhugh. It will not do at all."

"What won't do, ma'am?" Mr. Denholm inquired with resigned politeness.

"You know what won't do, you scapegrace. I'll not allow you to bring your doxy here."

Miss Thorpe gasped. Mr. Denholm's expression hardly changed. "You much mistake the matter, Aunt Kate. May I present—"

"Indeed you may not!" She lifted her cane and struck the marble floor with resounding emphasis. Then she turned her glass for a head-to-toe inspection of Miss Thorpe. Antonia's cheeks burned under the deliberate scrutiny. Her relief was indescribable when the glass again was aimed at Mr. Denholm. "What is going on here, Fitzhugh? This chit ain't Eugenia Lytton. Too young by half."

"I've been trying to tell you, Aunt Kate," Mr. Denholm began patiently but was once again pulled up short.

"So, you've taken to running off with schoolroom misses, have you sir? Well, I'll tell you here and now you'll not run off with 'em to my house. Take your lightskirt and be off."

"How dare you!" Antonia ceased to be intimidated and glared at the old crone.

"Oh, for God's sake, Miss Thorpe, don't put yourself in a taking, too." Mr. Denholm's patience had worn thin. "And, Aunt Kate, do be quiet long enough for me to present Miss Antonia Thorpe, Mrs. Blakeney's granddaughter. This old harridan, Miss Thorpe, is my great-aunt, Lady Thirkell."

The imperious glare had turned to shock. "Claire's granddaughter? This is Claire's granddaughter? Little Tonia? Oh, you have really done it this time, Nephew." She glared at Mr. Denholm accusingly. "This won't do, you know. Can't begin to tell you what this will do to Claire. Kill her, most likely. Nobody's such a stickler in these matters as she is. No, sir! It will not do!" She shook her cane in Denholm's face. "I will not allow it! You can't play fast and loose with Claire Blakeney's granddaughter. There's no two ways about it. You will marry the chit. Immediately!"

"He will do no such thing!" Miss Thorpe followed this passionate declaration with a sneeze.

"No one has asked your opinion, miss. You have no say in the matter. It's Claire I'm thinking of."

"Aunt Kate!" Mr. Denholm felt it more than high time to take charge. "Could we please move away from this doorway? And will you direct that ear-pricked butler of yours to provide me with a stiff brandy—and Miss Thorpe with tea and lemon? I'm sure she's famished—and exhausted—and unless I miss my guess, she's coming down with a case of the grippe."

"Serves her right. Traipsing around without a bonnet like some Covent Garden jade. You heard the man, Morton. In the blue withdrawing room. And I'll need a brandy too."

While Antonia gratefully imbibed her hot beverage she kept wrestling with the sensation that history was repeating, that she'd lived through all this before, which really was the outside of enough. Once was sufficient, thank you. But as the tea partially restored her equilibrium she recognized the source of the disturbing feeling. The room *was* familiar. Her grandmother had described it minutely, from the blue silk wall hangings, to the black marble chimney piece, decorated with night emblems in gilt bronze, to the mahogany armchairs with gilt enrichments in the style of Thomas Hope. And what's more, Grandmother had claimed it for her own, whereas in fact she was but a hired companion.

Antonia struggled to keep back the tears. Whatever was she going to do? She'd burned her bridges behind her with Uncle Edwin, expecting to find sanctuary with a grandmother whom she'd believed to be a nabob. Now she had discovered that same grandmother to be little more than a betweenstairs servant. It was all too lowering. She'd be out on the London streets in a matter of minutes once that old dragon got it properly sorted out that she was not her nephew's light-o'-love.

What a coil! She swallowed convulsively and felt Mr. Denholm's eyes upon her. The usually cynical blue gaze now looked concerned. She must be a pathetic sight indeed to trouble that cold heart. Denholm's speech, however, revealed the true source of his concern.

"First, Aunt Kate, let's make one thing clear. There's no question of my marrying Miss Thorpe." He held up a hand to forestall the storm. "You gave me your word," he admonished sternly, "that you'd allow us to refresh ourselves and then you'd hear me out. You're laboring under a grave misapprehension. I am not running away with Miss Thorpe to set her up in a life of sin. In point of fact, our acquaintanceship is but slight. She was on the London coach, coming to visit her grandmother, when it overturned. I was traveling behind it, and having previously met Miss Thorpe—her uncle's estate marches with ours—I felt it incumbent upon me to bring her into London myself. So, instead of casting me in the role of seducer quite so fast, you would have done better to think of me as a modern-day knight-errant."

What had begun as a derisive sniff turned into a sneezing spasm. When Antonia recovered and wiped her streaming eyes, the aunt and nephew were gazing fixedly at her. There was a decided warning in the gentleman's eyes. "The drawing master next to me had a bad cold," she offered by way of explanation.

"Beg pardon?" Mr. Denholm looked bemused.

"The drawing master. One of the passengers. He sat right next to me and had a bad case of grippe. I'm afraid I've caught it."

"I suppose you lost your bonnet when the coach overturned, then." Lady Thirkell was thawing noticeably. "For surely you did not embark upon a journey without one."

"Oh, no, ma'am. It matched my pelisse."

"I am pleased to hear it. Quite relieved, in fact. As I know your grandmother will be. Although one must make some allowances, I suppose, for any unfortunate reared abroad, neither Claire nor I would ever countenance a young lady traveling without proper headgear. Not in England."

"Nor in Belgium either, I assure your ladyship." Miss Thorpe ignored Mr. Denholm's odious grin.

"So you can see, m'dear, that such a solecism—bad enough in itself, but definitely compounded by arriving on my doorstep not only unchaperoned but in the company of a notorious rake—would count against you." It was now Antonia's turn to grin. She quickly hid it with a handkerchief as Mr. Denholm shot her a quelling look. "Your abigail, I take it, was injured in the accident," her ladyship continued. "An awkward circumstance, but under those conditions you did right, my dear, by allowing my nephew to bring you here," she observed with judicial condescension. "It's too bad that someone more respectable did not come along. But providence does not always provide in the way we'd choose. I trust no one observed your arrival here, Fitzhugh?"

"Oh, no, ma'am," Mr. Denholm remarked meekly, while Miss Thorpe, striving to stave off a fit of hysterical giggles, asked shakily, "May I see my grandmother, ma'am?"

"Certainly, my dear. Fitzhugh, please ring for Morton." Her ladyship nodded at the bellpull hanging next to the mantel. The prompt appearance of the butler suggested he'd been lurking in the hall. He was quickly dispatched upon his errand.

"I deliberately postponed your meeting until I was able to sort things out to my satisfaction. If what I'd first feared were true, well, it was my intention to spare Claire's feelings. Your grandmother, my dear, as you will discover, is a lady of delicate sensibilities. I am dedicated to protecting her from the harsher realities one is sometimes forced to deal with. But now I can see no impediment to a joyous meeting."

If Antonia thought privately that her grandmother's "delicate sensibilities," as well as her own nerves, might be best served by conducting their "joyous meeting" in private, she was too craven to say so. Mr. Denholm must have been thinking along those same lines, for he rose to his feet. "Well, then, I shall bid you both good day."

"Sit down, Fitzhugh," Lady Thirkell snapped. "You will do nothing of the kind." And to his great chagrin, he found himself automatically obeying. "Of course, Claire must meet you. She does, after all, stand *in loco parentis* for Antonia. Or, as grandmother, is she *parentis* literally? Well, never mind. She must meet you, of course."

If neither of the young people quite saw the rationale behind the "of course," it made no difference. The time to demur had passed. For the door opened and an elderly women stepped inside, then hesitated on the threshold.

In everything but age she stood in sharp contrast to her ladyship, and even there, she could have been ten years younger. She was small and dainty. Her face, while showing the ravages of time, still held some vestiges of a former beauty. Nor did she reflect any of Lady Thirkell's self-assurance. Instead, she managed, even while standing still, to appear quite ill at ease and fluttery.

"Oh, there you are, Claire," Lady Thirkell observed heartily. "Do come in, my dear. I think you must recall all the talk about me great-nephew, Fitzhugh. The one who disgraced us all by almost killing that sap-skull Lytton, then running off to the Continent with his wife. Well, guess who he's brought here to see you." Rather like a conjurer successfully pulling a rabbit from a hat, she swept her hand in a dramatic gesture. "This, my dear, is your granddaughter—little Tonia. Come all the way from Belgium!"

Mrs. Blakeney's lips parted, but for a moment not a sound emerged. Then, "Oh, no" escaped in a breathy little sigh.

Antonia's grandmother crumpled down upon the Aubusson carpet in a graceful swoon.

In the flurry that followed, while Mr. Denholm scooped up the prostrated Mrs. Blakeney and laid her on the couch-form sofa, while the granddaughter vigorously rubbed the grandmother's wrists (having heard somewhere that such action had a restorative power, though heaven alone knew why), while Lady Thirkell waved sal volatile underneath her companion's nose, Antonia had taken it for granted that her relative's collapse was the direct result of being caught out in her deception. How utterly shattering it must have been to realize that her granddaughter now knew that she was a mere hired companion and not the wealthy lady of the mansion in Grosvenor Square. Poor Mrs. Blakeney's sins had found her out. No wonder she had fainted.

Antonia was soon to discover, though, just how widely this assumption had missed the mark. Mrs. Blakeney's eyelids fluttered open and after a moment's bewilderment her baby-blue gaze came to rest upon her granddaughter. She moaned a piteous moan.

"Here, drink this, ma'am." Denholm pressed brandy to her lips.

"Oh, no. I couldn't." She shrank away.

"Don't be goosish, Claire." Her ladyship spoke firmly. "Think of it as medicine."

The dose Mrs. Blakeney obediently imbibed was liberal. She sat up coughing, then turned toward her employer. "Oh, Katie, I don't think I can bear it. Not to go through the whole thing again. I don't care if he is your great-nephew—and well-to-do—heir to a title—above her touch. I simply cannot bear it. Speak to him. Or, better still, speak to his father. Lord Worth could threaten to cut him off without a shilling unless he does the honorable thing and marries my little Tonia. She simply must not accept a carte blanche from him."

"Oh, for God's sake!" Mr. Denholm exploded. "Do we have to go through all this again? As for you"—he turned angrily toward Miss Thorpe, who was trying to bring a fit of near-hysterical laughter under control—"you're no help." But in spite of everything he found himself suddenly grinning, too.

"There, there, m'dear." Lady Thirkell sought to soothe her companion's agitation. "No need to put yourself into a taking. It's not what you think at all. Fitzhugh being here with your granddaughter is the merest coincidence. Antonia was on her way here, and the coach overturned. He happened along and drove her to London. That's all there is to that. At least that's what they say." She gave her great-nephew a flick of her shrewd dark eyes.

"And having discharged my duty, I must be going." Denholm rose from a kneeling position beside Mrs. Blakeney. Firmness, he had decided, was his only hope of extricating himself from Grosvenor Square. "Your servant, ma'am." He bowed to Mrs. Blakeney, whose color, he noted, was returning. "Aunt Kate." He bent for a moment over his great-aunt's gnarled, bediamonded hand, then turned to Antonia. "Goodbye, Miss Thorpe. Enjoy your stay in London."

"See him to the door, m'dear," Lady Thirkell commanded.

"I know the way better than she does, Aunt Kate."

"Run on with him, Antonia." Her ladyship's tone did not brook further discussion. Antonia dutifully preceded Mr. Denholm from the room.

"I expect she wishes privacy to decide what to do with me," she observed glumly once they were out of earshot down the hall.

"Don't worry. She'll not put you out into the street."

"You think not? It's hardly customary to receive a companion's relations into one's house."

"But then, Aunt Kate is hardly customary. Beneath that formidable bosom there beats a heart of gold. I think." He smiled to lift her spirits, but her eyes were fixed upon the row of Thirkell ancestors that lined the gallery.

"Well, perhaps her ladyship will allow me to be useful in some way for the next day or two," she said without much conviction, "or for however long it takes to secure my passage back to Belgium."

"To Belgium? You can't be serious."

"Entirely. I will not go back to Uncle Edwin. Indeed, I don't suppose I could even if I desired it. Which I don't."

"You don't read the papers, then?"

"How could I? I've not had a moment's leisure since I left home."

"Then, you don't know that Napoleon's escaped from Elba and is raising an army in France? English civilians are leaving Belgium, not going there."

Denholm could have bitten his tongue the minute he'd passed on this bulletin, for Antonia looked stricken. Still, it was none of his affair. He'd already been entangled with Miss Thorpe far longer than he cared to be. Even so, he found it awkward to extricate himself.

"Things are bound to look better tomorrow," he offered awkwardly, and got a pained look for the platitude. "Perhaps not, then. But your Uncle Edwin's bound to have regretted the tongue-lashing he gave you. He'll be begging you to return."

She chose not to comment. They walked side by side in silence down the staircase and neared the door where Morton stood impassively. "Well, good-bye, then, Mr. Denholm." It was on her lips to thank him for his assistance till it occurred to her once more that he'd been catalyst to all of her difficulties.

He read her mind. "I'm sorry for my part in your troubles, Miss Thorpe. I assure you, none of it was intended. Except," he amended, "for the curricle race that cost you your bonnet. That was a financial necessity. Too bad I had to put you through it, though."

She sneezed again, as if in memory. "Oh, no," she demurred, as soon as she'd recovered. "No need to apologize for that. It was the only truly enjoyable experience I've had since I arrived in this country. I liked it above all things." Suddenly her face flamed. Ensuing events had completely wiped the race's shocking finale from her mind. She sneezed again. "I d-did not mean . . ." she stammered. "You must not think—"

"I don't," he replied, looking faintly embarrassed also as he shrugged into his greatcoat. "Again, the fault was entirely mine. Well, good luck, Miss Thorpe." He bowed, more anxious than ever to be on his way. "My hat, Morton." The imperiousness of his tone was meant to cover his unaccustomed lack of ease.

"You were not wearing a hat, sir." The butler's gaze was not entirely free of censure.

Miss Thorpe's gurgle of spontaneous laughter was followed by another sneezing spasm. Denholm could still hear it after the door had closed behind him. As he jumped the three steps and raced toward his curricle, it did not occur to him to wonder just what it was that he was running from.

Lady Thirkell had made good use of the interval of time she'd arranged for. "Well, what do you think of your grand-daughter, Claire?" she inquired as soon as the young people had left the room. "I should imagine she exceeds your expectations, though I must admit to being shocked when she came calling without her bonnet and with my scapegrace of a nephew in tow. But she seems quite well-spoken, nonetheless. And pretty, too. Reminds me of you, Claire, when you were young. But why am I rattling on? She's your grandchild. What do you think of her?" She sat down beside her companion on the sofa and gave her hand an encouraging pat.

"What I think of Antonia is of no consequence. The question is, what must she think of me?" Mrs. Blakeney's eyes filled up with tears.

"Now, now. No need to put yourself into another taking. Even if I did anticipate it. That's why I sent Antonia from the room. To get our stories straight. I do wish you hadn't spun that silly Banbury tale. It has made things awkward."

"Well, I never expected to see little Tonia." A lacy handker-chief dabbed pathetically at her eyes. "And a girl ought to think highly of her grandmother."

"And so she shall. If I had only known you were supposed to be mistress here, I would have pretended—still, with me nevvy showing up here as well, it would not have done."

"It wouldn't have done anyway. Imagine anyone believing for a moment that you were my companion."

"Humph. Yes, I suppose you do have a point. Anyway, what's done's done. We must now decide—quickly—how we'll go on from here. Antonia, I'm sure, will understand and forgive your foolish desire to impress her. So, please, Claire, let matters rest there. Don't go rattling any other skeletons."

"But I can't deceive the girl! Oh, you needn't look so Friday-faced, Kate. It's not the same thing at all. For it's one thing to pretend to be other than you are in a letter, written out of the kindest of motives, to someone you never expect to see. Telling a falsehood under these circumstances would be another matter entirely."

"No one's asking you to lie, Claire." Lady Thirkell sighed, knowing that her usually placid friend also possessed a high degree of stubbornness. "I'm simply saying that for Antonia's sake I see no need for you to go baring your soul to her right away. At least, let the child grow to know you first. But quickly now, before she returns, what do you think of my great-nephew?"

Mrs. Blakeney appeared bewildered by the rapid change of subject. "Well, actually, Kate, I've hardly thought of him at all. How could you expect it, what with the shock of little Tonia's appearance—all grown up at that. Somehow I've continued to think of her as a child."

"Well, think of Fitzhugh. It's important."

"If you insist, then, I shall try." She closed her eyes and frowned in concentration. "He is quite good-looking."

"Of course. That has been half his problem. Go on."

"Well, he was most kind about the brandy."

"Yes, he was, wasn't he?" Mr. Denholm's relative nodded approvingly.

"Though a little impatient perhaps."

"A little. But then I expect it had been a trying day for him. I have a feeling that there was more to his and Antonia's encounter than they were admitting. But what other impressions did you get of my great-nephew?"

Mrs. Blakeney pushed her power to recall to the limit but came up empty. "Oh, really, Kate. I do have a great deal on my mind at present," she protested. "Besides, what does my opinion of Mr. Denholm have to say to anything?"

"Why, everything. You see, m'dear, I've decided that Fitzhugh shall marry your Antonia."

"Oh, but—"

"Shhh!" Lady Thirkell shook her head warningly. "I believe I hear her coming. We shall discuss this thoroughly tomorrow, Claire. It may take a great deal of doing on our part to bring the matter off."

When Miss Thorpe reentered the blue withdrawing room just seconds later, she found Lady Thirkell smiling complacently to herself and Mrs. Blakeney looking quite thunderstruck.

Chapter Seven

LADY THIRKELL WOULD ALLOW NO AWKWARDNESS CONcerning Antonia's position. Of course she must reside at Grosvenor Square for the remainder of her stay in England. Claire's granddaughter should have taken this for granted. As for Claire, who feared she might have inadvertently given the impression that she owned the house, well, what could be more natural, since this was, in every sense of the word, her home? The title "companion" was merely a sop for her absurd pride. What she was, in fact, was an old and valued friend. "I lean on Claire. Depend upon her absolutely," her ladyship declared. Antonia thought that as preposterous a statement as any she'd ever heard.

"We'll have a comfortable coze tomorrow, dear," her grandmother had said at bedtime when she'd lighted Antonia to her chamber. So far, there had been no opportunity for a private talk. Lady Thirkell had taken control of the conversation during their dinner and later in the drawing room before tea and early bed. She had used the time to quiz Antonia about life in Brussels but had tactfully avoided any references to her arrival in England and her brief stay in Kent. Antonia could only be thankful for the reprieve. Tomorrow would be soon enough to air that embarrassment.

But, as it developed, she never got the chance to explain just why she had arrived unheralded upon their doorstep. The old ladies were not early risers. Then, when they had finally dressed and breakfasted, there was the matter of the second footman, who was far too attentive to an upstairs maid, to be dealt with. Consequently it was afternoon before the threesome found time for a conversation. They had settled once more in the blue room. The elderly ladies had their needlework and had supplied Antonia with a tambouring frame and colored silks. She was steeling herself to explain why she had left her uncle's house in such a shocking fashion when Morton materialized to announce, "Sir Edwin Thorpe to see Miss Thorpe, m'lady."

"Oh, heavens!" Antonia gasped. "Not Uncle Edwin, here!"

"You do not wish to see your uncle?"

"Oh, no, ma'am. Yes, I mean. That is to say, of course I must."

"Then, Morton, show the gentleman in."

If Antonia had hoped for some miracle that might have soothed her uncle's choleric temperament, the hope died at the sight of him. If anything, Sir Edwin appeared more agitated than in their past encounters. And to make matters worse, his resentment and anger were overlayed with a new emotion. For as he surveyed the threesome, meanwhile tugging at his cravat to its detriment, he appeared ready to sink from sheer embarrassment.

The probable cause was that Lady Thirkell had riveted him in the doorway with an assessing stare that seemed to weigh his bright blue coat and red striped waistcoat in the balance and find his provincial tailor sadly wanting. "Antonia, m'dear, you may present your uncle," she at last condescended to declare.

"Your ladyship, Grandmother, may I present Sir Edwin

Thorpe? Uncle, Lady Thirkell and Mrs. Blakeney. Oh, but I expect that you and my grandmother have already met."

Sir Edwin, becoming more flustered by the moment, accorded her ladyship a deep, obsequious bow. Then with his eyes still fastened upon that august personage, he nodded in the general direction of Mrs. Blakeney. "May I please have a private word with my niece, your ladyship?" he asked.

"Anything you wish to say to Antonia can be said before her grandmother and myself. I shall go even further, sir. It *should* be said before her grandmother and myself. So, do sit down, pray." She indicated a caned-seat armchair, and Sir Edwin obediently perched himself upon its edge. "I have yet to ascertain," Lady Thirkell continued, "just how it happened that Miss Thorpe was traveling to London in a *public* coach." She paused to shudder at the term, then added as an afterthought, "Perhaps you do not keep a carriage?"

"Of course I keep a carriage." He was obviously affronted.

"Well, then, Sir Edwin, I can only say that I am shocked. For not only is a public coach a completely unsuitable mode of transportation for a young lady of Miss Thorpe's station, it also proved hazardous as well. Are you aware, sir, that the vehicle overturned?"

"I am" was the grim answer.

"Well, then, I rest my case."

"And are you aware, ma'am . . ."—being placed so unfairly in the wrong was causing Sir Edwin to lose some of his awe for the formidable Lady Thirkell—"that I had no say-so in my niece's choice of transportation or in her departure from my house? Are you aware, ma'am, that my niece stole from my house in the early morning hours without so much as a word to anyone? In short, ma'am, ran away?"

Antonia looked embarrassed and Mrs. Blakeney shocked. Lady Thirkell's black eyes snapped with interest. "No, I was not aware, sir, of the exact circumstances of Antonia's departure. But I will say that I suspected something of the sort. Now, then, what do you have to say for yourself?"

"What do I have to say for myself?" he sputtered. "What do *I* have to say?"

51

"Exactly. Antonia's father, your own brother, sir, an officer in His Majesty's service, who at this very moment may be locked in mortal combat with our country's enemies—"

"My brother is a doctor, your ladyship."

"The principle is still the same. Your brother placed his child in your protection. And you, sir, have failed that sacred trust."

"I have done no such thing! Why do you think I am here, ma'am, if not for my brother's sake? And for the sake of the honorable name of Thorpe."

A derisive sniff conveyed what Lady Thirkell thought of such pretensions. He paused long enough to look offended and then continued. "I am here to fetch Antonia back to Kent. As you can well appreciate, Lady Thirkell, a certain association will not do. For that reason I am prepared to forgive and forget her abuse of my hospitality and accept her once more into the bosom of my family." He avoided looking toward the sofa where Antonia and her grandmother sat side by side.

Lady Thirkell chose to misunderstand. "Are you implying, sir, that Miss Antonia Thorpe would be better served under your protection than under mine? What impudence! And how dare you speak to me of the 'honorable' name of Thorpe? I'll have you know that the late Lord Thirkell's family had long been noble when the Thorpes were still sniveling serfs. And you think to add to Miss Thorpe's consequence by taking her back with you? The notion is absurd."

"I think your ladyship is well aware," Sir Edwin observed stiffly, "that I cast no aspersions upon the name of Thirkell. I think you are also well aware, ma'am, that the association I refer to is the one between my niece and"—again the head jerked toward the sofa—"and—er, *Mrs*. Blakeney. My brother has never acknowledged any connection between them and has trusted me to concur with his wishes in that regard."

"Then, your brother is as big a fool as you are," Lady Thirkell snapped. Antonia longed to add a setdown of her own and to deny her uncle's right to speak for her absent father. The problem was, she hadn't the slightest notion of what he was talking about. She glanced uneasily at her grandmother, who sat still as death, her eyes fixed upon her folded hands. "Perhaps it will salve the plebeian sensibilities of both you and your brother," Lady Thirkell continued, "to learn that my dear friend Mrs. Blakeney and I have decided that Antonia shall remain with us as my relation and not hers. It is true, you know. We are connected. Antonia's grandfather and my husband were cousins."

"I am well aware of that relationship, m'lady, but under the circumstances, I should not think—"

"Oh, I doubt anyone will bother to work out the genealogy," her ladyship broke in impatiently. "And if they should, well, you may rest assured that my consequence is sufficient to overset any number of worn-out scandals. Antonia, sir, will remain with us."

While it was plain that Sir Edwin found a great deal to attract him in that arrangement, he was not a man who shirked his duty lightly. Therefore, even though he knew it was next to impossible to relegate Lady Thirkell to a secondary role, he nevertheless made another attempt to deal directly with his niece. "Your father placed you under my care, Antonia. He would be much distressed to learn of your defection. For his sake I am prepared to forgive and forget any former unpleasantness that passed between us. And"—he held up his hand to prevent interruption—"I am prepared now to admit that I was out of line with some of my accusations. Upon reflection I can see how you might have misled the Mr. Denholm quite unintentionally." He seemed unaware that Lady Thirkell's black bombazine rustled at that name and that Mrs. Blakeney raised her eyes to look directly at him. "Though, you must admit that to all outward appearances it did seem to be deliberate mischief-making on your part. No, please. Wait until I have finished. I have had a long talk with Lord Worth and we have both agreed that in our eagerness to form this alliance between our houses we have, perhaps, been too precipitate. The Honorable Fitzhugh Denholm had only just arrived in this country after a long absence. And as for Rosamond"—he groped for the right words—"well, as his lordship pointed out, she is quite young and inexperienced and inclined to be, err, intimidated by Mr. Denholm's, err, worldliness. Lord Worth thinks, and I agree, that she would be better prepared for marriage after a London Season. His lordship feels that a bit of town bronze would make her a more compatible wife for Mr. Denholm."

"Just one minute, sir!" Lady Thirkell, who had perhaps achieved her own personal record for silence, could contain herself no longer. "Do I understand you to say, sir, that Fitzhugh Denholm is betrothed to *your* daughter?" Her voice rang with disbelief.

"Not to say *betrothed* exactly," he answered stiffly. "There is, however, this understanding."

"On whose part, I wonder? But never mind all that now. Just please explain, I pray you, how all this involved our Antonia."

Her ladyship and Mrs. Blakeney listened spellbound while Sir Edwin reluctantly explained about the mixup of identities. At the conclusion of his recital Lady Thirkell whooped with laughter. "Do you mean to tell me the young nincompoop offered for the wrong young lady? Lord, what a farce!" She wiped her streaming eyes. "And did you accept, Antonia?"

"Of course not!"

"A pity. But do go on, Sir Edwin. I'm all agog to hear what scheme you and that pompous Worth have hatched between you."

"We have hatched no scheme, ma'am." Sir Edwin bristled. "We have simply agreed to give our children time to become acquainted before formalizing their attachment."

" 'Attachment'!" Lady Thirkell chortled. "An odd term to use when me nevvy doesn't even know the gel by sight. But pray don't let me interrupt you."

"I shall try not to, your ladyship. The point is, Antonia, that I have brought Rosamond to London to stay with her maternal aunt."

"In hot pursuit of Fitzhugh, I daresay."

Sir Edwin kept his eyes fixed firmly upon his niece and pretended not to have heard his hostess's latest sally. "Rosamond is to stay with her Aunt Lydia on Wimpole Street. Lydia will sponsor her come-out and has graciously consented to introduce you to Society as well."

"And just who is this person?" her ladyship inquired.

"Mrs. Samuel Whitcomb, ma'am. My late wife's sister."

"Mrs. Samuel Whitcomb. Of Wimpole Street, you say? Well, she can't be of any consequence, for I've never heard of her."

"Mrs. Whitcomb is a close friend of Lady Hartswell," he was stung into saying.

"That tradesman's daughter?" Lady Thirkell sniffed. "But never mind all that. I do agree that Antonia should make her come-out. Don't you, dear Claire?"

"I-I suppose."

"And it really would place too much strain upon us at our ages to do the thing ourselves. Don't you agree, Claire?"

"Oh, yes," the other replied faintly.

"Well, then, it's settled. Antonia will continue to reside here in Grosvenor Square with us. But we will permit Mrs. Whitcomb to bring her out. Along with your daughter, Rosebud."

"*Rosamond*. But—"

"I, of course, will supply the guest list. Mrs. Whitcomb will be quite useless in providing the kind of company Antonia should meet."

"I'm sure my sister-in-law will have her own ideas on that subject, ma'am."

"Well, then, it's up to you, sir, to dispel them. For you and I, it appears, need each other. You wish your daughter to marry Lord Worth's son. I wish, for her grandmother's sake, to introduce Antonia into Society. So I shall see to it that both young cousins are provided with the very pink of the ton, including the Honorable Fitzhugh Denholm. And after that, it's up to Rosalea to get her clutches into him as best she can. Pity, though, about Wimpole Street. Not really up to snuff. But can't be helped. Your sister-in-law has a large ballroom, of course?"

Sir Edwin nodded dumbly.

"Well, then, we're agreed. Antonia and your flower shall

55

make their come-out at Mrs. Whitcomb's residence under my sponsorship. I bid you good day, sir." Lady Thirkell rose dismissively to her feet.

Chapter
Eight

"GO TO BED, ANTONIA."

Miss Thorpe looked up in consternation from the sneezing fit she had had on the heels of her uncle's departure. Clearly Lady Thirkell and Papa were of one accord as to modes of punishment. But she was not still a child, however.

Lady Thirkell was looking at her kindly, though. "I should have insisted you not leave your room today. We cannot afford to have you ill. There is far too much to do. So go to bed, child. I'll send Maud in with Dr. Twiton's Receipt for colds."

"Oh, but it's only a slight one, m'lady. Papa says—"

"Nonsense. I will not have you ill. To bed, Antonia." The ebony cane pointed toward the bedchamber. Antonia sighed inwardly and gave in.

It was not the maid, however, who appeared a little later bearing the remedy. Mrs. Blakeney drew a chair up beside the four-poster and saw to it that Antonia licked every last drop of the disgusting brew from the spoon. "I know it's nasty, dear," she said sympathetically, "but quite efficacious. It was my own dear doctor's recipe. Lady Thirkell swears by it."

High praise, indeed! Antonia suppressed a smile. "Oh, do stay and talk to me," she pleaded as her grandmother rose to go. "Really, I don't know how I shall ever pass the time. And we've had no chance at all to become acquainted."

"Yes, I know," Mrs. Blakeney appeared troubled. "And, of course, after all your Uncle Edwin's hints, I do owe you an explanation. But perhaps that should wait until you're better."

"But I feel perfectly well. Oh, dear, I did not mean that you should——You owe me nothing at all, Grandmother. Please stay. We shall not talk of anything you don't wish to."

Mrs. Blakeney sighed. "No, it's much like Dr. Twiton's medicine. The longer you put it off, the worse things get. So, if you're sure you feel well enough. I must warn you, though: You may find what I have to say distressing. And dear Kate will be most displeased with me for confiding in you, for she feels it to be unnecessary. But though I do bow to her superior judgment in most matters"—she smiled faintly as Antonia murmured "Who doesn't?"—"I think she's wrong in her belief that scandals eventually blow over. She is so high-minded herself, you see, that she thinks others are fashioned the same way. But in this one respect I do know the world far better than dear Kate does. And there's no diversion, Antonia dear, that equals drinking scandal broth. And while the latest *on-dit* must have the greatest claim, of course, no scandal worthy of the name is ever really buried, but only laid aside to be picked up once more when the proper occasion arises. Your uncle certainly gave us proof of that today."

"My Uncle Edwin is a prig. A very brief acquaintance has taught me that. Believe me, Grandmother, I wouldn't refine the slightest upon anything he says. So we'll speak no more of it. I cannot believe you capable of any kind of scandal."

"That shows a proper granddaughterly feeling on your part, Tonia dear." Mrs. Blakeney's eyes grew misty. "But though it pains me to say so, I fear you much mistake the matter. The odd thing is, I never felt at all scandalous while your grandfather was alive. Not at any time. That was very wicked of me, I suppose, but there it was. Your grandfather was such a tender, loving man, you see. And so protective of us. I collect that's why I never felt at all like any of those terrible things women in my position are called. He was my true husband, you see, dear, in all save ceremony."

"You and Grandfather weren't married!" The shocked words popped out before Antonia could stop them. "I mean to say, how very interesting." She tried valiantly to erase the stricken look from her grandmother's face.

"No, Antonia, we never married. He already was, you see. And there was nothing to be done about that fact. It was a marriage of convenience, nothing more. His legal wife did not care for him. John and I had a house in Henrietta Street for twenty years and were completely happy. He was, as I said, the kindest, most considerate, of men. He died soon after your mother and father married. And"—she seemed in danger of breaking down completely—"though I know he'd intended to take care of me, it appeared no provision had been made. Kate, of course, is of the opinion that John's family simply ignored his wishes. She urged me to hire a lawyer. But I could not bear to drag John's name through the mud that way." She rose to pour a glass of water from the pitcher on the washstand and hand it to Antonia. "Your body needs fluids, dear." Realizing the real need was for Mrs. Blakeney to collect herself, Antonia obediently drained the glass. Her grandmother replaced it and continued her narrative.

"That was when her ladyship took me on as her companion. She was widowed, too, you see. Lord Thirkell and John were cousins and had been very close. Like brothers, actually. Anyhow, Kate insisted that I come stay with her. The way she put it was 'the thought of John turning in his grave over his family's treatment of you is making me positively giddy.' " She smiled wanly at the remembrance. "Of course, the Thirkell family was outraged. Dear Kate considered that ample payment, she said, for her charity to me. For John had been the only member of her husband's family she could abide. Well, now, Antonia, the family skeleton that your father and uncle were at such pains to hide from you is out of the closet, I'm sorry to say. I hope you are not too shocked."

"If you are the best the family can dish up in the way of skeletons, Grandmother, I shall consider myself fortunate indeed," Antonia said stoutly, hoping to hide the fact she was reeling from the blow. "Thank you for telling me. Now let's consider it forgotten."

"No, no, dear," Mrs. Blakeney said sadly, "that is the point I've been trying to make. It will not be forgotten. Oh, Kate is right in one respect. Her consequence will override most social obstacles for you. She possesses one of the largest fortunes in London, you see. She was wealthy in her own right when Thirkell married her, and he was very plump in the pocket. And both their families are old besides. So, you may be sure that her cards of invitation will be coveted, even though she hasn't gone out in Society for years now. And the ton will accept you as her relation regardless of which side of the blanket you come from." Antonia flinched, and her grandmother looked stricken. "I know, my dear. That phrase is quite unkind. But I wish to prepare you for the sort of whispering you'll hear. For there will be talk. There's no getting away from that."

"As if I'd care a fig." Antonia tossed her head, trying to make up for her initial reaction.

"Oh, one does care. One tries to tell oneself it does not matter. But it's galling to have one's character torn to shreds by people who haven't the slightest notion of your circumstances."

"Oh, Grandmother. It must have been terrible for you."

"No, no. As I said, your grandfather was the kindest—most protective . . . While he lived, my life was all I ever could have wished for. It was only afterward . . . Even so, I cannot regret anything for myself. I did grieve for your mother's position. For your father was never really comfortable with the situation. And now I am distressed that you should have to be made . . . uncomfortable."

"I shan't be, I assure you."

"It's quite all right for you to feel censorious, Tonia dear." Her voice was gentle. "For I wish to speak of something that will sound most odd, not even to say hypocritical, coming as it does from me. Whereas for myself I would not wish away the time I spent—under any circumstances—with John, it's impossible for me to lay too great a stress upon the importance of respectability. That is why I deceived you in my letters. I did not wish you to have any reason to feel embarrassed by your background. And I want respectability for you more than anything in the world. I want you to make a respectable marriage.

Oh, I know you will enter the marriage mart lumbered by my character and your lack of fortune. But you have your uncle's respectability behind you. Sir Edwin may be a tiresome, pompous man, but, all the same, his character will help offset my notoriety. And you must not underestimate the value of Lady Thirkell's sponsorship. The combination of these two circumstances should, I believe, just about nullify the harm I've inadvertently done you." She paused to wipe her eyes.

"Oh, Grandmother!" Antonia jumped out of bed and impulsively hugged her relative. "As if you could ever harm a fly. Don't ever say such a thing to me again." She, too, burst into tears. The two wept comfortably for quite a while in each other's arms.

During the next two days Antonia's case of the grippe flourished. Lady Thirkell insisted, over the invalid's protest, that she stay in bed. "It will pay in the long run. You'll see." Antonia was far too grateful to, not to say intimidated by, her ladyship to cross her. So she remained propped up in the huge fourposter listlessly turning through the copies of the *Ladies' Magazine* her hostess had supplied. "This should keep you occupied," her ladyship had said, "for you will need a new wardrobe suitable for the Season." Since the issues were hopelessly outdated, Antonia silently questioned their usefulness. But she turned their pages dutifully all the same. Would Lady Thirkell actually force her to make her bow in a gown that had been out of fashion for years? She shuddered at the thought but could not dismiss it.

When a maid popped her head in to announce a visitor, Antonia's surprise was overmatched by her relief from boredom. Who on earth? She'd barely had time to straighten her hair and fluff her pillows when her cousin eased into the room looking furtively around her. "Oh, thank goodness, Antonia, you're alone."

"Rosamond! What in heaven's name are you doing here?" The exclamation was hardly cordial. In the first place, Antonia was feeling little charity toward the cousin whose cravenness had landed her in such a coil. And in the second place, this was not the visitor she'd expected, even though the idea that her one London acquaintance might be concerned about her health was ridiculous in the extreme.

"I had to see you." Without removing the cherry *gros de Naples* pelisse she wore, Rosamond placed a cross-framed stool close enough to the bed for conversation, far enough away to avoid infection, and sat upon it. "Papa doesn't know of this visit. He has expressly forbidden me to come here."

"Oh? And why, may I ask, is that?" In her short acquaintance with Lady Thirkell, Antonia had picked up pointers on toploftiness.

"Well, you must have noticed what a stickler for propriety Papa is. And he now says my character lacks stability. He greatly fears I'm easily swayed by undesirable influences."

"And just what particular 'undesirable influence' did he have in mind?" Antonia sounded dangerous.

"Why, your grandmother, of course. Which is absolutely absurd. As though I'd let her influence me in the slightest. I wish to marry Cecil, not to live in sin with him. Besides, I think it's beastly of Papa to preach propriety to me and at the same time plan to wed me to a depraved libertine."

" 'Depraved'?" Antonia was diverted from her intention of removing her cousin bodily from the room. "Surely that's coming it a bit too strong."

"Not nearly strong enough. Cecil is convinced that Mr. Denholm is debauched."

"Well, I must say I'm beginning to understand my uncle's strong objection to your Cecil. No one would care to hear his candidate for his daughter's hand termed 'debauched.' "

"Oh, he never said so in Papa's hearing. Papa objects to Cecil because he's poor."

"Yes, well, that would lose out to 'debauched' any day, I suppose. But before this conversation goes any further, Cousin, let's get one thing clear. You may tear Mr. Denholm's character to shreds as freely as you please. But if you say one more word that discredits my grandmother, or if you show her anything less than complete respect, I shall have nothing further to do with you."

Miss Rosamond Thorpe's eyes widened with shock, then

slowly filled with tears. "Oh, Antonia, I never intended—I would never—while I cannot approve of—and c-certainly you could not expect Cecil to condone—a man in his position—a clergyman—but he'd never cast a stone—n-nor would I!"

"For heaven's sake, don't be so dramatic. I hardly thought you'd chuck rocks at her. I just want to make it clear that my grandmother is the dearest, kindest, sweetest person imaginable, and if you dare make her uncomfortable in any way, well, our come-out is canceled. My part of it, at any rate."

"But that would mean that Lady Thirkell would withdraw her patronage."

"Exactly."

The tears spilled over. "Really, Antonia, this is too unkind of you. I don't think I can bear any more. Papa is furious with me as it is. And now this will put Aunt Lydia in a taking. For she's been in perfect raptures over cohostessing with Lady Thirkell. She says that London's most tonish people will attend her party now. And that from then on her social position will be assured. And now you plan to ruin all that just because you think I shall be rude to your grandmother, which of course I should never dream of being. Really, Antonia, it is the outside of enough." She wiped her eyes with the fingers of her kid gloves and looked reproachfully at her cousin.

For some obscure reason Antonia felt guilty and, as a consequence, went on the defensive. "What actually was the 'outside of enough' was for your father to forbid you to come here. 'Undesirable influences,' indeed. If the whole thing were not so insulting, it would be ludicrous."

"That's what Aunt Lydia said. She said that in this case it was perfectly all right to disobey my father, for if he was too big a fool to know the advantages of being received by Lady Thirkell, she certainly was not. So, by all means, I was to come to see you. 'What your father don't know won't hurt him' is what she said. But I do hope he will not learn of it. Papa can be so difficult. Do take care not to mention to him that I've been here, Antonia."

"Since Uncle Edwin and I are hardly likely to be tête-à-tête, you worry yourself unduly. But was there any particular reason you wished to see me? In addition to calling in at Lady Thirkell's, I mean to say."

The sarcasm was wasted on her cousin. Rosamond merely looked grateful for the prompting. "Oh, yes, there is. I desperately need your advice, Antonia. What must I do about Mr. Denholm?"

"Do about Mr. Denholm? I'm afraid I don't understand."

"Why ever not? I explained it all before. I love Cecil. I cannot marry Mr. Denholm."

"And I explained that Mr. Denholm does not really wish to marry you."

"Oh, but he does. At least, it's what his father wishes. And Papa says Mr. Denholm's sure to wish for the match once he's seen me."

Antonia opened her mouth to argue that point, then closed it. She looked at her cousin's creamy complexion, glorious hair, limpid eyes. Perhaps her uncle was right. Gentlemen were not renowned for prizing intellect above beauty. Antonia found these reflections a bit dampening. "Well, you can always refuse him," she observed.

Such decisive action still had no appeal for Rosamond. But just as she was about to express her reservations, the cousins were interrupted by the reentrance of the maid, this time carrying a flowered hatbox. "This just came for you, Miss Thorpe." She placed the box beside Antonia upon the bed, then rather reluctantly withdrew.

"For me? But I did not—oh, Grandmother must have!" Antonia eagerly untied the string as Rosamond risked a case of grippe by daring to come stand beside the bed and see.

"Ooooooh!" both young ladies gasped together as Antonia lifted the milliner's creation from its nest. The headdress was fashioned in the style known as the "gypsy hat." It was made of British leghorn and ornamented with a full plume of ostrich feathers. Its saucy brim was turned up both in front and back. Its trim and ties were of deep blue satin ribbon.

"It's the most beautiful thing I've ever seen, not to mention owned." Antonia's eyes were shining.

Her cousin was too busy perusing the card that had fallen out upon the coverlet to comment. "Here's a replacement for your lost chapeau," she read aloud. "Consider it your part of the race winnings. Fitzhugh Denholm."

Rosamond stared at her cousin, openmouthed. "Antonia, the Honorable Fitzhugh Denholm has sent you a bonnet. Why on earth would he do a shocking thing like that? You must know—surely even in Belgium *anyone* would know—that it is most improper."

"Oh, but you mistake the matter. I mean you mustn't think—Really, Rosamond, you are too absurd. It's not like that at all. Mr. Denholm is not *giving* me a bonnet. He is merely replacing the one he lost."

As a rule, Rosamond Thorpe's mental processes were none too swift. Now she got to the heart of the matter with amazing speed. "You say that Mr. Denholm lost your bonnet? How on earth did he come by it in the first place?"

"Oh, dear." Antonia could see no help for it. She launched into a slightly expurgated version of the coach accident and the ensuing curricle race. The fluency of her recital was not aided by her cousin's increasingly scandalized expression.

When Antonia had finished her explanation there was a pregnant pause while Rosamond appeared to be thinking over what she had heard. "Papa will be quite displeased" was her considered judgment.

"Your papa will not hear of it unless you tell him," Antonia snapped.

"He will know when he sees the bonnet."

"Oh, for heaven's sake, Rosamond, don't be absurd. How on earth would he know that Mr. Denholm bought this bonnet? But never mind trying to answer that, for the question's academic. I do not intend to wear it anyhow."

Her cousin was still pursuing her own line of thought. "Papa was convinced that you were setting your cap for Mr. Denholm. I daresay he was right."

"I daresay he was not!" Antonia replied with considerable heat. "I will not be held responsible for my coach capsizing.

And how else, may I ask, was I supposed to get to London? Walk?"

"Really, Antonia, there's no need to scowl. I'm sure I don't mind if you have set your cap for Mr. Denholm. Goodness, I've told you at least twice that *I* don't wish to marry him. But I really don't think you've much chance of fixing his interest. For I got the distinct impression that he didn't like you above half. Still"—she paused—"he did send you this lovely bonnet. Oh"—she frowned in concentration—"did I hear you say, Antonia dear, that you do not intend to wear it?"

"You heard me."

"Oh, well then, may I?" And before Antonia could do more than gasp, her cousin had whisked off her own black velvet headdress and had placed the gypsy bonnet atop her flaxen curls.

Rosamond turned her head this way and that as she preened before the cheval glass while her cousin seethed. "You're quite right, Antonia. It is the prettiest bonnet ever. You're sure you don't mind if I wear it?"

"I most certainly do mind."

"But if you're not going to—Really, Antonia, it does seem rather selfish."

Antonia got a firm grip on herself. "I am returning the bonnet to the milliner, Rosamond. Surely you must see that you cannot wear it any more than I can without explaining its origins."

"But I can say I got it from you."

"And do you think no one will wonder why I gave away such an obviously expensive hat? And what would Mr. Denholm think if he saw you wearing it?"

"That you were tired of it?"

"No! The thing is, Rosamond, as you yourself so effectively pointed out, I cannot be the recipient of such a gift."

"I suppose you're right." Rosamond removed the bonnet with obvious regret. "Propriety can be a nuisance, can it not?" she observed as she carefully replaced the headgear in its flowered box. "Oh, dear, the time!" She counted along as the mantel clock struck three. "Aunt Lydia is expecting callers and particularly wished me to meet her dear friend Lady Hartswell.

I must rush or she'll be out of sorts. Oh, dear. We didn't get the chance to finish our discussion of Cecil and Mr. Denholm. I did so want you to advise me. I know we've barely met, Antonia, but I already feel fast friends, don't you?" Rosamond was putting on her own discarded bonnet. "And you are much more worldly than I am. You do seem to have the most astonishing adventures. I expect it's in the blood. From your mother's side, of course. Anyhow, I'm confident you shall be able to advise me, the very next time we meet, on just exactly what I should do. Good-bye, Tonia dear." She hurried from the room.

Antonia sank back against the pillows and thought of several things she might tell Rosamond to do. Her gaze fastened on the hatbox. She took the gypsy bonnet from its container and stared at it lovingly a while. Then she slipped out of bed to go stand in front of the cheval glass and try it on. Perhaps the nightgown that she wore was to blame. Or the fact that her nose was still slightly red from her bad cold. Whatever the cause, the stark truth was, the bonnet had looked much, much better upon her cousin Rosamond.

Feeling far worse than she had at any time since her first sneeze, Antonia removed the hat, packed it carefully away, and crawled back into her bed.

Chapter Nine

LADY WORTH'S VISIT TO HER SON'S LODGINGS IN ST. JAMES Street was ill-timed. The Honorable Fitzhugh Denholm had spent a late night at Watier's, followed by a visit to a barque of frailty and had been sleeping off the effects of both when his valet pulled the curtains to announce that his mother wished to see him.

He entered the withdrawing room some thirty minutes later, freshly shaved, wearing a deep gold dressing gown and a guarded expression.

"Fitzhugh, you do look dreadful!" his parent exclaimed, noting the bloodshot eyes, the pouches underneath them, and the way they squinted at the light streaming through the windows, evidence of a splitting headache.

"You don't appear top-of-the-trees yourself, ma'am." She was prostrated upon the sofa. A pretty woman, whose looks belied her years and gave no indication of the variety of ailments she was wont to suffer, Lady Worth had few interests beyond her imagined indispositions and keeping her irascible husband appeased. As her son suspected, it was the latter cause that had induced her to make the trip to London.

"Oh, I know I must appear a fright. The noise of Pulteney's Hotel was not to be endured. I did not close my eyes once for the entire night."

"You could have stayed here." A tea board lay untouched on the sofa table, the exertion of helping herself having proved too great for Lady Worth. Her son poured for them both and placed a Dresden cup in his parent's hand.

"Stay here? With you out carousing all night long? It is not to be thought of. And don't say I should have stayed with friends, for I am not up to doing the polite in my present state of health. I do not think you quite appreciate my delicacy, Fitzhugh. And while I do not like to reproach you, dear, the constant friction between you and your father is putting a dreadful strain upon my constitution. The doctor tells me that my heart—well, never mind that for the moment. The point is, only a matter of utmost urgency would have made me risk my health by traveling up to London. Fitzhugh, have you the slightest notion of what you've done?" The blue eyes, so like his own, looked at him accusingly.

"Lately?" he inquired, buttering a light wig.

"Please do not be flippant. Your father is quite beside himself. Fitzhugh, you have offered for the wrong girl entirely!"

While his mother proceeded to relate the matter of the mixed-up cousins, Denholm did his best to appear surprised by it. "How could you have made such a mistake, Fitzhugh? Your father is convinced that you deliberately set out to defy him."

"He mistakes the matter" was the icy reply.

"That is exactly what I told him. Oh, Fitzhugh!" Lady Worth pulled herself up to a sitting position and turned imploring eyes upon her son. "You cannot imagine how difficult living with Lord Worth has become. No one has more pride than he. You can never begin to know how dreadful all your earlier—escapades were for him. The notoriety!" She shuddered. "It was almost more than he could bear. Now all he wishes is for you to settle quietly in Kent. And Miss Thorpe—the *original* Miss Thorpe I mean, of course—seemed the perfect choice of a wife. Her estate borders on ours. Your holdings will be substantially increased. And while I'm the first to acknowledge that her background leaves a lot to be desired, well, as your father says, dear, you have placed yourself outside the social pale. No young lady of the first stare will have you."

"Oh, you think not?" her son asked dryly.

"I repeat your father's opinion." Her tone implied his words had been carved in stone. "But what I've traveled all this way to say, Fitzhugh, is that the matter can still be put to rights. Miss Thorpe has come to London. Miss *Rosamond* Thorpe, I mean. And please, please, Fitzhugh, do endeavor to keep the cousins straight from here on out.

"And while your father would have preferred for you to remain quietly in Kent, he concedes that perhaps this could prove advantageous in the long run. For when Miss Thorpe makes her come-out and the polite world gets the chance to see you form a respectable alliance—for no one is more respectable than Sir Edwin Thorpe, though I must own I find him a trifle too encroaching—well, you must see that it could do a great deal to restore your good name. And make your father comfortable once more. Then things could be back as they were before that—that—odious creature bewitched you into ruining all our lives. So, promise me, Fitzhugh, that you will do it."

"Do what, ma'am?" he inquired wearily.

"Dangle after Miss Thorpe, of course. Fix her interest. Offer for her again. Well, for the first time, actually. Oh, Fitzhugh," she implored, her eyes refilling with tears, "you owe it to your father. You can't know how his pride has suffered. As for me, well, I don't think I can bear his unhappiness any longer."

Denholm took a deep and steadying breath. While he had few illusions concerning his mother, he was fond of her. And though his father might not think it, he did have a strong sense of obligation to his name. "Very well, Mama. If you wish me to pursue Miss *Rosamond* Thorpe, I shall endeavor to do so."

"Oh, Fitzhugh, my boy!" Lady Worth, more animated than she had been for years, actually moved from the couch to throw her arms about her son. This tender scene was interrupted by the valet's entrance. "This just came for you, sir."

"Fitzhugh, that's a lady's hatbox!" her ladyship exclaimed after the valet had deposited the flowered container on a table and withdrawn.

"It's a hatbox all right, though as to its sex I could not say."

But his parent was already pulling the gypsy bonnet from its wrappings. "Oh, how lovely" was her involuntary reaction to it.

"Would you like it, ma'am?" he said, and received an outraged look.

"Wear the headgear you've purchased for some lightskirt! Fitzhugh, how could you?" She tried it on almost absently before a convex mirror that hung between a pair of sconces on the wall. "Your taste is impeccable," she said, sighing, as she regretfully removed it, "which only proves the point I've tried to make."

"I'm afraid I don't quite follow."

"Well, you should. No *proper* gentleman, Fitzhugh, would have the slightest notion of how to select a bonnet that any female would die for. Your father could never do so, that is certain. It all just goes to show that it is more than time you turned respectable and settled down. And Miss Thorpe will make the perfect wife for you. Your father and I shall count upon your fixing her interest before the Season's done."

His mother's visit had made Denholm's headache decidedly worse. His blessed reprieve from an early betrothal had been short-lived. Well, he thought philosophically as he dressed to go in search of congenial company to divert the blue devils lurking to pounce upon him, if Miss Antonia Thorpe's judgment was to be credited, Miss Rosamond was a beauty at any rate. And then the memory of Antonia's animated face as she urged him on to beat Lord Thayer and the feel of her lips upon his own rose unbidden to his mind. He wondered just what traits Rosamond might hold in common with her cousin.

"A gentleman to see you, sir." The valet cut short such unprofitable reverie. The unnecessary stress that Doggett the valet had placed upon the word "gentleman" somehow managed to imply that the matter was in doubt. Denholm finished his inspection of the *trône-d'amour* arrangement of his cravat and turned impatiently from the glass. "I don't wish to see anyone. Get rid of him."

But Mr. Burnside, who had anticipated just such a reaction on Mr. Denholm's part, was already in. He forestalled any impulse to throw him out by saying quickly—and unctuously, "I beg pardon, sir, for this intrusion. You must believe I would not impose myself upon you if I were not convinced that my business was of a nature that you'd be anxious to discuss. And, I might add, it should only take a moment of your time."

Mr. Denholm had been on the town too long not to know a sharper when he saw one. The tall, cadaverous-looking man seemed to be trying to ape the dandy set. His coat was tightly pinched in at the waist, its lapels enormous. But the inferior tailoring of this garment failed to conceal the layers of padding over narrow shoulders. His pantaloons also betrayed the artificial bulges over his skinny calves. Too fly by half and up to no good, Denholm mentally concluded.

"Have a seat, Mr. Burnside." He nodded curtly toward a chair and took another. "But pray state your business briefly. As you can see, I was just on my way out."

"Oh, I'll not detain you, sir. My business is the theater." He

70

smiled ingratiatingly but, receiving a stony stare, continued. "I, sir, wear many hats in that noble cause: occasional actor, sometime writer, and now and then, producer. It is in these last two capacities I've come, sir."

"Look, Mr., err, Burnside," Denholm interrupted, "if you wish me to put up the blunt for one of your projects, you're wasting our time."

"Oh, no, no, sir. Quite the contrary, in fact." His smirk was rather unpleasant. "Were you aware, sir, that Lady Hastings—Lady Lytton, as was—has authored a play?"

Denholm was too adept at cards to show his emotions now. The other looked a trifle disappointed when his expression did not change. "Eugenia? An author? You do surprise me. I had thought the lady could barely write her name. Or names."

"Well, in truth," the other acknowledged with proper modesty, "I did assist her ladyship with the actual composition. But it was she who"—he paused significantly—"furnished the plot."

"Well, that's all very interesting, I'm sure. But I'm due at my club." Denholm rose to his feet.

Mr. Burnside scrambled up also. "Pray hear me out, sir. It is to your advantage. As you may know, Lady Hastings has recently been widowed. And the late Lord Hastings's estate, while not impoverished exactly, is not adequate to support her in that style to which she has grown accustomed. And you, sir, would know more about that style than most." The silence that followed such observation caused him to speed up his narrative. "Her straitened circumstances have forced Lady Hastings to stop and consider all of her assets. It was then she came to realize the dramatic possibilities of her own history. As you know, few ladies of our era have had the fascinating love affairs that have enlivened Lady Hastings's brief career. And I can assure you that her adventures make good theater. Very good theater indeed. I'm confident the public will flock to see our production. By the by, we call it *All for Love*."

"Hardly original." Denholm sneered. "Now if you'll excuse me."

"But you see, sir, it did occur to her ladyship and to myself

71

that what with the tremendous cost of theatrical production these days—hiring the theater, paying the actors, not even to think of the settings required and all the costumes—that it might be more financially rewarding *not* to produce our little piece, if you take my meaning."

"I think I do." Mr. Denholm was drawing on his gloves with the greatest of care, smoothing the soft leather over each finger.

"And Lord Lytton agrees, you'll be interested to hear. He has already become one of the play's backers, in a matter of speaking." Mr. Burnside sniggered. "Only he's backing it right out of Drury Lane. His lordship was especially concerned with suppressing the scene in which he catches you making love to his wife, as he then considered Lady Hastings to be. It's the highlight of the play, as you can well imagine." Again there was no comment. "But the more her ladyship thought about the matter, the more she regretted her decision to suppress a play that's bound to give so much pleasure to the London public. She's seriously considering returning Lord Lytton's money. You can appreciate, I'm sure, the artistic temperament. And the cost in pain of hiding a creative work under a bushel, so to speak. Why, it would be like smothering her own child."

"Now I can only hope," Mr. Denholm drawled, "that you are finally coming to the point."

"Oh, you're a canny man of business I can see, sir. The fact is, that even though Lord Lytton has contributed generously to the suppression of *All for Love*, Lady Hastings still would like to see her drama upon the boards. But if you, sir, who cannot be any more anxious than his lordship to find your most intimate history made public property, were to see yourself clear to matching Lord Lytton's contribution, I think then that the financial considerations would win out over the artistic ones. In fact, I will go so far as to say you can depend upon me, sir, to guarantee that Lady Hastings will have a change of heart."

"Does that conclude your business?" Mr. Denholm started toward the door.

"It only needs the mention of a sum. Five thousand pounds is the going rate. Oh, naturally you needn't pay it all at once. We can work out terms to your satisfaction."

72

Mr. Denholm paused at his dressing room door and eyed Mr. Burnside with an expression usually reserved for the most repellent kind of crawly vermin. "Here, sir, are my terms. You can tell Eugenia to do her play and be damned."

Mr. Burnside, smarting from failure, left Mr. Denholm's lodgings upon that gentleman's heels and watched him drive away in his smart curricle. The entrepreneur could perhaps have profited by observing at that moment the technique of Captain Horatio Crosland of His Majesty's Third Dragoon Guards. The captain had just followed Miss Antonia Thorpe to Noble's Circulating Library wherein he behaved so charmingly, and referred to seeing her traveling alone with a certain notorious gentleman so obliquely, and assured her so quickly that her secret was safe as the Bank of England with him—her father in particular would never hear of it—that when Captain Crosland wrangled an invitation to the come-out ball, which was the talk of the town, he informed her, Antonia was scarcely aware she was being blackmailed at all.

Chapter
Ten

A S FAR AS ANTONIA WAS CONCERNED, THE ONLY CIRCUM-
stance to mar her come-out was the fact that her grandmother would not be present. When she had declared, "I will not go if you don't," Mrs. Blakeney, with uncharacteristic asperity had said, "Don't be absurd." And Lady Thirkell, when appealed to, had agreed. "Claire is right. It would not do. Your

73

social assets are questionable enough without uncovering ancient scandals."

But it was Mrs. Blakeney who supervised Antonia's toilette and, as her ladyship's ancient dresser rebrushed one of the blond ringlets that dangled before the debutante's well-shaped ears, declared with misty eyes, "My dear, you are a vision. You will easily be the loveliest female there."

Though she smiled at the exaggeration, Antonia, too, was pleased with herself. Her fears that she would be presented in a gown that had been all the crack during the last century had been unfounded. Her ladyship had consulted London's most fashionable modiste and allowed the Frenchwoman to hold sway. "Simplicity!" had been the decree. "The young lady has youth, beauty. We shall not detract." The modiste had chosen spider gauze of a delicate blue, liberally tamboured with silver that sparkled by candlelight. Tiny white silk roses ornamented the shoulders over the small puffed sleeves. A wreath of the same flowers formed Antonia's headdress. White kid gloves and white corded silk shoes completed the ensemble.

There was a slight altercation over jewelry. Lady Thirkell's generous inclination was to adorn her protégée with one of her own diamond necklaces, a heavy ornate affair that Mrs. Blakeney and the dresser both insisted detracted from the ethereal effect that had been created. For once, Lady Thirkell allowed herself to be overruled. Antonia was delighted to wear a small string of pearls, a gift from her grandfather to her grandmother. She herself supplied the tiny pearl drops to dangle from her ears.

Lady Thirkell had taken unaccustomed pains with her own appearance. She had forgone her usual black and was resplendent in lavender satin worn over a gold slip. An opera comb branched out above an elaborate knot of her still-abundant hair. Now, to the profusion of other jewels that she wore, she added the diamond necklace. "We'd best leave," she said when she'd regally accepted Antonia's compliments on her appearance. "I wish to view the ballroom before the guests arrive. Heaven knows what that vulgar Mrs. Whitcomb may have done."

Her ladyship found very little to displease her, though, in the decor of the ballroom at Wimpole Street. She had already overridden Mrs. Whitcomb's desire to convert the room into a huge tent of purple silk, to suggest a sultan's harem. And though piqued by the disdainful sniff that had followed her suggestion, Mrs. Whitcomb had been too overawed by her ladyship's consequence to protest her scheme's dismissal. Now all Lady Thirkell felt compelled to do was to have the footman remove the masses of flowers from the side walls and rebank them with the groupings at both ends. "There is always a crush when I give a party," she informed the offended hostess as she stalked across the parquet floor with her cane, intent upon rearranging the orchestra, much to the conductor's consternation.

Antonia had parted company with Lady Thirkell and gone upstairs. And when she first saw Rosamond in all her splendor, her instant reaction had been a prick of jealousy, squelched immediately, but wondered at. Since Antonia laid no claim to beauty, she rarely felt any rancor toward those who did. She was honest enough, however, to admit to herself that Rosamond's predictions as to Denholm's reaction when he saw the right Miss Thorpe could have had some bearing on the situation.

But if Antonia felt cast in the shade by the other's natural endowments, she took comfort in the fact that her own ballgown was at least as pretty as the dusky rose her cousin wore. And if Rosamond echoed Lady Thirkell's taste by wearing a fortune in diamonds on her generous bosom, what did that have to say to anything? "Oh, you look lovely, Rosamond," she said sincerely as her cousin rotated slowly to allow her dresser to make any final adjustments that might be necessary. "So do you," her cousin replied, adding ingenuously, "I had not realized you were so pretty."

At just that moment the clock struck ten. The cousins clasped hands for moral support and went to join their elders and greet their guests.

Lady Thirkell had not overestimated her importance. No one who had received a card of invitation, unless confined to a sickbed or experiencing a family death, stayed away. And if many of the guests were impelled by curiosity ("I thought the old dragon dead," more than one person was heard to say), it made no difference in the actual results. The requisite crush had been achieved. Mrs. Whitcomb, wearing purple crape and a tall headdress of ostrich plumes, was beside herself.

Antonia took due note of the Thirkell power as evidenced by the ball's attendance and kept waiting for her ladyship to fulfill her second promise to Sir Edwin and produce the Honorable Fitzhugh Denholm like a rabbit from a hat. So apparently did Sir Edwin, up from the country for the event, for he delayed as long as was considered proper before personally leading Rosamond upon the floor. Lady Thirkell had procured an ancient viscount to partner her protégée. The orchestra struck up an equally old-fashioned minuet. The ball was underway.

Captain Crosland, resplendent in his dress uniform, was quickest of the sizable number of young men who were waiting to claim Antonia's hand for the following set. The captain was so obviously enjoying himself and so very desirous of amusing her that Antonia quite forgot the somewhat dubious nature of his invitation. And when at the conclusion of their country dance he asked to be presented to Lady Thirkell, she was happy to comply. Nor did she try to correct the impression he gave her ladyship that he was a longtime family friend. When she was claimed by her next partner to join in a quadrille, she left him chuckling at her ladyship's wicked comments on the altered hair coloring of a certain guest.

Time passed quickly. Antonia never lacked for partners. Nor did her cousin, who, after her initial nervousness, appeared to be having a delightful time. It was nearly eleven-thirty when Antonia saw Rosamond standing up with a tall gentleman who seemed to have overawed and subdued her once again. And then when the movement of the dance caused the gentleman to turn her way, Antonia saw with a sinking heart that it was Mr. Denholm.

No one else in the room looked quite so distinguished as he did in the prescribed white satin knee smalls and dark long-tailed coat. It was easy to see, Antonia concluded, how any number of women might have run away with him. He lifted his eyes at just that moment as though he felt her stare. She quickly looked away. And later on in the evening she pretended not to notice when he stood up with her cousin a second time.

Certainly that fact had nothing to say to the matter when, a little later, Antonia felt an overwhelming desire to escape the crush. This need for a few minutes to herself was due, of course, to the buildup of excitement before the dance and the rush of partners during it, both of which had left her exhausted. She eased out of the ballroom after a cotillion, dodged past the withdrawing room where her elders were playing cards, and found sanctuary in a small morning room, where she collapsed in a chair, nearly hidden by its enormous velvet wings. Antonia leaned back, closed her eyes, and for several minutes slowly plied her crape-and-ivory fan.

"Bored?" a languid voice inquired.

Her eyes jerked open to behold Mr. Denholm standing over her, two punch cups in his hands. "Here." He offered one. "I'm afraid most of it's sloshed out. Blame the pack of swains trying to follow you." He pulled up a chair, sank thankfully upon it, stretched out his long legs, and took a sip. "Aaugh!" He wrinkled his nose in distaste. "Lemonade! This is worse than Almack's."

She laughed. "What were you expecting at a come-out ball?"

"God knows. I haven't been to one of these affairs in years." The tone implied that it had been a deliverance. "But why the retreat, Miss Thorpe? You obviously are an unqualified success. And may I compliment you on your gown?"

"Thank you. And I'm not in retreat. Or bored. In fact, I'm having a most marvelous time. It's just that I felt the need to get away by myself a moment. Oh, dear. I did not mean—"

"Never mind." He smiled. "I'll not be so easily routed. I've done my duty manfully in there and am entitled to an intermission. And since Aunt Kate will skewer me if I try to escape before supper, you shall not monopolize the only empty space I've discovered. And speaking of suppers, may I take you in?"

She strangled on her lemonade. "Oh, no!"

"Is the thought that appalling?" he asked dryly. "I do occasionally forget my reputation."

"Don't be ridiculous. It isn't that. It's just that Uncle Edwin would think the worst. And he's just coming round to halfway believing that I did not deliberately deceive you into thinking that I was Rosamond when you came to make your offer."

"Ah, yes, Rosamond." His face was enigmatic.

"She is quite lovely, isn't she?" Some self-destructive impulse caused Antonia to ask the question.

"Indeed. You did not exaggerate. She's everything you say. Tell me"—he abruptly switched the subject—"how does it happen that Captain Crosland is a guest? Aunt Kate tells me he's a close family friend. When he saw us at the inn, you gave me the impression you scarcely knew him."

"It's true. But he and Papa are in the same regiment, of course."

"But hardly intimate?"

"I couldn't really say." She looked uncomfortable. "I'm not acquainted with all of Papa's cronies."

"It just struck me odd to see him here. Tell me, was it his idea or yours?"

"Well—he did suggest it, I suppose. But it seemed the thing to do to ask him. Honor of the regiment and all."

"And the fact he saw you in my unsavory company had nothing to do with the invitation?"

"Oh, no," she said too quickly. "Of course not. The encounter, Captain Crosland assures me, is completely forgotten as far as he's concerned."

"Indeed?" His brows rose. "Well, Miss Thorpe, it hardly behooves me to tell you how to choose your friends. A case of the pot calling the kettle black you could say. But I'd be a bit wary of the ubiquitous captain if I were you. The fellow's a Jack Sharp or I miss my guess. Oh, by the by, what was wrong with the bonnet I sent you? Not polite to say so, but I thought it far superior to the one we lost."

"Oh, it was," she said earnestly. "And I do thank you for it. It was most kind of you. But of course I could not keep it."

"Why ever not? You're not making too much, I trust, of one impulsive kiss. I can assure you, the only stings attached to that headgear were its fasteners."

78

"I know that!" Her cheeks reddened. "I certainly did not think—"

"Didn't you? Then, I'm at a loss to see why you returned it—unless it did not suite your taste."

"Oh, but it did! In fact, it was quite the loveliest bonnet I've ever seen."

"So my mother said."

"Your mother? I don't understand."

"She happened to be in my lodgings when the footman returned it. And like you, she immediately thought the worst. Oh, don't look so alarmed. She didn't know I'd sent the hat to you. She assumed it was for some lightskirt."

"Oh, how awful for you." Her giggle robbed the words of sympathy. "I am sorry."

"You look it. I still don't see why you couldn't simply have kept the thing. After all, it didn't have a sign upon it, 'Purchased by the notorious Mr. Denholm.' "

"Oh, but it did. That is to say, it had a card, which my cousin Rosamond read. And she, too, thought the worst. So you can see that I had to send it back."

"Yes, I suppose so." He grimaced, then laughed rather wryly. "That's what comes of trying to make amends. It can't be done, as I should know by now. But I never expected such an innocent purchase to be so misunderstood. I'm slow to learn, it seems," he finished bitterly.

"Well, no one could have expected it to go quite so public." Her sigh was filled with regret for the ill-fated chapeau.

"Well, miss!" An imperious voice caused them both to jump. "I have been wondering where you were hiding." They had been unaware of Lady Thirkell's entrance. The dowager surveyed them, leaning heavily upon her stick. "This will not do, you know." But even as she scolded, she seemed slightly pleased. "Did you realize, sir, that you were expected to take Miss *Rosamond* Thorpe in to supper? Well, Captain Crosland has just done so, and Sir Edwin appears on the verge of apoplexy. At this very moment he's looking behind the palms and underneath the chairs for you."

"Oh, my goodness!" Antonia jumped to her feet. "Whatever will he think?"

"The worst, of course, if he finds you here," her ladyship cheerfully observed. "Oh, do hurry and claim Rosamond, Fitzhugh."

"Sounds a bit late for that. Allow me instead to escort you two ladies in."

"Not I, sir." Lady Thirkell smirked. "Lord Carstairs has that honor."

"In that case, Miss Thorpe, it appears you have no choice." Denholm offered his arm with mock gallantry and did not miss the reluctance with which she accepted it.

"Tell me, are we skulking?" he whispered a bit later as she tugged him into the midst of a large group of guests making their way toward the supper room.

"Yes," she hissed. "I'm trying to avoid my Uncle Edwin. I've already explained that he thought I'd set my cap for you. I certainly don't want to put him into that sort of taking once again."

"Don't worry. I intend to do my duty. Go join your cousin." He nodded toward a corner where Rosamond sat waiting for Captain Crosland to fill her plate.

It seemed that Antonia was barely seated, and her cousin had scarcely begun to exclaim over the great success of the ball, when Fitzhugh joined them bearing refreshments. And whether Rosamond's face fell because of the scant supply of food upon her plate or because of the plate's bearer, was anybody's guess. Then, when Captain Crosland materialized with overflowing bounty, he had no choice but to present one of the plates he carried to Antonia and sit down beside her.

The supper partners, thanks to the civilian outflanking the army officer, had, at last, been properly sorted out. But the only person who seemed really pleased by the arrangement was Sir Edwin Thorpe, whom Antonia spotted beaming at them from across the room.

Chapter Eleven

THE HONORABLE FITZHUGH DENHOLM HAD PLUNGED into the life of the Bond Street beau, seemingly determined to take up where he'd left off eight years before when his celebrated affair with Lady Lytton had resulted in their hasty departure for the Continent. This social round included all-night macao sessions at Watier's, compensating workouts with the famous pugilist, "Gentleman" Jackson, trips to Newmarket to bet heavily on the races, and occasional appearances at the informal parties on York Street given by Amy Wilson, the stylish demirep. Interspersed with all these typical bachelor pursuits, he still managed a rather perfunctory courtship of Rosamond Thorpe.

It only took a morning call or two at Wimpole Street and a ride in the park during the fashionable hour, where they were observed by all and sundry, for the word to spread that the beautiful Miss Thorpe was as good as promised to her country neighbor, the notorious Fitzhugh Denholm. This made Miss Thorpe an object of wide interest. Each morning, cards of invitation piled up on the silver tray in the Whitcomb hallway. Nor did Rosamond lack for swains to fill the void when Mr. Denholm was otherwise engaged. The fact that the beauty was bespoken made her all the more attractive to the young men-about-town who might, had the situation been otherwise, have been afraid of becoming leg-shackled to her themselves.

Antonia did not fare nearly so well after their come-out.

True, like her cousin, she was showered with invitations. Lady Thirkell's prestige assured her that. She was not, however, besieged by suitors. For the word soon spread that Miss Antonia Thorpe, while almost as pretty as her cousin, unlike her cousin, had no fortune. An early rumor that she was Lady Thirkell's heir died aborning when the social genealogists among the ton revealed that the relationship between her ladyship and Miss Thorpe was merely slight, if not actually nonexistent. "Fitzhugh Denholm," the gossipmongers whispered, "will likely be the Thirkell heir. Blood's thicker than water, after all, and Lady Thirkell has a *tendre* for rascals, besides."

Since Antonia had never rated her chances high on the marriage mart, she was not downcast by developments. Her London stay was merely an interlude, something to talk about when she returned to pick up her old life in Belgium. She was perfectly willing to spend most of her time in the company of her cousin, even when that company included Mr. Denholm. Though she thought it absurd that Rosamond still got the quakes in that gentleman's presence, she was glad enough to help her cousin over the rough spots. The addition of Captain Crosland to the group was also welcome. Antonia knew full well that the captain was too much an opportunist to be interested in her. But his easy charm of manner made him the perfect foil for Rosamond's shyness and Denholm's broodiness.

Therefore, when Mr. Denholm invited Rosamond and herself, chaperoned by Lady Thirkell, to join him for an evening at Drury Lane, the only surprise was that Captain Crosland, for whatever reason, was not included. And had she thought about it, Antonia would have attributed the silence that engulfed their box soon after their arrival at the theater to the ebullient soldier's absence. But she was too absorbed with looking around her to do more than note their party's heavy atmosphere.

The magnificence of the auditorium first claimed her attention—the elaborately carved half columns that flanked the stage, the gracefully curved four tiers of galleries, the crystal chandeliers that hung in such profusion. She was pleased that their box was situated on the side, so as not only to command an excellent view of the action on the stage, but to allow a full view of the auditorium as well. Her gaze swept from the orchestra, where the musicians were busily arranging their music sheets, on to the pit where the hoi polloi were perched on backless benches. She then shifted her attention to the balcony, where the pink of the ton were gathered, to see and to be seen.

Even Edmund Kean, the current rage of London, was going to have his problems competing with all this, Antonia decided as she ran her eyes around the boxes that sparkled with diamonds and quizzing glasses and glowed with the soft reflection of candlelight upon the variegated colors of satin and silk.

The audience was indeed resplendent. But Antonia found a silent satisfaction in the fact that their party had no reason to feel cast in the shade. Lady Thirkell's purple turban and the heavy emerald necklace she wore along with several ropes of perfectly matched pearls commanded instant attention. Rosamond looked unusually lovely in a white crape dress spotted with white satin and trimmed with bands of flowers and leaves of deep blue silk. She herself wore a gown of Urling's net over a pale pink satin slip. But, as always, she concluded, it was Mr. Denholm who distinguished their little group. The severity of his black and white evening clothes was perfectly suited to his inky hair, Antonia decided with something less than complete objectivity.

She was not as approving of his habitual hauteur, though, especially now that she had seen him abandon it upon occasion to become quite personable and human. But for some reason he seemed more toplofty than usual this evening, sitting in tight-lipped silence, seemingly unconcerned by any hostly obligation to his guests, his eyes focused on the closed stage curtain. Well, he was Rosamond's problem, thank goodness, and not hers. His moodiness was not going to interfere with her first taste of London theater.

Just as Antonia resolved this, she heard some timid remark of her cousin's remain unanswered. Even the ever-garrulous Lady Thirkell seemed to have lost her tongue.

Botheration! Rosamond's discomfort overrode Antonia's desire to be as boorish as their host. "Oh, who is that lovely lady everybody's looking at?" Antonia asked. To this conversational gambit she quickly added, "Oh, don't all turn your heads at once, for while everyone else is gaping at her, she is looking directly our way."

There was no need for this admonition. Denholm did not waver from his contemplation of the stage. Lady Thirkell had developed a sudden need to rearrange the numerous rings she wore. Only Rosamond appeared appreciative of Antonia's efforts to enliven their theater party. "What lady, where?" she asked.

"In the fourth box from the end, directly across. She must be someone quite famous, the way everyone stares. Royalty, do you suppose?"

The cousins gazed admiringly at the striking black-haired beauty, whose black evening gown was cut daringly low to expose a rather shocking amount of alabaster shoulders and seductive bosom. Small jet beads were her only ornament. Her hair was braided high in a coronet, topped with a green-jade ornament. Both Misses Thorpe felt suddenly quite young and gauche as they gazed at the sophisticate.

"Do you perhaps know who she is, sir?" Antonia was beginning to grow exasperated at the Denholm silence.

"Why ask him?" Lady Thirkell sounded waspish. "He's been out of London for years now."

"I was not so much seeking enlightenment as giving our host an opportunity to enter the conversation." Antonia immediately regretted the rash remark. It was just as well that at that very moment the curtain rose.

Edmund Kean's *Richard III* had dazzled the critics. He did not have the same effect upon Lady Thirkell. Her piercing black eyes followed his hunchbacked progress for several seconds, then she was heard to sniff, "Looks like a monkey," and after an even shorter interval, "Sounds like one, too." Someone in the adjoining box was heard to titter. When Antonia next glanced at Lady Thirkell, the dowager was sound asleep.

Rosamond soon lost the plot thread, wriggled in her chair, and mainly watched the audience. Denholm might have been carved from the same stone as the Grecian columns from the amount of animation he conveyed. Only Antonia seemed caught up in the villain's powerful emotion, as she leaned out over the railing of their box to watch with parted lips and widened eyes. When the curtain was lowered at intermission, it took several seconds for her to return to reality.

Lady Thirkell shook off the spell of Morpheus far quicker than Antonia escaped the spell of Kean. When the curtain dropped, her head snapped up, and with the help of the ebony stick she carried she rose quickly to her feet. "Lady Mary Harlowe's here. Better go speak to her. That way I can leave when I want to. If she comes to our box, she'll prose on and on and never go away." The black eyes fastened on Rosamond. "Miss Thorpe, you can take me."

Rosamond rose thankfully to her feet. Intimidating as Lady Thirkell was, she dreaded trying to make conversation with Mr. Denholm even more. "Oh, not you, Antonia." Her ladyship dismissed the other Miss Thorpe, who seemed bent on accompanying them. "You stay here and guard Fitzhugh."

"What on earth did she mean by that?" Antonia blurted out as soon as the velvet box curtains had closed behind the two. She and Denholm were on their feet. They moved together toward the back of the box, where they'd be less conspicuous.

"Do you mind if I blow a cloud?" he asked abruptly.

She did but decided it was politic not to say so since he might soon find her conduct equally distasteful. Still, she watched with undisguised disapproval while he pulled a cigar from the recesses of his coat and began puffing to ignite it. She placed a kid glove delicately over her mouth and coughed pointedly. The only result was that the blue eyes fastened unswervingly upon her face till the smoke he blew obscured them.

"It's just as well we're alone," Antonia said abruptly, "for I did wish to speak to you."

"What makes me suppose you're about to ring a peal over me? Your pointed remark about my lack of civility perhaps? I'm sorry if you feel I've neglected you, Miss Thorpe."

"Don't be ridiculous," Antonia snapped. "As if I care a fig about your behavior. It's Rosamond I'm concerned with.

You've put the poor girl into a proper quake with your distemper. And just when she was beginning to feel more comfortable around you."

"I'm sorry if your cousin thinks me an ogre. But it was an opinion already formed before I'd met her, you may recall."

"Well, all the more reason you should be at pains to dispel it. You do intend to offer for her, do you not?"

"I think that question would be a bit more appropriate from Sir Edwin than from you, Miss Thorpe." Her face flamed red. "But since you ask, yes, I do."

"I beg your pardon." She managed to keep both her temper and her voice level. "I deserved the setdown. But since I've already sunk myself below reproach, let me go on and say that unless you are deliberately trying to goad her into refusing you—as you did when you believed that I was she—then I think you should treat her with more kindness. Rosamond, as you yourself have noted, is rather inclined to be overset by your, err, worldliness. You might try and be more considerate of that fact."

"And just what, may I ask, is your particular interest in the matter? Are you afraid—or hoping—that if your cousin turns me down, offering for you will have become habit-forming?"

"I realize, Mr. Denholm, that you are trying to be deliberately insulting and shall therefore overlook it. What I do not understand, though, is just what has put you in such a temper."

Since he had no intention of enlightening her, it was just as well that they were rejoined by Lady Thirkell and Rosamond. Antonia's own temper began to cool when she noted that her rag-mannered lecture had not been wasted. Denholm was at some pains to seat both ladies courteously. He then proceeded to engage in small talk with her cousin. Rosamond was relaxed and smiling when the play resumed.

Lady Thirkell went immediately back to sleep. The Shakespearean drama had lost some of its power to enthrall Antonia as well, due entirely to her altercation with Mr. Denholm, she thought resentfully. So, when the play reached its tragic culmination and Lady Thirkell revived just as Richard the Third expired, she thought it considerate to suggest they leave.

"Leave!" her ladyship exploded. "After suffering through all of this? Don't be sap-skulled. Only came to see the farce!"

Rosamond, too, was all eagerness. There was no doubt that for her as well the more frivolous portion of the evening's theatrical fare held far greater appeal than Shakespeare. Mr. Denholm, who had seemed more than willing to depart, settled back down once more with a contrived smile that signaled to Antonia: "See how gracious I am being."

The farce lovers were doomed to disappoint, though, for the theater manager appeared upon the stage to announce a change in the evening's fare. Instead of *Devil to Pay*, as indicated upon the playbill, they were to be treated to a brand-new afterpiece, "never yet performed on this or any other stage," written by a brilliant new lady author, who wished to keep her identity a secret, and entitled *All for Love*.

Antonia, who had been covertly observing Mr. Denholm, seemed to imagine rather than see a look of consternation appear upon his face before it was wiped clean once more of all expression.

"Why ain't they going to do the farce?" Lady Thirkell complained to the world at large.

Antonia found the piece to be boring, too cloying for words. But when she looked around and saw the other patrons leaning forward, literally on the edges of their seats, giving this play a far more rapt attention than that accorded the brilliant Kean, she began to wonder if she had not allowed the accumulated fatigue from five acts of Shakespearean tragedy to cloud her perceptions. She returned her attention to the stage.

She remained mystified, however, by the general reaction, which was shared, she noted, by the other occupants of her box. True, the actor and actress upon the stage were personable. But the dialogue with which they declared their undying love and tragic circumstances seemed hopelessly stilted, if not plain silly.

Antonia squirmed a little in her seat and wished once more that they could leave. Small chance of that. Lady Thirkell, refreshed no doubt by napping during *Richard III*, was drinking in every word of the cloying dialogue, her hands clinched tightly upon her stick, her face suffering along with the pair on stage.

Antonia was less surprised that Rosamond looked stricken by the star-crossed lovers' plight. She was no doubt thinking of her curate. Antonia glanced past her cousin, expecting to find a fellow critic in Mr. Denholm. For, no matter what opinion she might have formed about some other aspects of his personality, she did hold his intelligence in high regard. Until this moment. For he seemed to have come under the spell of the maudlin drama as much as anyone. More perhaps. He was so intent and still as to appear mesmerized.

Completely mystified now, Antonia returned her attention to the stage, where the trysting lovers, locked in a passionate embrace, were interrupted by the entrance of the lady's husband with a pistol in his hand. How melodramatic. How predictable. How boring. Her eyes traveled aimlessly along the horseshoe of boxes as if seeking further confirmation of her judgment. Sure enough, she was not the only person in the theater whose attention now wandered from the play. In fact, more of the tonish occupants of the boxes seemed staring her way than were looking toward the stage. When the light then finally dawned, it was all Antonia could do to keep from gasping.

How could she have been so stupid! How could she have not realized! Why, even Rosamond was aware of what was happening. And she'd thought her cousin none too bright. She sank back into her chair, willing herself to become invisible.

The afterpiece seemed to go on and on forever, through duel, flight, and romantic exile. Antonia divided her time between wishing the balcony would collapse and end their misery and concentrating upon not looking Denholm's way again. One glance at his masklike face would most likely turn her into stone.

When the lovers on stage were finally wrenched apart by the heroine's sad recall to a higher duty, Antonia breathed a long, if silent, sigh of relief. They could soon leave this public box where they were pilloried. Rosamond was crying softly. From mortification, Antonia felt sure. And while she could certainly sympathize with that reaction, she did wish, for Denholm's sake, that her cousin could be more stoic. Oh, thank heavens it was finally over. The curtain closed to thunderous applause.

"Well, shall we go?" she asked, too brightly. "My bottom is quite numb. Oh, dear. I mean to say—" Her cheeks flamed at the unladylike observation. Well, at least some of the tension was broken now.

"Antonia!" Rosamond gasped, while Denholm's eyes strayed toward her afflicted anatomy. "Sit down, miss," Lady Thirkell hissed. "I could care less for the condition of your posterior. I will not have it appear that we've been routed."

The actors were taking their third curtain call, and a few patrons were leaving to avoid the crush when a voice from the pit cried "Author!" It was echoed by another, then by others, till the gallery took up the chant and soon the entire theater joined in to swell the cry to thunderous proportions.

Antonia, who had thought that nothing could possibly be more horrifying than the discovery than Denholm's life was being made public upon the stage, soon found herself looking back upon that period of the evening as an oasis of tranquility. For now the beautiful lady in black whom she'd admired and remarked upon earlier in the evening was rising to her feet and graciously nodding in response to the wild cheering. And then, slowly, deliberately, she turned their way, and, as all eyes followed her lovely gaze, she bent a smile, more enigmatic than *La Gioconda*'s, upon the shuttered face of the Honorable Fitzhugh Denholm.

Chapter
Twelve

THREE YEARS EARLIER, LORD BYRON HAD AWAKENED TO find himself famous. Now he was being temporarily replaced by a new romantic hero, Fitzhugh Denholm.

Whereas Society originally had sipped its scandal broth while rehashing the more lurid aspects of Denholm's notorious affair, now the teacups clinked to a different time. To know all, it seemed, was to forgive all. Denholm and Eugenia Lytton Hastings had been elevated to martyrs, their grand passion the victim of selfless duty upon her part and upon his, overweening pride. The ton flocked in droves to see the afterpiece at Drury Lane and, their appetites whetted by the drama portrayed on stage, watched with bated breath for the real-life final act. For had not the Honorable Fitzhugh Denholm returned to London? And was not the beautiful Lady Hastings now free? How long could even a Denholm's pride (though that family was noted for an inordinate amount of that commodity) prevent the course of true love from eventually running smooth? Society eagerly awaited the happy ending.

And Miss Rosamond Thorpe found her position even more intolerable. "Surely Denholm won't offer for me now, will he, Tonia?" she said over the cousins' own cups of tea, taken in Antonia's bedchamber a few mornings after their Drury Lane adventure.

"Why ever not? Nothing has really changed, has it?" She

wrinkled her nose distastefully. "Except for the fact that odious play has brought all the old scandal back to life."

"But that's just the point, don't you see? Everyone's saying that the only reason Lady Hastings agreed to bare her soul on stage was to present her case to Mr. Denholm. They say he had always believed she left him for the Hastings fortune and title. And you know how much false pride he has."

"I know he's proud. I've no way of judging its justification."

"Why, pride's a deadly sin," Rosamond pronounced virtuously. "Didn't they teach you that abroad? But never mind. The point is, Denholm didn't know why she *had* to leave him. How she was duty-bound to the man she had married when he was ill and needed her. And Lord Hastings loved her at least as much as Denholm did. I found his character heartrending, didn't you?"

"I suppose so. I also found Richard the Third villainous, but I did not forget for a minute that Shakespeare made him up."

"Good heavens, Tonia, didn't they teach you anything in school? There actually was a King Richard the Third. And Lord Roderick in the play was actually Lord Hastings. His character was real."

"If you say so. But I didn't see all that much resemblance between the play's hero and the real Mr. Denholm, did you?"

"Well, the actor did seem a great deal nicer." Rosamond sounded regretful. "Though the real Denholm's better-looking," she added with a strange loyalty.

"I can only hope that the real Denholm didn't keep sighing like one of Trevithick's new steam engines standing up. And, frankly, I can't imagine him mouthing all those ridiculous periods that actor kept uttering."

"But then, you weren't there when he was making love, were you? And do you have the slightest notion how a man in love might act?"

Antonia had to admit that she did not, and with that Rosamond steered the conversation back to the phase of the subject foremost on her mind.

"Oh, Tonia, what shall I do if—when—Denholm offers for me? I know people are saying that he will not, that now he knows just how true and noble Lady Hastings really is, they're bound to fall into each other's arms sooner or later. But the thing is," she explained as her pretty face grew more troubled, "the ones who are saying that have never met Lord Worth. Oh, Tonia, Denholm's father is the sternest man. He quite frightens me to death. And I don't care how touchingly romantic Mr. Denholm's elopement with Lady Hastings may now appear to the rest of the world, there's no use thinking Lord Worth will ever approve. For she was a married lady. And they did—well, you know—commit adultery—practically beneath the nose of her second husband. Well, he wasn't actually her husband, as it turned out, but that would have nothing to say to Lord Worth's attitude." She shuddered.

"Yes, but if, as they're saying, this is the greatest romance since Antony and Cleopatra, I'd hardly think Denholm would let his father's approval or disapproval stand in his way. It certainly didn't when he eloped in the first place. Really, Rosamond, I don't think you need worry."

"No?" The other looked unconvinced. "Don't forget, there's always his pride. That could be a bigger obstacle than his father. And if he does offer for me, Tonia, I'll know it's only because of the one or the other. And I don't think I can bear it. It was bad enough to contemplate marrying Mr. Denholm when my deep regard for Cecil and my abhorrence of the life Denholm had lived were the only obstacles. But now that I know he will be pining for another woman during every waking moment of our married lives . . . Oh, Antonia, I don't think I shall be able to bear it!"

Though Rosamond's romantic view of the protagonists in *All for Love* prevailed, there was a bit of minority dissent. For one thing, a scathing caricature caused tittering crowds to gather before a particular print shop window. There a drawing portrayed Lady Hastings, in Grecian costume, her beautiful countenance recognizable but avaricious to the point of repulsiveness, furiously writing upon a scroll, while her muse, who bore a strong resemblance to Mr. Burnside, whispered in her ear. Pots of money were stacked at the playwright's feet while Mr. Denholm and Lord Lytton, stripped to their smallclothes, cowered in the corner. Such a twisted version of the great romance of the day was ascribed to the acerbic Mr. Cruikshank. But since the drawing lacked a signature, this was the merest speculation.

Also, Lady Thirkell held the opinion that whether or not Denholm had ever been as besotted by that creature as the drama had portrayed him, no man could stand being placed on exhibition that way. Lady Hastings obviously had no shame. Tying one's garters in public couldn't touch it.

But as to how Denholm himself felt, those supposedly nearest to him could only surmise. For whatever reason, and for several days, he did not put in an appearance either at Wimpole Street or Grosvenor Square. Captain Crosland, a frequent morning caller to both establishments, was able to report, however, that Mr. Denholm, far from having gone into hiding, was very much upon the town. And Antonia and Rosamond were able to verify the truth of this assertion when, promenading in the park accompanied by the faithful captain, they were passed by Mr. Denholm's curricle drawn by a high-stepping pair. He was far too engrossed by the beauty seated on the leather seat beside him to notice them. But they had ample time to ogle him and correct their first impression that the vision beside him was Lady Hastings, a revision made simple by the fact her hair was golden to the point of improbability.

"My word, it's Venus Sheraton!" the captain blurted out, then wished he hadn't, from his expression.

"Oh?" Rosamond turned her troubled gaze upon him. "Who exactly is Miss Sheraton? I don't think I've ever heard of her."

"Oh, no one in particular." He looked uncomfortable.

"She's a cyprian, Rosamond."

The captain was disconcerted by Antonia's plainspeaking. Rosamond was shocked. But Antonia herself was less disturbed by the kind of company Mr. Denholm kept than by the fact that his ladybird was wearing her gypsy bonnet.

She was unusually subdued and thoughtful when she returned to Grosvenor Square to find a letter from her father waiting there. After reading it, Antonia abandoned any concern she may or may not have been feeling for Mr. Denholm's tangled affairs. He, she felt sure, would be able to sort out his own life. She would now have to face an issue she'd been avoiding—what to do about her own.

This problem occupied her thoughts for several days. In fact, she was so busy concocting various impractical schemes for her future that, as she crossed St. James's Square after an errand to the linen drapers, she failed to take note of a sporting rig that clattered past her and then suddenly pulled up. The driver had to address her twice. "Where's your abigail?" Mr. Denholm inquired when he'd finally gotten her attention. "You've no business out on the street alone."

"Why ever not? Will someone take me for a lightskirt? But I no longer have the gypsy bonnet."

"You saw that, did you?" Denholm was climbing down from a gleaming high-perch phaeton. "I wondered afterward if that was you we passed. Come on. I'll drive you home."

She thought of three reasons why she should not do so, then succumbed to the lure of the elegant equipage. "This is new, isn't it?" she asked after he'd helped her up and then retrieved the reins.

"Brand-new. Had a run of luck at faro."

Antonia sighed. "I must say, you do seem to contradict everything I was ever taught about the fruits of wickedness."

He laughed. "Don't you believe it. I've been known to pay dearly for my sins. Want to try this out? I was just going to the park."

"Oh, yes." She suppressed a brief version of what her grandmother might say with the comforting thought that Mrs. Blakeney need never know. For who would be in Hyde Park to see them at this hour? So with her conscience subdued and the threat of rain she'd noted earlier giving way to sunshine, she rechecked the strings on her cherry bonnet and relaxed to enjoy the briskness of the air as they tooled along. After a minute or two spent in discussing the various points of his rig and cattle, Denholm inquired, "What were you thinking of so hard back there? I almost ran you down, and you didn't even notice."

Antonia hesitated a moment, then rejected her first impulse

to be evasive. She needed to confide in someone. Grandmother and Lady Thirkell were far too involved. And asking advice from Rosamond would be useless. Certainly no one could be more detached and objective than her companion. "To be honest," she blurted out as he slowed the horses and turned into the entrance to the park. "I was trying to form some acceptable scheme for my future."

"Oh?" An eyebrow lifted underneath his jauntily cocked beaver. "Forgive my denseness, but what 'acceptable scheme' can there possibly be other than marriage?"

"Well, I'd always supposed that after my visit here, I would rejoin Papa and keep house for him."

"And now?"

"He's getting married."

"I see. That does upset things. Do you know the lady?"

"Yes." She did not quite succeed in sounding noncommittal.

"And you don't deal well together?"

"I cannot imagine that we ever could. Besides, Papa has made it clear that I'm not wanted." The hurt in her voice earned a look of sympathy that she missed. "Do you remember when you thought I was Rosamond?"

"How could I forget?" he observed while skillfully maneuvering round a barouche.

"Then, you may recall that whereas at first I thought you'd escaped somehow from your strait jacket, then I was ready to accept the possibility that Papa could have arranged my marriage behind my back. He was so eager to ship me off to England, you see. Now I know that it was his own he wished to arrange." She unleashed her bitterness. "And he urges me to make the most of my opportunities here. He doesn't even mind that I'm with Grandmother, though he's kept her secret from me all my life. The important thing is that I have Lady Thirkell's patronage. I tell you, I have never been so disillusioned. Why, there's not a penny's worth of difference between Uncle Edwin and my papa. He's practically ordering me to cast myself upon the marriage mart."

"I don't wish to appear as hopelessly crass as your relatives, but isn't that the fate of every young lady of our class?

And haven't you, in effect, already done just that—entered the marriage mart, I mean? This is, after all, the purpose of a come-out."

"Well, *I* did not consider it so. I only thought of it as an interlude, an adventure, if you will, before I took up my old life again."

"Where you eventually would have married."

"Not necessarily. At least, I would not have felt forced to do so. And Papa is saying that he is absolutely opposed to my marrying a soldier. And that I must take advantage of my opportunities here in London."

"Well, why not? I've never noticed any scarcity of young bucks dangling after you."

"Dangling, yes. But if you think one of them is going to come up to scratch and offer for a girl without a fortune, well, you certainly are a disappointment. Everyone's already saying how worldly you are. And if you think that, well, you're a green 'un."

"It's been known to happen. Remember the penniless Gunning sisters? They married peers. Right down to the final Gunning."

"There were only two of them, not a bevy. They were also nonpareils."

"I'll let that pass. I can't stand females who dangle after compliments."

"And I can't stand males you feel compelled to talk flattering fustian. I am serious."

"Yes, I can see that."

"And the thing is, even if I were a Gunning, I have yet to see a man I'd wish to marry. And I cannot go on indefinitely sponging off Lady Thirkell."

"I wouldn't worry about that too much. Aunt Kate can well afford it."

"But I've no claim upon her. It's enough that she supports Grandmother, which I long to do. I'd even dreamed of taking her back to Belgium. For what's to happen to her if Lady Thirkell dies?"

"You really are blue-deviled. I'm quite confident that Aunt Kate will have provided for her. Want me to ask her?"

"No! That would never do. Oh, would you? I mean, not directly. But could you hint? For if I knew that Grandmother was provided for, well, then, I could feel much freer about seeking a post for myself."

"What kind of post?" he asked as he whipped up his team. "Can you do anything?"

"Well . . ." She sounded doubtful. "I could be a governess to very small children, I suppose. Before they needed to be taught much more than their ABCs."

"I doubt there's much demand for that," he observed dampeningly.

"You're probably right. I should perhaps be a companion."

"And become a dogsbody? Believe me, the relationship between Aunt Kate and your grandmother is hardly typical. You'd hate it. Your father's right. You'd better marry."

She glared. "You haven't paid the slightest attention to what I've said, have you? I've just explained why I cannot."

He narrowed his eyes to study the gait of the leftside horse. "Would you like for me to offer for you? Again."

"I don't find that amusing. I know I've no right to dump my troubles upon you, but you did ask and could at least take me seriously. And I had thought it just possible, considering all you yourself have been through, that you might be a bit more understanding than the average, though why I should have thought so defies all reason. I collect I must have let that ridiculous play influence me. I should have remembered that that sensitive, caring man on stage was not really you."

"You're damned right he wasn't," Denholm snapped. "And if you'll climb down off your high ropes a minute, we—"

Whatever he had intended to say was interrupted by a horseman cantering past in the opposite direction. The rider abruptly reined in and shouted after them, "Fitz! Fitzhugh Denholm! Is that really you, or has your ghost come back to haunt me?"

Mr. Denholm abruptly pulled up his team, thrust the reins into Antonia's hands, and leaped down from the phaeton. "I won't be a minute," he called over his shoulder as he went to join the friend who was tactfully waiting at a little distance in case he did not wish to introduce his female companion. With a great deal of back-thumping and shoulder-slapping, each man explained to the other how he happened to be back in England and then arranged a more lengthy reunion for later on that evening. When Denholm returned to his rig five minutes later, he found that Antonia had moved over into his place.

"Could I please drive?"

"No. Scoot over."

"But I'd give anything to learn. Ladies do, you know. I saw two driving in the park just the other day."

"In a high-perch phaeton?"

"Yes. And the woman driving seemed a perfect hand."

"No doubt. But I daresay she didn't learn on that particular rig. Perhaps I'll let you drive my curricle someday."

"Driving a phaeton doesn't look so difficult."

"It is. Besides, I wish to finish our conversation, not wind up in the ditch."

"Our conversation is already finished as far as I'm concerned." She was reluctantly scooting across the leather seat to avoid being sat upon. "And, as for ditches, I've no intention of—oh, dear, my reticule." She had somehow swept her purse off the other side.

Sighing, Denholm dismounted again and walked round the rear of the phaeton to retrieve it. Then, just as he bent to do so, Miss Thorpe gave the reins a glorious snap and sprang the horses. He watched, cursing beneath his breath, while his team and its female driver galloped out of sight.

At first Antonia felt only exhilaration as the perfectly matched grays sped down the carriage road. It was the curricle race all over again, made even more exciting by her elevated perch and sense of power. Her bonnet was blown back off her curls, but this time the ribbons held and it bounced merrily against her back while the wind played havoc with the Grecian arrangement of her hair. Since the team showed a decided preference for keeping to the center of the road, it was most fortunate that the traffic was quite light. It was only when she tried to pull her horses to one side to avoid a landau that Antonia realized she might be in a bit of trouble. The pair refused to yield an inch. The coachman of the oncoming carriage headed for the open field while the lady passengers squealed and their escorts hurled oaths at the flying phaeton.

"So, I'm not yet quite ready for the Whip Club," she told herself aloud; "driving is famous!" Although she now recognized some of her inadequacy, it never occurred to her that she'd be unable to stop whenever she desired till she pulled hard upon the reins and shouted "Whoa!" and the pace accelerated. And as if this were not sufficient warning, the full import of her predicament was now brought home by the shocked expression of a horseman who had just roweled his steed to avoid her. "Help! Runaways!" Antonia screeched as she sped on by him.

Captain Crosland acted with all the courage, daring, and dispatch that had made England victor over the upstart Napoleon. He wheeled his horse and tore off in hot pursuit, overtaking the runaway rig and managing to grab hold of the harness and slow the horses down to a gradual halt. "Are you all right, Miss Thorpe?" he asked solicitously, noting her chalk-white face.

"C-certainly." Antonia did not protest, however, when Captain Crosland secured his horse to the rear of the phaeton and took the reins from her nerveless fingers. But she did recover sufficiently to give an edited explanation of her circumstance before they rounded the curve to the scene of her piracy. The captain heard her out, chuckled, and agreed to trade places with her, adding there was little danger of a repeat performance since the horses were now run quite off their feet.

Denholm, leaning against a tree and scowling, was thereupon treated to the sight of Miss Thorpe, her bonnet sedately in place, who was very much in command of the situation, while Captain Crosland lounged beside her, casually lighting up a brown cheroot. "I've had the most glorious spin," Antonia announced in a bright voice that was almost steady. "And look who I ran into—chanced upon, I mean to say."

Mr. Denholm held his pose while his narrowed eyes traveled from her chalky face, to the flecks of foam upon his team, to Crosland's dishevelment. With a Herculean effort he refrained from comment and merely nodded briefly to the captain as he strolled over to reclaim his rig. He had missed his opportunity, for Miss Thorpe chatted desperately of this and that all the way back to Grosvenor Square, never allowing him or Captain Crosland to slip in so much as a word.

Chapter Thirteen

T HE HONORABLE FITZHUGH DENHOLM WAS A GREAT DEAL more knowing than Miss Antonia Thorpe. He was well aware when he was being manipulated. But it suited him to act upon Captain Crosland's casually dropped regrets that he'd spent too much time in the army to gain admission to any of London's exclusive clubs. He invited him to be his guest at Brooks's that very evening. And after several hours of play in the Great Subscription Room, wherein the captain won a modest sum and Denholm fared ever better, they settled down with brandy and cigars to the real business of the evening.

Denholm allowed the captain to do his none-too-subtle probing first. And after a few inquiries concerning Miss Antonia Thorpe's status in the Thirkell household and Mr. Denholm's opinion of the rumors that her ladyship might make the girl her heir, when none of the answers proved satisfactory, he turned the conversation around to Miss Rosamond Thorpe.

Here the captain felt his way a bit more carefully. But he wound up with the confirmed impression that Sir Edwin's only child did indeed have great expectations and that, although nothing had been definitely settled yet, the nabob opposite, so casually regarding him through a cloud of smoke, was going to become a rival to Croesus through a marriage to the fair Rosamond. The world was indeed unjust, the captain concluded, when a here-and-thereian like Denholm had it all and a stout fellow like himself was forced to scrape by on his charm and wit.

But when it came to learning what one wished to know, two could play at the same game. Without needing to resort to the kind of digging the other had employed, Mr. Denholm was able to confirm his impression that Captain Crosland was a blatant fortune hunter and would not do for Miss Antonia Thorpe.

There was one thing, though, that had been puzzling Denholm about the soldier, and scorning the other's devious methods, he asked his question bluntly. "How does it happen, Captain, that with Napoleon on the rampage again, you've been able to spend so much time in England?"

"Well, it's not a thing I care to talk about." Crosland assumed an air of proper modesty. "Wounded, you know. Needed a good deal of time to recuperate. Bad timing on my part, of course. Hate to miss such a show." His expression now was downcast, and Denholm noticed as they left the club that his limp, heretofore unnoticeable, had become quite pronounced.

Sleep was slow in coming when the Honorable Fitzhugh Denholm finally blew out his candle in St. James Street. He found his troubled thoughts returning more than once to Miss Antonia Thorpe. What on earth had caused him to be so quixotic as to mention offering for her? Thank God she hadn't taken him seriously. The question he couldn't answer was whether or not he had been. Oh, there was no doubt in his mind that he'd much prefer to be married to her than to her vacuous cousin, but since the only purpose in marrying was to please his long-suffering parents, such a preference had nothing at all to say in the matter. Lord and Lady Worth might prefer Antonia to Eugenia Lytton—*Hastings,* he should say—but only barely. No, that particular alliance was not to be considered.

But he continued to think of Antonia anyhow, in order to avoid more painful thoughts; so he surmised. And he realized that he was quite concerned for her. A step up, he mocked himself, from his usual absorption with his own self-inflicted problems.

He had never before considered the plight of the gently bred young female who had no fortune. Few, if any, in that category had been flung at his head back during the interlude when he'd been considered the biggest catch on the marriage mart, before Eugenia Lytton had tossed her cap over the windmill and run off with him. No, Antonia was right. Money married money. In the main, at least. But there were exceptions. Men did now and again lose their heads over certain women. He—and his smile was bitter there in the darkness—was living proof of that. Antonia Thorpe was hardly a femme fatale, though. Still, she did have a rather unique appeal. His smile changed character as he recalled once more the way she'd cheered him on during their curricle race and the sly way she'd left him eating her dust after she'd made off with his rig that morning. But those particular episodes might not endear her to every man, he realized. Denholm frowned and began to make a mental listing of his eligible friends. He came up with a few who just might be interested in a fortuneless young woman of unusual style. It wouldn't hurt him to take a few coves calling at Grosvenor Square. After that, it was up to Antonia Thorpe to make the most of the opportunities he provided.

Denholm felt quite virtuous after this resolve, and he expected the altruistic decision to help him fall asleep. But the thoughts he'd striven to keep at bay came back to torment him. And once more he watched the jackanapes who had portrayed him cavort upon the stage, and through a red haze of anger he saw the gorgeous, triumphant face of Eugenia smiling her knowing smile. He swore vehemently. Then relighted his candle and picked up his sketchpad.

Miss Antonia Thorpe's own first choice for keeping unwelcome thoughts at bay would have been increased activity. But one could not always be paying or receiving calls, and Lady Thirkell's enormous staff of servants precluded making herself useful around the house. As a consequence, Antonia was a frequent visitor to the circulating libraries.

On one such visit, as she edged her way around the shelves, scanning titles, she felt that she was under surveillance. But when she turned to glance at the few other patrons present, she concluded she was imagining things. No one was looking her way. Nor did she recognize any acquaintance. Antonia returned her attention to the serious business of book selection; still, she could not shake the feeling she was being watched. This time she turned more quickly and spied a soberly dressed young man staring her way.

He reddened and approached her. "Pray forgive my boldness in addressing you, Miss Thorpe. Miss *Rosamond* Thorpe said I might find you here and that, under the circumstances, you would not require that we stand on ceremony."

"Oh, are you Mr. Hollingsworth?" Antonia was unable to conceal her astonishment that this was Rosamond's curate, so little did the pale young man with his pale hair and eyes match the Adonis image Rosamond had painted.

"Might I have a private word with you?" From his nervousness, Mr. Cecil Hollingsworth appeared to consider this a most improper suggestion.

"Why, of course." Antonia smiled to set him at ease and, indicating an unoccupied table, went to take a seat. There was a slight delay before the curate followed and sat across from her. He had deemed it necessary to bring along a book as subterfuge and chose to whisper at her across its open pages.

"Miss Rosamond Thorpe tells me that she has made you her confidante." He blushed above the plain white stock he wore.

"Why, y-yes." Antonia's hesitation was not due to contracted nervousness, but to the fact that it had been so long since the curate's name had cropped up in her cousin's conversation, she had almost forgot those early transports. Now she looked expectantly at the young man, waiting for him to come to the point.

But his pulpit training did not permit such directness. He built up slowly to a climax, dwelling at whispered length upon the high regard in which Miss Rosamond held her cousin and the admiration that she accorded the other's ability to take decisive action. "Miss Rosamond Thorpe herself would have never been able to slip away from the Hall and embark for London on the public stage as you did. Nor would I wish her to." In fact, Mr. Hollingsworth could hardly hide his horror at the notion. "But while as a man of the cloth I cannot approve of such a drastic course for any gently bred young lady," he felt obliged to say, "I must at the same time acknowledge the degree of courage such an action showed."

Antonia was about to protest that there was nothing particularly heroic about boarding a coach when the curate forged ahead. "And I must also add that as much as I naturally abhor flouting parental authority, I can see how in Sir Edwin's case you were goaded to do so. He is not an easy man to deal with."

Antonia did wish the prosy young man would not find it necessary to absolve her character before coming to the point. "Why did my cousin wish you to speak to me?" she asked.

He looked a bit offended at such directness. "Rosamond— Miss Thorpe, I should say—feels that anyone as resourceful as you is sure to find a way around our difficulties."

"And just what specific difficulty did she have in mind?"

"Why, in the first place, how to save Rosamond from being sold to that—that—devil's disciple!"

"Mr. Denholm?"

"Of course Mr. Denholm." The curate was beginning to think that his beloved's faith in her cousin's acumen was misplaced. "You are aware of Sir Edwin's ambitions in that regard, are you not, Miss Thorpe?"

"Oh, yes. Of course. Certainly. I'd just never heard Mr. Denholm described in quite those terms before."

"Pray forgive my lack of delicacy. I should not perhaps have done so. But when I think of my sweet, pure Rosamond bartered to such a man, I am beside myself."

"Well, yes, I can see that," Antonia said hastily. His voice had risen from a whisper to an impassioned squeak, and heads were turning toward them. "I do sympathize with your position, Mr. Hollingsworth, but I really don't see what I can do about it."

The curate was looking more and more disillusioned. "We had hoped you could persuade your uncle to see reason. Mr.

Denholm can only make dear Rosamond miserable. I could make her happy."

"Well, yes, I suppose so." Antonia had not intended to sound so doubtful on the second score. "But the thing is, as you've just noted, Uncle Edwin and I do not deal well together."

"Ah, yes." As a man of the cloth Mr. Hollingsworth was probably not in the habit of playing aces, but his tone of voice would have been appropriate for such a contingency. "But you have a most formidable ally—Lady Thirkell. It is Rosamond's impression that her ladyship does not wish Mr. Denholm to marry her. If this is so, could you not persuade her to make her desires known? Sir Edwin, according to Rosamond, stands in great awe of her."

"*Everyone* stands in great awe of Lady Thirkell," Antonia retorted. "Including me. And I can hardly see myself persuading her of anything."

"Well, I must say that Rosamond will be very disappointed." The curate was decidedly huffy by now. "She relied on you. I don't think it even occurred to her that you would be so unsympathetic."

"I'm not unsympathetic," Antonia was stung into declaring. "It's just that I feel it would be an abuse of her ladyship's hospitality for me to meddle in her family affairs." What she didn't confide to the curate was that she feared her ladyship might find her motives suspect. She had awakened to the fact that Lady Thirkell was developing an alarming tendency to throw her at Mr. Denholm's head. "No, it would be quite improper for me to try to influence her ladyship. And I've no chance whatsoever in changing Uncle's mind." She raised a hand to cut off whatever new reproaches were forming on the curate's lips. "But I will promise to think on the problem very seriously." She rose to her feet dismissively. "And then I'll discuss the matter with Rosamond." Since the curate's expression suggested a prisoner denied his stay of execution, Antonia was moved to add, "Come now, cheer up, Mr. Hollingsworth. Things cannot be as black as they now appear. Love will always find a way."

Antonia could not believe that such a preposterous bromide

had actually emerged from her own mouth. Was it perhaps a line from *All for Love*? It certainly rang as false as the rest of that cloying drama. She glanced at Mr. Hollingsworth, braced for a scathing setdown.

The clergyman, however, was looking at her with new respect. His pale eyes glowed. There could be no doubt about it. Mr. Hollingsworth was most definitely heartened.

Chapter Fourteen

Mrs. Blakeney thoroughly approved of Captain Crosland. He was everything she desired in a grandson— handsome, charming, attentive to old ladies. She had decided that he would be perfect for Antonia. After all, they came from the same background, he knew of her straitened circumstances, and he obviously had private means. The fact that he was on such easy terms with so many of the ton suggested at least a competency, if not actual wealth. He had just been entertaining Antonia and several morning callers with a lively account of an evening at his exclusive club. When the others had left and the captain was still there, the scheming Mrs. Blakeney contrived to leave him and her granddaughter alone together.

Well, not literally alone or it would have been much too improper to excuse herself to tend to a domestic matter. Lady Thirkell was with them, ensconced in her favorite wing chair, her feet resting on a painted cross-framed stool. But her ladyship had been receiving visitors for the better part of two hours, and her head was beginning to nod. Mrs. Blakeney was sure that in a few moments' time the attractive young couple would be entirely private, a state of affairs she knew the captain yearned for.

Her deduction proved correct. As Captain Crosland prosed on at length about the play in Brooks's Subscription Room, his narrative was soon punctuated with snores. He broke it off. "Miss Rosamond has made me her confidant," he said, being careful not to change his tone of voice.

"I beg your pardon?" Antonia had not been attending. In fact, she had almost followed their hostess's example. "Confided about what, I mean to say," she rallied.

"About the monstrous coil she's in—forced into a marriage she finds abhorrent while her heart belongs to another."

"Oh, yes, that. Of course." If Antonia was a bit surprised that her shy cousin had been so open, she thought it impolite to say so.

"And she tells me that you mean to help. I think that's splendid of you."

"Well . . ." She glanced at Lady Thirkell, whose chin was now resting on her collarbone. "Yes, I have said that I would try. And, to tell the truth, I've thought of little else. But I don't really see how. Uncle Edwin has his heart set on this match, you know."

"Yes, I do know." Captain Crosland leaned toward her and lowered his voice. "And I agree with you. On the surface, matching Miss Rosamond with the man of her choice seems hopeless. We need to approach the problem from another angle."

Antonia did not miss the "we." But she was no further enlightened and said so.

"Really, Miss Thorpe, it's very simple. We must see to it that Mr. Denholm weds someone else."

"Perhaps you think that's simple. But I certainly don't see how *we*,"—she stressed the pronoun—"can possibly do anything of the kind."

"Merely by providing the opportunity. After all, Denholm already loves another. He is, in fact, the victim of a grand

107

passion that makes Miss Thorpe and her curate—pray do not repeat this to your cousin—seem like two young mooncalves."

"Oh? And has Mr. Denholm also confided in you?"

"Not in so many words." His knowing look implied an understanding between gentlemen. "But you were in Drury Lane. At Miss Rosamond's insistence I went myself the other night. Can you doubt the depth of the attachment?"

"Well, no, I suppose not."

Antonia had no desire to pursue that subject any further, but the captain seemed unaware of her reluctance. "It's obviously only pride that stands in the way. Lady Hastings tells me that is the major obstacle to their happiness, the thing that makes Denholm determined to keep avoiding her."

"You know Lady Hastings!"

"Shhh!" In her astonishment Antonia had allowed her voice to rise. Lady Thirkell raised her head, looked all around the withdrawing room, then nodded off once more. "Yes. After my conversation with Miss Rosamond I took it upon myself to gain an introduction to Lady Hastings in order to discuss your cousin's situation. And I must say her ladyship's gratitude for my doing so was most touching. She had heard rumors of an understanding between Denholm and Miss Rosamond and is convinced that such a match could only cause great unhappiness to the parties most concerned. She's quite sure of Denholm's love, you see." He broke into his train of thought to ask, "Have you ever seen Lady Hastings?"

"Yes. From a distance."

"Then, you can well imagine that any man could easily fall under her spell. And one who, like Denholm, has been on such intimate terms with her ladyship—pray forgive my candor—could not easily free himself from that spell. If it were not for his fierce pride and all-consuming jealousy—"

"You must forgive me, Captain Crosland," Antonia interrupted rather rudely. She was finding this conversation more and more distasteful. "But I really don't see what all this has to do with me."

"That's what I'm trying to explain." He frowned. "To put it simply, we must find a way to bring those two parted lovers back together. And since you seem to have considerable influence with Denholm—"

"That's ridiculous," she protested. "I've no such thing."

But as if to disprove her words, Morton appeared at that moment to announce, "Lord Thayer Edgemon and Mr. Denholm, your ladyship."

"Oh, there you are, Fitzhugh." Lady Thirkell snapped to, adjusted her cap, which had slipped down upon her forehead, and fastened her wide-awake gaze upon her nephew. "Thought you'd probably gone into hiding after that odious woman's odious play. Glad to see you ain't. Best to outface the gossip-mongers, I always say."

"What I like most about you, Aunt Kate, is your remarkable tact and delicacy." Mr. Denholm, looking unusually elegant in a blue tailcoat with brass buttons worn over a fawn waistcoat, nodded at the others and strolled over to kiss her cheek. "You remember my friend Thayer, of course."

Lord Thayer, despite his tailor's efforts to minimize his slightly rotund figure with dark-blue superfine worn with gray, still fell far below his friend's sartorial splendor. Under the old lady's stare, he turned pink and bowed.

"Of course. Couldn't forget him, more's the pity. Helped you liberate me parrot. Nasty little boys, both of you. Antonia, ring for more tea. Oh, never mind, here it is." The butler had made a reappearance. "But you don't know my companion's granddaughter, now, do you? Antonia, this is Lord Thayer Edgemon. Thayer, Miss Antonia Thorpe. And the military gentleman is Captain Crosland."

His lordship murmured a polite acknowledgment to both introductions, but his amiable face had grown bemused. Antonia was feeling most uncomfortable, whereas the captain found the situation intriguing until he realized her ladyship was looking pointedly at him as she poured out only four cups of tea and was reminded that he had flagrantly overstayed the prescribed twenty minutes for morning calls.

After the captain's departure, Lord Thayer returned his puzzled gaze to Antonia and inquired politely. "Ain't we met before, Miss Thorpe? Nearly sure of it."

"I pointed Miss Thorpe out to you when we were out riding," Denholm offered, and suppressed a smile as the light finally dawned upon his friend.

"Oh, *that's* who you are. Didn't realize. What I mean to say is, you don't look the same. That is, I didn't expect to find you here. Couldn't have, of course, just having seen you riding in the park that way," he finished lamely.

"And speaking of driving," Denholm chimed in none too subtly, while taking a proffered cup from his aunt's hand, "Miss Thorpe here has expressed a burning desire to learn to drive a curricle, Thayer. And since you're so devilish proud of your new equipage and inclined to show off at every opportunity, it occurred to me that you are the very one to teach her. I assure you, Miss Thorpe, no one's more qualified than his lordship to be your instructor. His prowess as a whip is legendary."

"Oh, I say," Lord Thayer protested.

"Really, Mr. Denholm." Antonia glared.

"Nonsense!" Lady Thirkell thundered, and got the floor. "What's the meaning of this, Antonia?"

"Miss Thorpe wishes to learn to drive, ma'am." Denholm forestalled whatever answer Antonia might have made. "More and more young ladies are doing so. It's quite the thing, in fact. I hope you've no objection."

"I've no objection to Antonia learning. Think it's a capital notion, in fact. Been thinking of getting a sporting rig. She can drive me. What I object to is having Thayer teach her. Now, no need to look offended," she said soothingly to her titled guest, "I'm sure you're a dab hand, boy. But me nevvy's coming it too strong when he says no one's more qualified to teach Antonia. Pack of nonsense. He is."

"Thank you for your vote of confidence, Aunt Kate. But the thing is, it will not be convenient for me to teach Miss Thorpe." He gave his relative a speaking look that was entirely wasted.

Denholm had been rather proud of this scheme to bring Lord Thayer and Miss Thorpe together. Thayer had no need to marry money. He was also painfully shy where the ladies were concerned. Driving was his greatest passion. Denholm, therefore, had counted on Miss Thorpe's own enthusiasm for that sport to break down Thayer's bashfulness and give them a common interest to counteract his usual tongue-tied state. Trust Aunt Kate to blow the gaff!

"Well, then, it's settled," that autocrat pronounced. "You'll teach Antonia to drive, Fitzhugh. Call for her at nine tomorrow."

"No, Aunt."

"Too early, eh? Humph. Planning to be on the town all night, I collect. Oh, very well. Make it nine-thirty, then. No later. Won't do to let the traffic get too heavy."

"What won't do, Aunt Kate, is for me to teach Miss Thorpe to drive." Denholm's exasperation was evident. Antonia's initial annoyance had turned to amusement. She took a quick sip of tea to cover up her smile. "To be as blunt as you are wont to be, dear relative, have you forgotten my reputation? Surely you don't wish to make Miss Thorpe grist for the gossipmongers' mill?"

"She won't be," Lady Thirkell said complacently. "Nothing could be more natural than for you two to be seen together. Everyone knows that Antonia is my ward and you are my heir."

"I didn't know it!" Lord Thayer Edgemon blurted out, as Antonia strangled on her tea. "Never knew either one of those things. The ward business don't surprise me. But hadn't the slightest notion you were her ladyship's heir, Fitz."

"No, I expect you didn't, for it isn't true. Any more than it's true that Tonia—Miss Thorpe—is her ward. My aunt will stop at nothing, including the most out-and-out rappers, to get her own way."

"Oh, very well." The old lady looked sheepish. "You've caught me out. But the true or false of the thing don't signify. Your concern was with what people will say when they see you two out driving together at nine-thirty A.M. sharp. And that's what they'll say. Or would if they saw you, which they won't, for no self-respecting member of the ton will be in Hyde Park at such an ungodly hour.

"Now do run along, Fitzhugh, and take Thayer with you. For I need me nap. And Mrs. Blakeney is the only person I know of who actually would be shocked if I left her grand-daughter alone with a man of your reputation. By the by, Antonia, no need to mention this driving business to her. Shouldn't say so, for she's me dearest friend, but your grandmama's too strait-laced by half. I tell you, there's nothing like leading a scandalous life to turn an otherwise normal person into a pattern card of virtue."

Chapter Fifteen

"HOW DOES IT FEEL TO HAVE BEEN HOIST BY YOUR OWN petard?" Antonia inquired as they turned into Hyde Park. The morning was chill and damp with fog, making her envy Denholm's five-caped greatcoat, more suitable to the capricious weather than the light pelisse she wore. Hers were the first words spoken since a perfunctory greeting when he'd arrived at Grosvenor Square promptly at nine-thirty. Antonia had been ready and waiting but had not actually expected him to appear. Since she deduced from his haggard face he'd been up for most of the night, his presence was a tribute to Lady Thirkell's forcefulness. Even a confirmed rebel didn't dare to cross her.

"Just what petard was that?"

"Oh, don't play the innocent. I'm well aware you've been flinging suitors at my head ever since I told you of my father's marriage plans. And I suppose that kind of reaction to my Cheltenham tragedy serves me right. And I'll even go so far as to suppose that you mean well by it. But I find it all rather hu-

112

miliating. Poor Lord Thayer! He was quite ready to sink. As for me, I've learned my lesson. I'll never tie my garters in public again. So, pray try to forget that I ever confided in you."

"I've been wondering about that." He pulled his team to a halt and turned to look at her. "Why did you?"

"I've asked myself the same question," she replied candidly. "And the truth is, I haven't the slightest idea. You were there, of course."

"That's certainly one requirement of a confidant."

"But I suppose the main thing was that it was perfectly safe to do so. Or at least I thought so."

"Safe?"

"Well, for one thing, you weren't likely to overset me by being too sympathetic, as my grandmother might have done."

"Thank you."

"And you certainly give the impression that anything told you would be treated with all the sanctity of the confessional. You are probably the most private person I've ever met."

"*Private*, Miss Thorpe?" His lip curled. "You'd best consult Mr. Johnson's dictionary. I am in fact the most *public* person you'll likely meet. How many others of your acquaintance can boast of having the most intimate details of their lives dramatized on stage?"

"But that's exactly what I mean. It's bound to have been simply awful for you. But you don't betray your feelings. And so, I had believed that you'd respect my—outpourings—and not betray them."

"Surely you don't think I did?" he protested. "I can assure you—"

"Oh, I know you haven't gossiped about me. But what you have done is almost worse. For you were the last person I should have expected to turn matchmaker. There is one thing you need to understand, Mr. Denholm. You do not have an exclusive claim to pride. I have my share as well. And I find it humiliating to become an object of your charity."

"Charity!" The word became an epithet. "Is that what you think? Well, you're quite wrong, Miss Thorpe. But your point is well taken, nonetheless. In the future I shall remind myself to

mind my own business—which at the moment, God help me, is to teach you to drive. So, let's get on with it." He then imprudently leaped down from the driver's seat and winced when the impact jarred his aching head.

"Shot the cat last night, did you?" Antonia observed without much sympathy as she scooted into the driver's seat. "Well, I did not intend to put you into such a taking."

"A taking? Me?" He climbed up beside her. "Whatever gave you such a maggoty notion? I'm the man who never shows his feelings, so you just said. Those, Miss Thorpe, are the reins. Now pick them up."

The lesson proceeded in near silence except for the necessary instructions succinctly delivered and promptly acted upon. Antonia, who was beginning to regret so much plain-speaking, devoted herself to being as apt a pupil as was possible. And from her own point of view she succeeded so well that she soon forgot all else but the joy of handling such a superb team hitched to the smoothest running rig it had ever been her privilege to ride in.

So pleased was she with her progress, in fact, that when a foppish young man in a natty bright red curricle pulled alongside intending to pass them, she gave him an impish grin and whipped up her horses. The young man gleefully accepted the challenge and urged his own team on.

"What the devil! Have you lost your mind?" Denholm reached for the reins and got his wrist slapped. "God help you, then, if you damage my cattle or so much as scratch this rig," he growled. And then with a raw courage that would have done justice to a Spartan, he braced his feet, folded his arms, and let his pupil have her head.

Antonia's enthusiasm proved contagious. Denholm's detached disapproval lasted all of thirty seconds before he fell victim to her sparkling eyes and delighted laughter as they pulled a few paces ahead of the red curricle on the tree-lined avenue. He grinned back at her and began to issue rapid instructions.

On the straightaway there was no contest. The superiority of the Denholm cattle compensated for Antonia's inexperience.

But when the road curved sharply, the tutor felt it time to intervene. He put his arms around the driver, his gloved hands closed above her own and reined the horses in. The red rig swept around them with a triumphant shout.

"Oh, how could you be so craven? We could have won. Easily."

Denholm was about to retort that what they could have done was land the curricle in a ditch with themselves hurled God knows where, when he suddenly abandoned the whole idea of explanation. Antonia's lips were entirely too near for such reasonableness. He kissed them. And met a response so intense that it took his breath away and destroyed the last vestiges of his common sense.

There was a sweet desperation in Antonia's kiss. For while her emotions were acknowledging the truth her mind had sought to hide, her intelligence still operated enough for her to know that this was all she could ever expect from such a misguided attachment, and she should do her best to make a memory good enough to last.

After their first widened start of surprise her eyes had closed, her fingers had sent his beaver toppling to entangle with his hair, and she had simply surrendered to the wonderful, heavy glow that overpowered her. She would never have dreamed that the mere touch of lips, the teasing of tongues, could turn the balance of nature topsy-turvy, bringing stars out in mid-morning to spiral and cavort and calling the larks home early from their winter quarters to warble a serenade. All she really knew was that she wanted the moment to last forever—and for this man to love her.

Both notions were ridiculous, of course. As Fitzhugh Denholm soon demonstrated. Though it did seem to take considerable effort to disengage himself, he managed. And his rather dazed expression as he gazed into her equally bemused eyes quickly turned to self-reproach. "I knew it was sheer insanity for me to teach you to drive," he said huskily.

"Well, no need to reproach yourself." Her smile was forced. She'd been wrong when she'd spoken of his skill at hiding what he felt. Emotion was written large upon his face. And of all the things he might have been feeling at the moment, the revealed reaction was the one she wished for least: he seemed completely overcome with guilt.

"I do reproach myself. My God, you're just a child. You probably think by now that every curricle race ends in a kiss. That it's part of the ritual."

"Like cutting off the fox's brush at the end of a hunt? Don't be absurd."

"Don't joke. I'm trying to be serious. The point is, Tonia, I came back to England thinking I could straighten out my life. Well, I was wrong. It's in a bigger mess than ever. There's my father's matchmaking. Eugenia's theatricals. God knows, all that would be coil enough for any normal man. But what do I do but complicate things further by making love to a schoolroom miss. No, do be quiet for one minute, Antonia. What I'm trying to tell you is that I'm the last man on earth you should be entangled with. But since matters seem to have taken their own turn, let me say—"

A kid glove was clapped none too gently over his mouth. Blue eyes glared. "Denholm, don't you dare offer for me again. It will be the third time, and I call that the outside of enough. No wonder you ran off to the Continent. If your conscience can goad you into proposing marriage over a simple—well, let's not call it that—over a *complicated* kiss that no one knows of but us, I can well see why, under those circumstances, you felt you had to elope. No, do be quiet! The only thing you've said so far that makes any sense is that your life is in disarray and you shouldn't make things worse. Do you know what I think?"

"No, but I'm sure you're about to tell me."

"I think you should declare a moratorium on offering anything to any woman—marriage, elopement, carte blanche, whatever. For at least a year. Till you can learn to overcome your odd bent toward chivalry. Really, Denholm, your reputation as a rake seems undeserved. You haven't the slightest notion of how a scoundrel operates. Good heavens, even I— schoolroom miss or not—know that no one gets compromised by a mere kiss. You act as though you'd made me *enceinte*." She punctuated this shocking remark by skillfully cracking the whip and springing the horses. His arms were around her once more, his hands on the reins.

"Please don't do that again." To her mortification, tears stung her eyes.

"Don't worry" was the grim answer as he tugged the horses to a halt once more. "The only thing I intend to resume is the driving lesson. And here's the final, most important pointer of the day. Never let your emotions affect your driving. A good whip never takes his anger out on his cattle. Now, then. I'd say this has been more than enough instruction for one day. I declare the lesson finished. Scoot over. I'll drive."

He remembered how she'd left him high and dry before, so he took no chances. Instead of climbing down and around, he scrambled across her knees and displaced her none too gently. "A good instructor never takes his anger out on his pupil," she mimicked as he flicked his reins. "By the by, you've lost your hat."

"Blast!" He clapped a glove to his head in confirmation, then set to work smoothing his disheveled locks. "Well, what could I expect? Isn't that a part of the ritual, too, when we ride together? Losing hats. My turn again."

"We could go back and get it," she said practically.

"I've got others. It's more than time to get you home."

They rode in silence, sitting as far apart as the seat allowed, neither glancing back as carriage wheels approached.

"Oh, I say, Denholm!" A male shout behind them caused both to turn. Denholm's response was to increase their speed. Nothing of the previous lesson had been lost on Antonia, though. She reached over, grabbed his hands, and tugged on the reins. "It's Captain Crosland. He's got your hat."

Seconds later, Antonia regretted her impetuosity. Unlike her driver, she'd failed to recognize the captain's passenger. Crosland skillfully guided his phaeton up beside them, placing Mr. Denholm and Lady Hastings close enough to touch.

A close-up view of the famous Eugenia Lytton-Hastings put the final touches on Antonia's rotten day. From a distance the lady had seemed merely beautiful. Nearby, she took one's breath away. Never mind that she was well beyond the first blush of youth. "Age cannot wither her, nor custom stale," Shakespeare had once written. Well, actually Lady Hastings wasn't all *that* old. The point was, she seemed the reincarnation of Cleopatra—or Helen—or Calypso—any of those females equipped to lure men to their dooms. A young Denholm would never have stood a chance. With a sinking sensation in her stomach pit, Antonia watched the seductively mocking smile play on the beauty's lips as she studied her ex-lover. "I see this is your hat, Fitzhugh." Her voice was warm and husky. "I can't imagine how you came to lose it." Her knowing smile belied her words.

"No, but I'm sure you'll try, Eugenia," he answered levelly, taking it from her but managing to avoid the intended contact with her hand. "Thank you very much." He clapped the beaver on his head, then tipped it. "Your servant, Eugenia. Captain."

But Lady Hastings reached across and seized his arm before he could flick the reins. "Please, Fitzhugh," she pleaded softly. "Don't run away. You've avoided me at every turn. Refused my letters." The lovely dark eyes brimmed with tears. "It isn't like you to be so cruel. All I ask is a few minutes of your time. And I should not ask that if it were not absolutely vital. If Miss Thorpe would change places with me. You would not mind, would you, Miss Thorpe?"

"Oh, not in the least," Antonia managed to say with forced politeness. But as she started to climb down, a vise-like grip on her arm prevented it. How absurd we must look, she thought inanely, she holding him, he, me.

"Miss Thorpe may not mind, Eugenia, but I do." Denholm's voice was still coolly civil, but he shook the beauty's hand off as though it were some species of vermin that had landed on his sleeve. "As I have endeavored to make clear—but then, you always were a bit obtuse—we've nothing at all to say to each other."

He sprang the horses so abruptly that Antonia feared her neck had snapped. She bit back a protest just in case he proved dangerous. There was no doubt about it, Mr. Denholm was in high dudgeon. She longed to repeat his maxim: A good whip

118

never takes out his anger on his cattle. But she bit that back as well. Antonia was learning prudence fast.

But when he halted his winded team in front of Thirkell House, she considered the tension eased enough to ask, "Don't you think you were rather rough on Lady Hastings?"

His look almost blasted her off the seat. "No, I do not."

"It wouldn't have hurt you to talk to her a minute."

"You know nothing of the matter." He jumped down and reached up an impatient hand to help her alight.

"I know she loves you. All of London knows that."

"And I would be grateful if you and all of London would stay out of my affairs. Good day, Miss Thorpe."

He nodded curtly, climbed into the curricle, and cracked his whip, leaving her standing on the cobblestones, gazing thoughtfully after him as he recklessly took the corner on two wheels.

Arriving back in his own lodgings did little to improve Denholm's mood. The brandy his man presented him might have helped if it had not been accompanied on the silver tray by a letter from his father. Denholm read the epistle twice before consigning it to the fire.

The news of the London theatrical sensation had filtered down to Kent. This latest chapter in Fitzhugh's sordid history had put his mother to bed, so his father had informed him, and might well prove to be more than her much-tried constitution could overcome. As for his lordship, his son would never know the pain and humiliation that gentleman had suffered, for unlike Fitzhugh, he cringed at making a public spectacle of himself.

The point of the letter was not to dwell upon his or his dear wife's pain, however, his father continued, but to consider what might be done to salvage the few shreds of dignity left the Denholm name. So after talking the matter over with Sir Edwin Thorpe (there had been several lines devoted to Sir Edwin's magnanimous attitude; not every gentlemen would wish to see his daughter married to a man lumbered with such scandal), they had decided that the quickest way to stop tongues wagging was for Society to read the notice of the Honorable

Fitzhugh Denholm's betrothal in the *Gazette*. That should scotch all speculation about an alliance between Fitzhugh and "that woman." Sir Edwin was writing to let his daughter know his wishes in the matter. Instead of finishing out the London Season, Miss Thorpe was to accept Fitzhugh's proposal and come home. Lord Worth concluded by hoping he might rely upon his son to respect his father's wishes in this one matter and offer for Miss Rosamond Thorpe with all dispatch.

After the letter had flamed, curled into black carbon, and then disintegrated, Denholm sat for a long time staring into the fire and drinking deep. If the desired numbness didn't come to alleviate some of the pain that he was feeling, at least the brandy, or time, brought resignation.

Perhaps marrying Rosamond Thorpe was the best thing that could happen. It would be a marriage of convenience, in the classic mode—"convenient" for both of them to see as little of each other as the business of producing an heir would allow. True, having to give up her curate might go hard with Rosamond for a while. But Denholm was well enough acquainted with that spoiled young lady to know that life with an impoverished cleric would not suit her for very long. Of course, her father wouldn't likely leave her destitute. But unless Denholm missed his guess, some of the curate's luster had already begun to fade as Rosamond herself acquired town bronze.

Yes, he and she might deal well enough together. For the fortunate thing was, she didn't love him. A picture of her cousin's face at the conclusion of their kiss came back to haunt him. And despite the way Antonia had rallied her forces to hide her feelings and stop him making a foolish declaration, he was far too worldly not to realize she'd fallen in love with him. And though at this moment his deepest desire was to tell his father to go to blazes, that he planned to marry the other, ineligible Miss Thorpe, he knew he could not do it. Rosamond might appear to be the weaker of the two cousins, but she was well armed against him. She didn't love him. Ergo, he couldn't hurt her. Whereas Antonia was very vulnerable indeed. And while he might think now at this very moment he would, perhaps, be able to make her happy—he refilled his glass and quickly drained it—it was no good. For he had no faith in his constancy at all.

Chapter Sixteen

SIR EDWIN THORPE HAD NOT RELIED UPON THE MAIL coach to convey his wishes to his daughter. He had personally come up to London to avoid any misunderstanding.

There was none. But after he had gone, poor Rosamond was in such a quake over Mr. Denholm's looming proposal that she sent a message at once to Captain Crosland appealing for his help. It was his advice that she absent herself as much as possible from Wimpole Street until they could work out a strategy. Mr. Denholm could hardly propose if he could not find her home.

The two sought out Antonia. "I'm convinced Denholm really loves Lady Hastings" was Captain Crosland's voiced opinion. "We merely have to get them together long enough for her to break down his stiff-necked pride. Eugenia has suggested that we arrange an outing with him to Vauxhall."

"Oh, but I couldn't go there." Rosamond looked shocked. The gardens, a favorite gathering place for the hoi polloi, had gained a rather unsavory reputation.

"Not you, Miss Rosamond. I rely upon your cousin to persuade Mr. Denholm to take her to Vauxhall Gardens."

The captain overrode all of Antonia's objections. "In the first place," she'd protested, "I can't really accept your premise that Mr. Denholm is in love with Lady Hastings. You observed him in the park. I'd come nearer to believing he hated her."

"Of course that's how it appeared. You should know that there's a fine line between love and hate. Now, if he were indifferent, that would be quite another matter."

"Perhaps you're right," she reluctantly conceded. "But in the second place, I doubt I can persuade him to go."

"Of course you can." Rosamond's eyes were large and trusting. "Mr. Denholm quite likes you, Antonia."

So in the end she had agreed to try and lure Mr. Denholm to Vauxhall Gardens, since they'd come up with no other plan. "It will have to be quite soon," the practical captain pointed out. "Rosamond can only dodge Denholm for a few more days before her father learns of it."

Her cousin's touching gratitude for her cooperation made Antonia squirm. For as much as she was sickened by the thought of Denholm married to Lady Hastings, she liked the thought of his being married to Rosamond even less. Hence her willingness to help.

The following day their silly scheme seemed even more rackety, however, and she decided to postpone sending a message to Mr. Denholm until afternoon. He'd not likely stir from bed all morning anyhow. In the meantime she could be thinking how best to persuade him to accompany her to Vauxhall. And, she decided, a visit to Spring Gardens might clear her brain for that distasteful effort and at the same time lift her sagging spirits. So after receiving permission from Lady Thirkell, Antonia engaged the coachman to drive her to Pimlico.

The drawing exhibition there had the desired effect of wiping everything else but its beauty from her mind as she walked through the various rooms studying the array of paintings jammed together upon the walls—three, four, even five deep, depending upon the size. Antonia craned her neck to observe those next to the ceiling and squatted ungracefully to examine those near the floor. Then when fatigue finally broke through her absorption, she seated herself at a table provided in the center of the room and settled in to concentrate on those works of the late, great Sir Joshua Reynolds that were grouped within her view.

After spending some time trying to commit the artist's techniques to memory, Antonia had a better notion. She laid her sketchbook open on the table, helped herself to the pen and ink so thoughtfully provided, and with frowning concentration began to draw.

"That's not bad." The voice that caused her to spoil a line sounded surprised. "You never told me you were an artist." The Honorable Fitzhugh Denholm sat down beside her and cast an appraising eye over her sketch, then studied it intently. "Not bad," he repeated. "Perhaps if you tried this, however." He took the pen from her nerveless fingers and with a few deft strokes altered her drawing until it reflected the essence of the masterpiece upon the wall.

"Damnation," Antonia said.

Denholm looked slightly shocked. "I do beg pardon. I've spoiled the picture for you. I had no right."

"No, you haven't spoiled it. Quite the contrary, in fact." She was mortified at her unladylike exclamation. "It's just so aggravating. Is there anything you can't do?"

"Oh, the list is endless."

"It doesn't seem to be." Her disgust got the upper hand again. "Here I was, thinking seriously that my greatest asset was an ability to draw and that perhaps I could employ myself by giving lessons; then you happen along and with five strokes of the pen show me how absurd my notion was."

"Oh, come now. You make me feel like a monster. I said your work was good."

"Actually, what you said was that it wasn't bad. Then clearly demonstrated that it was. There's no use hoping anyone will take me seriously as an artist when any foppish"—she stared pointedly at the brand-new coat of bottle-green he wore, set off by a flowery buttonhole—"dilettante who comes along can immediately outdo me."

"No need to be insulting. I said I was sorry." His twinkling eyes, however, belied a true repentance. "Besides, I take exception to your name-calling. Oh, I grant you 'foppish.' Weston will be pleased that you noticed his latest creation. It's all the crack. And my valet insisted on the buttonhole. But I'm no dilettante." He had reclaimed her sketchbook and was drawing furiously with one eye on the wall. "Some people would say that I can even out-Reynolds Reynolds." He pushed the drawing toward her, and she laughed out loud, causing heads to turn curiously their way. What he had produced was an absurdly comical caricature of the artist's work "Mrs. Siddons as the Tragic Muse."

"Oh, really, this is libelous!" Antonia whispered. "Poor Sir Joshua is no doubt turning in his—" She broke off suddenly to stare at him. "That was your cartoon at the printshop, wasn't it?"

"Damnation!" It was his turn to voice disgust. He didn't pretend not to know exactly what she meant.

"It never occurred to me—or to anyone else, I daresay— that you'd done that wicked drawing."

"I hope not. And I'd appreciate your keeping it to yourself. I was immediately sorry for it. It was a petty—womanish, if you'll forgive me—sort of revenge."

" 'Womanish'!" she bristled. "Well, perhaps you're right. It was subtle. And funny. And made its point. What would 'manly' be? A duel? That was your earlier recourse, as I recall."

He studied her thoughtfully. "You really do have your dagger drawn today, haven't you? But since you bring it up, actually I've never been enamored of the art of dueling; though, if you'll forgive my adding to your grievances, I am good at it. But my only indulgence in that activity was forced upon me.

"What I should have preferred to do after I saw that play was plant a few levelers. I'm also good at that. But one can't hit a weakling. And certainly not a female. Hence the cartoon. Oh, yes, I got drunk as well. Neither reaction very laudable, I fear."

"Maybe not. But still a great improvement over pistols at dawn."

"Don't patronize me. But to get back to our earlier discussion, and none too soon, I don't see why my ability, or lack of it, with a pen should have anything to say to your ambitions to be a drawing teacher. My superiority to you in that area is doubtful. Sir Joshua's . . ."—he nodded toward the wall—"is an established fact. You didn't let him discourage you. Why me? It makes no sense."

"It certainly does. I can't even compete with amateurs."

"Forgive—once again—my immodesty. I'm not precisely that. That is, if you define 'professional' as one who's paid and don't judge by quality: you see, I did work as an illustrator in Italy."

She stared in amazement. "Did you really?"

"Oh, yes. I've several books to my credit. Or 'discredit,' if you will. Again I rely on your discretion. I'd hate for my father to learn of this other blot on the Denholm escutcheon. He would probably find my venture into commerce a greater disgrace than my womanizing. At least, there's precedent among the ton for the latter pursuit."

"Your father is sap-skulled, if you'd pardon my saying so. I think what you did is famous. Oh, I know—you informed me when we first met that I'm little better than a cit. So, I suppose my attitude only proves your point. But I really don't see how anyone, gentleman or not, could bear to be forever idle. I'm glad you found something interesting to occupy you while you were abroad. For I don't suppose," she added thoughtfully, "that even the grandest passion would make one wish to make love exclusively and have no other interests."

"One does reach a saturation point," he observed with a near-straight face.

"I shouldn't have said that either." She sighed. "But I do find it difficult to stand on points with you. From the moment we met, our association has been so—bizarre—that it seems impossible to put things back on a proper footing."

"Antonia, I would not have you changed for all of China's tea."

"You're roasting me, of course. I realize I should change. But it hardly seems worth the effort since I doubt we shall be seeing each other very much longer." This observation struck Antonia as such a lowering prospect, that she rushed on to say, "Do tell me, please, how does one become an illustrator? Do you think I'm good enough to do it? Does it pay well? I must say it sounds a great deal more pleasant than instructing children. Don't you agree?"

Denholm seemed almost as anxious as she to move the conversation from the muddied waters of their relationship. He willingly launched into a discourse upon the illustrator's craft, which he concluded with a promise to explore the London possibilities for her. And as Antonia was expressing her gratitude for his offer, she suddenly recalled the mission she'd been entrusted with. "Oh, dear. This is terrible," she blurted out. "I've another favor to ask of you. Will you escort me to Vauxhall Gardens tomorrow night?"

"No. Nor at any other time."

"No? Oh, dear. I did so very much wish to go there." Antonia fairly choked on the whisker. "And Lady Thirkell will only give her permission if you take me."

"Then, my aunt has taken complete leave of her senses. Vauxhall Gardens is no place for you. And particularly not with me."

"Oh, but you would be the perfect escort. You've just admitted that you're a dab hand in a mill. You'd be well able to protect me against any rough element I might meet there."

"Yes, but who'd protect you from me?"

"Don't be absurd. I'll need no such protection. Not unless we drive in your curricle and race someone on the way. That's the only time we behave improperly."

Her attempt at humor failed. There was no responsive smile. "I'll not take you to Vauxhall." Denholm rose to his feet. "It's no place for a lady. Trust my judgment on that score at least. My aunt is out of touch, or she wouldn't dream of encouraging you to go there. Not with anyone."

Antonia looked so distressed that he reached out and lightly touched her cheek. "I wouldn't disappoint you without good reason, Tonia." He smiled crookedly. "You really must learn not to play with fire. Good day."

He turned abruptly and strode from the gallery, leaving Antonia confused as to whether it was Vauxhall or himself he was warning her away from.

Chapter
Seventeen

ROSAMOND THREATENED HYSTERICS WHEN SHE LEARNED of Antonia's failure and was warned that if she didn't hush that instant Mrs. Blakeney was sure to reappear to see what was wrong. Captain Crosland, though, received the news that Mr. Denholm had flatly refused to escort Miss Thorpe to Vauxhall Gardens with surprising equanimity. He and Rosamond had come calling at Grosvenor Square that afternoon to find out if Antonia had succeeded in contacting Mr. Denholm (and, not incidentally, to insure that if the Honorable Fitzhugh Denholm came calling at Wimpole Street, he'd find Rosamond out). They were in the withdrawing room huddled over the tea tray, deep in conspiracy.

"Don't be distressed," the captain spoke soothingly to Rosamond. "No campaigner goes into battle without a contingency plan. If Denholm had agreed to accompany Miss Antonia, it would have made matters simpler, that's all. But it will amount to the same thing in the end. And that's what counts. Miss Antonia, I will personally escort you to the gardens. Lady Hastings can make her own arrangements."

"But what's the point of going without Denholm?" Antonia protested.

"He'll be there. Leave that to me."

"But I needn't be. And I certainly do not wish to."

"Oh, but you, Miss Antonia, are absolutely vital to my scheme. Now here's what we shall do."

Antonia thought little of the captain's plan, which involved sending Denholm a note, supposedly from Lady Thirkell, saying that Miss Thorpe had gone without her permission to Vauxhall and asking him to set out in hot pursuit.

"What if Denholm is not at home?" she objected.

"Why, then, the footman will track him down."

"But what if Mr. Denholm checks first with Lady Thirkell?"

"The note will make it clear that he should waste no time in rescuing a foolish young lady from the perils of Vauxhall."

After more debate along similar lines, Antonia returned to her main objection. The purpose of the exercise was to throw Lady Hastings and Mr. Denholm together. Why was it necessary for her to actually go to Vauxhall?

By this time the captain's patience had worn thin. "There's no need at all if you're willing to have Mr. Denholm know you've plotted the whole thing."

"He'll know anyhow."

"Why should he? You've convinced him you wish to visit Vauxhall. He wouldn't take you. I'm more accommodating. The fact that Lady Hastings will just happen to visit the gardens that night is sheer coincidence."

"Why doesn't Rosamond come, too?"

Her cousin looked shocked. "Papa would kill me."

"We don't want Rosamond there reminding Denholm of where his duty lies, now, do we? Really, Miss Antonia, I certainly don't claim my plan is foolproof. But your cousin does not have much time. The only way I can see to prevent her disastrous marriage is to bring about this reconciliation. Now, if you have a better idea of how to achieve that, we'll try it."

But in the end, all their scheming proved academic. For Denholm had a sudden change of heart. He kept remembering how upset Antonia had seemed when he'd refused to take her to Vauxhall. But most of all he kept remembering how she'd said they'd not be seeing each other much longer. He was surprised at just how blue-deviled that prospect made him feel. And so, he'd gone calling on his great-aunt the following day.

Lady Thirkell looked over her spectacles in surprise and put down her needlework. "Well, Fitzhugh, it's been a long time since I've entertained a handsome gentleman in my bed-chamber. To what do I owe this honor?"

"I'd like a private word, ma'am." He refused the offer of tea and, ignoring the chair she indicated, went wandering about the room, picking up bits of bric-a-brac, examining the reading material by her bedside, pulling back the damask curtains to peer out the window, and, finally, inquiring absently about her health.

"At eighty-two my health is precarious, Fitzhugh" was the testy answer. "There's a good chance I may not survive long enough for you to disclose the purpose of your visit. Do sit down. You're making me positively giddy."

He grinned and obediently plopped down in a carved and gilt armchair, a twin to the one she sat in. "I was trying to find a subtle way to worm some information without you knowing what I was up to. I give up."

"And a good thing, too. I admit to old, but deny senility. Come to the point, lad."

"I want to ask about your will."

"So, that's the way the wind blows." She gave him a hard look above her spectacles. "Strapped then, are you? Wondering if I've made you me heir?"

"No, of course not, to both questions. Oh, the devil! I am making a mull of this. But you don't actually think I'm after your fortune, do you? Good God, such a thing never occurred to me. I may not be the nabob you are, Aunt, but I'm quite plump in the pocket, thank you."

"Is that so? Heard a rumor that old Paxton bypassed Worth and left you his fortune. True, then?"

"As a matter of fact, yes."

She chuckled wickedly. "Lord, I wish I could have seen Worth's face when he found out. Paxton never could abide him, now I recall it. Thought your father too platter-faced by half. And he was right. Even as a boy Worth was a hopeless prig. And your uncle Paxton always did have a soft spot for rogues."

"Thank you."

"Oh, you're welcome. But if you've no need for a fortune,

clear up this mystery. Why on earth are you dangling after that insufferable Thorpe chit?"

"Which one?"

"Don't be impudent. You know perfectly well I would never describe Antonia so. I mean Rosamond, of course. Do you intend to marry her?"

"Yes."

"For God's sake, why? You'll never suit."

"We should rub along as well as most couples, I collect. But I did not come here to talk of my affairs."

"It's Worth, I suppose. You two have been at daggers drawn ever since you came out of leading strings. Seems a bit late to try to please him now. But never mind. Before you wish me to the devil I'll admit it's none of my affair. But now then, sir, suppose you tell me just why you're poking your nose into what is my affair. My will, I mean."

"I'm wondering if you've left Mrs. Blakeney provided for."

"No, of course not" was the acid rejoinder. "I've consigned her to the workhouse. Good God, boy, what do you take me for? Of course she's provided for. And though I'd like to believe you've developed a touching concern for indigent old ladies, well, I wasn't born yesterday, you know. If it's Antonia you're concerned with, why not say so?"

"It amounts to the same thing, doesn't it?" Denholm, feeling rather guilty as he did so, went on to confide some of Antonia's concerns about the future.

"So her father's remarrying. Hmmm. Antonia did well to hide that from her grandmother. It will break Claire's heart. Though why it should is more than I can say. It's remarkable that Thorpe stayed single this long. Handsome fellow as I recall. But a lightweight. Antonia, thank God, takes after her grandfather. Now, there was a man!"

"He must have been, to maintain two households. I'm sorry. That was in poor taste. From me, especially."

"You'd best apologize. For I'll not hear one word against John. And as for Antonia's future, Claire will be more than able to look out for the girl. Not that it will be necessary. All men aren't fools. Antonia will make a match. Mark me words."

"Oh, undoubtedly you're right." The young man did not appear particularly cheered by this reassurance. "But why don't you do this much, Aunt Kate. Tell Antonia what you've done. Let her know she doesn't have to be forced into marriage just to support herself."

"I'll do no such thing. I don't want the gel feeling obliged to me. Besides, having money doesn't nullify bad marriages. As you're determined to demonstrate."

"Touché. Go ahead and ring for tea if you wish, Aunt Kate. For there's one more thing I want to ask you."

If Lady Thirkell found the concluding part of her tête-à-tête with her great-nephew even more puzzling than the first, she refrained from saying so. Instead she agreed to Denholm's plan with an alacrity that surprised them both.

It was left up to Antonia to express amazement after his departure when she was summoned to the dowager's bedchamber. "Mr. Denholm has invited you, Grandmother, and me to Vauxhall Gardens? Surely not!"

"Not only that, at your grandmother's suggestion, he has expanded the party to include Rosamond and Captain Crosland. I don't wonder you look amazed, m'dear. I know that Vauxhall is no longer considered quite the thing. But there's still some wholesome amusement to be had there. And for a party such as ours, well the outing must be considered unexceptionable."

"Oh, I am sure of that, ma'am." Antonia struggled not to laugh.

Captain Crosland, however, did not share her sense of the ridiculous, as he made clear on the evening of their expedition while he, Antonia, and Rosamond stood waiting for the others to join them in the hall. "Oh, come now," Antonia protested when the captain had refused to abandon his plan to bring Lady Hastings and Mr. Denholm together. "You surely don't think you can insinuate Lady Hastings into our group. With Lady Thirkell and Grandmama? That's too absurd."

"Of course not. We will not include Eugenia Hastings. We shall simply rid ourselves of Denholm, which sounds simpler, I must say, than luring him there would have been. You should be able to detach him from our party with little difficulty."

"Me!" she squeaked as his choice of pronoun sunk in.

"Shhh!" He frowned and shook his head. Lady Thirkell and Mrs. Blakeney, escorted by their host for the evening's outing, were coming down the stairs, Mrs. Blakeney touching the banister lightly and Lady Thirkell gaining moral support, at least, from both her nephew and her cane.

If Antonia had not already anticipated an awkward evening, the business of disposing themselves in her ladyship's old-fashioned crested coach would have pointed in that direction. Lady Thirkell had a fear of drafts. Mrs. Blakeney could not ride backward without getting ill. Rosamond seemed determined not to sit by Denholm. In the end, Lady Thirkell, tightly enveloped in a fur-lined cloak, even though the evening was actually warm for May, sat flanked by her companion and her nephew, facing forward, her knees all but touching Crosland's. Antonia herself spent the entire time of the seemingly endless journey trying to look anywhere but straight into Denholm's eyes.

But in spite of all, once Denholm had paid the two shillings apiece admission price and ushered them inside, Antonia found herself enjoying Vauxhall. As long as she could forget their covert reason for being there, it was easy to become entranced by the brilliantly illuminated walks where myriads of tiny colored lamps decorated trees and arches, where pavilions glittered, water cascaded, and romantic grottoes abounded. They strolled leisurely along, being entertained by jugglers, rope dancers, tumblers, and sword swallowers, pausing now and again to refresh themselves at the various stands or to purchase souvenirs at exorbitantly high prices. Rosamond declared Vauxhall the most famous place she had yet seen in London and Lady Thirkell unbent so far as to congratulate her nephew for arranging such a treat.

Captain Crosland seemed the only one of the conspirators whose mind remained fixed on their main objective. The fatigued party had gathered for supper in one of the long rows of boxes provided for that purpose and were partaking of the chicken, beef, and proverbially thin slices of ham that Vauxhall was noted for, the gentlemen washing the food down with

132

the equally famous Vauxhall Nectar, a mixture of rum and syrup with an addition of flowers of Benjamin. When a nearby band struck up a raucous tune, the captain, who had abandoned Rosamond for the first time that evening to sit beside Antonia, whispered in her ear, "You can make your move during the fireworks display."

Really, Antonia thought, he was the most impossible man! From his cloak-and-dagger approach they might be planning to stab Caesar.

"What move?" she whispered back, annoyed with herself as well when she waited for a covering drumroll to do so.

"When we go to watch the fireworks," he instructed from behind a concealing apple tart, "you must lure Denholm away to the Dark Walk."

"What!" Antonia forgot to whisper and as a result had her soft shoe nudged none too gently by a Hessian boot. She noticed Denholm watching them curiously from down the table and just managed to tone down her "Ow!"

"I can't do that," she hissed as Denholm turned his attention back to Rosamond, who was keeping up a constant stream of chatter in his ear, fearing to pause lest he make an offer of marriage then and there. "I could never make such a shocking proposal. What would he think?"

"If he's the man I take him for," the other said, leering, "he'll jump at the notion. But don't look so horrified. You won't actually have to go on the Dark Walk with him. Lady Hastings will be waiting there. You can slip back before you're even missed."

Antonia had not actually made up her mind to go through with Crosland's rackety scheme, but then fate seemed to conspire against her better judgment. At ten o'clock, when all the pleasure-seekers gathered to watch the fireworks display, the crush was so great that it became impossible for their party to stay together. Antonia was elbowed aside by a law clerk with a wife and brood of children intent upon a better vantage point to view the pyrotechnics. Mr. Denholm was the only member of their group left in the vicinity.

Together they watched the sky come alive in myriad fiery

patterns, bursting, twirling, cascading, as if the firmament had marshaled all its stars and planets to appear at once, then caused them to go berserk for their amusement. Antonia could have been content to stand spellbound, but duty nagged her. And so she screwed her courage to the sticking place and tugged at Denholm's sleeve to drag his attention earthward. "Could we go to the Dark Walk now?" Her smile was meant to be provocative.

"I beg your pardon?" A rapid series of explosions had made Denholm doubt his ears.

"I'm longing to see the Dark Walk. Could you take me? Now?"

He gestured toward the heavens, where the spectacle defied belief. "Are you bored, Miss Thorpe?"

"No, of course not. It's just that the Dark Walk is the most famous part of Vauxhall Gardens, and if we don't slip away now while my grandmother's attention is on the fireworks, I'll not get to see it. I doubt that she'd approve."

"So do I," he answered dryly. "You do know why people go there?"

"Of course." She tried to sound coquettish. It was hard to tell from his expression whether the performance was convincing. He was studying her intently.

"Come on, then." He made up his mind abruptly and took her hand. They weaved their way in silence through the throng.

As they finally broke clear Antonia walked swiftly. "You are eager," he commented.

"Well, I don't dare be gone long." He still held her hand, but she was almost dragging him.

"Then, I suggest we change directions. The Dark Walk's this way." He gave a jerk that prevented her from taking a wrong path in the mazelike garden.

The lovers' rendezvous was well named, Antonia discovered, as they left all the sparkle and glitter behind them. The effect should have been romantic, mysterious; somehow it missed the mark.

"Scared?" Denholm inquired.

134

"No, of course not," she answered stoutly, but clung more tightly to his hand nonetheless.

They were approaching the entrance to the walk where the thick foliage that lined the path obscured what little light had managed to seep into the surrounding area. The squeals and giggles coming from behind the hedges made it all too clear that they were not the only ones to take advantage of the general preoccupation with the fireworks. It was all in the spirit of fun, of course, Antonia told herself. No need to feel it was somehow demeaning, perhaps disgraceful even.

"Want to go back? You can always say you've seen the Dark Walk?"

"Oh, no. 'In for a penny, in for a pound.' We have to go inside." She led the way into the entrance.

The giggles were funneled toward them now. Punctuated with an occasional playful slap. And there were other sounds she did not care to identify. She also closed her ears to the suggestive remarks that came from some young men lounging back against the hedges, waiting for unescorted female prey.

"Don't you think we've gone far enough, Antonia? I hardly think this is your sort of thing."

"Just a little farther." She led him on with grim determination. Where was Lady Hastings anyhow? She should have been near the entrance. Antonia was feeling more like Theseus in search of the Minotaur. And then, just as she'd decided that in all good conscience they could now turn back, they rounded a bend where the hedges formed a grotto with a convenient bench for lovers, and there in the gloom sat a female figure who rose slowly to her feet as they approached.

"Ah, there you are at last." Lady Hastings's voice was husky, sultry. "I'd almost despaired of seeing you, Fitzhugh."

Antonia felt Denholm stiffen. His grip on her hand now made her wince. "So, that's what this has been about all along, Miss Thorpe," he said softly between clenched teeth. She was thankful the darkness made his expression difficult to read.

"Miss Thorpe has been a dear friend, Fitzhugh." As the beauty moved toward them, Antonia stepped away, or tried to. The grip on her hand increased. "She knew I'd perish if I didn't get to talk to you—to make things right again." Lady Hastings pressed against him. Her hands rested on his shoulders. Her eyes gazed imploringly into his. "Oh, Fitz, my darling, you can't stay angry always. You know you're the only man I've ever loved." She suddenly grew aware of his appendage and spoke sharply. "You can go now, Miss Thorpe. I'm ever so grateful to you."

"By all means, Miss Thorpe." Denholm dropped Antonia's hand like loosing a hot coal. "Your decoy duty is over. May I congratulate you on a job well done?"

Antonia ran. Tears stung her eyes and made seeing impossible. She blundered into the hedge as the path curved. Why she should feel like a Judas defied all understanding. Cupid was the role she'd meant to play. Or maybe that was what made her so miserable. She'd succeeded all too well, and it was herself that she'd betrayed.

"Got you!" Rough arms seized Antonia. A male body pressed hard against her own. A dim face leered. She smelled the brandy-breath as the parted mouth bent toward her. She screamed. Then screamed again and struggled but was quickly overpowered. Her arms were pinned. The slack, wet mouth met hers with a repulsiveness that sickened, made her long to faint even while she knew that she could not. She kicked and stamped, but the soft shoes she wore made such tactics ineffectual—mere annoyances that only served to increase her assailant's passion. Then, just when it seemed she might succeed in fainting after all, her attacker was jerked roughly around and a well-aimed blow sent him buckling to his knees.

"Come on." Denholm tugged her by the hand. "If you've had quite enough of the Dark Walk, Miss Thorpe, I'll return you to your party."

He rushed her along the path so fast she felt her feet might fly out from under her. She kept rubbing at her mouth with the sleeve of her walking dress, thinking never to rid herself of the feel of those disgusting lips. When they emerged into the open, Denholm pulled out a handkerchief and gave it to her, watching in silence while she rubbed her lips till they were almost raw. "Come on," he said abruptly, not taking her hand again.

"You mustn't leave Lady Hastings alone in there," she gasped. "It isn't safe."

"Your concern is touching. Eugenia will manage. She always does. She can fend off all comers till I get back."

"Oh, you are going back, then?" They were hurrying toward the crowd. The fireworks were building to a grand finale.

"Of course. That was the general idea, wasn't it? The motivation behind your burning desire to visit Vauxhall—and all your eagerness to explore, with me, the Dark Walk? Oh, you are quite a matchmaker, Miss Thorpe. Again, my congratulations.

"I see Crosland over there." He pointed toward the tall captain's curly beaver, which stood out above the crowd. "You can make it the rest of the way on your own, I'm sure. Convey my apologies to my guests for leaving them so abruptly. I'm sure you'll think of some explanation for my boorishness. Deception seems to be your forte, Miss Thorpe."

Chapter Eighteen

"OH, WHAT ARE WE TO DO, ANTONIA?" ROSAMOND wailed. The curate's appeal was no less desperate for being mute; his face was just as stricken. The three of them had met, as arranged, in the lending library. And the star-crossed lovers were gazing at Antonia as if she were their last frail hope. She longed to shake them.

"The only thing to do is what you should have done in the first place. I don't know how we ever allowed ourselves to meddle so in Mr. Denholm's affairs." All they'd accomplished, it seemed, was to make him despise her.

"But Captain Crosland was so sure," Rosamond protested. "And Lady Hastings was so sure that Mr. Denholm truly loved her. It only seemed a matter of simply throwing them together. No one could have known he'd bite his nose off to spite his face."

"Pride is indeed a deadly sin." The curate was perhaps thinking of next Sunday's homily.

"Oh, Antonia"—Rosamond took up the thread again— "Captain Crosland says Denholm actually told Lady Hastings he wants her out of his life once and for all. He p-plans to marry me. That's what he said. And I can't go on avoiding him forever. What shall I do?"

"Run off and get married right away."

"You mean elope?" Rosamond seemed horrified.

"Of course. Really, if you had simply done so ages ago, none of this mess need have happened."

"We wouldn't have made our come-outs either," Rosamond retorted. "Besides, an elopement's quite out of the question."

"Why should it be?" The cousins were coming close to daggers drawn. Antonia had lost all patience with anyone who, if too great a fool to wish to marry Fitzhugh Denholm, was also too fainthearted to run off with the suitor of her choice. "Oh, your father will cut up rough for a while, but he'll come around. You're his only child. He's hardly likely to cut you off with just a shilling."

"Do you know, Rosamond," the curate said thoughtfully, "I think your cousin is right. Believe me, your aversion to elopement does you credit. And you can surmise how repugnant such a course seems to a man of the cloth like myself. But nothing," he said, his voice choked with emotion, "is as repugnant to me as the thought of you married to another."

It should have been a touching moment. Certainly Rosamond seemed deeply moved. Perhaps it was unworthy of Antonia to feel that Rosamond's inheritance was the motive for the curate's decision to throw caution to the wind.

"Well, Rosamond, what have you decided?" She sounded

far too brusque and businesslike. But those two might go on gazing soulfully at each other the remainder of the day. "Is it Gretna Green or not?"

"Oh, I don't know." Poor Rosamond struggled with her conscience. "It just does not seem the thing to do."

"Well then, I promised to go shopping with Grandmother at Grafton House. I must be going."

Rosamond caught her hand as she stood up. "Oh, Tonia, don't be angry. Stay just a moment longer. I've decided now. I will do it. Cecil, we shall go to Gretna Green!"

But once that monumental decision had finally been reached, it seemed that the romantic pair hadn't the slightest notion of how to set about eloping. They turned their imploring eyes once more upon Antonia. "Oh, really!" she snapped. "This is the outside of enough. I must be going. You two work it out." Simultaneously their faces fell; then Rosamond suddenly brightened and clapped her hands. "Oh, I know! I shall consult with Captain Crosland. He is an expert when it comes to planning any sort of action. He's bound to tell us exactly how we must proceed."

Antonia's relief at shifting the burden of responsibility to the captain's broad shoulders proved short-lived. He sent round a note early the next morning saying he'd be in the library at ten and it was absolutely imperative that she meet him there. And though the assignation filled her with foreboding, it seemed craven not to go.

I do hope he won't ask me to break the news to Uncle Edwin, she thought as she hurried toward the library, after sending her maid off on an errand to Wedgwood and Byerley's in York Street. Surely, though, Rosamond will leave a note.

It was far worse than she'd imagined. "Go along on the elopement! You're funning, of course." She looked across the library table at the captain's face for a sign of the jokester's twinkle.

The captain, though, was serious. Rosamond absolutely refused to make the journey to Scotland without a chaperone, he told her.

"But Mr. Hollingsworth intends to make an honest woman of her! How ridiculous!"

The captain shrugged and allowed himself a tiny smile. "I fully agree. But then, you're aware of Miss Rosamond's excessive sensibility. She is, after all, Sir Edwin's daughter."

"And has Sir Edwin's daughter thought of how I'm to get back to London with *my* character intact? Oh, never mind." The question was academic. No need to worry about the local gossipmongers, for she'd made up her mind to return to Belgium as soon as possible anyhow. Papa and his new bride might not welcome her with open arms, but they'd have to take her in. And the arrangement would be a temporary thing. It would be far easier, she'd decided, to find a position as a drawing mistress among the English expatriates than here in London. The standards could not be nearly as high.

She listened intently, if reluctantly, as the captain went on to explain in a low voice the plan that he and Rosamond had agreed on. Antonia must say that she intended to spend the following night with Rosamond. Rosamond would tell her Aunt Lydia that Antonia had invited her to stay the night in Grosvenor Square. That way neither would be missed for several hours. In the meantime they would meet tomorrow afternoon at one o'clock in Oxford Street, where the Reverend Hollingsworth would pick them up in a hackney coach.

"One o'clock!" Crosland glanced at the people milling about the library and frowned a warning at Antonia, who lowered her voice. "Shouldn't we be leaving early in the morning? We can't travel at night. There'll be no moon."

The captain had a bit of difficulty keeping his face straight. "I pointed that out, thinking Miss Rosamond would wish to avoid an extra night in an inn. But she wouldn't be budged. She's ordered some new gowns and refuses to leave London till they're delivered sometime tomorrow morning."

"Saints preserve us!" Antonia echoed a favorite expression of her ladyship's Irish maid. Then she caught the captain's eye, and they both dissolved in laughter. She was to recall the reaction later on and wonder how she could have found anything at all amusing in the situation. Disgust would have been the emotion of choice, if only she had known.

After a near sleepless night when she'd tossed and turned, then definitely decided she would not go with Rosamond to Scotland, Antonia wound up arriving early for their rendezvous. She felt most conspicuous backed up against a shop window with a portmanteau in her hand. She prayed that she'd see no acquaintance who might expect an explanation.

When a nearby clock struck the hour of one, and neither Rosamond nor the chaise had appeared, Antonia did not know whether to be relieved or angry. Then, when she saw her cousin hurrying toward her, lumbered with no more than a reticule, relief predominated. Rosamond had obviously changed her mind.

"Of course we're going." Rosamond looked bewildered by her cousin's greeting. "I'm here, am I not?" Then, when Antonia pointed out that the bride had not brought along a traveling bag, Rosamond seemed convinced the other had taken leave of her senses. "I could not possibly marry and take a honeymoon with just the clothes I could cram into a portmanteau. That really would be shocking. I packed all my boxes myself and put them in the carriage house," she said with a touch of pride. "Captain Crosland slipped them out last night and will see to it they are put aboard the coach."

Captain Crosland's responsibilities did not end there, however. When the hackney coach came rattling down the street a few moments later, Antonia glanced briefly at the coachman, then jerked her head back to stare. "Crosland's driving!" she gasped.

"Yes. It's so kind of him. Cecil does not know how, you see."

The coach had pulled to a stop in front of them. The curate peeped out a furtive head, glanced around, saw that the coast was clear, then jumped out and practically pushed his fiancée inside. "Oh, do hurry, Miss Thorpe," he snapped at Antonia.

But she had balked. "It is one thing," she snapped back, "to accompany you and Rosamond. It is quite another to make a foursome with Captain Crosland all the way to Scotland. To say nothing of the fact that the two of us must come back alone. I'll not do it."

The result of this declaration was to send Rosamond into hysterics. "Now see what you've done!" the harassed bridegroom hissed. Passing shoppers were turning to stare their way curiously. The coachman climbed down to join them.

"I know my being here's a shock, Miss Thorpe," he said soothingly. "But Miss Rosamond did not want a hired coachman along who'd make her uncomfortable and gossip later. And Hollingsworth, you see, doesn't drive." The captain sounded scornful.

"Well, I can and will." Antonia's pronouncement only served to increase her cousin's hysteria. As far as an inconspicous departure went, the elopement was proving to be a dismal failure.

"I can understand and sympathize with your attitude, Miss Antonia." Despite all the pressures, the captain took time to be diplomatic. "But I don't think we can discuss the matter here. I know what we'll do!" He snapped his fingers as inspiration struck. "We'll hire a maid—a farmer's wife—a respectable female of some description—at the very first posting house, to accompany us and serve as chaperone."

"B-but—"

The captain forestalled Rosamond's sobbed objection by another masterstroke. "And no fear of any tale-bearing there. We'll give false names. Now, do get in, Miss Thorpe. We're beginning to collect a crowd."

Antonia was to look back on their awkward departure as the best part of the journey north. For, once having begun to weep, Rosamond made no attempt to stem the tide. The clergyman divided his time between patting her hand ineffectively and glaring at Antonia as the cause of her upset.

Then, once they'd left the metropolis behind, the sobs gradually subsided to be replaced with reproaches of another kind. Could Mr. Hollingsworth not have provided them with a better coach? Rosamond weighed the hackney against her father's well-sprung carriage and found it sadly wanting. Really, she had never been so jolted in all her life! The ordeal was giving her a headache. She'd daresay that her cousin had never experienced such an ill-sprung coach, not even on the Continent. "Have you, Antonia?" And not only was the hackney miserably sprung, it was dirty. Heaven only knew what types of people had ridden in it last. If they did not succumb to all sorts of horrid diseases, it would amaze her. And worst of all, the carriage smelled. Really, she felt quite ill. Rosamond clapped her perfumed handkerchief to her nose.

Antonia, who had been gazing sightlessly out the window, absorbed in her own thoughts, awoke to the situation and turned her cousin's way. Goodness, Rosamond was decidedly green. She leaned far out the window and shouted for the captain to stop the coach.

And from then on it was stop-and-go, stop-and-go, with stop predominating. It seemed that the only way Rosamond could possibly tolerate the journey was to leave the coach at frequent intervals, gulp great breaths of air, and sit by the side of the highway till her head stopped swimming and her stomach settled once again. Really, Antonia thought, at this rate we'll not reach Scotland before Christmas. She did not, however, express the thought aloud. Mr. Hollingsworth was less prudent. "Could you not put your mind on other things, Rosamond dear?" There was some justification for the curate's peevishness. They had broken their trip for the third time within the hour. "I find that reciting elevated passages to myself will often blot out discomfort."

This well-meant suggestion brought on a new storm of tears, followed by the announcement that he was too insensitive for words if he did not realize she was doing everything within her power to continue this odious journey. If only he had provided them with a respectable equipage, instead of being so cheeseparing as to expose his betrothed to such excruciating torture.

Despite the impropriety of their situation, Antonia was thankful for the captain's presence. His patience was inexhaustible. He seemed to know exactly the right thing to say to calm even the worst of Rosamond's high fidgets. And after several stops to rest along the wayside, he suggested that walking in a nearby field might be more beneficial than simply sitting, and supported the wilting Rosamond with a steadying arm while they paced to and fro, talking earnestly, in the spring-green meadow. Antonia, in the meantime, stood by the horses. The curate stared balefully after them with folded arms.

Then, when the twosome returned from this exercise with Rosamond looking rather more the thing, neither the curate nor Antonia could quarrel with the captain's logic when he suggested they put up at the next posting house they came to, rather than continue on till dark as they had planned. "All of this has put too much strain upon Miss Thorpe's delicate nervous system," he said soothingly. "And it's little wonder. She will be much better for some quiet rest. Then, I daresay, we'll find we can make capital time tomorrow. We'll more than make up for the delay, I promise you. And it's not as if anyone will be chasing after us. We've covered our tracks quite well, I'd say."

Recognizing her cousin's growing dependence upon Captain Crosland, Antonia seized the opportunity to suggest she drive. The curate was aghast at the idea and said so. Rosamond, however, would welcome the captain's comforting presence inside.

"No need to be alarmed, Hollingsworth," he said. "Why, the horses could drive themselves on this stretch of road. I'll take over before we reach the inn." The curate reddened at the patronizing tone.

With this new arrangement in effect, they were actually able to cover the final stretch of the day's journey without stopping. Antonia began, almost, to enjoy herself. Whether due to being freed from Rosamond's complaints, or to the uninterrupted view of the countryside she was afforded from the coachman's perch, or to the fact that it was fun to hold the reins of even these poor specimen of cattle hitched to this much disparaged coach, or to a combination of all these things, this interlude was definitely the high point of her day. She spied the sign of the Old Bull and Horn Inn in the distance but scorned the notion of changing places with Captain Crosland. Her passengers were too self-absorbed to notice that they were about to reach their destination. Before they awakened to that fact, Antonia had tooled the hackney into the crowded inn yard with as much style and dash as such a ramshackle equipage could manage. Curious heads turned, and jaws came crashing down at the sight of a young lady wearing a modish bonnet and stylish pelisse perched on the driver's seat.

But no one in the assembly was half so surprised as Lord Thayer Edgemon. His lordship, in the act of springing his matched grays, froze with his whip in the air to stare at what he at first believed was a hallucination as Captain Crosland came leaping out of the coach to hand Antonia down.

Later on that same evening he expressed some of this astonishment to Mr. Denholm when he happened upon his friend at Brooks's. He had come strolling into the club just as a game of deep basset was breaking up. He and Denholm were now sharing a bowl of punch.

"Damnedest thing," Lord Thayer remarked. "Couldn't believe me eyes at first. Thought I was seeing things. Imagining, you know. But I rubbed me peepers hard and sure enough I was still seeing what I saw."

"Thayer, what are you raving on about?" Denholm was looking rather the worse from too little sleep of late along with having shot the cat a bit too often.

"Trying to tell you of this odd thing I saw, old man." Lord Thayer was noted for his patience. "Was coming back from Derby today. Told you I'd been up to rusticate with Whitcomb, didn't I? Well, then. I'd stopped in at the Old Bull and Horn. Know it, don't you? You can get a damn fine arrack punch there. Well, anyhow, as I was just about to spring me horses, here comes this hackney coach turning into the yard with Miss Antonia Thorpe driving the thing."

Denholm, who had taken a deep draft of punch, choked suddenly.

"Watch it, Fitz. Damned near sprayed me. New coat, too. Knew you'd be surprised."

"Miss Thorpe driving a hackney!" Denholm expostulated when he'd sufficiently recovered. "The Old Bull and Horn *must* make a damned fine arrack punch."

"Knew you'd not believe it. Didn't myself at first. But told you. I made sure. It was her and no mistake. But you ain't heard the queerest start of all. Guess who got out of the carriage she was driving—bold as brass."

"I've no idea," Denholm said faintly.

"That Captain Crosland, that's who. Friend of yours, perhaps, but frankly I never could quite stomach the fellow. There's something—can't say what exactly—that ain't quite the thing about him."

"Did you speak to them? Find out what they were doing there?"

"Of course not. What do you take me for?" Lord Thayer looked offended. "The very last thing they'd want would be to see me, and be seen by, some cove they knew."

Further discussion of this topic was made impossible by three friends who joined them at their table. The conversation soon turned to a mill between Ferocious Frederick and Barton the Bruiser, which was to take place the following week. And though the discussion grew quite heated, Mr. Denholm was not a participant. Indeed, he simply stared off into space for several minutes, then rose, excused himself, and left the room.

Chapter Nineteen

ANTONIA WAS ROUSED BY A BANGING ON THE DOOR. IT was broad daylight. She poked her head out from under the pillow where it was buried to see if Rosamond would answer. She, after all, was on the side of the bed nearest the door.

Her cousin was gone. Antonia sighed and reached for her

dressing gown as the knocking continued. "Just a minute," she called, and it stopped. Rosamond had locked herself out, no doubt. She had been restless all night long, up and down, up and down, till finally in desperation Antonia had clapped her pillow over her ears and slept. It's going to be another one of those days, she thought as she clutched her robe around her and stumbled toward the door. Since she hadn't gotten the rest Captain Crosland had prescribed, Rosamond was bound to be as difficult as before.

As Antonia opened the door, the curate, fully dressed, pushed past her. "They've gone!" he croaked, waving a sheet of paper in her face.

"Who's gone?" Antonia closed the door, which, even in his agitation, he had left wide open for propriety's sake.

"Rosamond and the captain, you numskull! Who else is with us?"

Antonia looked at Mr. Hollingsworth with some alarm. He was beside himself. "Have you looked in the dining parlor?" she asked soothingly. "They're probably just having an early breakfast."

"They've eloped!" the curate screeched. "Of all the underhanded—treacherous—despicable—Here, read this." He thrust a paper at her. Antonia frowned down at the hasty scrawl.

My dear Cecil,
    Captain Crosland and I have just discovered—quite in the nick of time—that we have loved each other always and have gone on to Gretna Green to be married there. Try and forgive me, Cecil. In time you will come to thank me. As dear Horatio has pointed out, we should not have suited.

Yrs. most truly,
Rosamond

"Good God!" Antonia sank weakly down upon the bed and reread the letter.

"That cad! That blackguard! He intended this all the time."

The curate paced up and down the room. Antonia had never actually seen anyone tear his hair before. "He meant to steal her from me from the very first. The man's nothing but a gazetted fortune hunter."

"I expect you're right," Antonia said thoughtfully.

"And I hold you entirely to blame."

"Me!"

"He's your friend. You're the one who insinuated him into her life. Nothing has been right since you came to England. Rosamond was always so sweet—so sheltered—so pure. Then you descend upon her with your scandalous background—"

"Scandalous background!" She was on her feet. "How dare you? And as for everything being my fault, if I hadn't come to England, Rosamond would be married to Mr. Denholm by now. For, heaven knows, you would never have lifted a finger to prevent it. And if you had managed to plan your elopement and drive your own equipage, there would have been no need for the captain to become involved. Oh, Rosamond's married the better man all right! Oh, my goodness." She stopped her tirade. "There's no point in our haranguing each other this way."

But she had opened another wound. "The coach!" he said bitterly. "Do you realize they are on their way right now to Scotland in the hackney that *I* paid for?"

Antonia immediately regretted her spontaneous giggle. "What do you mean to do?" she asked solicitously to cover it. "You could perhaps still catch them. Rosamond's not exactly a good traveler, as we can testify."

He gave her a withering look. "I will not demean myself. Rosamond has made her choice. I shall return to Kent. And I pray God that no breath of this scandal shall ever reach my parish. I shall be ruined. Good day, Miss Thorpe."

"Good day?" she echoed. He might as well have said "good riddance." "You feel no responsibility for me, then?"

"My responsibility is to my calling," the man of the cloth replied. "And the fact that I forgot my higher duty and embroiled myself in such a disgraceful coil shall be a thorn in my flesh forever. So, don't ask me to risk sure disgrace by traveling, publicly, in your company, Miss Thorpe. Again, I say good day."

After first opening the door a crack to make sure no one was there, Mr. Hollingsworth eased out into the hall. The door shut softly behind him.

Antonia read Rosamond's letter one more time to assure herself of its reality. She sighed and reached for her reticule. A quick count confirmed what she'd concluded. She had just enough money to pay for her room (for she'd bet a monkey Rosamond hadn't done so) and her coach fare back to London, if she was lucky. But there was no way her meager resources were going to provide for breakfast.

While Antonia had been obliviously asleep, Lady Thirkell and Mrs. Blakeney were up and drinking tea. Lady Thirkell was wearing a brilliant purple dressing gown. Mrs. Blakeney's costume was more subdued but gained a certain dash from the curl papers she was wearing. Mr. Denholm had recently roused their household, then gone storming off, after making sure that Antonia wasn't, after all, safe home in her bed.

"What I do not understand," Mrs. Blakeney spoke peevishly, "is why he has taken it upon himself to go after them that way. I know elopements are not quite the thing, but it is not as though Captain Crosland will not marry her."

"Oh, Captain Crosland has no intention of marrying Antonia. That man's been dangling after a fortune from the very first."

"Oh, dear." Mrs. Blakeney put down her teacup and clutched her heart.

"Quit jumping to conclusions, Claire," Lady Thirkell snapped. "If Thayer saw what he said he saw, the only reason for Antonia to be driving a hackney coach with that captain fellow inside it was that there was another passenger. Crosland's eloped with Rosamond, of course."

"Oh." Mrs. Blakeney tried to cope with conflicting emotions, relief that her granddaughter was not embarked upon a life lived in the shadows, and disappointment that the dashing captain was lost to her forever. "Then, it's Rosamond that Mr. Denholm's chasing after."

"Nothing of the kind! Fitzhugh is pursuing Antonia."

"Don't tell me that *he* intends to offer my granddaughter a carte blanche."

Lady Thirkell sighed. "Really, Claire, your mind does seem to travel a well-worn path. Of course he won't offer Antonia a carte blanche. When he gets around to thinking logically—if a man in love can ever reach that happy state—he'll offer for her. Right now the only thing on his mind is to stop her from eloping with Crosland. For I doubt it will occur to him either that Rosamond's along. And to think I used to consider him the only intelligent member of his generation in the family."

"Well, I can't say much for *your* intelligence if you think Mr. Denholm will marry Antonia. He's promised to Rosamond and in love with Lady Hastings."

"In love with that trollop!" Lady Thirkell snorted her contempt. "Anyone who ever looked at him and not just at that sap-skull in the trollop's play would know he's no longer in love with her. And furthermore, it's my opinion that he never was."

"Well, Kate"—Mrs. Blakeney, who was beginning to feel a bit more the thing, poured out fresh cups of tea—"you've always been much better at reading human nature than I. But we both know that Worth will never approve."

"I don't think Worth's approval or disapproval will have anything to say to their marriage. But it will make things much more comfortable all around if he gives them his blessing—which of course he'll do when he learns Antonia's inheriting my fortune."

Mrs. Blakeney all but dropped her teacup. She managed finally to set it down with shaking hands. "You mean you've actually made Antonia your heir?" she gasped.

"Well, actually, no. Fitzhugh's that. Thirkell named him when the boy was still at Eton. Never told him, though. Thought it better not to. But there's no reason Worth shouldn't think everything's meant for Antonia. Amounts to the same thing in the end, and it will do marvels in smoothing the gel's way. For there's no use thinking otherwise. The Thirkell fortune will make Sir Edwin Thorpe's seem paltry. That jacka-napes!" She chuckled wickedly.

The only bit of good fortune Antonia had had all day was to secure a seat by the window in the public coach. Not only was she able to contemplate the view, but she was spared a bit of the aroma of the large man next to her, who, besides having an aversion to soap and water, seemed immoderately partial to garlic. She occupied her time by thinking up, and then discard-ing, various explanations of her complicity for use when her grandmother and Lady Thirkell should learn of Rosamond's rackety elopement. And as for Uncle Edwin (Antonia shud-dered, causing her neighbor to ask solicitously if she had a chill), if he did not have her head delivered on a platter, she'd be much surprised.

Traffic on the London Road grew heavy. The coachman made frequent use of his horn to announce their approach as they bore down on a loaded cart or rounded a blind curve. An-tonia was glad to trade her morbid thoughts for the distraction of observing and being observed by the passengers in the other carriages who were traveling the way they'd come.

She became even more distracted when their coach's progress grew suddenly erratic. The inside passengers gave one another knowing looks, not untinged with fear. The gar-lic person expressed aloud what each was thinking: "One of them flash coves up there has took over the reins, or I'm a Dutchman."

Antonia nodded. At the last posting house she, too, had no-ticed the pair of well-dressed young gentlemen, on holiday from school most likely, who had joined the passengers on top. They must have greased the coachman's palm for the privilege of driving. The blare of the horn grew louder, more frequent. The one not holding the reins was obviously in charge of the "yard of tin."

With her newly developed expertise, Antonia assessed the substitute coachman's skill and found it sadly wanting. "Brace yourselves," she warned her fellow travelers. They were tak-ing the curve much, much too fast. What's more, they were

151

straying well across the highway's center. The horn blared frantically.

Denholm, in his speeding curricle, did his best. He heard the tinny warning and coach wheels coming fast. He took the curve as close to the edge of the highway as safety would allow. All might have yet been well if the young stage driver had not panicked and jerked the reins. The four horses swerved suddenly to their left. As Denholm tooled his team expertly round the careening coach, he heard someone scream his name and glimpsed a familiar, badly frightened face. He tugged and cursed his horses to a halt while he watched with sickening, helpless horror as the stagecoach headed for the ditch, where it rocked back and forth precariously before coming to rest at last on an acute angle against an apple tree. As Antonia was knocking the garlic breath out of the fat man with the impact of her body, Denholm came leaping from his curricle and sprinted toward the wreck. "This has become a habit," he observed as he dragged her up and out. "Are you all right?"

Chapter Twenty

FITZHUGH DENHOLM RELUCTANTLY SET ANTONIA THORPE upon her feet. He returned to help the other passengers out of the tilted coach and then, by combining manpower with horsepower, succeeded in getting the vehicle back on the road again. Once assured that no real damage had been done to passengers, cattle, or coach, Denholm's intention had been to give the greenhorn driver and irresponsible coachman a good dressing-down, if not actual levelers. But he soon discovered that the angry passengers were sufficient unto themselves in that department. He returned instead to Antonia, who stood a bit apart, obviously still shaken.

"Where's your luggage? Or do you have any?"

"Up there." She pointed to the coach top. "But you mustn't concern yourself with me. I'm sorry I shouted. You should not have stopped. They've got a tremendous head start on you as it is. Go on now. I'll be all right. That idiot won't drive again."

Denholm climbed up, pulled her portmanteau out of the pile of baggage, then took her none too gently by the arm and steered her toward his rig. "Do you know that I haven't the vaguest notion of what you're raving on about? Or why you were in that coach alone? But we can sort it out while I take you home." He more lifted than handed her into the curricle.

"But you mustn't waste time with me," she protested as he climbed aboard and picked up the reins. "Oh, don't turn around, you gudgeon! Scotland's that way."

"I know my geography, Miss Thorpe," he snapped. "But you aren't going to Scotland. Where's your pride, girl? Give it up, I tell you."

"I'd be glad to," she spit back as he sprang his horses in the London direction. "Goodness knows I never wanted to go there in the first place. But I refuse to be blamed when you don't catch up with Rosamond."

He turned to stare. "What the devil does Rosamond have to do with this? No, wait; don't answer. First things first. What the devil have you done with Crosland? I can only hope you came to your senses and left him high and dry. I know how worried you've been about your future, but how you could have even considered running off with that—that—toadeater is beyond understanding. I never thought you lacked for sense, Antonia."

It was her turn to stare. "Are you saying that you think *I* eloped with Captain Crosland? But that's ridiculous. I'd never do such a ramshackle thing. And when it comes to that," she added fairly, "he'd certainly not elope with me. The man's a fortune hunter. What ever gave you such a rackety notion anyhow?"

"Why, Thayer saw you and him together at the Old Bull and Horn. Oh, my God!" Relief was struggling with chagrin. "What an idiot I've been. I went off half-cocked and never took the time to sort things out."

"You mean you came chasing after me?" Her eyes were wide.

"Oh, yes."

"Grandmother sent you, I daresay."

"Not at all. I think she would have been most contented with the match. Aunt Kate, of course, doubted that Crosland would actually marry a penniless girl."

"Oh, I see." Antonia sounded decidedly let down. "It was Lady Thirkell who sent you after me."

"Wrong again. It was my own idea entirely. I only rousted them out of their beds in order to make sure you weren't in yours. Thayer isn't the most reliable of witnesses, you see. Or so I thought. But if my brain had only been working, I'd have stopped to sort out what he said. For he told me he saw you driving a hackney and then saw Crosland climb out of the coach. I should have been able to deduce from that odd displacement that the good captain was keeping someone else company inside. My God, what a fool I've been!" He slapped his forehead. "I should have realized that little miss meddlesome was up to her old tricks, helping her cousin elope with the dashing captain."

"Well, not exactly. But that's close enough."

"Oh, Lord, wrong again. I don't think my self-esteem can bear it. But, go on. Don't spare me. Just what the hell were you up to, Antonia?"

"I was helping Rosamond elope with the Reverend Hollingsworth."

"Rosamond ran off with the curate? I wouldn't have thought either of them had that much enterprise. But then, of course they didn't." He sounded resigned. "That would have been where you came in. But Thayer surely couldn't have mistaken Hollingsworth for Crosland. Not even he could get that confused. I fear to ask—but why was the captain along?"

She sighed. "Must we go into all of this? Yes, I suppose we

must," she added quickly, since he looked dangerous. "But, I warn you, you're going to think I've made the whole thing up, for such a pudding-hearted approach to an elopement defies belief even to the average person. And for an old campaigner like yourself who, alone and unabetted, managed to seduce a married woman, fight a duel with her husband, then run away with her to Italy, well, you aren't likely to countenance a word of what I say."

"What I'm likely to do is throttle you if you don't get on with your recital. Only first let me say, ungentlemanly though it may be, that you've got my history right except for one minor point. I was not so much seducer as seducee."

"Oh."

"But we were discussing Crosland's part in your latest escapade." The reins were slack now in his hands, and the horses could have been mere plodders, so snail-like was their pace.

"Well, yes. As you know, Rosamond has never wished to marry you." She assessed his expression and hastened on. "So, when Uncle Edwin wrote that you were told to offer for her right away, her first hope was that you yourself would go back to Lady Hastings. But then her ladyship informed Captain Crosland—"

"At last! The captain!"

"Lady Hastings informed Captain Crosland—they've become good friends, you know—that you had told her you intended to marry Rosamond. So she—Rosamond, I mean to say—decided that there was nothing for it but to run off to Gretna Green with the Reverend Hollingsworth.

"Looking back on matters now, I should have known from all the obstacles she threw in our path that Rosamond really did not wish to wed the curate. But then, Rosamond's sense of propriety is so overblown—for instance, her attitude toward your past history always seemed decidedly excessive—oh, for goodness sake, don't fly off into the boughs again. I'll get to the point. Well, as I was saying, when Rosamond refused to go to Gretna Green alone with Mr. Hollingsworth and insisted that I accompany them, it did seem absurd but entirely within character nonetheless."

"Crosland!" Denholm said between his teeth.

"I'm coming to him. Heavens, we've miles to go yet. Oh, very well. Arranging an elopement, as it happened, was completely outside the curate's scope. I suppose it isn't the sort of thing they touch on in theological preparation. So Captain Crosland was forced to make all the arrangements: drive the hackney coach, collect Rosamond's baggage—you'd not believe the number of boxes; oh, never mind—work out the route, decide where to change horses, which inns to patronize. And then Rosamond did not wish to hire a coachman for fear he'd gossip about them, and Hollingsworth could not drive." She came close to sneering. "I volunteered to do so myself, but Rosamond would not hear of it. Now, of course, I know the reason why."

"I can think of several."

"Well, you'd be mistaken, for as your friend observed, I did drive partway, and most skillfully, if I do say so." After this setdown, she seemed to think her narrative was finished.

"Antonia!" She was jerked from her reverie to find Denholm glaring at her.

"Yes?"

"Are you going to explain why you were on the public coach while the other three, I presume, continued on to Scotland, or must I choke it from you?"

"Oh, that. I thought I'd made it plain. When I woke up this morning, Rosamond was gone. She'd run off with Captain Crosland."

Denholm stared incredulously. "You're bamming me! You're not!" Suddenly he doubled up with laughter. It proved infectious. Antonia joined in.

After they'd subsided, she wiped her eyes. "I t-told you it was all too absurd. But after I'd got over the shock of the thing I couldn't help but feel it was for the best. Rosamond and Captain Crosland should deal well together. At least, they will if Uncle Edwin doesn't cut them off, which I doubt he'll do, once his anger cools. Oh, I know the captain's a gazetted fortune hunter. But he does have the patience of Job, and I think he really cares for Rosamond. If you could have seen his solici-

156

tude when she was getting sick every mile or so and he had to stop the horses." Denholm went off into whoops again, and again she joined him. "And as for Mr. Hollingsworth," she continued once they'd recovered, "I don't care if he is a curate, I've rarely known such an odious man."

"You're saying, then, that Rosamond did well to change horses at the posting house?" He struggled to keep his face straight this time, then succumbed once more. "Well," he was finally able to say, "I hope you've learned a lesson."

"Whatever do you mean?" Antonia bristled. "I had nothing to say to any of this."

"Oh, did you not? It seems to me that you've been busy as a bee of late promoting disastrous matches. And while we're on that subject, do you mind telling me just why you were so eager to fling me at Eugenia's head?"

"I wasn't. What I mean to say is, it was all Captain Crosland's notion that you and Lady Hastings would fall into each other's arms once you were brought together."

"And you wished for that happy conclusion, did you?"

"No. Yes. Oh, everybody was convinced that you really loved her—and only pride stood in your way. So I thought it was the right thing to do. Help you along, I mean. Besides, I know it's not a cousinly admission, but having you married to Lady Hastings would have been easier to bear than having you married to Rosamond."

"I see." He gazed at her thoughtfully. "Everybody was wrong, you know."

"I beg your pardon?"

"The 'everybody' that was convinced I loved Eugenia was all wrong. Our history, I'm afraid, does me no credit." His face reflected the misery he was feeling. "And telling it is ungallant to the point of caddishness. But you have to hear it. Oh, damn it all, Tonia, I was a twenty-year-old green 'un when I met Eugenia. And well, you've seen her."

"Oh, yes." She sounded as miserable as he looked.

"And, well, she made advances—that I was more than happy to comply with. Often. But the truth was, I was pretty

157

well bored with the whole affair and looking for a gentlemanly—if you'll pardon the use of such a term—way to break it off when her husband caught us, and the rest is history. Or drama, if you like. Of course, I had to take her to Italy with me then. We stayed together for a little while. And I kept on supporting her when she found more entertaining companions. It was a fortuitous escape for both of us when Hastings turned up again and inherited that title. So you see"—his smile was twisted—"it's all a pretty sordid story. I'm a far cry from that romantic hero on stage at Drury Lane."

"Thank goodness!" The comment was soul-felt. "I thought him insufferable."

"Did you, by God?" He grinned, then quickly sobered. "In fact, what I've most feared I am, Tonia, is inconstant. I've grown to doubt, you see, that I could ever love any woman for very long."

"Yes," she answered thoughtfully, "I can see where you might feel that way, having fallen out of love with such a diamond of the first water."

"But I've given the matter considerable thought since you first started to plague my life."

"What an odious thing to say."

"I know. Hardly romantic, is it? But I don't know how else to describe my state since that morning I walked into your uncle's library and interrupted your letter-writing. I've not been the same man since. You've been full of surprises, Tonia. And, well, I can't bear the thought of not knowing what you'll be up to a month—a year—thirty years from now. I know this is a negative way to put things, but whereas before the thought of having to live a lifetime with one woman seemed intolerable, the thought of not spending the rest of my days with you is totally unacceptable. What I'm trying to say, and making such a mull of, is that I've come to realize there's a world of difference between real love and mooncalf infatuation. Do you think you could marry me, Tonia, warts and all?"

She stared up at him. "Are you offering for me? For *me*?"

"Why all the surprise? It's hardly the first time."

"But you can't possibly marry me. Your father—"

"Damn my father. If he's too big a fool to realize you're the most wonderful thing that's ever happened to me, he's not worth pleasing. I love you, Tonia. I want you for my wife. For the fourth or fifth time, will you marry me?"

Whatever she might have answered was interrupted by the sound of a rig approaching fast. Another curricle drew up beside them with a young sprig of fashion holding the reins. "Oh, I say, sir . . ."—he gave Denholm an impish grin,—"devilish fine-looking cattle you have there. Appearances can be deceiving, though. Since you're practically limping along, I take it they ain't goers."

Antonia leaned forward and asked sweetly, "Are you wishing to find out, sir?"

"Antonia!" Denholm scowled a warning.

The young gentleman's grin widened. He recognized a kindred soul. "Would you care to wager a pound that my pair'll beat yours to a church about a mile and a half from here?"

"Done!" cried Antonia.

"Now!" The young man cracked his whip and flew.

"Spring 'em! He's getting away! Do hurry!"

Denholm sat with folded arms. "Not till you say you'll marry me."

"Of course I'll marry you. But what does that have to say to anything?" She lunged for the reins, which he managed to keep just out of reach. "Either spring those horses, you widgeon, or let me do it!"

"Yes, ma'am." His long whip snaked out with the crack of a dueling pistol just above the horses' ears. They were off like a bullet from that same weapon as Antonia's bonnet went spiraling from her head. Fresh as though they'd just come from the stables, the team of horses galloped down the highway. Antonia began to cheer as the distance rapidly closed between the curricles. When a small white church with an overweening steeple came in sight, Denholm made his move. He sped past the other vehicle while the love of his life gaily waved her handkerchief in a taunting farewell.

The Honorable Fitzhugh Denholm swerved into the church-yard and pulled up his scarcely winded pair. He turned with a grin toward Antonia, who flung herself into his arms, her cheeks flushed with victory, her eyes sparkling. "Oh, that was famous. You really are a none-such."

"In all departments," he murmured as his mouth met hers.

So eagerly did she cooperate, so absorbed did they become, that neither noticed the other curricle draw up beside them. The young gentleman cleared his throat politely and, getting no response, watched with interest for a moment, then shrugged and tossed the pound note upon their carriage seat and left.

Much, much later, Denholm reluctantly released his betrothed and stared at her speculatively as she sought to straighten her disarranged garments and smooth her tangled hair. "Tonia, love," his voice mused tenderly, "effective as it is, we really must find another aphrodisiac."

" 'Aphro'—what? I haven't the faintest notion what you're talking about."

"I mean, it's simply not going to be practical to get out my rig, harness my team, and find some young fool to race us neck-or-nothing every time I wish to make love to you."

"You really are absurd." Her face was scarlet nonetheless as they circled the little church and returned to the London highway.

On the outskirts of the city they stopped again to watch a glorious sunset that boded fair. When the last streaks of red were dimming in the sky and the lamps of London began to twinkle in the distance, Antonia, who for some time had been quite thoughtful, now observed, "It's odd, isn't it, how people's characters and their lives can be so contradictory. Take Grandmama, for instance. Her life has been a scandal. Yet no one's more anxious for propriety than she is. And now here you are—a notorious rake—bent on becoming a veritable pattern card of virtue."

"Disappointed?"

"Not in the least." The smile she flashed him caused his pulse to race. "But it does make one wonder what the gossipmongers will find to chew on now while they sip their scandal broth."

"Well, there's always your Cousin Rosamond."

"Oh, yes, Rosamond." She chuckled. "Now there's a case in point. No one—with the possible exception of Uncle Edwin—has ever been more concerned with doing the proper than my cousin. And how does she, in the final analysis, live up to her principles? By eloping with two fiancés at once! My heavens, that almost rivals your own Lady Eugenia Lytton Hastings! I think I'll write a play about it."

"You do and I'll throttle you. No, cancel that threat. I'm not worried about you in the least, my love. For I have a foolproof scheme to keep you out of mischief." He flicked his reins and guided his horses off the verge where they'd been standing. Once firmly on the high road, he cracked his whip and urged the team to an incredible burst of speed.

"What on earth do you think you're doing?" Antonia clutched his sleeve to keep from sliding off the leather as they went flying round a curve.

"Looking for another curricle to race!" he shouted, and grinned lasciviously. "There's bound to be one on up ahead there somewhere. I can hardly wait!"

The whip cracked again as the smart sporting rig went tooling on toward London and toward a future that, like the fading sunset, boded fair.

A Question
of Class

Chapter One

"**B**ATH IS NO PLACE TO MEND A BROKEN HEART."
Lady Stoke's mouth pursed in unaccustomed disapproval as she looked over the throng collected in the Pump Room. Her situation beside the Tompion Clock offered an ideal vantage point. Just above it, in an alcove, the statue of Beau Nash also watched the crowd, though rather more benignly.

"But I don't have a broken heart, Aunt Louisa." The young lady who shared Lady Stoke's settee was modishly attired in a gray muslin round dress topped by a blue spencer against the cold. She looked at her relative with fond exasperation. "Why do you keep insisting upon a physical impossibility? I've assured you no end of times, that particular organ is perfectly intact."

"Of course your heart's broken. Your engagement was."

This logic was indisputable in the older woman's eyes. Her companion seemed to find it somewhat lacking. But Lady Venetia Lowther managed to bite off the rebuttal that she realized was futile. "I suppose heartbreak is the conventional attitude," she compromised.

"Of course it is. And the only cure for a romance gone sour is to plunge into another as soon as possible. Trust me, Venetia. I'm not entirely without experience in these matters." Lady Stoke's expression caused her niece to think of cats and cream.

"But as I was saying," her ladyship continued after a reminiscing pause, "Bath is the last place on earth your father should have sent you. But then, Lowther never had a brain for anything except politics."

"Father didn't send me," Lady Venetia explained patiently. "As I've told you, Aunt, it was my own idea entirely."

"But you could not possibly have known what Bath is like. You were raised abroad." Lady Stoke contrived to make "abroad" sound like one of the moon craters. "Of course," she added fairly, "I suppose Lowther had no idea himself what Bath's become. It used to be England's most fashionable watering place. But that was eons ago. Now just look around you." A wave of her gloved hand encompassed the full scope of the room, from pump to people. "Every soul here is either an Ancient or an Invalid. Or most likely both. Bath is nothing like it used to be," she said with a sigh, casting her eyes upward toward the statue of Nash, who had presided over the resort in its eighteenth-century heyday when in the eyes of the Beau Monde only London could surpass it in importance. But in 1816, as Lady Stoke was fond of pointing out, the situation was much changed. "You'll find no one but retirees here now, m'dear. Lawyers, doctors, clergymen, half-pay officers. All suffering from some complaint or other that they delude themselves into believing this vile mineral water will cure." She sighed lugubriously, then added in a confidential whisper, "Which, between us, is exactly why I chose to live here. It's a perfect place for a lady in her, er, *middle years* to find male companionship."

Clearly Louisa Stoke did not classify herself as either an Ancient or an Invalid but as the exceptional Bath resident that proved the rule. She admitted to being "fiftyish" but had in truth surpassed her sixtieth birthday the month before. And she could almost get away with it. Her pink silk walking dress and rose-trimmed bonnet of gros de Naples were bravely youthful. She possessed the perfect degree of plumpness to smooth out wrinkles. Her hair defied the laws of nature with dogged goldenness. Her blue eyes were childlike. Her face was amiable.

"Sooner or later, you see," her ladyship continued, "every gentleman of a certain age winds up, glass in hand, over there." She pointed toward the windowed alcove that contained the famous pump. "But this won't do for you, my dear. You really don't wish to wind up marrying some Ancient and fetching his nostrums for him just because your *young* man proved unreliable, now, do you? Trust me. Marrying out of one's generation is no fun at all. I do know whereof I speak, Venetia, for my first husband was a full thirty years my senior. Still," she added fairly, "I can't complain, for he went on to his reward after only ten years of marriage and left me mine—a fortune for my lifetime. But you can't count on being that lucky, Venetia. Besides, I was considerably younger than you, m'dear, when I married Lord Wincanton.

"Anyhow, all that is completely beside the point that I wished to make. My second husband, you see, was only four years older than I, and that marriage was far more satisfactory, if you take my meaning. The point is, the only possible reason to marry an older man, Venetia, is for financial independence. And since you have that already, you should not look for a husband here."

"But I'm not looking for a husband."

"Well, you should be. And London's the proper place to do it. Your aunt Ellis, I'm sure, would be more than happy to—"

"Aunt Louisa," Venetia interrupted her firmly, "please don't start up again. I absolutely refuse to cast myself upon the marriage mart like some chit straight from the schoolroom. The idea's repugnant to me. Not even to mention ludicrous."

"Don't talk fustian. You're not an old maid quite yet."

" 'Quite yet.' See? Even you have me tottering on the brink. Well, I intend to tip right over and accept my single state. There are worse conditions, I assure you, and I'm thankful to have escaped at least one of them."

Lady Stoke opened her mouth to reply but delayed her rebuttal in order to greet a passing dowager weighed down with pearls and weighing down a weary companion by leaning on her arm. Once assured that these acquaintances were out of earshot, her ladyship took up the conversation where they'd left off.

"Being twenty-four years old hardly puts you in your dotage," she said severely. "But one would expect you to be a bit more worldly than a schoolroom miss. If you will forgive my saying so, Venetia, you do seem a bit naive. It comes, I'm sure, from your having lost your dear mother at such an early age. Had you had an older, wiser female to guide you, I'm convinced you never would have broken off your engagement so precipitously. Certainly had I been there to advise you, I should have counseled against any such action. Oh, please don't think me unfeeling, Venetia. I know it must have been upsetting for you to discover that the man you were betrothed to was keeping a mistress. But after the initial shock had worn off a bit, you could have been led to see the advantages to that sort of thing."

Venetia's expression wavered between amusement and disgust. "You really are serious, aren't you, Aunt? Personally I should hate to contemplate reaching a stage where I'd be content to share a husband with some—some—lightskirt. Spinsterhood sounds most attractive compared to that."

Her aunt sighed heavily. "If you think that, m'dear, you really are deluded. Marriage, any kind of marriage—excepting, of course, to some brute, which in your case has no application—is far superior to a single state. A married woman has all sorts of social latitude denied the spinster. She can do pretty much as she pleases—as long as she's discreet, that is. And it never hurts if her spouse's attention is diverted elsewhere. Providing, of course, that one isn't madly in love with him, which would put an entirely different complexion upon the matter." She paused expectantly.

Venetia merely smiled enigmatically and wished her aunt would drop the subject. Had she been in love with Fletcher Langford? She really was not sure. She must have been a little, she supposed. But certainly not madly so.

The young secretary to the British ambassador to Spain had, at the time, seemed the perfect Beau Ideal—handsome, charming, of good family, assured of a brilliant career—especially with her fortune behind him, she added cynically. But when, after a twelve-month betrothal, she had discovered her fiancé's three-year liaison with an opera dancer, it was her pride more than her heart that had suffered, she suspected.

"Perhaps your problem is that you expect too much, my dear," Lady Stoke continued. "Here I've been thinking that your heart surely must be broken, but you assure me that it is not, an attitude that struck me at first as decidedly unromantic. But perhaps your problem is that you are *too* romantic, that, as I said, you expect too much. If so, I lay the blame squarely upon those novels all you young women read nowadays.

"Thank goodness I was never so misguided in my youth. I had no taste for reading at all, I'm glad to say. For no mortal man could ever live up to those impossible heroes who sigh and die for love twenty-four hours out of every day. It's been my experience that gentlemen for the most part—at least after the excitement of pursuit and conquest has worn off—are far more concerned with their dinners and hunts and mills and cards and races—or, if they're of a serious turn of mind, their politics and their estates—than they are with being in love. So it's really foolish of a woman to take the whole thing too seriously.

"Let me put it another way, Venetia. It's all well and good for a woman to be romantic. Why, I've been in love too many times to number and I've certainly no intention of breaking the habit now just because I've reached the age of, er, fifty. But it's when you confuse romance and marriage that the difficulties arise."

"Are you trying to tell me, Aunt, that one should never marry for love?"

"Well, I should not go quite so far as to say 'never.' I was terribly in love with my second husband. And it did make things quite pleasant. For a while, at least. But later, when he was not quite so . . . attentive . . . No, I would not consider that my most successful marriage. There are better reasons for marrying than being in love."

"That, Aunt Louisa, is the most cynical remark I've ever heard you make."

"Cynical?" Lady Stoke mulled the word over and then

rejected it. "Certainly not. Worldly, perhaps. I am merely trying to give you good advice, my dear. Above all, a marriage should be comfortable. And for all its appealing qualities love, I can assure you, is seldom that.

"So you really need to adopt a more practical view of life, my dear. All this talk of spinsterhood is foolishness. You must marry. And to do so you must be where the eligible men are—"

"Aunt Louisa!" her niece broke in firmly. "If you wish to be rid of me, just say so and I'll set up my own establishment. But what I will not do is go off to London—or anywhere else, for that matter—in blatant pursuit of a husband. I know you mean well, but frankly this conversation has stiffened the resolve that my former fiancé forced upon me. I will not marry for the 'convenience' of an unfaithful spouse. Oh, I don't doubt you're right in one respect. It would be naive of me to expect a love match. And by the by, I don't really think of myself as a heroine out of one of those novels you think so little of. But since I don't have to marry for financial reasons, I see no point—" Lady Venetia broke off here, aware that her aunt was no longer attending.

Lady Stoke was leaning forward on the edge of the settee, squinting through the crowd at a new arrival. Venetia looked in the direction of her aunt's narrowed gaze. It was targeted upon a portly gentleman in a bright-blue tailcoat who was staring at the assembly through a quizzing glass.

"Why, I do believe it's Porge! Porge Carstairs!" Lady Stoke exclaimed. "Yes, it's bound to be. Who else would wear such a monstrous buttonhole this time of year? What did I tell you, Venetia?" her ladyship crowed as she rose to her feet, waving her hand in circles above her head to draw the gentleman's attention. "Sooner or later every gentleman a bit beyond my own age bracket either comes here on his own accord or is sent here by his quack. Oh, famous! He's seen me!"

Indeed, the quizzing glass held steady, a huge smile split the corpulent face, and then the gentleman came bearing down upon them as fast as a rather mincing gait would allow.

"Would you look at that," Lady Stoke hissed in her niece's ear. "What did I tell you? Case of gout or I'm a Dutchman."

"Louisa, by gad, it is you!" The gentleman, panting a bit from so much exertion, beamed down at her ladyship. "What a stroke of luck! Had begun to think there was no company worth bothering with in Bath, and here you are, like something fetched up by a genie from a bottle. You're a sight for sore eyes, gel. Lovely as always." Lady Stoke was being smothered in a bearlike embrace while her niece looked on curiously.

What she saw was an elderly gentleman whose immense girth and thinning hair had by no means diminished his propensity for dandyism. Even brighter than his coat was its nosegay of flowers. Canary pantaloons strained across his stomach and hugged his bulging thighs. Hessian boots gleamed like mirrors, their tassels brilliant gold. Shirt points starched stiff as plaster forced his several chins upon an upward slant. He was just saved from appearing ludicrous, Venetia decided, by an expression as amiable as his apparel was affected. After an enthusiastic buss upon the cheek, the gentleman released her aunt and turned his interested gaze to Venetia as Lady Stoke made the introductions.

"M'dear, allow me to present one of my oldest and dearest friends, Sir George Carstairs. Porge, this is Lady Venetia Lowther, me brother Victor's daughter. You remember Victor, of course."

"Charmed, m'dear." Sir George bent over Venetia's hand as gallantly as the creak of his corsets would allow. "Knew your father slightly. Didn't move in the same circles, though. He was younger than me, for one thing. And too brainy by half. Always studying something or other. Couldn't've been less like Louisa here. But then families are that way. Take me own brother, for instance—"

"Oh, do let's sit down, Porge dear," Lady Stoke interrupted. "Is it gout?" She gestured toward the foot he was favoring. "I thought as much," she continued, her diagnosis having been confirmed. "And you will insist upon wearing those tight Hessians in spite of all your sufferings. Well, I cannot say I blame you, for you always were all the crack, Porge. A regular Brummell. And one should never allow minor infirmities to force a lowering of standards. But still, there's no need to stand around when we can be comfortable." She spied a group leaving a nearby table. "Oh, good. There's an empty place. Now we can all sit together and have a coze. Do hurry before some other party claims it."

"Oh, but that's not necessary," Venetia quickly interposed. "Let Sir George sit here beside you on the settee. I know you old friends have a great deal to talk of, and this will give me the opportunity to visit the circulating library without feeling guilty about deserting you, Aunt Louisa." She smiled mischievously. "I need to replenish my supply of those dreadful novels that you've been at pains to warn me against."

The old friends watched her departing back in silence. "Demmed fine-looking gel." Sir George pronounced his verdict once Venetia had left the room. "Can't hold a candle to her aunt, of course," he added gallantly, "but you've no call to blush for her, m'dear. No cause at all."

Lady Stoke fastened her large blue eyes intently upon him. "You ain't just doing the polite, are you, Porge? You do really mean it?"

"About the gel not holding a candle to her aunt? Of course I mean it," he declared a shade too heartily. "Why, you don't look a day over thirty, Louisa. No, by gad, make that twenty-nine."

"Oh, for heaven's sake, Porge dear, I was not referring to all that fustian about me. Although you mustn't think I'm indifferent to it. I'll gladly accept all the Spanish coin you care to fling my way. But not right at this moment. Now I'm concerned merely with Venetia. Did you mean it when you said that she's attractive?"

"Of course I meant it. It's obvious enough, I'd say. Neat figure, nice expression. And that combination of fair hair and dark eyes is most striking. The girl's no diamond of the first water, perhaps, but well above average certainly."

"Would men think so?"

"What the devil's that supposed to mean? What do you take me for, a cabbage?"

"Don't dissemble, Porge. You know exactly what I'm asking. Anybody can decide whether a female's features are all

172

they should be and if her complexion's up to snuff. But what I want to know is, would a man look at her in that certain way? Oh, botheration! Why am I being so missish with you, of all people? What I want to know is, would you wish to go to bed with her?"

Sir George was shocked. "Good gad, Louisa, have you lost your mind? The idea's monstrous. Why, the gel's barely out of leading strings."

"She's twenty-four when it comes to that, but of course I don't mean you specifically. I was speaking figuratively. I merely wish to know if you think men in general would find her appealing in that way."

"Someone's bound to. At least in my experience, coves find all sorts of odd females attractive. Not to say that your niece is odd," he clarified. "Merely making the point that if freakish females can find men who wish to bed 'em, certainly your Venetia can. But what the devil are you up to, Louisa? This kind of talk ain't quite the thing, you know."

"I do know, Porge." Lady Stoke sighed heavily. "But you see, I'm quite determined to do something about Venetia. Indeed, I *have* to do something about Venetia before she drives me to distraction."

"My word! Like that, is it?" Sir George's eyes widened in surprise. "Seemed a pleasant-enough chit. But then you never know."

"Oh, she is quite pleasant. You must not jump to the wrong conclusion, Porge. I like the girl prodigiously. Why, I couldn't think more highly of her if she was me own daughter. Though it's hard to imagine that this conversation would be necessary if she was. The thing is, George—" And Lady Stoke proceeded to fill her friend in on the details of Venetia's broken engagement.

"I don't understand any of it," she concluded, shaking her head in bewilderment, setting the roses on her bonnet into motion. "You see, it seems to me, Porge, that if Venetia was really up to snuff where the male sex is concerned and if she was bothered by the fact her fiancé was supporting a mistress, she should have had no difficulty at all in persuading him to send the trollop packing—for the first few months, at least, by which time she might be just as glad to see her reinstalled. But not only did Venetia refuse to put up a fight for the man she was betrothed to, but she's quite determined to be an old maid. And what's worse, she's going to be it here with me!

"Oh, Porge, Venetia is the kindest thing." Lady Stoke's countenance was stricken. "She cossets me. She's solicitous. She fetches things. I swear it, Porge, I've never felt so *old*. There, now. I've said it. The thing is, I've never, ever wanted a companion. But if I did desire one, it would be some female of my own age or older who would not make me feel like Methuselah. I vow, Porge, it should not surprise you if any day now you see Venetia pushing me down Stall Street in a Bath chair!"

"My God!" Her friend was horrified by the outburst. "Send the chit packing!"

"No, Porge dear, I can't do that. I will not hurt her feelings. For I really do like the girl, you see. And she's suffered a most severe blow. To her pride, if not her heart, which might take longer to heal, actually. No, Porge, what I wish to do is marry Venetia off. That's why I asked your opinion of her desirability. For it would be best if I could find someone to fall in love with her. Frankly, I don't think she'll tolerate being courted a second time just for her fortune."

"Well, if the fellow's worth his salt, she wouldn't have to know it."

"That's so, of course. But the immediate problem is to find some eligible males to throw at her head. She refuses to go to London and, well, just look around you." Lady Stoke repeated the sweeping gesture with which she'd earlier dismissed Bath's male population. "You're the only attractive male in the whole assemblage, Porge, and I quite refuse to share you with Venetia."

Sir George *pshaw*ed the compliment but looked pleased by it all the same as he bent his none-too-powerful intellect upon the problem. "Why, it's simply another case of the mountain and Mohomet, m'dear," he pronounced after a few moments' thought. "That's it, pure and simple."

"I beg your pardon?"

"You must know the saying."

Since apparently Lady Stoke did not, he went on to enlighten her. "If the mountain won't come to Mohomet, Mohomet must go to the mountain, or some such thing."

"Don't you have that backward? But never mind, for really, Porge, I don't see what bearing some heathen proverb has on Venetia's problem. The girl will be back here any moment. I don't need senseless sayings. I need advice."

"I'm giving it," he explained patiently. "Simply trying to say that if there ain't any young men to be had in Bath, you'll have to import 'em."

"And just how am I expected to do that, pray tell? You don't order up a dozen eligible young bachelors like oysters."

"Don't need a dozen, actually. One will do for starters."

"Well, I don't have one. That is to say, not one I know well enough to ask down here on his own. Too obvious, anyhow. Venetia wouldn't sit still for it. I suppose I could give a house party." Her face assumed a martyred look. "Though I'd hate it above all things. No, we'd best dismiss that notion. It won't do. No one under fifty would come to a house party held in Bath."

"No need to have a party. Send for Wincanton. The very ticket."

"Wincanton?"

"Oh, come now, Louisa. Surely you ain't forgotten your heir."

"Of course not. I've also not forgotten that he's been in the army for donkey's years. With Wellington. Chasing Bonaparte. In Belgium or some such place, the last I heard."

"Well, he ain't there now. Friend of mine saw him in Brooks' just last week. Said he's quit the army. Nothing left to do now. Surely, Louisa, you must've heard of Waterloo. Even in Bath."

"Gareth Wincanton's in London? Oh, Porge, it just might do at that. But do you think he'd come?"

"I think he'll have to if you ask him," the other replied simply. "Got no choice. Duty-bound, you know."

"Me, ask him? Oh, no, I think not." The world was looking

a great deal rosier to Lady Stoke. "I'll do better than that!" She clapped her hands and crowed. "For it pays to be subtle in these things, Porge dear. I'll simply let his mother do it."

Chapter
Two

THE PARTY GATHERED AROUND THE PUNCH BOWL IN A private parlor at Brooks' Club in London could not be described as "convivial," in spite of the fact that the four gentlemen had been drinking deep. The problem was that both the host and his special guest were decidedly blue-deviled. This twosome, along with their companions, had come to the exclusive club directly from Drury Lane Theatre for the specific purpose of shooting the cat. But the punch, though potent, had not had the desired effect of lifting the party's spirits.

The host, Major Gareth Wincanton, late of His Majesty's cavalry, had perhaps the greater claim to an acute case of the dismals. Affairs of the heart are traditionally given precedence over other kinds of woes, such as suddenly losing one's source of livelihood, as was the case with Mr. Nicholas Forbes, his guest.

In the ordinary way of things, Major Wincanton and Mr. Forbes would not have been thrown together socially. And certainly in the ordinary way of things Mr. Forbes would not have been admitted into a gentlemen's club, since by no stretch of the imagination did he qualify for that high honor. Indeed, the only degree of merriment the party had thus far managed to achieve came from recalling how Mr. Forbes had been foisted off as Major Wincanton's cousin. "Distant" cousin, actually, was the nearest relationship that the major had been able to force himself to claim. Then, perhaps to make up for such half-heartedness, he'd gone on to add that he and his "cousin" had had the honor to serve in the same regiment. This embellishment was almost their undoing, for it sent his cronies off into sudden spasms, since they all knew that while the statement was literally true, the major had served on Wellington's staff, whereas Mr. Forbes had been the merest ranker.

It was a capricious fate that had thrown these two unlikely candidates for comradeship together. Fate in the guise of the comely, provocative, romantic leading lady of Drury Lane, Miss Amabel Fawnhope, who was lusted after by Major Wincanton and "sister" to Mr. Forbes.

For shortly after selling his commission and arriving back in London, Major Wincanton had attended a performance of *The Fatal Marriage*, gazed down upon a black-haired, violet-eyed goddess, and lost his head completely. And it had come as a severe blow to his self-esteem when his suit had failed to prosper. The major had never before been rebuffed by any female of a certain stamp, which was the only type of female he pursued, having no desire to forfeit a bachelorhood he was enjoying to the hilt. Wincanton was personable, he was rich, he was an earl's grandson and a war hero—a combination that should have assured him spontaneous success. But in the case of Miss Fawnhope, actress, it had failed to do so.

Not that Miss Fawnhope spurned him. Far from it. She was warm and caring and in their more tender moments had been known to whisper words of deep affection into his ear. The rub was, Miss Amabel Fawnhope drew the line at consummating their relationship, and none of the major's considerable powers of seduction had thus far been able to break down her iron-willed resistance. She had even breached the rules of conduct generally accepted in this type of situation by hinting broadly that marriage would be the only means to the major's desired ends. A circumstance that was, of course, quite unthinkable.

It was after his courtship had reached this impasse that Major Wincanton had begun to cultivate Mr. Forbes, who was as close to being family as Miss Fawnhope could claim. It was the major's hope that Forbes, a rather rackety here-and-thereian but a man of the world nonetheless, could make Amabel see reason. Now even this support was about to be taken from him.

"What are you going to do now, Nicky?" he asked. Recalled to his hostly duties, he refilled the others' punch cups.

"Damned if I know." Forbes shrugged. "Head for the provinces, I expect. Put in a season or so there. Then maybe Covent Garden can use me."

"Rotten luck, old man," said "Sprig" St. Leger, corpulent and thirty, who was so named not for his youth or size but for his fashion excesses. "Terrible thing, getting booted out like that. Unfair. Didn't think you were all that bad myself."

"Don't read the notices, then, do you?"

This comment—from the fourth member of the company, Owen, Lord Piggot-Jones, an effete-looking young man with pale eyes, pale skin, pale hair—earned Piggot-Jones a darkling look from the actor, who was sensitive about his reviews. "Mr. Forbes's lack of histrionic talent was mercilessly exposed by the beacon of Kean's brilliance," the *Times*'s critic had observed.

"Nicky's performance had nothing to say in the matter," Wincanton interposed diplomatically. "His looks were his problem. You know how sensitive Kean is about his height—his appearance in general, for that matter. He's not about to let someone tall and handsome share the stage with him."

Nicky Forbes gave his host a grateful look, but the Sprig, who was more than a bit disguised, had a fit of the giggles that ended up in hiccoughs. "You only say so, Wincanton," he finally managed, "because you two are dead ringers for each other. Just a roundabout way of puffing your own self up, if you ask me."

This physical resemblance between the major and the private had been the subject of much discussion among the party earlier. Indeed, it had been the impetus for insinuating Nicholas Forbes into Brooks' Club in the guise of a Wincanton relative.

It was a resemblance that both involved parties publicly accepted but privately denied—the actor because he considered himself better-looking than the aristocrat, and the major because he found it intolerable to be look-alike to a Cit. "We're hardly 'dead ringers,' " he said shortly now. "All ginger-pated coves get lumped together."

"All ginger-pated coves don't have the same blue eyes and cleft chins, though. By gad, it's uncanny." The Sprig became convulsed once more as an idea struck him. "You sure you two ain't actually cousins after all? Or brothers, even? Oh, I say, Win, could it be that you ain't the first of your family to lose your head over some actress? How about it, Nicky? Tell us— who's your father?"

The Sprig's face turned a deep, dark red as the actor leveled him with a set-down look that the great Kean himself might have envied. "Sorry," Mr. St. Leger mumbled. "Devilish poor taste."

Nicky nodded a curt acceptance of the apology while mentally examining, then rejecting, the other's insinuation. He could come up with three—or possibly four—good candidates for the post of his progenitor. Not one of these had the slightest Wincanton connection.

"You couldn't stick around London for a fortnight or so longer, could you, Nicky?" The actor's dubious parentage held no fascination for the major. His mind had reverted to his own problems. "Perhaps Amabel could—" He cut himself short, then shied away from the suggestion he was about to make, that Miss Fawnhope would most likely be happy to house Nicky temporarily. Somehow the idea of those two living together held little appeal to him, even though they'd done so as children. "Amabel will miss you," he amended.

"I doubt that. She won't have time."

"Oh, God, you're right. And I'd counted on you to act as a sort of chaperon to keep the other coves away while I'm gone. Of all the curst luck." Wincanton gave a heartfelt groan, then ladled out more punch to one and all. "As if it weren't bad enough to have to leave London myself just when Amabel was beginning to come around, now you won't be here either to protect my interests. That swine Leacock's just waiting for me to turn my back so he can make his move. Of all the damnable timing, this has to be the worst."

"Oh, you're going away, Win?" Lord Piggot-Jones stopped drinking deep to ask.

"My God, Owen, where have you been all evening?" the Sprig inquired. "Win's off to Bath. That's what this wake's all about, for heaven's sake."

"Bath? Why on earth would anybody go to Bath? Last place I'd want to go, I'll tell you."

"I don't *want* to go," Wincanton said impatiently. "I *have* to go. My father insists I pay a duty visit to Lady Stoke. I'm the heir, you see."

The others, with the exception of Mr. Forbes, murmured sympathetically.

"Cut you off without a shilling, would she, if you didn't show?" the actor asked.

"Oh, no. She can't do that, actually. It's her husband's fortune. Or was. He's dead, of course. No, it isn't that. It's just that the old lady's heard I'm out of the army and her nose is out of joint that I've not been to see her. Don't know why it should be. She hasn't clapped eyes on me since I was at Eton. But if she wants me, I'll have to go. Devilish bad ton not to, you know. Besides," he added, "if I don't go do the polite, my father will be coming to London to learn the reason why. And that's all that's needed. I can imagine the dust-up when he discovers I'm dangling after an actress. Waterloo won't touch it for fireworks. Oh, lord, what a coil."

"Well, look on the bright side." Piggot-Jones spoke soothingly. "Since Nicky here's being banished, too, you two could travel down together. Or does Bath have a theater, Nicky? Wouldn't surprise me any if it didn't."

"Well, yes, as a matter of fact. Quite a good one, actually. The Theatre Royal. Come to think on it, that would be as good a place to start as any—especially if I can wheedle a ride, Major." He brightened at the thought of the savings in coach fare.

"I've a better idea!" The Sprig, who was most definitely castaway, clapped his hands with sudden inspiration. "Why don't you go in his place?"

"I beg your pardon?"

"Of course! Why didn't we think of it before? It's the very thing. You have to leave London. Win don't want to. You take his place."

"You really must be foxed, St. Leger." Despite this observation, Wincanton poured them all more punch.

"No, I ain't. At least foxed's got nothing to say in the matter. You coves are the ones who must be disguised past all reasoning. Use your noggins, why don't you? What have we just been talking about? That you two are dead ringers for each other, that's what. Oh, very well, then," he reacted to his host's expression, "maybe you ain't just alike precisely, but there is a decided resemblance, you can't deny. And didn't you just say that your aunt, Lady Whosoever, hasn't seen you since your school days? Well, then, there you are."

"Where exactly are we?" Wincanton asked sarcastically.

"I'm simply trying to point out that there'd be nothing to it. What's the old lady going to remember about you? The color of your hair, that's what. And maybe after that, your eyes. And they're near enough a match with Nicky's. My dear fellow, no one, but no one, looks the same as he did during his school days. And thank God for it." He shuddered. "Nothing but a mass of spots back then myself."

Wincanton was beginning to look thoughtful. "Well, I'll grant you," he said grudgingly, "that he might get by with an impersonation as far as appearance alone goes. But he couldn't pull off the rest in a million years."

"Why not? Knows you too well, does she? Your aunt, I mean."

"No, that's not it. Aunt Louisa and I were never together all that much. She was Uncle's second wife. After he died, she married again. So Aunt Louisa was never all that close to our family, actually."

"Well, then, there you are," the Sprig pronounced thickly. "She ain't likely to be dragging up odd bits of your family history, then, that Nicky here wouldn't know about. And if she asked about some of your kith and kin, he could simply make up the answers and she'd not know the difference. And if he did get stumped on something or other"—his enthusiasm mounted—"he could fall back on the war. He could claim that the whole horrible business of Waterloo wiped everything else out of his memory. Happens, you know. By Jove!" He tried to snap his fingers, but they just missed making contact. "It all fits. You were wounded, weren't you, Win?"

"Yes, as a matter of fact. In the leg. Which hardly makes me a candidate for loss of memory."

"Where you were hit ain't the point, old man," Mr. St. Leger explained patiently. "It's the horror of battle you wished to wipe out of your mind. And in managing that, you just overdid a bit, that's all, and wiped out a lot of other stuff as well."

"Don't be an ass, Sprig." The major, a consummate soldier, had never had the slightest desire to wipe out one moment of a military engagement that had changed the course of history.

"Oh, well, then, if that's the way you feel about it." The Sprig sulked a moment, but was loath to abandon the idea. "Well, then, look at the thing another way," he tried again. "What's the thing that you and Nicky here have in common? Besides Miss Fawnhope, that is. The war. Waterloo. My word, you both go all the way back to the Battle of Salamanca, don't you? Well, then, that's it. What else does anyone want to hear about? Females especially. Anytime the conversation gets a bit sticky, he can talk about the war. Safe as houses." He looked around the table in a challenging manner. Lord Piggot-Jones hiccoughed and nodded.

"Well, then, there you are." The Sprig was enjoying his role as barrister. "You don't want to go to Bath. Nicky's an out-of-work actor needing a part. Hire him to play you, and all's right and tight for both you chaps."

Nicholas's befogged mind had tended to wander somewhat during the exchange, but the word "hire" now gained his full attention.

Wincanton was thinking. Then after a pregnant pause he shook his head. "No, I tell you. It would never work."

"And why wouldn't it?" the Sprig asked.

Major Wincanton looked embarrassed. "Beg pardon, Nicky. Don't wish to appear offensive, but what I mean to say is, there's the *gentleman* thing, you know. It's not just something a cove can assume. He has to *be*."

"For heaven's sake, Win, the man's an actor!"

The word seemed to hang suspended in the air while each member of the party examined it, two recalling the performance they'd just witnessed, another remembering the reviews. Mr. Forbes, who despite his state of advanced intoxication missed nothing of the general reaction, looked miffed.

"St. Leger's right, dammit. I am an actor! Oh, I know what you're all thinking. That I ain't been exactly the critics' darling. But on the other hand"—he gave the major a haughty look that was intensified by the fact he was seeing two of him—"if you don't mind me saying so, Major Wincanton, you ain't exactly Hamlet the Dane, you know. What I mean to say is, I could play you in a breeze. Nothing to it. All a cove would have to do is stare right through common folk and never see 'em and talk like a toff, then limp a bit to peg down your character. Why, I'd be willing to wager anybody that aunt of yours would be calling me 'nephew' in no time flat."

"So would I!" the Sprig chimed in. "Look at it this way. We passed him off as a gentleman here, didn't we? And I'm sure your aunt can't be any more of a high stickler than our Charles is. By Jove, I'm sure Nicky can do it. And I've got a thousand pounds that says Nicholas can impersonate you, Win."

At the magic word "wager," Piggot-Jones had come to life. What had merely been an academic discussion, and a fairly boring one at that, now took on all the heady elements of a horse race or a boxing mill. "Oh, I say, if Forbes here did take your place, Win, how long would he have to do it?"

Nicholas thought the question amazingly intelligent, considering the source.

"Why, for the whole of February. You see, I'm supposed to squire Aunt Louisa around to the assembly rooms, take her to the theater, that sort of thing."

The actor, who had been thinking more in terms of a fortnight, stifled a groan. But his professional pride, which had

183

taken a severe drubbing of late, reasserted itself. "Since this is just another acting job far as I'm concerned, what would it pay?"

"What do actors earn?" Wincanton countered.

Mr. Forbes gave the matter thought, then, without blushing, came up with a figure that would have caused a star of Drury Lane to jump for joy.

"Well, then, how about it, Win? Is it worth that much blunt to you to stay here in London and storm Miss Fawnhope's citadel and repel all other boarders?" the Sprig inquired in a clash of metaphors.

A long draft of the powerful punch made up the major's mind for him. "Yes, by gad, it is!"

"Well, then, I'll take your wager, Sprig," Lord Piggot-Jones declared. "My thousand pounds against yours that Forbes here will be unmasked long before a month's up."

To Nicky's disgust, St. Leger hesitated as if his brain had suddenly unclouded. His "Done!" when he finally uttered it and extended his hand lacked the true ring of conviction to his listeners' ears.

"You don't sound too confident, Sprig," Wincanton observed dryly.

The actor was stung by his champion's sudden attack of cravenness. A man had his pride, by Jove. "He has no cause for concern, Major. By George, I'm more than eager to back my own performance. What would you say to a thousand pounds?"

This reckless bravado was aimed at Wincanton, who merely arched an eyebrow at the notion of the actor commanding that kind of blunt.

It was Lord Piggot-Jones who shouted "Done, by God!" and stuck out a hand. And before Nicky could retract his question, his own fist was being pumped vigorously up and down.

The Sprig motioned to a waiter who'd been hovering nearby, hoping the party would soon go home. The betting book was fetched and the wagers duly entered.

Mr. Nicholas Forbes was of a sudden sober and feeling more

than a trifle ill. It was all that he could manage not to cast up his accounts right then and there in Brooks' exclusive club for gentlemen.

Chapter Three

T HE POUNDING ON HER DOOR FINALLY PENETRATED THE dream of Miss Amabel Fawnhope. She was standing before an altar, plighting her troth. Though the face of her bridegroom kept perversely changing, there was no doubt at all of the most salient fact: He possessed both rank and fortune.

Miss Fawnhope murmured a futile "I do," then reluctantly cracked open her lids and squinted at the day. It was morning, sure enough, but what o'clock? She opened her eyes wider and focused on the ormolu timepiece that had the place of honor on her bedchamber mantel. Eight! Who would dare? The pounding increased. "Gareth!" she breathed, her eyes taking on some of the sparkle that made them so appealing by stage candlelight. She reached for the dressing gown draped around the bedpost and hurried eagerly toward the sound.

Her face fell as she unlocked the door. "Oh, it's you."

"Well, thanks ever so much." Nicholas Forbes entered her small hallway. "And it's nice to see you, too, love."

"Oh, don't be so goosish, Nicky." Miss Fawnhope rose on tiptoe to plant a kiss upon his cheek that did very little to mollify him. "It's just that I—"

"I know. You were expecting someone else." He made no effort to sound less aggrieved.

"Well, you are the last person in the world I'd expect to rouse a working actress from her beauty sleep. Oh, heavens, Nicky, I didn't mean . . . Don't look like that. I wasn't thinking."

" 'Working actress.' That's right, Bella. Go on. Throw it in my teeth." Martyrdom sat heavily upon him. "You're the only employed member of this family now. I'm well aware of that."

"Oh, for pity's sake, Nicky, don't be so touchy. Here I haven't seen you for three whole days, and I've been worried about you. Come sit down. I'll ring for tea. I just hope the shock won't kill Nellie. She ain't used to any exertion before noon."

It said a lot for Miss Fawnhope's rapid rise in the theatrical world that at the age of twenty she could hire a house in Russell Street and keep a maid. True, the rent on the former was often in arrears, and the latter, an out-of-work actress in her declining years, was more than content to take on her less-than-rigorous duties merely for her keep. Still, Nicky thought with a stab of jealousy as he looked around the little parlor, which was charmingly, if cheaply, furnished with secondhand pieces and some stage discards, there was no denying the fact that Amabel was doing well. Very well indeed.

As the maid came in, bearing a tray that gave off a promising aroma and a cloud of steam, Nicky continued to gaze around himself, partly to avoid looking at Nellie, who was putting the tray down with a thump while muttering darkly about folk who ought to know better than to rob an actress of her much-needed sleep, not even to mention servants what stayed up to all hours to do their duty by the young, who had no proper notion of what it was like to be old and feeble, thinking old age was a condition as would never happen to the likes of them.

"Oh, do go on back to bed," Amabel said with a sigh, "and quit jawing at poor Nicky here. He's got trouble enough without you ringing a peal over him, too."

"Don't I know it." Nellie, who had known both the young people since their leading-string days, suddenly forgot her own grievances and looked fondly at the young man. "But never you mind, Nicky darling. Any man as 'eartbreaking 'andsome as you've turned out is bound to get back up on the stage. Talent be blowed. It's looks what counts. As others in this room can testify.

"Of course, now," she pontificated as she poured out the steaming brew into mismatched cups, "that scoundrel Kean is the exception what proves the rule. All he's got is talent. Jealous as anything of you, Nicky, the meanspirited scapegallows." She yawned prodigiously. "Well, I'm off to bed again. Never you fret, Nicky love. Something will turn up for you. It's bound to." The words were more optimistic than the doleful shake she gave the gray head under the dirty nightcap as she left the room.

"How do you put up with the old harridan?" Nicky kept his voice low as he picked up his cup and took a restoring swallow.

"How can you ask? She was your mother's closest friend, in case you've forgotten. Besides"—Amabel dimpled fetchingly—"she's useful when I need a chaperon."

"Which is most of the time, I don't doubt." Nicky sized up his "sister" from across the tea table with the eye of a connoisseur. It still amazed him that the scrawny brat he'd known when he'd enlisted in the army ten years before had turned into this beauty. Even though he'd managed to see her from time to time on his infrequent leaves (including a fortnight when his mother had died and he'd arranged for Nellie to keep an eye on the child), he'd not been prepared for this transformation. Bella was a nonpareil, no mistake.

She grew aware of his intense appraisal and pulled her dressing gown, which carelessly exposed an improper amount of creamy bosom, more decorously around her. "For heaven's sake, Nicky, put your eyes back in your head," she said reproachfully. "Surely I don't have to stand on points with you."

"You don't have to watch your manners, if that's what you mean," he answered shortly. "But you'd do well to keep your clothes on. I'm male and human, for God's sake."

"But you're family!"

"If you say so."

"I do say so!" The gorgeous violet eyes were intensely serious. "You're my big brother, Nicky. That's the most important thing in the world to me, so don't you ever forget it. And I was

187

sure you felt the same. Why, you've always been there for me—even when you weren't," she continued with a total lack of logic. "I mean I always knew I had a *family*, as long as there was you. Can you understand that, Nicky?"

Well, yes, he supposed he could if he was forced to. Amabel's father had been just one more in a steady succession of lovers whom his actress mother had enjoyed during her foreshortened lifetime. The only thing that separated him from the other "uncles," in Nicky's mind, was that when he had moved in with them he had brought along a tiny daughter and when he had moved out he had left her behind, neither of which occurrences perturbed Nicky's mother in the least. Little Amabel was simply absorbed into their third-rate touring company, with Nicky given responsibility for the child when his mother was otherwise engaged, which was most of the time. He bearled her and she adored him, an arrangement that suited him quite well.

But after his discharge from the army, he had a great deal of difficulty in dealing with their changed status. Even the fact that Amabel had wheedled the manager of Drury Lane into hiring him had been something of a pill to swallow, although at the same time he was grateful.

Her success with the opposite sex had been even harder to contend with than her theatrical achievements, perhaps because his self-acknowledged jealousy had taken him completely by surprise. Now, as he dipped one of the light wigs Nellie had supplied into the steamy tea, he looked around him with a jaundiced eye. Every table in the room was abloom with flowers. "This place looks like a curst hothouse. Can't imagine how you ever manage to breathe. You would think that some of your nabobs could put their blunt to better use. Why don't they give you something that don't die off right away? Something you could hock."

"It's not *they*. It's *he*. Major Wincanton. And he sends flowers because I've told him they're the only gifts that I'll accept," Amabel said.

"Are you daft? Why, the man's rich as Croesus. He could buy you anything—diamonds, pearls—you name it. He's good

188

for any of that stuff. Why, the major's a walking actress's old-age pension. God knows what he's worth, with more to come. Use your head, Bella."

"Please don't call me Bella. I've told you before, it's common. And I am using my head, brother dear, because all those jewels you speak of, and carriages, too— By the by, did you know he's offered to buy me a curricle with a pair of matched grays to pull it?"

Nicky's eyes opened wide, followed by his mouth. He knew exactly the kind of rig she referred to. He'd left a similar one around the corner with a small disgruntled tiger in charge of it.

"But you see, Nicky," Amabel continued, "all those gifts have strings attached, and I'm not interested." She directed a small, complacent smile toward her teacup. "You see, I mean to marry Major Wincanton."

"Don't be a fool."

Nicky had spoken much too sharply and instantly regretted it as the actress raised her chin and gave him a frigid look.

"I'm sorry, Bella—Amabel—for such plain speaking. But you'd best get it into your head that the Wincantons of this world don't marry the likes of you. Oh, I know he's besotted." He waved his hand to take in the bouquets of flowers. "But not beyond all reason. He's a swell, Bella. A toff. Stiff-rumped as they make 'em. And he ain't likely to forget his obligations to his family. Or to his class, when it comes to that. No, the major won't marry someone off the stage."

"It's been known to happen."

"Yes, on rare occasions. And usually by young sprigs of the nobility too green to know what's what. I tell you for your own good, Bella. I know Wincanton, and he's too fly by half to let himself be leg-shackled to a Cit, no matter how in love he fancies himself."

"Oh?" She tossed her tousled dark curls and her brilliant eyes flashed, and for just a moment his deep conviction began to waver. To him she had never appeared lovelier than in this early-morning dishabille, with her hair tumbling every which way and her well-worn dressing gown inclined to slip its moorings. As far as he was concerned, all the regal gowns and paste

189

jewelry she'd worn on stage couldn't touch her present costume for desirability. If Gareth Wincanton had seen her like this, God knew what the upshot would be. No! He pulled himself up short. No use both of them becoming bird-witted. He was right. Wincanton would never marry Amabel, and that was that.

Disconcertingly, she read his mind. "Would you care to make a wager?"

"I would not!" After the fiasco at Brooks' Club, Nicky had sworn off betting. He came close to breaking out in a cold sweat once again as the image of his signature in that betting book came floating before his eyes.

With an effort he changed tack and adopted a more conciliatory tone. "Look, I don't enjoy being the one to have to say you've got maggots in your head. But I don't want to see you hurt, love. And you will be if you go on thinking the major will marry you."

"He'll marry me if it's the only way he can get what he wants. And believe me, it is."

Amabel Fawnhope was a stage phenomenon—a desirable young woman whose looks were her greatest asset but who still managed to keep her manager, her fellow actors, and an adoring public at arm's length. Shortly after arriving back in London from the Continent, Nicholas himself had made a halfhearted attempt at seduction, feeling slightly incestuous at the time, and had had an ear-boxing followed by a good tongue-lashing.

"I think your scheme would work," he now conceded, "on almost any other of those gentry coves who are dangling after you. But not Wincanton. You'll never bring him up to scratch. Why not switch to someone else?"

"You don't like him much, do you?"

This was a question he'd not previously bothered to think about, but no, by Jupiter, he guessed he didn't. "What I think of the major's got nothing to say in the matter," he replied aloud. "The thing is, Bella, I know the man, and he's as high in the instep as they come. But you could do worse," he went on seriously, partly from a reluctant conviction and partly because

190

he'd agreed to do so before he'd parted from Wincanton, "than to let him set you up in style somewhere. The man's not exactly my cup of tea, I grant you, but he ain't tightfisted. He'd see you fixed for life. I'd stake my own on that."

"He'll see me fixed for life, all right." Miss Fawnhope leaned toward him. "But not the way you mean. I intend to marry, Nicky. I'm *determined* to. You, of all people, should appreciate that ambition. We've both seen enough of the other kind of life. And I'm not having it."

"You surely ain't comparing being set up by Wincanton with the life my mother led."

"A mistress is still a mistress, while a wife's a wife," she said stubbornly. "But enough of this. Let's change the subject. It's not my affairs that need discussing; it's yours. What do you plan to do, Nicky? You can move in here, of course."

"No, that's what I can't do, Bella."

And even if there had been no wager, he still could not have done so. For though he was not averse to being a sponge under other circumstances, the notion of letting Amabel support him was somehow unthinkable—a leftover, no doubt, from the period in their lives when she hero-worshipped him. "Thanks anyhow, Bella, but I'm off for Bath. Just stopped to say goodbye, as a matter of fact."

"The Theatre Royal? That's a famous idea! Mr. Powell's down there, did you know? He was Mama's special friend when we played Bristol years ago, remember? He's bound to put in a good word for you."

It took all Nicky's self-control not to wince at that piece of news. Well, he'd just have to put a wide berth between himself and the theater, that's all.

"Would it help if I wrote the manager there?" Amabel asked.

"It might, but I'd rather you didn't," he replied rather shortly.

"Hoity-toity! You are the proud one, aren't you? And you call Major Wincanton high in the instep! Well"—she looked him over carefully—"I doubt my say-so would make much difference anyhow. And even if I was another Mrs. Siddons, it'd still be unnecessary. Just look at you. You've 'leading man' written all over you. And where did you find your new tailor? I've never seen you looking so bang-up-to-the-nines." She gazed with approval at the bottle-green coat he wore along with fawn-colored breeches and white-topped black boots. "If I didn't know better, I'd say Weston made that coat." In truth the famous Bond Street tailor *had* done so—for Major Gareth Wincanton, however.

"You should have no trouble getting hired, Nicky. Of course, you may have to work backstage awhile till the proper part comes along.

"Do you know," she continued thoughtfully, "this could all be for the best in the long run? You getting the sack here, I mean. A season or so in the provinces won't do you any harm. It'll give you a chance to really learn your craft."

"What do you mean, 'learn my craft'?" he said, bristling. "I was shoved onstage soon as I could toddle, the same as you."

"Lor' love us, ain't we touchy!" She threw up her arms in mock dismay. "The difference between us, brother dear, was that I wanted to perform and you fought it all the way. Why, you could hardly wait to run off to the army. Whatever possessed you, Nicky, to give the theater another try?"

"I learned an important lesson while fighting for my country." He grinned a crooked smile. "The worst they throw at actors is rotten oranges, which beats cannonballs and bullets by a mile."

She laughed. "Oh, but you were so heroic-looking in your uniform. And you *were* heroic, I've been told."

Nicky tried to look modest, which actually wasn't all that difficult, since he entertained a certain ambivalence about his military exploits. He certainly had no cause to blush for his service record. He'd been as brave as any man whose chief objective was to emerge from the conflict alive could be, he supposed. But heroic? Never!

"Anyhow," Amabel was saying, "I can see why it suited you to leave the army now the fighting's over. But you could have knocked me down with a feather when you decided to come back on the stage. There are other choices, you know."

"Such as?" He rose to his feet. "Name one, Bella, that

192

doesn't involve grubbing for a living and I'll consider it. But in the meantime, I'm off."

"Oh, Nicky!" Amabel wailed. "I will miss you." She jumped up and ran around the table in order to plaster herself against him in a manner he found most disconcerting. "I'd just got used to having you around again"—she sniffled into his shoulder—"and now you're leaving. It's just like it was before, when I thought I'd die of it." Her eyes were full of tears as she raised her face to look reproachfully at him. Nicky bent down and kissed her.

Vaguely he had intended for the kiss to be brotherly. But the whole thing got out of hand. His lips were soon traveling with a feverish intensity from her lips to her ear, by way of her cheek, then down her throat; they had targeted her breast when he was given a fierce push and sent careening back against the door.

"Nicky!"

He was glad to note that she, too, was breathing heavily, and not just from the exertion of her shove.

"It's possibly a good thing you're leaving." She gathered her dressing gown around her firmly, one hand clasping the pale pink satin together underneath her chin.

"No, it wouldn't do to mess up your ambitious marriage schemes, now, would it?" He'd meant to strike a light note and had wound up sounding churlish. Lord, the critics were right. He was a lousy actor.

"No, it wouldn't." She tilted her chin defiantly. "I intend to make our fortunes, Nicky."

"*Our* fortunes?"

"Of course. We always look out for each other, don't we?"

Did they? He wasn't sure. He'd left her in the lurch before. Still, he'd always sent her a good portion of his meager pay. But urging her to let Wincanton give her a carte blanche? Damned if he knew whether that was looking out for her or not. Well, one thing was certain. It was a damned sight better for her than what he'd had foremost in his mind a moment earlier.

Nicky's hand was on the doorknob, but he turned back once

more to face her. "You've not said, Bella. Tell me. Do you love him?"

"Love Gareth?" She frowned as she studied the question. "I honestly don't know. I'm not even sure what love is. Sometimes I think it's just something we've made up on the stage. I'm not sure what I feel. Oh, I won't lie to you. What I think about the most is what he can do for me—the posh life I'd lead and all of that. There are times, though, when that doesn't even enter into it and when I begin to wonder if I don't actually *love* him after all—whatever that word means. And do you know when those times are, Nicky?"

He shook his head.

"The times when he reminds me most of you."

Nicholas Forbes thought that was the most lowering statement he had ever heard.

Chapter Four

"WELL, AT LEAST YOU AIN'T COW-HANDED."
These were the first words spoken after several miles of silence, and the first sign, albeit grudging, of approval that the diminutive tiger had accorded his bogus master.

"Why shouldn't I know horses?" Nicholas retorted. "I was in the cavalry, for God's sake."

The two were seated side by side on the leather seat of a sporting black curricle with bright yellow upholstery and wheel spokes of the same vivid color. They were traveling down the Bath Road at a rapid clip on an overcast, bone-chilling day.

"I realize you and horses are well acquainted, gov'nor, but shoveling what comes out of one end of 'em don't necessarily qualify you to manage the bit in the teeth of the other." Jocko Hodges doubled up at this witticism.

Nicholas waited for him to subside. Then when the small man, who looked like a child but was actually Nicky's age, twenty-eight, finally straightened up and wiped his eyes, Nicky remarked conversationally, "You know, sport, this scam wasn't my notion. Major Wincanton's got a bigger stake in my pulling it off than I have." Or he would have if I hadn't been so sap-skulled as to wager my life away, he mentally amended. "So what I fail to understand is why the devil he had to saddle me with you."

"That's easy enough, I'd say. To make sure you don't take this pair"—Jocko nodded toward the perfectly matched team of grays—"and head for the border with 'em. All right, all right. Just funning. No need to look so brass-faced, guv. To answer your question—somebody's got to see to the cattle, ain't they? And no telling what sort of stable old Lady Stoke may keep, or even if she keeps one. Besides, having me along gives you the proper touch of class."

"Having you along is like carrying my own personal Jonah."

"Watch it, guv!" The tiger was deeply offended. "I'll admit the major's friends greased me fist to keep 'em posted on your progress—or lack of it, most likely. But you're dicked in the nob if you think I'll blow the gab to her ladyship. Wouldn't be sporting, now, would it? Besides being completely unnecessary." He broke into a gap-toothed grin. "I've ten pounds wot's said you'll land arsy-varsy without any help from me, guv."

"Thank you for that much-needed vote of confidence."

"I'm only telling you the God's own truth. Oh, you look like the genuine article, I'll grant you." Jocko appraised the tall man beside him, drinking in the elegance of the major's five-caped greatcoat. "And you even talk like a gentleman. But the plain truth is"—the tiger, who was well acquainted with the other's origins, paused dramatically—"you and me has got a damned sight more in common than you and those swells

195

you're going to be visiting has. And if they don't find you out in the first half hour, well, then I'm a Frenchy."

Nicholas, still dwelling on the Jonah parallel, struggled with the impulse that bade him to pick up the little man and cast him overboard. He restrained himself and retreated once again into his thoughts.

They were not pleasant. Jocko Hodges had voiced only a fraction of the qualms he himself was feeling. Nor had Major Wincanton's attitude fired his confidence.

The morning after the disastrous betting at Brooks' Club, the major had sent Jocko to fetch him to St. James's Square. Nicky had been ushered into a luxurious parlor, where he'd found the major berating himself for being ten kinds of a fool. "I should never have agreed to this ramshackle scheme," the tirade had climaxed.

"Well, then why not call the whole thing off?" Nicky, who had had time for more than second thoughts, had considered the question reasonable but found himself impaled by a look that lost not one whit in scorn from the fact the major's eyes were bloodshot.

"That's exactly what I mean," Wincanton had said frostily. "A gentleman would have known better than to ask that question. We've wagered on it. The matter's closed.

"Oh, God, how could I have let myself get into such a coil?" Wincanton had continued his self-flagellation. "Even if you should somehow manage to fool Aunt Louisa into thinking you are I—for an entire month"—he had groaned at the sheer impossibility—"just what the devil am I supposed to do when I actually do see her? Lord, I must have been totally disguised to have let myself be bamboozled into this."

"Well"—Nicky had abandoned his own problems to give the other's serious thought—"once I've paid your duty visit, so to speak, there's no reason you should be seeing her, is there? Not for years, at any rate. And she's an old woman, didn't you say? Well, then, with luck she could pop off before the occasion ever arises."

From Wincanton's second scornful look Nicky had concluded he'd done the ungentlemanly again. He'd found himself growing a trifle nettled. Devil take the man! Dammit, he wasn't Private Forbes anymore. He'd pulled himself up to his full height, which gave him a half-inch advantage over the aristocrat, and matched Wincanton's toplofty tone. "Well, I doubt there are any proper rules of conduct spelled out in the gentlemen's code as to what to do if we're discovered. My own suggestion would be for you simply to deny you've ever heard of me and tough it out. But since that only makes sense, I'm sure there's an unwritten law somewhere against it. So it appears to me that we'd be well-advised to stop all this breast-beating and get on with seeing to it that I'm not found out."

"You're right, of course," the major had handsomely admitted. He'd gone on to pull the bell rope and order up strong coffee. Upon its arrival he'd set to work, acquainting his pupil with details of his former life and background.

And in this area Nicky felt extremely confident. Whatever else might be lacking in his acting qualifications, he was certainly a quick study. Even as a child he'd caused his elders to marvel at how soon he was able to get his lines. So he was confident of remembering what he'd been told. It was the omissions that worried him now.

Five miles out of Bath they rested their cattle for the final time before resuming the last leg of their journey. "Get back on the perch, where you belong, Jocko," Nicky growled as he cracked his whip.

"I'm going, I'm going. No need to bite me 'ead off. I tell you again, guv, it ain't me as you needs worry about. Far as I'm concerned, from 'ere on out you're Major Wincanton as I ever knew 'im."

When they approached the city, the sun made its first appearance of the day in the act of dipping low. It bathed the pale stone that gave Bath its distinction with a golden light. Nicholas pulled his grays to the roadside and shaded his eyes with his hand to drink in the scene. They focused first on the abbey tower, then moved on toward other church spires and chimney pots. The view was impressive, he had to admit. And ominous. Had Napoleon stood thus on the eve of battle and gazed at the fields of Waterloo?

"Thinkin' of turning tail, then, was you?"

Nicky gave the tiger a quelling look, then flicked the reins.

Reaching his destination posed no problem. He simply weaved his way toward the imposing crescent that was clearly visible on Lansdown Hill. And when he drew alongside the elegant, curving row of houses, it seemed just one more circumstance put there to daunt him that of all the dwellings that comprised the Lansdown Crescent, Number Twenty was the most imposing of the lot. Lady Stoke's residence was situated on the west end of the crescent, with a five-storied elevation and a semicircular bow to distinguish its facade.

Jocko jumped from the curricle to hold the horses, and Nicky pointedly ignored the impish grin as he climbed down stiffly from the driver's seat. As he headed for the entryway, which led to a side lane, his newly acquired limp was rather more pronounced than the one the bona fide major's stiff knee usually produced.

"Other leg, guv!" the tiger hissed behind him.

Nicky turned in consternation, to find Jocko convulsed.

"Just funnin', guv!" he mouthed while Nicky made a firm and solemn vow to horsewhip the rascal at the earliest opportunity.

"Major Wincanton to see Lady Stoke."

Well, that had sounded authoritative enough, and the starchy butler hadn't turned a hair. In fact, there was exactly the proper note of deference in the majordomo's "Come in, sir" and in his manner as he relieved Nicky of his beaver and greatcoat. "I'll tell her ladyship you're here, sir." The butler ushered the caller into a very modern withdrawing room.

Though the room was actually quite large, it did not initially seem so, for it was cluttered with a profusion of furniture that had been placed in helter-skelter fashion with no attempt at any formal arrangement. At least that was Nicky's first impression, and he found himself at a loss among such an array of choices when bidden to sit down. Chairs, sofas, settees, couches, stools, abounded, seemingly abandoned on the spot by exhausted movers. Candle stands, sconces, all sorts of tables, were scattered here and there. A pianoforte graced one end of the room; a harp, another. And everywhere he looked he discovered what he dismissed as bric-a-brac but what actually translated into vases, urns, china jars, candlesticks, busts, snuff-boxes—an infinite variety of objets d'art worth a considerable fortune.

There was some method to the madness, though, he finally concluded as he chose one of the chairs placed near a rosewood-inlaid table awash with books. The plan would be, Sit here if you wished to read. And there were other groupings, it appeared, for music of each type and for conversation.

Nicky picked up a leather-bound volume from the table and examined it, hoping to divert his mounting panic. *Mysterious Warnings,* the gilded title read. He took it as an omen and almost bolted.

"Gareth Wincanton! I don't believe it! Can it really, actually be you?"

Oh, dear God, unmasked already! Nicky rose unsteadily to his feet and turned to face the door. A plump, pleasant-looking lady who was past her middle years but certainly not the relic he'd expected stood on the threshold, looking him up and down. Her baby-blue eyes widened with surprise, and he held his breath. "Why, Gareth"—she came sailing toward him—"you quite took my breath away. Who'd have believed that such an unpromising and, frankly, quite horrid little boy, not to mention a Wincanton of any stripe, could have actually turned into an Adonis!

"Why, my dear, you're actually blushing! 'Struth—your face is every bit as red as your delightful hair. Bless me, but I find that charming." Her ladyship extended a beringed hand to be kissed. Nicky was happy to linger over it in order to pull himself together once again.

"Do come sit back down, Gareth dear," she said as she reluctantly retrieved her hand. "I may call you, Gareth, may I not? But of course—what a foolish question. I am your auntie, after all. By marriage only, though. And in truth I do feel rather odd about the relationship, if you'll forgive my saying so. Your uncle was much, much older than I, you see."

"That explains it. For, to be honest, I had not expected such a youthful aunt." Nicky managed the required gallantry with ease, since it was literal truth. "And please call me Win, if you don't object to such informality," he added as she beamed at him across the table. "My friends all do."

"Then Win it shall be. I much prefer it to Gareth. Whatever possessed your parents to give you such an outlandish name? And you must address me as Louisa. I refuse to be called 'aunt' by the handsomest man in Bath—especially since I've no real claim to the relationship.

"But oh, do forgive me, m'dear. Here I am, prattling on, and you must be famished. We had early dinner, but I'll ring for a cold collation. And oh, my heavens, what an addlepate you must think me! Has Hope seen to your baggage yet?"

Nicky made a protesting murmur about not wishing to impose and declared his intention of putting up at the White Hart. But as the major had prophesied, her ladyship was scandalized by the mere suggestion. "Of course you'll stay here." She spoke with finality. "Put Major Wincanton in the blue room, Hope," she ordered as the butler appeared in answer to her ring.

"I've already seen to the major's things, m'lady, as well as to his equipage and his, er, groom." The butler, who had been forewarned by her ladyship of a possible visit from her nephew, seemed awesome in his efficiency. His employer merely nodded, unsurprised. "And bring a supper tray in here, Hope. The dining room's so cold and formal," she confided to her visitor. "No place to get acquainted. And while you're eating, I'd like us to be able to have a comfortable coze."

Even though he'd just realized he hadn't had a bite since Amabel's makeshift breakfast, this prospect routed Nicky's emerging appetite. But when the simple repast of cold partridges, oysters, hare, glazed neat's tongue, accompanied by a host of side dishes, was set before him, along with a decanter of port and the promise of coffee and chocolates to follow, in spite of his impending doom he set to work with a will.

And as he ate, his hostess talked. He had expected an inquisition. He got a monologue. She filled him in on Bath society—or the lack of it. On the entertainment to be found there—or the dearth of it. And went on to expound on the theme that now that the fates had accorded her a double blessing—his arrival and the fact that one of her oldest, dearest friends had just taken up residence in the Royal Crescent—all the aspersions she had formerly cast on Bath were now just so many words she'd be forced to eat. For with the handsome Major Wincanton and the distinguished Sir George Carstairs among its company, Bath was sure to become the most delightful of places. "Why, it will not surprise me in the least if the Prince Regent gets wind of our gaiety and abandons Brighton to build himself a new pavilion at Bath.

"But oh, goodness, what a rattle you must think me. I haven't allowed you the chance to get in a word. Tell me. How have you been spending your time in London?"

Then, before Nicky could swallow the mouthful he was chewing—he must remember: bad ton to take such bites—Lady Stoke had gotten a second wind and was well and truly launched into a satirical description of the various types who flocked to the Pump Room at set times of the day to drink their prescribed courses of the waters there.

Nicky was only thankful for her garrulousness. It never occurred to him as he ate his steady way through the repast that her chatter covered a nervousness almost equal to his and gave her opportunity to consider just what tack to take. By the time he'd reached the coffee stage and she'd poured out for both of them, Lady Stoke had made up her mind.

"I do believe that in the long run honesty is much the best policy, don't you?"

He'd just taken a large gulp of the steaming liquid and strangled on it. "I beg your pardon?" he managed to gasp when he'd recovered from his fit.

"It's what that Franklin fellow wrote. At least I believe he was the one. You know, that American chap with all those tedious sayings. Or was it Aesop? Well, never mind all that. It was one of those prosy types, at any rate, and in this case I expect that whoever said it was dead right. Honesty usually is the best policy. Don't you agree?"

He nodded dumbly, turning pale.

"Well, so do I, and I collect I'd best be candid in this instance and make a clean breast of the situation. For now that I've met you, I'm certain that you'll be all understanding and realize that what I'm going to say is in the best interests of all concerned and can in no way be taken as idle gossip-mongering."

He was still frozen at the moment of realization that *she* was the one who was supposed to make a clean breast of things, and had taken nothing in beyond that point. But he saw that her eyes were fixed upon him expectantly and felt obliged to utter. "I don't quite understand," he managed to say.

"I know you don't, dear," she replied kindly. For Lady Stoke had just concluded that although the major outstripped the rest of the Wincantons as far as looks were concerned, he lagged somewhat behind that family's average for intellect. "I haven't gotten around yet to explaining. But the more I think of it, the more convinced I become that it's the thing to do. That tedious man was right—that is, if he was the one to say it—honesty is the best policy after all, and you will keep everything I say in the strictest confidence, will you not? I wouldn't wish her to know I'd been so forthcoming. But how else can I get your cooperation?"

Again she paused expectantly. But Nicky was remembering Major Wincanton's dictum "When you don't know the proper thing to say, for God's sake keep your mouth closed." It seemed to apply to the present moment. Indeed, Nicky began to fear he might be forced into perpetual muteness.

Lady Stoke's mind had been diverted, however, from ethical considerations to more immediate ones. "Oh, my goodness, I hadn't thought. Here I'd simply taken it for granted that you yourself—so recently back from the Continent and all—must be unattached. Tell me, Win. Do you have an understanding with anyone?"

"An understanding? Am I betrothed, you mean? Oh, lord, no. Nothing like that, I assure you."

"Good. That *would* be unfortunate."

It could have been, however, that Lady Stoke picked up on some insincerity in his answer, for she was moved to probe a little deeper. "A tendre, then? A man like you must be con-

202

stantly falling in love. Is there a particular young lady who has perhaps already fixed your interest?"

"No." Again that bit of hesitation. "There's no young . . . lady."

"Well, then I'm much relieved to hear it. A man in love is so . . . so . . . unobjective. And I need you to tell me what's to be done in a certain situation."

"And just what situation is that, Lady—er, I mean to say, Louisa?" Nicky asked with mounting apprehension.

"Well, you see, my boy, you are not my only visitor. Although in her case 'visitor' is not what the French call the mot juste. What I fear I have acquired is a companion. Which is the last thing in the world I ever wanted. You've no idea of how awkward it is to have someone always under foot. And now especially, with Porge living in Bath. I've no privacy at all to— Alas, the young are so censorious. Don't you agree? But how absurd!" She laughed. "I'm speaking as if you were of my age, instead of a mere lad. But then, you're a man of the world, Win. Not to be compared with—

"But goodness, how selfish you must think me. I vow it's not my own interests I'm most concerned with. For it's very lowering, I tell you, to see someone one really cares for fossilize before one's very eyes when there's a world of dances and assemblies and plays and concerts and routs and all the rest out there just waiting to be enjoyed, though perhaps not in Bath. But anyhow, Win dear, that's where you come in. And why it's such a very fortunate coincidence that you should have unexpectedly taken the notion to come here. Oh, my heavens!" She broke off in consternation at the sound of rapidly approaching footsteps. "We must not be caught discussing—" she whispered conspiratorially. "Quick! Speak of something else!"

"Yes. Ah. Hmmm. Oh, well, yes, do tell me, Lady Stoke, how is the theater here?"

Nicky savagely cursed himself for reverting to type. He'd completely lost his Wincanton character, if indeed he'd ever had it.

But Lady Stoke did not seem to find the question odd.

Indeed, she picked up on it gratefully. "Ah, the theater! I'm so glad you asked." She spoke in animated, carrying tones. "For that's one feature of Bath society that we need not blush for." She turned from him and smiled as a young lady wearing a dark violet pelisse and bonnet hurried into the room. "Ah, Venetia, my dear!"

"I'm back, Aunt Louisa. I did not wish to worry you, but— Oh, I am sorry. I did not realize you have a caller."

Nicky rose slowly to his feet, trying valiantly to appear debonair and nonchalant, while feeling like a trapped fox with the hound pack circling. Who the devil was this female? And why hadn't he been told about her?

He found himself being coolly appraised by a pair of beautiful dark eyes that seemed to see right through him. And the owner of the stare, with her cheeks flushed pink from walking in the cold and her blond curls wind-blown where they peeped from underneath her modish bonnet, quite took his breath away and called to mind vague recollections of statuary he'd once seen of young Greek goddesses. Not, perhaps, that this newcomer quite possessed a classic beauty. It was her aristocratic mien, no doubt, that caused her to appear Olympian and placed her high above mere mortals like himself.

"This is no ordinary caller, Venetia dear," Lady Stoke was saying with a heartiness that sounded artificial even to Nicky Forbes's benumbed ears. "Win here has actually torn himself away from the delights of the metropolis to keep his auntie company for a while. But heavens, what can I be thinking of? I'd forgotten you two have never actually met. Venetia, pray allow me to present my nephew, Major Gareth Wincanton, who has just returned to this country after ridding the world of that Corsican monster. And this, Win dear, is my niece, Lady Venetia Lowther."

"Charmed," Nicky murmured as he bent low over the goddess's hand. "I'd no idea," he continued with perfect truth, "that I even possessed such a lovely cousin."

He glanced up at the sound of a disdainful sniff. The young

lady's eyes were no longer appraising. They had come to judgment. And the look he was impaled with was disbelieving, scornful, and, above all else, hostile.

Chapter Five

MAJOR WINCANTON'S EYES WERE GLUED UPON THE stage, but his mind was miles away in Bath and centered upon Nicky Forbes. Unconsciously he grimaced with distaste.

He had lately begun to develop an acute dislike of the actor after an initial impression that had been quite favorable. As an officer, Win had had opportunity to assess Forbes the soldier and had found him quick-witted and courageous, though inclined to shirk responsibility whenever possible. But Private Forbes's chief claim to fame, the major now recalled, was as a womanizer. He'd been a menace to the female population for the length and breadth of the Iberian peninsula.

It was this aspect of the other's character that Wincanton was inclined to dwell on as he sat in his box at Drury Lane while the plot of *The Fatal Marriage* unfolded. He had no need to follow the action. He'd seen the production a score of times before and could, if pressed, recite great chunks of the dialogue himself. He vowed every day not to return to the theater that night and found himself every evening once again ensconced in the stage box. But at least he felt no compunction to follow the progress of the drama except for those electrifying times when Miss Fawnhope appeared onstage. But since she was not there at this moment, he was at complete liberty to follow the direction of his thoughts. And perversely they returned again and again to Nicky Forbes.

It wasn't enough that Wincanton was concerned with the shambles the actor was no doubt making of his reputation. What really was galling to contemplate was a fact that he'd lately been forced to acknowledge: he, Major Gareth Wincanton, officer and aristocrat, was actually jealous of a common soldier. A Cit, no less. An actor, to boot. And a god-awful actor at that.

The acknowledgment of this degrading emotion was an enormous blow to Wincanton's considerable pride. But he was far too honest to pretend that the jealousy did not exist or to avoid analyzing the cause of it.

For one thing, he resented all the constant references to a nonexistent physical resemblance. Oh, he'd grant the hair. But why make so much of it? If they'd both had brown or blond hair, no one would comment. And outside of that one attribute, he could see little basis for the comparison.

He was convinced that his irritation with the subject of their looks had nothing to do with the fact that the actor held the edge. Wincanton had no desire for handsomeness. Let Forbes have that asset for the stage. God knew he needed all the help that he could get. No, the plain truth was, it galled him to be look-alike to a member of the lower class. And why so many people insisted on making the comparison was a mystery. Even Amabel had done so. On more than one occasion.

That was it, of course. Therein lay the rub. Major Wincanton had not built his distinguished military career upon false assessments. He was able to look a fact directly in the face, no matter how distasteful it might be. And his growing dislike of Mr. Nicholas Forbes, he now acknowledged, was based almost in its entirety upon the actor's relationship with Miss Fawnhope.

When the actress had first presented her "brother" to him, he'd been pleased to recognize a fellow veteran of the Napoleonic Wars. Besides, he badly needed an ally in the siege he was laying against Miss Fawnhope's unexpectedly strong defenses. Her own brother was the very ticket. And the ex-private seemed more than willing— eager, in fact—to whisper into his sister's ear a good word on his ex-major's behalf.

But little by little, as he recalled his relationship with his own sisters, Wincanton began to wonder whether Nicholas and Amabel weren't too close by half. And he'd discovered after a bit of inquiry that the two were no blood kin at all. In fact, they had no claim even to an in-law relationship, since their parents hadn't bothered to legalize their liaison.

It was at this point that the green-eyed monster had made its appearance and Wincanton had begun to wonder just what sort of game the "brother-sister" team was playing. Certainly if Nicholas was pleading his major's case the way he claimed to be, there'd been no results of this advocacy so far. Wincanton found that fact suspicious. For he had no doubt at all of the actor's influence on his "little sister." Sometimes the major felt she could talk of nothing else. It was "Nicky this" and "Nicky that" till he was ready to grind his teeth at the very sound of the other's name.

No, Win thought as he stared blankly toward the stage, he'd found no ally in the former Private Forbes. Why he'd ever trusted the scoundrel was past all understanding. He had no doubt now that the two were in collusion against him, playing deep. Well, if they thought they could maneuver him into marriage, they were due a rude awakening. Or any long-term commitment, when it came to that. He'd cut his eyeteeth long ago and was not about to be taken in by any bit of muslin, no matter how lusciously appealing. The major smiled sardonically to himself. But just then Miss Fawnhope made her entrance, to the sound of wild applause, and Wincanton felt his pulses begin to race while at the same time all his resolution melted.

"You're very quiet, sir." Three hours later Amabel Fawnhope gave Wincanton a searching look as she nibbled at a chicken wing. She had worked her way ravenously through sweetbreads, lobster patties, tongue with cauliflower; now her hunger was sated enough for her to notice his unusual silence and lack of appetite. "And you've eaten nothing."

"No, I'm not hungry."

He never failed to be astounded at the amount of provision the sylphlike Miss Fawnhope managed to put away without any noticeable damage to her alluring figure. He did, however, wonder just how much longer such a happy state of affairs could go on. Once, when she'd seen his eyes widen as she ate, she'd explained that acting required an enormous output of energy and left her famished. But it still occurred to him now and then that she had possibly passed beyond the bounds of ladylike behavior.

"Blue-deviled?" she inquired as she put the chicken bone upon her plate and licked her fingertips daintily with her enticing tongue. "Or are you still pouting over coming here?"

"I never pout." He smiled as he reached for the iced champagne and filled both their glasses.

There had been a time when he'd had high hopes for that particular potable, expecting it to soften Amabel's resistance. Now he knew that the actress would always stop well short of intoxication. He could do worse, he reminded himself, than to profit by her example. He felt a keen desire to get roaring drunk but recalled only too well the penalty for that particular overindulgence.

"And even if I were subject to pouting fits," he continued, "a most unmanly—not even to mention unsoldierly—pursuit, I'd certainly not indulge myself because of an argument we've had every evening since I've met you. Don't I always extend a gracious invitation to you to visit my rooms, where, believe me, the hospitality is far superior to this?" His scornful look took in the appointments of the private parlor he'd engaged in the Hummums Hotel and the remains of the repast she'd been enjoying. "And don't you always refuse?"

"Yes, because we both know just what that hospitality would include, don't we?"

"It would include a supper prepared by the finest cook, bar none, in London. Wine far superior to this pap we're drinking. And as to what other, er, *diversions* the evening might provide, well, that would be entirely up to you. I am, after all, a gentleman."

"And gentlemen never lose their heads, I suppose?"

"Gentlemen never force ladies to do anything against their wills."

"Oh, well, then. There you have it. It's my own weak nature that I must guard against. You're a very attractive, persuasive man, Major Wincanton, so I collect it's best to stay with the inferior, but far safer, hospitality of the Hummums."

"Do you know, Amabel"—he gazed at her thoughtfully as he twirled the crystal stem of his wineglass between his fingers—"I think you're developing into a deliberate tease."

"And I deny it." She tossed her head. "Teasing has nothing to say in the matter. I'm not one of your highborn ladies, Gareth, with all sorts of social conventions set up to guard my reputation. I'm an actress. Which means I have little enough reputation to begin with. But I value what I have. The problem is that I do want your company. You've quite turned my head, in fact. I've deserted all my old friends just to be with you. But I am not prepared, Win darling, to throw my cap over the windmill for you. Or for any man."

He believed about half of what she was saying. She'd resisted all his attempts to bed her, and he'd begun to recognize that she had no intention of ever weakening. It was the latter part of her declaration that he doubted. It was difficult—if not impossible—for him to believe in an actress's chastity. True, there'd been no rumors about Amabel, and, God forgive him, he'd made inquiries. But now that her "brother," Nicky, had come back into her life, well, who knew what went on in that free and easy—and intimate—relationship? Just the thought of it put Wincanton's blood on the boil. For some absurd reason, he felt cuckolded.

Even as she changed the subject to chat of this and that, underneath her easy manner Amabel was also doing some serious thinking. She was more concerned over Wincanton than she planned to show. She had not seen him like this before. He had avoided her for two whole days and nights. And now that he'd picked up where they'd left off, he seemed entirely different.

Was there someone else, perhaps? Amabel was well acquainted with the fickleness of the other sex. Still, some instinct told her his obsession had not waned. She began to have uneasy second thoughts about her campaign tactics.

As if he read her mind, Wincanton said abruptly, "I can't marry you, you know, Amabel. That's out of the question."

Those who thought Miss Fawnhope had reached her leading-lady status on the boards simply by her beauty much mistook the matter. She was an actress and thus was able to suppress her true reaction to that flat, bald statement and substitute one more appropriate to her purposes. "Of course not." She smiled enchantingly. "The idea's unthinkable. Why, what would your dear mama say?"

In spite of knowing she was being deliberately provocative, he was nettled. "My mother's reaction has little to say in the matter. It's the polite world in general I'm concerned with."

"I know you are, Gareth." She dropped her teasing manner and was suddenly all seriousness. "Society's opinion is all-important to you. Which goes to prove one thing: you don't love me. If you did, you wouldn't care a fig what anyone thought about a misalliance."

She paused, waiting, perhaps, for him to deny what she'd just said. But in all honesty he couldn't. She smiled once more, this time with a trace of bitterness. "So it seems we've reached a stalemate. Is that the right term, Win?"

"It will do."

"You do understand, of course, why I cannot give you what you wish." When he merely shrugged without answering, she chided him gently, "Well, you ought to understand. And even if you do not, since my refusal only affects your vanity and not your heart it's really a small matter after all. There are plenty of other girls prettier than I who would be more than happy to satisfy your . . . appetite. And if my refusal to do so pricks your self-esteem, well, I've told you time and time again that it should not do so." Her gaze was melting as she met his eyes across the table and held them. Her voice was low and husky.

"For I've told you time and time again that I find you—almost— irresistible. And if there were any man at all that I was willing to live in sin with, well, it would be you."

It was a touching moment. The look she gave him was wistful, longing, tinged with regret, and almost convincing. Damn her lying little heart, he thought viciously. Why did I ever involve myself with an actress, anyway?

Amabel sighed at his continued silence. "That was intended to salve your pride, Gareth. Which, as I've just said, is the only emotion of yours involved. Come now." She reached a hand across the table and covered his. "Can't we still be friends?"

He shook off the hand as though it burned him. "No, Amabel, we cannot be friends. I don't want you for a friend. I'm well supplied with friends. Thank you all the same." He rose abruptly. "Come on. I'll take you home."

They walked the short distance to her house in silence, ignoring the crowded gin shops they passed and the ladies of the evening casting out their lures to the rash young bloods out for a night of adventure. Amabel's mind was racing furiously. What happened next was crucial if she hoped to keep him dangling after her. When they reached her door, she turned to gaze up at him. Her face, in the glow of a nearby street lamp, was tortured. "It's just as well that I can't ask you in tonight," she whispered.

"Since you never have, I'll hardly notice the omission."

"But I've explained all that. Nellie insists on waiting up for me. She's like a second mother. Watches me like a hawk."

In all likelihood, of course, Nellie was at the Queen's Head Tavern, swilling gin with her cronies. Amabel only hoped she wouldn't come reeling around the corner before the major left.

"But as I was saying, it's just as well that I can't be tempted to ask you inside, for I've come to a dreadfully difficult decision. I don't think we should see each other anymore."

"It does seem rather pointless."

Although this certainly was not the cue she'd expected, Miss Fawnhope, the trooper, did not muff her mentally rehearsed lines. "That's too true. And for me, well, our association has grown far, far too painful. Frankly, Gareth darling, I don't

211

know how much longer I can find the strength to hold out against you. So it's time we drew apart. Good-bye, my dearest. Pray, do not forget me."

Tears spilled down her face as the little actress rose on tiptoe to place her lips on his.

The kiss was long and passionate. She pressed her body provocatively against him. Then, when inevitably his lips and hands began to wander, she allowed them liberties they'd never enjoyed before. But just as he'd begun to entertain thoughts of dragging her off behind the shrubbery, Amabel wrenched herself free of his embrace and leaned, gasping, against the door. "Oh, you do see what I mean, Gareth love. This *has* to be good-bye." And before he could get his own hard breathing under control to answer her, she'd eased through her door and shut it in his face.

Major Gareth Wincanton stood glaring at the oak portal for a moment, then turned and walked unsteadily away, his limp far more pronounced than usual. He was cursing fluently underneath his breath. And his oaths were all directed at one source—the beautiful, provocative, unscrupulous Miss Amabel Fawnhope.

For the major had no illusions about the scene that had just been enacted. "The little trollop's hooked me well and proper," he muttered viciously to himself, "and now, by God, she's playing me like a fish."

Chapter Six

W HEN NICHOLAS FORBES CROSSED THE THRESHOLD of the breakfast parlor and realized that Lady Venetia Lowther was its sole occupant, he almost beat a hasty, ignominious retreat. But before he could suit action to the impulse, she glanced up from the boiled egg she was cracking and bent a smile upon him that was as cordial as it was unexpected.

Nicholas had spent a fretful night tossing and turning on his fine linen sheets and—despite the fact that he'd landed in more luxury than he ever knew existed—wishing himself almost anywhere, up to and including the fields of Waterloo, than where he was. And the chief reason for his unease was Lady Venetia Lowther.

In the first place, her ladyship had been completely omitted from his briefing. Nicky still didn't know just who the devil she was. His initial stab at establishing the creature's identity had brought on her hostile atmosphere and a "Don't be ridiculous, Win dear—you know she's not your cousin" from Louisa. After that, they had settled in for what proved to be a most uncomfortable half hour of stilted conversation while Lady Venetia continued to look daggers at both Nicky and her aunt. This awkward interval had been terminated by the arrival of a Sir George Carstairs (another member of the dramatis personae the major's tutoring had omitted) dressed in evening clothes to collect Lady Stoke for a party that she had forgotten completely.

It was suggested that Lady Venetia and the major accompany them. The former icily pleaded the headache and withdrew, while the latter claimed fatigue as his reason for forgoing the proffered entertainment. There was no civil way, however, that he could have avoided keeping Sir George company while Lady Stoke hurried off to change.

But all in all that tête-à-tête hadn't gone too badly. Sir George showed no inclination to doubt his bona fides. And like his lady friend, the elderly gentleman seemed perfectly content to carry the lion's share of the conversation. When he did at last get around to probing for mutual acquaintances, Nicky was able to come up with "Sprig" St. Leger, whom they spent some time discussing. After that, Sir George seemed content to attribute any apparent memory lapses to the major's long absence on the Continent.

So Nicky felt that on the whole he had acquitted himself quite well in that encounter. Then, when a rather breathless Lady Stoke entered the withdrawing room, wearing a crimson crepe evening gown and a toplofty headdress of matching ostrich feathers, there was no time for more than her thrice-repeated apology for deserting her guest so soon after his arrival—"If it were anyone else but that odious Countess De Wint giving the party, I'd cry off. But she's bound to take offense, which would never do"—and a whispered aside after she'd proffered a cheek for him to kiss: "Never mind about Venetia, dear. I'd meant to prepare you for her. She'll come around. Though it may take a while."

Well, judging from the way Lady Venetia sat at her breakfast, smiling his way, she had done just that. And in record time. Nicky looked at her ladyship warily.

"Oh, do come get your breakfast, Major Wincanton. I won't eat you. In fact, I've been framing what I trust will be a handsome apology."

Even with that heartening forecast, Nicky still had little appetite as he looked over the array that crowded the sideboard. He settled on ham, rolls, butter, and chocolate and carried his plate over to the table, where he resisted the impulse to distance himself as far from her ladyship as the breakfast table would allow and, instead, sat down beside her. He took a sip of the chocolate and studied her covertly.

He was able to reestablish the impression he had made upon first seeing her, before her hostility had made him think of harridans and harpies. Lady Venetia was a very attractive woman. Indeed, were she less elevated in station and were he the same old Nicky Forbes as ever was, he couldn't have asked for a more desirable breakfast companion. But she wasn't and he wasn't, and he did wish his stomach would unknot and that he knew just what the devil was going on.

"You must have thought me rude past all redemption when we met last evening," she remarked.

He was pleased to note that she actually sounded embarrassed. It made her almost human. His stomach unknotted one small notch.

"Well," he answered tentatively, "I must admit to being a trifle puzzled by your attitude. People usually have to know me a great deal better to dislike me all that much." He produced a crooked, charming smile, and she laughed spontaneously.

"Believe me when I say it was nothing personal. Or, at least, in a manner of speaking it was not. I merely took exception to the reason for your being here. But after our aunt rang a peal over me and I had some time to think things over, I came to realize that was no excuse for being uncivil to you. Nor to Aunt Louisa. For exasperating as I find all her maneuvering, I do need to keep in mind that she's only acting from the kindest of motives— Oh, my goodness!" She broke off suddenly. "I fear I'm beginning to sound just like Aunt Louisa!"

"I must admit the both of you tend to make the head spin, if you'll pardon me for saying so."

"Well, then, I must try to regain the habit of plain speaking. Though too much candor is a particular vice of mine, I'm told. Goodness, there I go again! What I'm trying to say is that now that I've had time to cool down a bit, I realize how churlishly I behaved. And I have also come to realize that Aunt is right. Just because I've been burned once, I can't go on avoiding fire forever.

"Oh, dear, what a mull I'm making of all this. And after my

brave declaration about plain speaking. But it *is* humiliating, as you must understand, to have Aunt Louisa out beating the bushes to find suitors for me. And it did seem the outside of enough that just when she'd given up on Bath and I thought I could relax a bit, she's begun to import gentlemen for me. But last night, in lieu of sleeping, I came to realize that the poor dear is not half so desperate on my account as on her own." She smiled a self-deprecating smile. "She wants me off her hands. And while I'd like nothing better than solitary independence, I realize that spinsters, for the most part, are barred from that sensible course of action. Therefore, I've resigned myself to the fact that I must marry. And so, Major Wincanton, I'm quite prepared to pretend that you're dangling after me for my beauty, wit, and charm and are not influenced in the slightest by my handsome fortune. Oh, my word! I say, are you all right?"

"Major Wincanton" had strangled, sent his chocolate spraying across the table, and was now having a coughing fit. Venetia sprang up and thumped him between the shoulder blades till he finally subsided. "Here, sip this slowly." She thrust a water goblet into his hand and resumed her seat.

"Oh, dear. I am sorry. As I said, I've been taken to task repeatedly about my odious habit of plain speaking. Fletcher was most eloquent on that point right after I'd told him just what I thought of his cozy little love nest. Proper females, he informed me, choose to overlook such unpleasantries. So I am aware that a lady should always believe she's being pursued for herself alone. But I don't seem to have the knack of self-delusion. If you'll be patient with me, though, I'll try to cultivate it."

Nicky's coughing had gradually subsided. As had his apprehension. For he'd come to realize that the charade he'd embarked upon was hopeless. Even if there were only Lady Stoke to fool, the situation would have been touch and go. But now, with this latest development, there was no way he could get by with the impersonation. His situation was far, far worse than the actor's nightmare of being onstage and forgetting his lines. Hell, he didn't even know what play they were doing! But along with despair came calm. He felt the sort of resignation he'd felt in battle. Since he was about to be annihilated anyhow, he'd go out with flair.

And so, for the first time, he looked at Lady Venetia as he might have looked at any garden-variety female—and lord knew he had plenty of experience with those types. "Just who the devil is Fletcher, and where did you get the maggoty notion that I'm interested in either you or your money?" he inquired. "I never even knew of your existence until last night. Oh, I'll take your word for it that you're worth a fortune, though just why you think that's something that should send me jumping through hoops eludes me. My God, woman, I'm a regular nabob myself."

Well, now, a gentleman, he supposed, would not have made that speech, but he'd certainly taken the wind out of her nibs's sails and caused her chin to drop. By Jupiter, he felt his appetite returning. He picked up his plate and walked back to the sideboard, where he piled it high. When he returned to his place, she continued to stare in amazement, he noted, but at least she had closed her mouth.

Lady Venetia watched in silence as he attacked his beef ribs. Then, after a bit, she seemed to make up her mind. "I don't think you do know why Aunt Louisa sent for you. She didn't tell you about me, did she?"

"*Nobody* told me about you. And Louisa didn't send for me. This visit was my parents' idea entirely. My father wrote a blistering letter about how ungrateful it appeared for me to have been back in England for weeks now without visiting my uncle's widow. I am his heir, as Papa reminded me. He also informed me that Louisa was feeling quite neglected."

"Well, I do see our aunt's fine Italian hand at work," Venetia observed shrewdly. "But I can also see that I've done you an injustice." Her face turned pink. "Heavens, what you must think of me! Tying one's garters in public doesn't begin to describe what I've just done."

Nicky was enjoying her discomfort as he chewed his beef bones slowly. "Well, it's a bit late to stand on points now, don't you agree? So let's back up a bit. Just who is Fletcher?"

"My fiancé. My ex-fiancé, that is. We—I—called off our engagement."

"I see. And this Fletcher fellow. What makes you so certain it was just your fortune he was interested in?" Nicky was sizing her up with the eye of a connoisseur. "It strikes me that you could have mistaken the matter."

She colored a bit more under his appreciative gaze. "Oh, no. There was not the slightest doubt on that score. You see, I discovered that he kept a mistress. Had done so since before I met him."

"But he planned to give her up to marry you, of course."

"That's what he said. Though I doubt he actually would have done so. I think he was quite in love with her. At any rate, I did not care to put the competition to the test."

"I see." He paused to mull that over. "And did you love him?"

"My, you are direct." She grimaced. "Do you know I can hardly believe we're having this conversation? But since it's a bit late for missishness at this point, no, I don't think I ever did love Fletcher. Oh, he quite turned my head at first with his attentiveness." The light tone of voice she tried to adopt rang the least bit false. "For he was very good-looking. And charming. An incorrigible deceiver." Here Nicky barely managed not to wince. "But as I've tried to explain to Aunt Louisa, it was my pride that suffered the greatest blow. But she still insists upon believing I have a broken heart. Hence her desperate roundup of suitors."

"Like getting right back up on a horse once it's thrown you, I collect."

She laughed. "I wouldn't have put it just that way, but yes, I suppose I have been thrown."

"Don't you think that you're just possibly blowing the whole thing out of proportion? Oh, perhaps not the mistress part," he quickly qualified as she bristled. "But the fortune thing. After all, there's nothing so unusual about that. Don't most of the people of your—*our* class marry for convenience? And there's nothing more convenient than a fortune."

"Oh, you're right, of course. And Aunt is, too. I have far too many romantic notions for a female of my years. And so, during the wee hours of this morning, I decided that I'd turn over a brand-new leaf. I shall make myself as available as anyone could wish and accept the next 'convenient' offer that comes my way."

She was gazing at him speculatively. He willed himself not to tug at his cravat, which all of a sudden felt quite constrictive. For after an all-too-short-lived reprieve, Nicholas Forbes was beginning to grow decidedly uneasy once again.

Chapter Seven

"OH, MY! IF YOU COULD SEE YOUR FACE!" LADY VENETIA laughed across her teacup, while Nicky could only manage a sheepish grin. "I can assure you there's no need for panic. I haven't the slightest intention of setting my cap for *you*. And you must not allow Aunt Louisa to browbeat you on my behalf.

"But now that I think of it, you must be accustomed to having females thrown at your head, self-confessed nabob that you are."

"Actually, no. There was little opportunity for matchmaking where I've been."

"Of course. How stupid of me. When Aunt Louisa was raking me over the coals for being so rag-mannered, she did say you took part in the most dreadful part of the fighting and behaved most heroically."

This was a subject Nicky would have been quite happy to

expand on, feeling more at home on the fields of Waterloo than in the muddied waters of their relationship. But she denied him that opportunity. "So you haven't had much chance, then, to be viewed as quite a catch. How long did you say you've been in London?"

"Six weeks."

"Oh, well, then, I was wrong. That's ample time for the debutantes at Almack's and their scheming mamas to besiege you. A fortune and handsome, too! You're far too valuable a prize to escape for long. La, I'm amazed they ever allowed you to leave town."

"Well, to tell the truth, I've never been to Almack's."

"You astound me! I know its exclusiveness is legendary, but I cannot believe you were denied admittance, given your pedigree *and* your nabobery."

"You're roasting me, ain't you? I daresay I should not have mentioned my wealth."

"Oh, indeed not. Frightfully bad ton."

"Well, you goaded me into it. Besides, you admitted to being an heiress."

"I know. I share the blame. But I can't believe that you've spent six weeks in London without visiting the most famous marriage mart in the kingdom. You really must be gun-shy. And to think that Aunt Louisa despairs of me!"

"I will admit I've little desire to become leg-shackled. At least, not yet." Whether speaking as Wincanton or himself, Nicky had no problem achieving the ring of conviction.

"Then we are well met, sir." Venetia's smile quite took his breath away. "So now that we know where we stand, can we not put Aunt Louisa in high gig by appearing to fall in with her little scheme? Shall we begin this campaign immediately? Allow me to be your guide on a tour of Bath. I expect us to set the town agog."

She excused herself to dress for their expedition. He sat at the breakfast table a little longer, seeking the fortification of two cups of tea while trying to assimilate this new turn of events.

A half hour later, they emerged from the Crescent. Lady

220

Venetia was becomingly attired in a French gray walking dress ornamented with white lutestring, and Nicky looked most dapper in his brand-new maroon spencer jacket worn over a black tailcoat. She stopped short at the sight of a sporting curricle with a diminutive tiger who was suitably expressionless except for his lively, inquisitive eyes and who held the horses' heads. "Oh, dear. Is that your rig?" He nodded. "I had no notion that you'd ordered it. The day's so fine, I'd thought we'd walk. We can see so much more on foot. Oh!" She broke off in consternation. "I quite forgot. Your leg. How thoughtless of me. Of course we'll ride."

"No, no. It's not at all necessary, I assure you. As a matter of fact, I'd much prefer to walk."

There was no question of his sincerity. He disliked the thought of making conversation in front of Jocko Hodges. "Believe me, my leg seldom pains me at all."

"That's right, m'lady," the irrepressible tiger chimed in. "Why, the major here can walk a treat when he's a mind to.

"Oh I say, *sir*"—he gave the title rather too much stress for Nicky's liking—"how about if I exercise these beasts just a bit before taking 'em back to the stables? Not to disappoint 'em, you might say." Jocko grinned impishly, looking forward to tooling through the town and turning the heads of pretty serving maids with his bang-up-to-the-nines equipage.

"Go ahead," Nicky answered, trying hard not to grind his teeth but looking forward to the day when he could connect the sole of his boot to the groom's derriere.

"What an odd little man," Venetia observed as the tiger sprang the horses. "Doesn't he seem rather overfamiliar?"

"A little, I suppose. But he's a dab hand with the cattle."

As they walked down Lansdown Hill, Nicky experimented with his limp, trying to reduce it to the minimum without abandoning it altogether. It had occurred to him that this mode of walking might wind up actually crippling him before they'd covered all the miles Venetia seemed to have in mind.

She noticed his erratic progress and asked anxiously, "Are you sure you're quite up to this?"

"Perfectly," he replied as he settled into a more rhythmic

form of "dot and carry one." And noting the edge in his voice, Venetia judged it more tactful not to refer again to his infirmity.

She proved an excellent guide, new enough to Bath herself to find it interesting and charming. Also she was an indefatigable walker. Nicky was surprised to discover that athletic trait in a member of her class and sex.

They approached the heart of the city by way of the Royal Crescent, which she'd insisted he positively must see. And he was suitably impressed by the younger John Wood's masterpiece. Thirty houses of golden oolite stone were joined in a semiellipse, with Ionic columns supporting a continuous frieze. "It's magnificent, " Nicky pronounced as he limped past.

"Yes, isn't it. Aunt Louisa's friend Porge— Oh, my heavens, I must not call him that. What I meant to say is Sir George Carstairs has just moved in there."

Nicky barely restrained himself from asking what it might cost to live in such elegance. Instead, "By the by," he asked, "just what is his relationship with our mutual aunt?"

"Close, I assume," she gurgled. "It's my suspicion, Major Wincanton—"

"Please, call me Win," he interrupted her. " 'Major Wincanton' sounds so formal. After all, we are practically related."

"Very well, then, *Win* it is. But to continue my gossipmongering, I really do suspect that our mutual aunt, to use your term, has led a life best described as scandalous. No wonder she finds me so . . . dampening. And it's my guess that at one time Sir Porge was one of her— Oh, bother! I'm groping for some term that will sound halfway respectable."

"Something in French, perhaps?"

"What a good idea. I'm sure they must have a perfectly marvelous word, if only I could think of it. They do have a flair for putting the best possible light on that sort of thing."

"Yes, it's devilish hard to sound sinful in French, isn't it? The best the frogs can manage is attractive wickedness. But in plain English, I take it you're trying to tell me they were lovers."

"Oh, I'm quite convinced of it. And though it really does seem improbable at their ages, I suspect they'd like to be again.

222

Only Aunt is so well chaperoned. By me. Now have I scandalized you?"

"Quite the contrary. Considering their ages, I find the situation decidedly heartening. Something to look forward to, you could say."

She giggled, then realized the conversation had strayed into quite improper channels. But she found it difficult to stand on points with this gentleman. For although they'd only just met, she'd rarely been as open with anyone as she had been with him in that astounding breakfast conversation. And she had enjoyed the openness. She looked up appreciatively at her tall companion and found his eyes fastened upon her with something of the same approval reflected in them. She hoped she wasn't blushing. The habit was too odiously missish by half.

Venetia reverted to her former role of tour guide. "Oh, here's the Circus. It was begun by the elder John Wood, then finished by his son." She and Nicky had been sauntering down Brock Street and were now approaching another monument to the Wood architectural genius. As the name implied, the Circus consisted of a complete circle of houses designed with three tiers of columns. And like the Royal Crescent, it was joined with one continuous frieze.

Recognizing his companion's need to shy away from their former intimacy, Nicky observed solemnly, "Look—they've used a different type of column for each story. I wonder why. Couldn't make up their minds among Doric, Ionic, and Corinthian, or just showing off their classical knowledge, do you suppose?"

"I think you're the one who's showing off. However did you happen to know a thing like that?"

"Oh, well, now, I'll admit I didn't learn a lot at school, but a few classical details did penetrate my skull and stay there." The "scholar," who had helped build the sets for various Greek tragedies in his adolescence, tried to look modest.

Venetia had begun to notice that the major's limp was growing decidedly more pronounced and that there were tiny pain lines around his eyes.

The condition was brought on not by applied techniques of

223

acting but from the fact that the genuine major had insisted that Nicky take his new Hessian boots, since there was not time enough to have some quality footwear made to the actor's measure. These were rubbing a blister on his heel.

Venetia was much concerned and tactfully steered them toward Milsom Street, insisting that she must rest a bit and that he, despite his ample and recent breakfast, could not remain in Bath one moment longer without visiting Molland's Pastry Cook Shop and sampling the buns the town was famous for.

And it was while his mouth was crammed with this delectable pastry that Nicky realized he'd become the subject of an intense scrutiny. A tall, ramrod-straight elderly man of distinguished, albeit flashy, appearance was staring at him from across the patron-filled room.

Oh, God, no! Nicky quickly averted his eyes and appeared to be listening with absorbed interest to his companion's description of other Bath treats held in reserve, to be produced like rabbits from a hat during the remainder of his visit. Meanwhile, out of the corner of his eye he watched the gray-haired man begin to move implacably his way.

"Nicky! Nicky, lad! Can it really be? Why, I'd no idea you were in Bath. Heard you were in the army. Well met! Well met, me boy!"

The rolling, pear-shaped tones caused all heads to turn their way as the gentleman proffered a hand, which Nicky stared at as though it were a cobra. He pushed his chair back from the small table he and Lady Venetia shared and rose to stand slightly behind his companion.

"I think you must have mistaken me for someone else, sir," he observed frigidly while he tried to convey with his facial expression that he much preferred not to be recognized.

His pantomime served only to bewilder the old actor, who had been in a touring company with Nicky's mother before his talents had taken him on to better things. "Why, aren't you young Nicholas Forbes?" he inquired. He looked to Lady Venetia for possible assistance and became more mystified than ever by her obviously well-born appearance. "But oh, dear, how embarrassing!" He at last picked up on Nicky's frantic if mystifying signaling. "Pray, do forgive me, sir, for this unpardonable intrusion. I mistook you for an old acquaintance, you see. Quite silly of me, for now that I see you closer, there's not the slightest resemblance between you and my old friend. Vanity!" He smiled with a charm capable of enveloping an entire theater. "Blame this intrusion upon the vanity that forbids me to wear my spectacles in public. Your servant, sir, madam." He bowed gracefully in their direction and withdrew while Nicky sank back weakly into his chair, hoping Venetia wouldn't notice that he'd broken out in a cold sweat. But since her eyes were following the actor's back as he left the pastry shop, Nicky was able to blot his forehead surreptitiously with his handkerchief before she turned to look at him.

"How very odd," she observed. "He seemed so sure at first that he knew you."

"It's not really all that odd." Nicky managed to sound quite nonchalant. "In fact, it's always happening to me—being mistaken for some other cove."

"Really?" She looked surprised. "I can't imagine why. I'd say your appearance is quite uncommon. Distinguished, one might say."

"Thank you." He smiled disarmingly. "It's the hair, you see. When you have a carroty mane like mine, you find that people tend to focus upon it to the exclusion of all else. At first, at any rate. I fear it's the fate of redheaded people to be interchangeable."

She laughed. "Yes, I can see how that might happen. But do you know who I believe that was?"

"Haven't the slightest notion," he lied.

"I'm sure it's Mr. Powell, the actor. He's appearing on stage here as King Claudius. I haven't seen this *Hamlet* yet, but I've heard it's very well done indeed. Yes, I'm almost sure that was Mr. Powell. Aunt Louisa pointed him out to me in the Pump Room soon after the play opened. We really must go see it, Win. They tell me that the performances at the Theatre Royal are every bit as good as those in London." She grew enthusiastic. "Yes, I'm quite determined to become a theatergoer again as a part of my social redemption. Come now, sir. I've put you

225

squarely on the spot. As a gentleman you've no recourse except to say that it will be your greatest pleasure to escort me."

"It will be my greatest pleasure to escort you." Nicky spoke with apparent sincerity while inwardly he vowed at all costs to forgo that particular treat. The acting fraternity was not really that large. And even given his long absence from England, who was to say who else among the performers and stagehands might see and recognize him?

The encounter with the elderly actor had left him shaken. While he was fairly confident that Venetia's suspicions had not been aroused by it, another case or two of "mistaken identity" and the fat would well and truly be in the fire. The vision of Brooks' betting book came back once more to haunt him. If he lost the wager, he was ruined. The acting fee Wincanton was paying for this impersonation wouldn't cover even a fraction of his indebtedness.

"I beg your pardon?" He came back to the present, vaguely aware that Venetia had just addressed him and was waiting for a reply.

"Goodness, you were off woolgathering. I've just asked if we shouldn't plan a theater party with Aunt Louisa and Porge."

"Capital idea!"

"I was going to suggest that we go this Wednesday. But I suppose I should leave that up to Aunt Louisa to decide. Or do you have a preference?"

"No, no. Any evening you fix on will be all right with me."

And it would be, at that. For no matter which night they settled upon, that would be the evening when Major Wincanton's old war wound would become so excruciatingly painful that the veteran would have no choice except to forgo the promised theatrical treat and take groaningly to his bed.

Chapter
Eight

M AJOR GARETH WINCANTON WAS IN THE BLACKEST OF
black moods. This interval in his life, between soldiering and settling down to the serious business of civilian living, was intended to be carefree. It was turning out to be anything but that.

He lay in bed in the middle of the morning, puffing on a cigar and thinking of the coil he'd become involved in. The actor had been impersonating him in Bath for over a week now. He'd had no word from Jocko Hodges, so he assumed that Forbes had not yet been unmasked. The first few hours should have been most crucial. How could that fifth-rate actor have managed it? His Aunt Louisa must have really reached her dotage to believe that jackanapes was the outcome of centuries of breeding and the acquired polish of England's finest public schools.

And then, inevitably, his thoughts moved on to the cause of all this curst tomfoolery. Miss Amabel Fawnhope! He puffed savagely on his cigar at the thought of that particular beauty. Clouds of smoke billowed underneath the brocade canopy, making the major's four-poster bed look like an illustration of the Great London Fire.

He had never been so outdone by any female. Their relationship was not a love affair; it was more like a military engagement, all tactics and maneuvers. And he, by God, was being outcampaigned by an amateur.

He thought back to the last time he had seen her, when she had led him on, only to shut the door firmly in his face. His counter to her blatant sexual teasing had been to fall back and regroup. Let the little baggage cool her heels awhile, he'd decided. Let her wonder if her fish had wriggled off the hook after all. So he'd spent the past few evenings in his club, willing himself not to succumb to the nagging desire that would have driven him to visit Drury Lane.

But his withdrawal, by all reports, was not having the desired effect. Instead of leaving the theater each evening dejected and alone, Miss Fawnhope, his friends had gleefully reported, had been squired by a different gentleman every night. Her bevy of admirers, quick to observe his absence, were queuing up, by God, to take his place.

The major viciously ground out his cigar. To think that he'd been worried about that old roué Sir Horace Leacock, with his wife and brood of children permanently in the country while he went whoring around the town. Amabel could handle the Leacocks of this world. Did the breed include him? the major wondered, but dismissed that disturbing thought as quickly as it had come. It was her latest swain that alarmed him. The one, he'd been told, who had stepped to the head of the line and claimed her hand for two evenings in a row—Lord Desmond Keating, fresh-faced and down from Oxford, a green one not yet dry behind the ears. Just the type to throw all caution to the winds and actually marry an ambitious young coquette if that was what she wanted.

If that was what she wanted! He flung the covers back and, shouting for his valet, got out of bed. Of course that was what she wanted! And any gudgeon of **his** class would do. All her talk of being in love with him was just so much moonshine. Well, the devil take little Miss Conniving Fawnhope!

The major was in a flaming temper all that day. His servants gave him as wide a berth as their duties would permit and, when together, discussed its possible cause. Some were inclined to believe his leg wound was bothering him. His limp, these observed, was more pronounced than usual. But the valet, who was a knowing one, shook his head sagaciously and intoned *"cherchez la femme,"* a foreign phrase that earned him the admiration of servants' hall.

It finally came as a great relief to the major's staff when, after slamming around his house in St. James's Square all day and merely toying with the sumptuous repast Cook had prepared for his dinner, he called for his evening clothes and went out. He did not, however, go to Drury Lane. Perversely, he told his driver to take him to Covent Garden Theatre instead.

The scene he observed when he arrived there was a familiar one. He'd seen others like it countless times before without remarking on it. It was the way of the world, that was all, and not such a bad way at that from his former perspective. Now he viewed through new eyes the numerous barques of frailty positioned strategically about the saloon, vying for the best advantage posts to cast out their lures. And his emotions varied. He felt revulsion at an old and raddled type compelled to cling to the game long after nature had declared her unfit; pity for an obviously frightened young ladybird, a child merely, who might have run away except for the gimlet-eyed madam watching like a hawk from across the room; and a fleeting erotic response to the smile of a provocative goddess dressed in a blue riding habit almost as brilliant as her eyes.

Later, as he composed a note to be carried from his box to the titian-haired opera dancer he'd singled out in the burletta that was sandwiched between the tragedy and the farce, he thought of the tableau he'd witnessed in the saloon. He refused, though, to make comparisons between the commerce there and his own behavior.

Major Wincanton arrived at the Hummums Hotel around midnight with the beauty clinging like a limpet to his arm. It did not improve his disposition to discover that the private parlor, which he'd come to view as his own preserve, was preengaged. When the major took strong exception to this arrangement, the poor landlord was cast into a quake. The last thing he wished was to offend this wealthy member of the ton. But to preempt Lord Desmond Keating's arrangements was even more unthinkable.

And then, in one moment, it seemed that all the years devoted to being a genial host, to building up the type of clientele dear to any ambitious publican's heart, had become wasted, that indeed the entire edifice of the hotel was going to come crashing around his ears, when the young lordship in question came through the door with the lovely Miss Fawnhope's glove resting lightly upon his sleeve. For the landlord's greatest fear had become reality. Lord Desmond Keating had not only commandeered the major's parlor, but taken over his lady friend.

But the fireworks the innkeeper was braced for never happened, thanks entirely to the actions of Miss Fawnhope. For while the major continued to look like an impending storm and the noble calfling turned a trifle pale and the opera dancer looked quite confused, Miss Fawnhope broke into a dazzling smile. "Gareth!" she crooned. "How lovely to see you again. It's been ages. May I present Lord Desmond Keating? Oh, I see you've met. How nice." She paused expectantly, looking pointedly and pleasantly toward the beauty who was upon Wincanton's arm. Then, following a grudging introduction, she was cast into raptures by this chance meeting with a fellow artist, for she was dying to hear all the latest on-dits from Drury Lane's greatest rival; for instance, was it really so that Mr. Kemble was beside himself with jealousy over Mr. Kean?

When she suggested to his lordship that the foursome share the private parlor, the landlord wiped his brow and looked upon Miss Fawnhope as a female Solomon. But the major's curt refusal of this diplomatic gesture cast him back once more into nether gloom. Lord Desmond did not appear to share his host's dejection. Relief was writ large upon his face. The dancer, though, seemed disappointed, while Miss Fawnhope managed to look appealingly contrite.

"Oh, dear. What a perfectly goosish suggestion. What must I have been thinking? You two wish to be alone, of course. Pray, forgive me, Win."

Well, at any rate the crisis had been averted. The major accepted the landlord's second-best accommodation with a modicum of grace, and the host scurried off to the kitchen to make

230

sure that the supper served would in all respects atone for any slight the major might have felt.

But only the opera dancer appreciated the feast laid out before them. She interspersed bites of lobster and sips of iced champagne with valiant attempts at conversation but got no help at all from Major Wincanton, who toyed with his food, his mind clearly elsewhere. When his wandering attention did occasionally return to her, it was to wonder why the devil he'd ever embarked upon this juvenile course to make Amabel Fawnhope jealous. The actress had seen right through him and was beating him soundly at his game. As for the dancer, he'd concluded that she was not nearly as stunning when seen up close as she'd appeared to be upon the stage. Too vapid by half, as well. The creature was, in fact, a bore.

And since the young woman was at least as disenchanted with her brilliant catch, there was relief all around when at the conclusion of their supper Wincanton had the innkeeper whistle up a chair to take her home. Major Wincanton morosely watched her off, then pulled up the collar of his cloak against the fine mist that was falling and began to make his way toward Russell Street.

He was comfortably ensconced in a wing chair in Amabel's withdrawing room, his feet propped on the fender of the fireplace, where he himself had set the logs ablaze, when he heard the sound of footsteps on the walkway and then a low murmur of voices just outside. He smiled mockingly when the front door opened and closed almost immediately. At least Lord Desmond had not been treated to the lingering, passionate farewell that had marked his last parting with Miss Fawnhope.

Swift footsteps and a rustle of satin crossed the hallway. "Oh, Nellie—" Amabel halted abruptly on the threshold. "How the devil did you get in here, sir?"

He didn't bother to rise but gazed at her sardonically. "I bribed—*Nellie,* did you say?—that's how. Oh, she didn't come cheap, mind you. Cost me a bundle, in fact, to get her to unlock the door. Seems she was in a big hurry to get to the tavern. Funny thing, you know, she mentioned that she goes there practically every night. Like a mother to you, I believe you said? Or was it a watchdog? Anyhow, I did get the distinct impression that she was the reason you always— oh-so-reluctantly, of course—denied me entrance."

If he'd expected Miss Fawnhope to look disconcerted, he was doomed to disappointment. She merely shrugged. "What's a poor actress to do? I can't entertain male guests unchaperoned. And as you've just found out, Nellie flatly refuses to play that role. But since I don't wish to hurt anyone's feelings, I pretend otherwise. And"—her smile was meant to be disarming— "it's only a harmless little taradiddle, after all."

There was no answering grin from Major Wincanton. He continued to study her thoughtfully. "Yes, I'm sure you're capable of much better lies than that."

She flushed a bit but otherwise kept her composure. "I'll not rise to bait, Gareth, if you've come to quarrel. And now I must insist you leave. I'm sorry if you paid dearly to gain admittance, but indeed you should not have done so. You knew my stand on that. And besides, I'm very tired. I have a performance tomorrow and need my sleep."

"Oh, I won't take up a great deal of your time, Amabel." He indolently crossed one white-silk-clad ankle over the other. "But I did feel the need of privacy for our conversation. You see, I've come to tell you that you've won."

"I've won?" She walked into the room, tossing her Norwich silk shawl across a sofa back, and came to sit in an armchair opposite him. All her considerable thespian ability could not quite dampen the triumph in her eyes, though she spoke carelessly. "You should know that I haven't the slightest notion of what you're talking about. What have I won?"

"Me, of course. Let's speak plainly, Amabel. I'm tired of fencing. You'll not deny that the object of the game you've been playing was to bring me to heel?"

"I've played no game that I'm aware of."

"Oh, have you not indeed? Our courtship—if one could call it that—has been a veritable game of chess. Advance. Retreat. Attack. Followed by another strategic withdrawal. Then when the poor widgeon pursues, entrap him."

Her eyes narrowed. "You, sir, are being deliberately insulting."

"On the contrary. I'm being deliberately complimentary. Really, Miss Fawnhope, you should write a book on how to ensnare a reluctant gentleman. It would become a hornbook for the female sex and make your fortune."

"You're foxed, aren't you? I should have known." She rose to her feet. "Forcing yourself in here this way, spouting nonsense. I should have realized at once that you're disguised. But you do hold your drink like a gentleman, Major Wincanton. Could you not also behave like one and leave now?"

"Oh, do sit down, Bella."

"Don't call me Bella. You've picked that up from Nicky. I keep telling him I hate it."

"Then sit down, *Amabel,* my darling. Please. I promise you I'm not foxed in the slightest. And I beg pardon if I appeared insulting. I can only repeat that it was not my intention. Believe me, I am all admiration. You've done what I was determined you should not do. You've beaten me, Amabel. Thoroughly. Completely. I'm here merely to surrender."

She leaned forward in her chair; her eyes were shining. "Oh, Gareth. Do you really, truly mean it?"

"Oh, indeed I do. Really. Truly."

"Oh, darling, darling Gareth! You've made me deliriously happy!" Amabel cried as she jumped up and threw herself into his arms.

The interlude was brief but stormy, with much of the passion Wincanton had held in check now unleashed and Amabel responding with an enthusiasm that fueled his desire. It was only when he rose with her in his arms that she pulled her lips away. "Oh, no, Gareth," she managed to breathe huskily. "No, dearest. Not in there."

"Damnation, woman." He paused on the threshold of the dining room. "Where the devil is your bedchamber, for God's sake?"

But she was busy wriggling free of him, then standing on her own two feet. "Just never you mind about the bedchamber, Major Wincanton," she scolded him playfully. "After all we've

233

been through together, I insist on doing the thing properly. The bedchamber can wait. We've the rest of our lives for that."

"Easy for you to say," he said, glaring. He personally might well expire at any moment from thwarted lust. But then he shrugged with resignation. "Oh, the hell with it. I've waited this long. A little longer won't kill me. Perhaps."

He let her lead him by the hand back to the sofa. There she untied his cravat, which had been crushed past all recognition of the Mathematical tie his valet had taken such pride in hours before, and fetched a cross-framed stool and placed it underneath his low-cut evening shoes. "I'll make us tea"—she smiled down at him tenderly—"and then we'll talk about our future."

God, but she was a coldhearted little baggage!

But later, after a half cup of the steaming, restorative brew, Amabel sensed that he was feeling much more the thing. She snuggled closer beside him, tucking her feet underneath her and letting her head rest against his shoulder. "First, where shall we live?" she muttered.

"Why, I collect I'll buy a house around here somewhere," he answered vaguely.

"Around here!" She stared up at him in surprise.

"Well, yes. Won't that suit?" His surprise matched hers.

"I'm amazed that you'd choose this particular neighborhood, that's all."

"Actually, I hadn't given that part a great deal of thought. I just supposed it was something you'd decide. Where would you prefer to live, then?"

"Grovesnor Square" was the prompt reply.

"Grovesnor Square!" Her answer jolted him. He almost blurted that he didn't like the notion above half. Still, he supposed it was not unthinkable. "But wouldn't that be a bit inconvenient for the theater?"

"Well, it's never stopped the carriage trade that I've ever noticed, so why I should not be able—" She broke off suddenly. "Surely you don't think I'll keep on working!"

Once again, he'd not thought that far. "Well"—he proceeded delicately—"I had just supposed you'd wish it. You've

234

always seemed so dedicated to what you do. So ambitious. You talked of becoming another Mrs. Siddons, as I recall."

"And you wouldn't *mind*?"

"Why, no. At least I don't think so. Oh, I'll admit that I've always been a little jealous of your love scenes. And of the way the men in the audience ogle you. But at the same time I'll admit I've been proud, too. But you certainly don't need to perform if you don't wish it," he hastened to add as she continued to stare in disbelief. "You certainly will not need to. I plan to settle two thousand pounds a year on you, Amabel."

"Two thousand pounds!" she gasped. "Two thousand pounds!"

At first he thought she was simply overcome by his generosity. Slowly he realized she was incensed. "Come now," he protested. "I call the sum handsome. It's certainly far more than you're earning now. More, I suspect, than you ever will earn—at least for any length of time. You do realize I'm talking about a settlement for life, don't you? And as I was saying, you'll not have to continue on the stage, but if you choose to, well, then the peak of your earnings could put you fairly near the nabob class. But that part's up to you. For in either case you should be able to live comfortably—luxuriously, you might say. And any, er, *issue* should be well provided for."

"Issue?"

"Offspring. Oh, well then, dammit, *children*." He looked a bit embarrassed. "It's almost bound to happen. So I took that into consideration in arriving at a figure."

She was now sitting bolt upright and had distanced herself far enough to be able to look him directly in the eye.

"Now, let me get this all quite straight, Major Wincanton," she said with silky sweetness. "You are offering me a house— wherever—and two thousand pounds a year for life?"

"That's right."

"A carte blanche, in other words."

"You may call it that if you desire."

"A carte blanche!" Her voice rose in volume, quivered in anger. "And that's what this interview has been about? All your talk of surrender—capitulation—and you were thinking of a carte blanche? And just what did you think you were surrendering, Major Wincanton?"

"My freedom, dammit! God knows this kind of domestic arrangement was the last thing on earth I ever expected to enter into. But I've come to see I owe it to you, Amabel. Anything less than a commitment on my part would be unthinkable."

"Anything less than making me your mistress?"

"Anything less than putting our relationship on a permanent basis and seeing that you don't come to harm from it."

"You are all heart, Major Wincanton," she said between clenched teeth as she reached for the china teapot. The instinct that had saved him in many a hand-to-hand engagement did not fail him now. He dodged the missile and was on his feet when the pride of Josiah Wedgwood shattered on the wall.

"What the devil's come over you, Amabel?" he shouted. She reached for another projectile, and he began backing toward the door. "I'd thought to make you happy, and you've gone berserk." He sidestepped the flying cup, which then smashed into the paneling behind him. "God, but you're impossible— melting in my arms one minute, a termagant the next. Two thousand's more than handsome, Amabel. No use thinking you can do better—from me or from anyone—especially from that moon calf Keating. My God, woman, be reasonable. What did you expect?"

He thought it prudent to step through the door and slam it. A heartbeat later he heard the remaining cup and saucer explode on the other side. Nor was the heavy oak nearly thick enough to drown out her sobs.

"Expect? What did I expect? I expected you to marry me, you louse!"

236

Chapter Nine

NICHOLAS FORBES WAS STILL IN BED, RELUCTANT TO GET up. It wasn't the luxury of that magnificent canopied and domed piece of furniture that seduced him, though he did realize he was growing far too fond of a mode of living almost as far out of his reach as a chance to become king. But it was the desire to think that kept him lying there.

And his thoughts turned to his "little sister," though he sniffed aloud at the inappropriate term. Lovely little Amabel, with her air of fragility and her will of iron. Even when she was a child her ability to get her own way had been the stuff of legend. He grinned at the memory of the small face grown red with screaming and of the tiny, stamping feet. He'd paddled her little bottom once or twice himself, as he recalled—an occupation not without a certain appeal even now. He let that thought die aborning.

Amabel's methods for getting her own way had changed considerably, of course. But her determination to achieve that end was not one whit abated. He was sure of that. And he wondered how she was progressing in her plan to trap Wincanton into marriage. Nicky was certain—almost—that she'd met her match there. True, a cove should never predict how any man might behave around any woman. The laws of probability never seemed to apply to a confrontation of the sexes. But he was too well acquainted, partly through observation, more by reputation, with Wincanton's legendary coolness under fire to think that he would ever lose his head enough to form the sort of misalliance that Bella had in mind. Still, if anyone could bring it about, she could. That conclusion brought no joy. Nicky cursed himself for his dog-in-the-manger attitude. He should be wishing little Amabel success, instead of secretly hoping Wincanton would suddenly decide to renounce the world and enter a monastery. Small hope of that. With all his aristocratic ways, the major was a lusty one, no mistake.

Nicky's thoughts continued to dwell sourly upon Wincanton, and he took some small satisfaction in discovering that demigod's feet of clay.

For instance, he'd certainly been wrong about his Aunt Louisa. The idea of portraying her ladyship as a doddering old lady with failing senses—hardly able to see or hear, much less know what's what! If Wincanton could have seen his "ancient" aunt the way Nicky had when he'd blundered into the gold saloon, unaware that anyone was in there! Her clothes had been all every which way, and her cap had been lying on the floor behind the sofa arm as she and Sir George scrambled, red-faced, to their feet. He grinned to himself at the recollection. So much for the antique old crone he'd been sent to gull. Still, to be fair about it, Wincanton hadn't seen her ladyship since his school days, and to a lad of that age, anyone over thirty was tottering hopelessly on the brink.

Nicky took a few moments to wonder just how well the major and his aunt might have dealt with each other if Wincanton had come to Bath himself. Not half so well as he and she had done, he'd bet a monkey. He took no small satisfaction in scoring off the aristocrat in at least one area.

For he and Lady Stoke had become the best of friends. There was nothing high in the instep about Louisa. Of course, she was actually no blood kin to the major, which probably accounted for it. She was, in fact, a kindly, lusty, fun-loving woman. And lady or no, she put him very much in mind of his own mother.

As he and Lady Stoke had left the outskirts of Bath recently, with him driving the curricle and the tiger riding behind, and were tooling down the road toward Weston village, her ladyship had come directly to the point. "I wished to get you alone to discuss Venetia."

Nicky had grown justifiably proud of the way he was learning to ape the manners of the gentry—a quick study, by Jove, if he did say so. But there was one area in which he had failed and could never hope to master, the ability of the aristocrat to make a nonperson of anyone in the servant class. Clearly the tiger's presence had not inhibited Louisa's conversation. Nicky, though, had been aware of the little thatch gallows's ears flapping all the while.

"I must say, my dearest Win," Louisa had continued, affectionately laying a gloved hand on his sleeve, "it's a delight to behold the change that's come over my niece since you arrived. No more silly talk about wearing caps and having nothing more to do with the other sex. I vow she's a different person altogether. And the transformation can be laid at your door entirely."

"Oh, I'm sure it would have happened anyhow," he'd answered modestly. "Time has a way of—"

"Oh, no," she'd interrupted him. "You do yourself an injustice if you believe that. Surely you must realize what an attractive young man you are, Wincanton. What lady could resist you for long?"

Nicky had heard a sudden snort behind them and had been hard put not to turn and give Jocko a set-down glare.

"Yes, it's easy enough to see the effect you've had on dear Venetia. What I wish to discover is the effect she's had on you." Her ladyship had then paused expectantly.

Nicky had thought it best to proceed cautiously. "I don't think I quite understand."

"Of course you do, Win dear. And I also understand you perfectly. You're thinking I'm meddling where I've no business to. But where Venetia's concerned, you see, I now stand *in loco parentis*."

"I beg your pardon?"

"Goodness, Win. Didn't they teach you any Latin in that expensive school of yours?"

"Er, yes, of course. At least they tried. But I fear mine's gone a trifle rusty. The Frenchies rarely shouted any Latin as they charged."

She'd chuckled. "Well, to put the whole thing in plain English, then, what with Venetia's father being a world away, I feel obliged to take his place and sound you out about her."

Nicky had begun to feel a constriction around his throat that had nothing to do with his carefully tied cravat. "Well, actually," he'd managed to say, "I really haven't thought that much on it."

"I know you haven't, m'dear," Lady Stoke had replied patiently. "That's the object of this little talk. To get you to do just that. You like Venetia, don't you?"

"Yes, certainly." He'd had no problem there with sincerity.

"Well, then, that's all that's required, actually. What I wish to suggest—and, mind you, I'm not trying to push you into anything against your will—I simply wish you to consider making an offer for Venetia. Oh, I don't mean right away. I realize you need time to get accustomed to the notion. But I've grown more and more convinced that the two of you would deal quite well together. You enjoy each other's company. Your backgrounds are perfect for each other. You're both attractive—and of an age. And you're both excellent catches. I think it's a very good thing when neither party has to feel too obligated to the other in a marriage, don't you, Win? I don't know if you're acquainted with the size of Venetia's fortune, but—" And here Lady Stoke had gone on to mention a sum that had caused Nicky to suck in his breath and the tiger behind them to murmur, "Cor!"

"So you do understand, Win dear, just why I think you should seriously consider offering for Venetia. I know it would please your parents no end. And Venetia's father would be in raptures over such a match. Now, I don't wish to seem to pressure you. For there's no hurry about the thing. None at all. I only wished to put this tiny flea in your ear. For I'm convinced that a word to the wise is sufficient. Oh, I say—did that odd American who shocked himself with his silly kite say that, too?"

"Oh, God." Nicky now groaned aloud at the memory of that

interview. "What a coil!" He roused himself to tug at the bell-pull beside his bed. The chambermaid looked a bit surprised when he asked for tea to be brought in. He'd heretofore preferred to dress and go down to the breakfast parlor. But he did not feel up to confronting Venetia quite yet. He only hoped that Lady Stoke had not put a flea in her ear as well.

He took advantage of his privacy to blow on his scalding tea while trying to recall every syllable of Lady Stoke's unsettling conversation. And for a bit he allowed himself to dream of being married to all that money. But he soon put a period to that fantasy. On stage the plot might unmask him as a pretender and then allow Lady Venetia to declare her undying love despite his humble origins, but in real life such a story line would never play. Oh, gentlemen did occasionally lose their heads and marry actresses. Amabel wasn't completely daft for pinning her hopes on the remote possibility. But a lady, marry a common actor? If such a thing had ever happened, he'd not yet heard of it.

So what the devil was he to do? Nothing.

After wrestling with the problem to the bottom of his teacup, he finally concluded that his best course of action was none at all. Lady Stoke had promised not to rush him. He had only a fortnight of impersonation left to go. Surely he could spend that length of time in Lansdown Crescent without being forced into any sort of declaration. After all, he'd been avoiding matrimonial traps for years. The only difference here was a matter of degree.

True to his latest resolution, Nicky managed to avoid being alone with Lady Venetia all that day. And when evening came, he pleaded the difficulty of standing around on his "game leg" as an excuse for not attending a private ball with their ladyships and Sir George Carstairs. The threesome was waiting for him in the hall, cloaked and expectant, when he limped heavily down the stairs and begged off apologetically.

"Oh, I say, Louisa," Porge broke into the ladies' sympathetic release of the suffering major, "do the rest of us have to go? Nothing but a boring crush, all Frederica's parties. We've got the perfect excuse, ain't we? Bad form to go off and leave an ailing guest."

"Oh, I quite agree," Venetia seconded him. And so it was decided they'd all stay home with the invalid and provide their own entertainment.

In deference to the wounded hero's sensibilities, the evening began in a most sedentary manner. Venetia went to the pianoforte and began to play a soft and mournful air, while Lady Stoke pulled her tambouring hoop and a variety of colored silks out of the work table. Sir George was soon nodding in his chair and Nicky had smothered several prodigious yawns when Louisa protested, "For heaven's sake, Venetia, Win only has a hurt leg. He ain't dying. Don't you know anything but dirges? Or, better yet, why not come read to us?" She indicated the volume *Mysterious Warnings*, which still lay on the table, untouched since Nicky had examined it upon his arrival.

"Here, allow me." He roused himself and reached for the novel, feeling a need to exert himself before he drifted off with Sir George, who was now snoring rhythmically.

"Come over here by the light." Lady Stoke indicated the chair on the other side of the Egyptian-style candelabrum. "That is, if you're certain you feel up to it."

Nicky did. And the remarkable variance of his tone as he assumed the voices of different characters, plus the sepulchral way in which he read the creepy parts, soon had even Sir George wide-eyed and the ladies quaking in their chairs.

"Oh, do stop it!" Lady Louisa clapped her hands over her ears as Nicky emitted a low, prolonged, and ghostly moan. "I vow I'll not sleep a wink tonight as it is." She shivered pleasurably. "You've quite frightened me out of my wits, Win dear. I've never known anyone to read better, have you, Venetia? He actually brought the book to life. Why, I could see it all as if it were taking place before my very eyes." Again she shivered. "We must do something else to get my mind off it, or else I'll be awake with the candle lit all night. Oh, I know! Charades! That is, if you don't think the exertion will be too much for your poor limb, Win dear. It might be best if you confine yourself to the guessing part and don't do any of the acting out. We'll excuse you this time, won't we?"

Though the other two agreed, it was not in Nicky's nature to be so retiring. He was soon caught up in the spirit of the game and insisted on taking his turn, during which he amazed them with the virtuosity of his performance. His enactment of the Seven Deadly Sins—without the aid of any makeshift stage props or costumes—earned him the spontaneous applause and vocal accolades of his tiny audience. Unaccustomed as he was to such an enthusiastic appreciation of his performances, Nicky was basking in the moment with professional pride when his euphoric mood was rudely shattered.

"I vow, Win," Lady Stoke gushed, "for an instant I thought I must be in my box at the Theatre Royal. Why, if you'd been born a Cit, think of the career you might have had upon the stage!" She gurgled at her own absurdity.

"Yes, it's wonderful that a military officer would be possessed of such a talent." Lady Venetia was looking at Nicky rather oddly, or so he imagined. "Certainly your reading was the most moving that I've heard. And now your pantomime casts the rest of us entirely in the shade. You never cease to amaze me, Major Wincanton."

Nicky managed to mumble some modest disclaimer, followed by an admission of having participated in his school theatricals. And then, when it was again his turn to do a charade, he lowered the level of his performance to such a degree that his audience finally had to admit they hadn't had the slightest inkling he was trying to do the Labors of Hercules.

"Could've sworn you were that Hannibal cove crossing the Alps with a group of clumsy elephants," Sir George grumbled as he helped himself from the laden tea board that a footman had just placed before him.

And so the day ended for Nicholas Forbes as it had begun, with him lying in bed, reviewing his situation. You came close to blowing the gab, you curst loose screw! he berated himself as he tossed and turned. No telling what seeds of suspicion you may have planted.

He found consolation in another thought, however, as he

blew out the candle and prepared for sleep. Of course, you did cover yourself quite well. The bit about school theatricals had shown quick thinking, and that god-awful turn at charades had made them forget all about his earlier, brilliant pantomime. Besides, why shouldn't a soldier like Wincanton have some acting talent? Look at that strutting peacock Napoleon. Now, there was a man who could have made it on the stage!

His mind, having been set at ease, now reverted to his drawing-room performance. By Jove, I was good tonight, wasn't I? he congratulated himself. No Edmund Kean, of course. Yet. But damned good, if I do say so.

Nicky basked for a moment longer in the memory of the others' admiration, then sighed heavily. Two more weeks to go. He turned on his stomach and buried his head beneath his pillow, ostrich-style. Well, a clever chap like him should be able to brazen it out for another fortnight without winding up arsy-varsy. Just as long as he kept out of the way of old acquaintances and didn't give in to another hen-witted acting urge.

Chapter Ten

MAJOR GARETH WINCANTON HAD JUST ACHIEVED HIS objective—seeing Miss Amabel Fawnhope alone—by the simple expedient of grabbing Lord Desmond Keating by the collar and throwing him out of the actress's dressing room. It was not an auspicious beginning for their interview.

Miss Fawnhope was seated at her dressing table, removing the heavy stage makeup that she wore. The gaze she fixed upon the major in the glass was steely. "You had no right to do that," she said.

"How else was I to get a word with you? Don't worry—the moon calf won't go away. Yet." He gave weight to the final syllable.

"And what is that supposed to mean?"

"Simply that you've a head full of maggots if you expect Keating to marry you. Oh, I don't doubt he's willing enough." He staved off the retort forming on her lips. "Oh, asked you already, has he? Well, then you'd better get him to Gretna Green in a towering hurry, for someone's bound to have informed his papa, who should arrive any moment with the horsewhip to fetch his heir back home."

She wheeled angrily to face him. "You did that? How odious! How utterly despicable!"

"Climb off your high ropes, Amabel. You know I did no such thing. I hope I'm too much the gentleman to throw that kind of rub in your way. But I'll never know, for believe me, I wasn't even tempted. That sort of news doesn't need my help to travel fast. Some scandalmonger is probably banging his old lordship's ears right now. No, Amabel, *ma belle,* I fear you're backing another wrong 'un. If you're absolutely dead set on marriage, you'd best focus your chances on some Cit who's made a huge fortune in trade."

"Thank you for your advice, Major Wincanton," she replied with icy hauteur. "Now, having delivered yourself of it, will you kindly leave my dressing room?"

"Not till I've finished what I came to say."

"Then pray, be quick about it. I have a supper engagement, and if I can believe you, my escort may be snatched away before we come to the first remove. So don't detain me."

He lounged back against her doorway, which he'd locked, and ignored the fact that Lord Desmond's ear was undoubtedly pressed against it. "Am I to take it, then, that your attitude hasn't changed? I'd hoped that after you'd had a chance to cool down a bit, you'd see reason, Amabel."

"Reason?" Her voice rose an octave. "You think it *reasonable* to be your mistress?"

"Damn reasonable. You'd be established. And I can't—won't—marry you. I'd very much like to share your life, however."

"You'd like to go to bed with me, you mean. Come now, Major, let's not shy away from truth at this stage of the game."

"Very well, then, I'd like to go to bed with you. I've never denied that's mostly what this is all about. But you've other attractions as well. God knows you aren't exactly dull to be around." His smile was wry. "And perhaps if I were the country-gentleman type I'd snap my fingers at convention and we'd go rusticate together on one of my estates. But I've learned a few things about myself, you see. I found that I wasn't content to be a peacetime soldier, and I know I'll not be content to be a Bond Street beau for long. I need a challenge. Some kind of conflict. So I've decided on a political life, Amabel. And, to make no bones about it, a marriage to you would put a period to that particular ambition."

"Whereas keeping a mistress would speed your career right along!"

He shrugged away her indignation. "It wouldn't harm it. That's unjust, I know. But this is an unjust world. Think about it. You know my offer, Amabel."

"Indeed I do!" she blazed. "And I daresay you wouldn't be making it if my brother were still in town! I've half a mind to send for him. He'd give you what-for! Gentleman or no. Nicky would take a horsewhip to you, sir!"

"Nicholas is well aware of my intentions. And approves of them, let me add."

"That's a bald-faced lie!" Her hand closed on a rouge pot. "Nicky wouldn't hear of me being anybody's mistress!"

"Don't be goosish." He eyed her warily. "Any man of the world would be quick to see the advantages for you. But never mind now about Forbes. He has nothing to say in the matter. It's your decision." Wincanton was unlocking the door as he spoke. "I'm through playing games, Amabel. I'm here for your final answer."

He got it. She flung the pot at him just as he'd jerked the door wide open. It struck Lord Desmond in the chest, where its

246

contents played havoc with the black superfine of that dandy's long-tailed evening coat and detracted from the intricate folds of his pristine starcher.

It had been Lady Venetia Lowther's idea that "Major Wincanton" must see Prior Park, Nicholas Forbes's that the treat should be shared by Lady Stoke and Sir George Carstairs, and Lady Stoke's that the young couple should be left to their own devices.

The shared carriage ride to the stately home, built in the mid-1700s by Ralph Allen, a former postmaster and social leader of Bath and owner of the Bathstone quarries, rather frustrated Lady Stoke's scheme for the afternoon but suited Nicky to a tee. It was his notion to avoid all possible pitfalls for the remainder of his stay. This included keeping clear of the city and of the danger of running into old acquaintances, either his or the major's, there and nipping in the bud any opportunity that might lead to a romantic entanglement between himself and Lady Venetia.

He had, however, underestimated the strong-willed determination of Lady Stoke. Upon arriving at the park, the foursome left their carriage as a unit. They stood together upon the mansion's terrace, gazing at the panorama it overlooked. Mr. Allen, under the influence of Alexander Pope, so it was said, had planted trees on either side of a valley that sloped downward from the mansion, so that the eye was automatically focused, as though peering through a giant spyglass, upon the distant white-stoned lovely city of Bath.

After admiring this breathtaking view for a few awed moments and speculating upon the possibility of rain, the party set out—still together. Their walk wandered through the trees that lined one side of the grassy expanse where cattle grazed. It would eventually lead them to the Paladian Bridge, one of the chief wonders to be seen at Prior Park.

But they had not traversed three-quarters of that distance when Lady Stoke, spying a convenient rustic bench, turned an ankle and declared herself unable to walk another step.

Nicky was all for making an "armchair" with Sir George's

help and carrying her back to the carriage. But her ladyship would have none of it. Not for anything would she spoil the opportunity for her guest to explore the grounds. Dear Porge, who like her had been there countless times before, would keep her company. But Venetia must act as dear Win's guide. And on no account must her trifling injury be allowed to ruin their outing. As long as she kept her weight off her tiresome ankle, she could assure them, it pained her not at all.

Nicky had no choice. He set out alone with Lady Venetia. But when he realized that all her interest was fixed upon the marvels of the park, which she delighted in previewing for him, he soon relaxed and began to enjoy their sightseeing. One treat they must not miss, it seemed, was a spot known popularly as Pope's Grotto, copied from one in the poet's Twickenham estate. What's more, the very dog that the great man had presented to Mr. Allen was buried there, with a touching inscription, "Weep not," engraved on a flagstone by Pope himself. It was Nicky's opinion that, poet or not, he personally could have come up with something a great deal better, but in light of his guide's enthusiasm, he decided to keep that sentiment to himself.

Just as Venetia and Nicky left the shelter of the trees, the low-lying clouds that had almost dissuaded them from making this excursion decided to open up and do their worst. "Oh, my goodness!" she exclaimed, and with an alacrity that both astonished and impressed her companion, she ran for the Paladian Bridge.

The rain was coming down in sheets now, wind-driven, and when Venetia reached the covered structure, the sole of her half boot slipped on the wet stone floor. This could have caused a very nasty fall indeed, had not Nicky been right there to catch her. As it was, the results of this timely intervention were even more disastrous.

For upon finding the delectable Lady Venetia encircled in his arms with her face uplifted toward his in gratitude, Nicky completely lost his head and kissed her. The kiss, despite the water streaming from her bonnet and the curly brim of his beaver hat, turned out to be such an agreeable occupation that the thought of terminating it never even occurred to him.

And after the initial shock of being so accosted had quickly fled, to be replaced by other, far more interesting sensations, Venetia had no impulse, either, to put a period to this enlightening experience. For it had come to her as a complete surprise to learn that she had never actually been kissed before. Oh, she had thought that she had been. And had considered the activity decidedly overrated. Now she knew that the cool and calculated busses Mr. Fletcher Langford had planted upon her cheek and, rarely, upon her lips could not even qualify as imitation kisses. Major Gareth Wincanton, however, was assuredly delivering the real thing.

There was no way of knowing just how long this pleasurable state of affairs might have continued, had it not been interrupted by the unexpected arrival of Sir George and Lady Stoke.

The downpour had wrought a miraculous cure. Her ladyship had discovered not only that she could support her weight on the injured ankle but that she could outdistance Sir George to the shelter of the Paladian structure and arrive a step before him while Nicky and Venetia's lovemaking was still at a fever pitch.

"Oh, my goodness, Porge!" her ladyship called to her winded companion while clapping her hands with delight. "Would you look at this! Well, what have you to say now, sir? Did I not predict that we'd soon be wishing these two lovebirds happy?"

The two lovebirds sprang apart—Venetia, embarrassed; Nicky, appalled.

"Yes, indeed you did, Louisa. Congratulations, m'boy." Sir George, deeply moved, clapped Nicky on the shoulder. "Couldn't be more pleased, b'gad, if you were me own son."

"Oh, I say!" Nicky tried to protest but choked.

Venetia, recovering more quickly, filled the breach. "Oh, really, Aunt Louisa, you mustn't jump to such conclusions. You much mistake the matter, I assure you. Win has not offered for me."

"Only because we blundered in and interrupted" was the arch reply. "Pray, don't mind us, Win dear. Go right ahead."

"I say now, really! That's hardly—"

"Necessary?" Sir George chuckled. "I should think not myself. Not after the way you two were going at it. Fair put us to the blush, didn't it, old girl?"

"Yes, and I shudder to think, Venetia, what your dry stick of a father would have to say. Well, the sooner I send a notice to the *Gazette*, the better it will be for all concerned."

There was a long and pregnant pause. Lady Venetia was the one who finally broke it. "If it's what Win wishes," she said, feeling her way tentatively.

"Well, we all know what Win wishes." Lady Stoke's laugh was bawdy. "La, if we hadn't come along just when we did, I vow he'd have had you on the floor, like as not."

"Aunt Louisa!"

"No use coming all over missish at this late date, Venetia. You were enjoying every minute of it."

Nicky felt himself being swept away like the rainswollen waters that were gathering momentum underneath the bridge they were standing on. He made a last, valiant attempt to save the situation. "Oh, but you mustn't notify the paper just yet, Louisa. I mean to say it wouldn't be the thing. I'll need to write Venetia's father for permission."

"Nonsense! All the way to Brazil and back? Why, that would take you donkey's years. And it ain't as though Venetia's not of age. The sooner the better, that's what I say. Don't you agree, m'dear?"

She turned toward her niece, who hesitated just a fraction longer before murmuring agreement.

"Well, then, that's all settled." Lady Stoke beamed with satisfaction. "Do you suppose Cook included some champagne in the picnic basket? If not, we'll simply toast the happy couple with claret, Porge. Look—the rain's let up. Does anyone see a rainbow anywhere? There ought to be one to mark the occasion. Oh, well, never mind. One can't have everything. Do let's hurry back before the rain starts up again. I'm sure we've seen all we need to see of Prior Park."

250

Her ladyship kept up a constant stream of congratulatory chatter all the way back to their carriage. She overflowed with plans and predictions for the young couple's future happiness.

Nicky, however, could not hear a single word of it above the persistent roaring in his ears.

Chapter Eleven

IT WAS FORTUNATE THAT AMABEL FAWNHOPE HAD NOTHING at hand to throw but the copy of the *Gazette* she was reading when she saw the notice of Lady Venetia Lowther's engagement to Major Gareth Wincanton. She hurled it viciously, but, in the manner of paper, it merely flapped its way across her counterpane to land on the floor at the foot of her four-poster. She immediately retrieved it to read the notice once again. Having satisfied herself that no hallucination was involved, Miss Fawnhope let loose a flood of tears, more in rage than in sorrow, then spent most of the afternoon lying in bed with a wet cloth over her eyes, trying to repair the damage from such self-indulgence.

The treatment did not work as well as she might have wished, which proved a very good thing, for her red-rimmed eyes gave credence to her story of the death of a dear, dear friend when she asked for leave to attend the funeral.

Major Wincanton learned secondhand the news of his betrothal. He was drinking a thoughtful second cup of tea, after having polished off a breakfast of ham and eggs, when Lord

Piggot-Jones and Mr. Bertram "Sprig" St. Leger ran the disapproving gauntlet of his butler and his valet to interrupt his reverie.

Two minds with but a single thought, they had converged on the doorstep of Number Four, St. James's Square, each clutching his copy of the *Gazette*. Now they vied with each other to see who would be first to break the news.

In the end, since Wincanton's glare was hardly encouraging, they both simply thrust their copies toward the major, index fingers pointing to the cogent paragraph.

Major Wincanton prided himself on a superior intellect. But in this instance he was slower to comprehend than Miss Fawnhope had been. He was forced to give the item a third reading, with no time out for throwing, before he fully took it in.

His friends waited anxiously for an explosion that did not come, however. It belatedly occurred to both that their eagerness might be their undoing, should this turn into a classic case of "kill the messenger," so they backed off a discreet distance as he read. But whereas the soldier had first turned white, then fiery red, he otherwise managed to keep a tight rein on his emotions.

After a lengthy silence, the Sprig dared to break it. "By gad, he's won it!" he crowed unwisely.

Wincanton's furious eyes impaled him. "What the devil are you talking about?"

"The wager. He's pulled it off! He's won it! What an impersonation! I never dreamed he'd be able to carry the thing so far. And you actually said, Piggot-Jones, that Nicky couldn't play Little Jack Horner if you gave him a Christmas pie. Those were your very words!"

"He ain't won yet," the other said darkly. "What he's done, it appears, is overreach himself, the cocky devil. The time ain't up yet, by any means. And he'll never be able to keep up the impersonation now. Too complicated by half is my opinion. Oh, I say, Win, just who *is* Lady Venetia Lowther?"

"How the devil should I know?"

The vicious retort sent the visitors off into gales of laughter, despite the ever-present threat of a combat hero's temper put on the boil.

"Oh, lord," the Sprig managed to gasp as they subsided, "that's rich. He's no notion at all of the gel that he's betrothed to."

This sally set them off again. Then, when they'd partially recovered for a second time, Piggot-Jones managed to ask, "What are you going to do about it, Win?"

"Go to Bath."

"But you can't do that!" St. Leger protested, suddenly sobered. "The wager! Have you forgotten the wager? You'd be throwing a rub in Nicky's way. Ain't sporting to interfere in any way that might decide the outcome of a bet."

"Damn the bet!" Major Wincanton spoke through teeth that were tightly clenched.

An hour later, in a curricle hired from Tattersall's, he was speeding down the Bath Road at an alarming rate.

His two friends, driving Piggot-Jones's rig, followed at a discreet distance, ostensibly to see that the terms of the wager were not violated, but covertly determined to miss none of the fun.

And at five o'clock the following morning, after having been assessed three halfpence per pound for five pounds of baggage over the limit, Miss Amabel Fawnhope boarded the public coach. She, too, was bound for Bath.

Chapter
Twelve

A s Major Wincanton proceeded down Bath's Cheap Street in the late afternoon of the day following his arrival, he caught sight of a familiar vehicle. He skillfully weaved his way through the congestion of carriages, horsemen, carts, and crossing pedestrians and managed to pull abreast of his own curricle. It was necessary for him to shout "Jocko!" in an imperious voice to get the driver's full attention, which was firmly fixed on the barque of frailty he was striving to impress. The tiger looked around with some annoyance.

"Can't it wait, guv? I'm bloody busy. Oh, I say, where'd you get the rig? Oh, my God, it's you! Beg pardon, sir. I thought—"

"I know what you thought. I need to talk to you."

They pulled off the busy thoroughfare, and while the tiger's companion held the horses, he jumped down to secure the major's cattle. His employer joined him at the horses' heads. "You might begin by explaining what you're doing tooling that light-skirt around town in my curricle."

It was not an auspicious beginning to what could only be an awkward interview, but Jocko did his best. "Why, exercising the beasts, that's wot. You've no notion, guv—*sir*, I means to say—of 'ow that imposture neglects 'em. I knew as 'ow you'd want 'em kept fit, sir."

"And I suppose you also knew I'd want you to parade that

baggage around Bath in my rig. But never mind that just now. What's been going on?"

"Well, I daresay as 'ow you must know the meat of the matter, else you wouldn't be 'ere." The tiger's attempt to suppress a grin was only partially successful.

"If you mean I've read the notice of my betrothal, then you're right. So enlighten me. Who the deuce is Lady Venetia Lowther?"

After the tiger had filled him in on the background and appearance of his fiancée, Wincanton asked drily, "Aside from his obvious romantic success, how has the actor gotten along? Would you say my aunt's at all suspicious?"

"Lor' no, sir." Despite all better judgment, Jocko gave the grin free rein. "Plays you to a treat, 'e does. Much as I 'ates to admit it, I must say I underestimated the fellow. Lady Stoke's fair eating from his 'and, and 'e's nailed down a fortune in Lady Venetia as I've 'eard tell would make King Midas jealous. You might go so far as to say 'e makes a more thorough job of being Major Wincanton than you do, sir."

"You might say it if the actor paid your wage. As he or someone else may soon need to do," Wincanton snapped. "Now, I suggest you get rid of your doxy in short order and see to it my grays are properly rubbed down before they're stabled."

This time Jocko Hodges's "Yes, sir" was a model of subservience.

"And one more thing," the major called as he climbed aboard his hired curricle. "Don't tell the actor that you've seen me. I think it best if I throw him that particular cue."

The trouble with that notion was that for probably the first time in his life, Major Wincanton found himself at a loss as to how best to proceed. He'd come haring down to Bath, blood in his eye, but what the devil was he to do now that he was here?

His inclination was to drive straight up Lansdown Hill to the Crescent, expose the actor for the fraud he was, confess his part in the hoax, break the engagement, and take his medicine. That was what he'd like to do, but he knew he couldn't. And it was not the presence of Piggot-Jones and St. Leger who'd come to

255

Bath to ensure that he do no such thing that stopped him. Wincanton knew the code without their prompting. He could not intervene in any way that might influence the outcome of the wager without earning the condemnation of his acquaintances. He'd have to watch his step very carefully. His honor as a gentleman was at stake.

When he emerged from the White Hart the next morning, Wincanton was still mulling over how best to proceed. He was depending upon a brisk walk to clear away some of the cobwebs resulting from a near-sleepless night and was mentally composing a note to Forbes, asking the actor to meet him in some out-of-the-way place, when his thoughts were interrupted by a female voice hailing him.

He had paused and turned before he was struck by the folly of responding to "Oh, Major Wincanton!" He now saw, hurrying his way, an attractive young lady who wore a cherry pelisse and was laden down with parcels. She was almost upon him when he saw her dark eyes widen in surprise, followed by a confusion that rapidly turned into embarrassment. "But you aren't! Oh, I do beg your pardon! I mistook you for my fiancé."

Venetia continued to look Wincanton up and down in some bewilderment while he appraised her just as closely. Well, at any rate he couldn't fault the actor's taste. She was a very personable young lady.

"I'm flattered by the mistake, ma'am." He recovered enough to reply in a manner worthy of Nicholas Forbes. "Your fiancé is a most fortunate man."

His obvious admiration was rather disconcerting to Venetia. "It's astonishing how much you do resemble him. Why, you even have the same slight limp. Oh, I beg your pardon." She was aghast at her tactlessness. He might be sensitive about his infirmity.

"Not at all. That really is a coincidence." A limp, for God's sake! Trust an actor to overdo.

"And then there's the same hair coloring. Win says that redhaired people—but of course!" The light had begun to dawn. "Why, you must be Mr. . . . Forbes, was it? I believe that was the name. Yes, I'm sure now of it. Are you by chance Mr. Nicholas Forbes?"

It was on the tip of the major's tongue to emphatically deny it. But instinct told him that a third look-alike in the farce his fellow club members had created would strain credulity a bit too much. "However did you know?" he inquired cautiously.

"Why, some friend of yours made the same mistake that I did—in reverse, of course. Oh, I say, are you by chance an actor?"

"No!" He realized he'd been a shade too vehement, but he was damned if he was going to take on Forbes's identity. The name was bad enough. He smiled to correct the impression that he'd just been insulted. "Actually, I'm a soldier. Or was, I should say. That's why I thought you really were addressing me," he said, improvising. "I didn't quite catch the name but did hear you say 'major.' "

"This really is the oddest thing."

"Isn't it? I say, I noticed a tearoom back there, the way we came. Couldn't we have a cup of tea and discuss it further?"

Venetia's conscience began to form polite excuses, for what he had suggested was totally improper. On the other hand, she was formally engaged now. If, as Aunt Louisa claimed, a married lady could do whatever pleased her, well, surely an affianced one was allowed a little license. Besides, she convinced herself, she was simply parched with thirst.

The major ended her vacillation by the simple expedient of relieving her of her parcels and taking her elbow.

When they were settled in at a small table with a pot of Indian tea and a supply of the ubiquitous Bath buns, he said, "Tell me more about your fiancé. I must admit it's a strange feeling to learn I have a double."

"Actually, the resemblance is only slight, now that I've seen you better. But you are both of a height"—she delicately skirted around mentioning the limp again—"and most of all, there's your hair. Major Wincanton's is of the same brilliant shade."

"But then, of course, he's better-looking," Wincanton offered before he thought.

She appeared to think it over rather seriously. "No, I would not say so" was the verdict. Then, for some inexplicable reason, she blushed. "Were you on the Peninsula?" she asked to cover her confusion.

Not wishing to overdo the parallels between "Major Wincanton" and himself, he started to deny it. But the devil with coincidence, he decided. It was a large army, after all. "As a matter of fact, I was." He went on to elaborate.

Lady Venetia proved to be a marvelous listener. She had long been fascinated by Wellington's campaigns, but her curiosity had gone largely unsatisfied. Her fiancé, it seemed, had spoken little of his experiences, and she'd been reticent about quizzing him.

The major was rather surprised at this revelation. He would have expected Nicky Forbes to be expansive on that particular subject, since it was the one place that the actor's background meshed with that of the man he impersonated. Wincanton's conclusion was that the ex-private was afraid of revealing too much of the common soldier's point of view in any account he might give of the Peninsula Campaign.

The major was impressed with the intelligent questions his listener asked and with her keen interest in the political aspects of the Napoleonic defeat. It pleased him to learn that her father was a diplomat and that she'd spent several years in Spain. Their tea grew cold as they traded their impressions of that fascinating country. Later Wincanton realized that this was a first for him. He'd never had a serious conversation with a woman before, let alone given such credence to the judgment of a member of the other sex.

"Oh, my goodness, the time!" Venetia woke up to the fact that she'd spent the better part of an hour in the tea shop. "My aunt will wonder what's become of me. I'm to fetch a particular silk she needs for her tambouring. Oh, well"—she smiled— "Aunt Louisa is an indifferent needlewoman and may be just as glad to have had an excuse to stay idle." She rose from the table and thanked the major politely for the tea. "You must call soon." She found refuge in formality. "My fiancé is also staying with our aunt. I'm sure he'll wish to meet you. You have so much in common, you're certain to become friends."

That was a possibility he'd not bet on, no matter how foxed, he told himself as he escorted her ladyship outside. "Thank you. I shall be pleased to call," he lied, "if you'll give me your direction."

Here was just one more devilish complication, he realized as she gave him her address. He didn't dare come face-to-face with his Aunt Louisa. She was bound to grow suspicious if she ever saw Forbes and him together, and it wouldn't take her long to sort them out. The Sprig was right. He should never have left London. Still, when Venetia smiled up at him shyly and said good-bye, he found it difficult to regret his folly to the degree required.

As he walked slowly back to his hotel, Major Gareth Wincanton was feeling more confused and less in charge of circumstances than he ever had throughout the course of his entire life. He sought the sanctuary of his room, anxious to blow a cloud and spend some time in quiet thought. But this bit of escapism was denied him. He opened his door, to be greeted by the accusing faces of his friends.

Lord Piggot-Jones fired the first volley. "I must say I'm shocked."

Right behind him Mr. St. Leger brought up his guns. "Ain't the thing at all, Wincanton. Not gentlemanly. Unsportsmanlike."

"What the devil are you two ranting on about?"

"No use acting the innocent with us. We saw you in the tea shop. Chattering away like anything. And we know who the lady was."

"And so?"

"And so you are deliberately interfering with the outcome of our wager. That's low, Win, it really is." The Sprig was awash with righteous indignation. "A gentleman would have stayed in London."

"A gentleman would not have entered into a betrothal as someone else."

"Yes, but then Nicky *ain't* a gentleman. We all knew that when we put up our blunt. Couldn't expect *him* to behave like

259

one, now, could we? But yours is a different case entirely. And we're disappointed in you—there's the long and short of it. I could halfway understand your need to talk to Nicky and find out what's what. But to introduce yourself to your fiancée right off the bat, that really is the outside of enough. By the by," he came down off his high ropes long enough to ask, "how did she take it?"

"She didn't. That is to say, of course I didn't tell her who I am. And if you had come along a little earlier, you'd know I didn't seek her out. She spoke to me." He went on to explain what had happened.

"Thinks you're Nicky, eh?" Lord Piggot-Jones suddenly peered at Wincanton through his quizzing glass as if to establish his true identity. "Gad, this is confusing."

"No, she doesn't. That is to say, she believes Nicholas Forbes is my name, but not all the rest of it— Oh, the devil. You know what I mean."

"Can't say I do, really," the Sprig said, sighing, "but I am relieved to hear you didn't blow the gab. Still and all, it certainly would've been a dashed sight better if you'd stayed in London with your little ladybird, where you belonged."

Wincanton's eyes narrowed dangerously. "If by any chance, St. Leger, you are referring to Miss Fawnhope, pray, use her proper name."

"Beg pardon, I'm sure." The Sprig turned scarlet. The major nodded a curt acknowledgment of the apology and offered port. When the friends parted company a little later, an uneasy truce prevailed.

Nicholas Forbes, however, was not as fortunate in his mental state at the conclusion of an interview that took place at approximately the same time. Lady Venetia had returned from her shopping expedition and found him reading in the library.

"Oh, there you are, Gareth. I've been looking for you everywhere. The oddest thing just happened. You can't imagine whom I met on Milsom Street."

Chapter Thirteen

THE COUNCIL OF WAR THAT TOOK PLACE IN THE WHITE Hart that afternoon was unsatisfactory to all parties concerned. After Lady Venetia's bombshell burst, Nicholas Forbes had come rushing down Lansdown Hill at the first opportunity. He'd been spotted entering the inn by Lord Piggot-Jones and Mr. St. Leger, who were lolling in the public parlor. They had insisted upon accompanying him to Major Wincanton's rooms in order to protect their interests.

The two red-haired men eyed each other with stony faces. It was the genuine Major Wincanton who was now grateful for the hours spent over cards that had schooled him to hide all emotion. For he was jarred by the change in Nicholas Forbes, a change that he'd have been hard put to define but that nonetheless was evident.

There had always been something entirely too flash about the actor, a showiness smacking of the stage. So of course the exquisitely understated gray coat and biscuit pantaloons he himself had provided made a difference. But this did not begin to account for all the change. It was as if in playing the gentleman, Nicholas had become one.

It occurred to Wincanton that Lady Venetia just might marry the actor anyhow, once he'd been exposed. Forbes was a good-looking devil; there was no denying that. Wincanton refused, however, to draw any parallel between his own infatuation with Amabel and Lady Venetia's possible feelings for the actor.

No, by God, it had to be Major Wincanton, scion of one of England's oldest families and grandson of an earl, that Venetia had agreed to marry. What was it Jocko had said, though? "He makes a more thorough job of being Major Wincanton than you do." Well, it was time to put a period to this kind of thinking. Self-doubt could prove habit-forming. He'd had enough of it.

"How's Amabel?" Nicky asked abruptly as he commandeered the wing chair closest to the fireplace and let his two companions make do with an upholstered mahogany settee.

Wincanton, however, refused to be upstaged and remained upon his feet, lounging against the mantel. "Amabel's quite well," was his nonrevealing answer. He'd be damned if he'd advertise his failure in that department, too.

"Well, what's to be done?" The Sprig tried to cut through the small talk and stared expectantly at Wincanton.

The major could have told him the half-baked plan he'd formed during his ride down from London. It had been simple enough. He'd meant to tell the actor to get out of Bath as soon as his month was up, leaving a note behind, confessing his impersonation. The note would explain that he'd been out of work and out of funds and had seized upon a known resemblance to Major Wincanton in order to worm his way into their household for free board and lodging. In no way would Wincanton have had to be connected with the deception. He could show up innocently upon his aunt's doorstep anytime he wished.

But that plan was worthless now. Today Venetia had met him as "Nicholas Forbes" and would know that he had been a party to the flimflam. She was bound to despise him for it. He found the thought of that too lowering to dwell on.

"I asked you, Wincanton, what's to be done?" the Sprig repeated.

"How should I know?" was the terse reply.

"Nicky?" The Sprig's expectant look was a tribute to the actor's resourcefulness. But Nicky's shrug was eloquent. The Sprig looked shocked, then sighed heavily and took charge himself.

"I think we should consider that the terms of the wager were violated by extenuating circumstances. What I mean to say is that when Win here came to Bath, as he'd no right to do, it put a spanner in the works. I thereby declare Nicholas Forbes the winner."

A howl of protest rose from Lord Piggot-Jones, who stood to lose a bundle. "Now, just you hold on, St. Leger. 'Extenuating circumstances' be damned! What I mean to say is, when you place a bet on something or other, you simply take it for granted there'll be extenuating circumstances. Why do you think they call it gambling? Because of all those extenuating circumstances, that's why. Your horse pulls a tendon. That's an extenuating circumstance. Your dog gets sick before he kills more rats than the other cove's mongrel. That's an extenuating circumstance. The bruiser you put your blunt on in the ring—"

"We get the picture, Piggot-Jones," Major Wincanton said, breaking in upon the tirade.

"The point I'm making"—the other stuck doggedly to his guns—"is that it ain't fair to call off the bet now. Nobody ever actually said you couldn't go to Bath if you took the notion. And you've just explained that you didn't blow the gab to Nicky's fiancée, which would really be too low for words. I say the wager stands."

A fierce argument then broke out. The two men most involved took no part but eyed each other surreptitiously.

"I think we have to let Nicky off the hook," the Sprig insisted for the dozenth time.

"Why the devil should we? No one told him to offer for the girl. Talk about your extenuating circumstances! Now, there's a— My word, Nicky, you don't actually mean to marry her before your time's up, do you?"

Judging from their expressions, Nicky could see that the gentlemen present hadn't thought of such a horrifying possibility.

"Of course not. Don't be a gudgeon." The Sprig recovered first. "He couldn't marry as Wincanton. Wouldn't be legal—not even to mention moral—don't you know."

But the three were glaringly aware of the golden opportunity afforded the penniless actor. Such a marriage would be illegal, right enough. But it also would create a climate for blackmail, the high price of hushing a scandal.

"I'd never let you get away with it," Wincanton said between clenched teeth.

"Get away with what?" Nicky asked innocently as he rose to his feet, drawing on the major's best pair of gray kid gloves. He was well aware of what was going on in the others' minds and was thoroughly enjoying their agitation. "I plan to carry out the terms of our wager as set down in Brooks' betting book. And if any of you *gentlemen*"—he sneered at the word— "interfere in those terms in any way, well, it will behoove me to report that breach of faith to whoever's in charge of that sort of thing. Surely the club has a review committee to see that everything's right and tight? If not, they can always form one."

That seemed a good-enough speech to exit on, so the actor did so, closing the door emphatically behind him.

On his way back up Lansdown Hill, Nicky chuckled to himself over Major Wincanton's discomfort. Let the stiff-rumped toff stew in his own juice a bit. Do him good. Nicky took pleasure in dwelling on the major's out-of-joint proboscis; it gave him a reprieve from his own problems. But halfway to the Crescent he reluctantly began to review his own situation.

For it wasn't the bet alone that was holding him in Bath. And the others wronged him gravely when they thought he'd go through a marriage with blackmail in mind. He'd seen the opportunity right away, of course. He was no fool. Nor was he a blackguard. The truth, which he now acknowledged for the first time, was that he was being downright quixotic. Chivalrous. Or, better yet, a hopeless idiot. Nicky could hardly believe it of himself, but there it was. He simply couldn't bear the thought of being the second fiancé in a row to humiliate Lady Venetia Lowther. He was convinced she'd never recover from such a double blow to her self-esteem. He was buying time now to allow her to call off the engagement to "Major Wincanton" of her own volition. Not because she was once more forced by a shattering discovery to do so but simply because she would have decided that they wouldn't suit. Then later, if she should ever find out she'd been deceived, at least she would have the satisfaction of knowing that she'd sent the scoundrel packing. She might be angry, but she would not be hurt by the experience.

His instinct told him that Venetia was already regretting their betrothal as much as he was. For from the moment that Lady Stoke had sprung her trap, their relationship had changed. The free and easy friewndship they'd developed had deteriorated into awkward politeness. And on the rare occasions when they were alone together, Venetia carefully avoided mentioning their engagement, a state of affairs that Nicky welcomed.

But it was not only the subject she avoided; he was convinced she was avoiding him as well, a second circumstance that he rejoiced in. The only time she had actually sought him out was after her meeting with Wincanton.

Nicky mulled that over as he walked along, still limping out of force of habit. She hadn't seemed at all suspicious of the coincidence. If he hadn't just become a reformed punter, he'd bet on that. Still, when she'd had more time to think about it— Damn Wincanton's eyes! The Sprig was right. He'd no business leaving London. Things were already at sixes and sevens without him coming on the scene to mess them up still more!

From the bow window of her bedchamber, Venetia watched him walking down the Crescent and caught her breath. "Oh, it's only Win, you pea goose." She corrected her misapprehension, at the same time acknowledging to herself that she'd actually been watching for Mr. Forbes to pay his visit. Her cheeks burned at that damning bit of insight. It was almost four o'clock, late now for morning calls. He wasn't going to come. And she didn't feel up to facing Wincanton at the moment. Perhaps exercise would help clear up some of the confusion she was feeling. She quickly put a rose gros de Naples spencer jacket over her pale pink round dress and chose her most becoming high-crowned bonnet to wear with it.

Venetia would have vowed that her direction was aimless, her route chosen from force of habit. When she did wake up to the fact that her feet had carried her to the heart of the city, it became necessary, for her peace of mind, to invent an acceptable reason for having done so. Hence she was hurrying to Smith's haberdashers when Gareth came driving down Stall Street and spied her.

"Lady Venetia!" he called, and she didn't really need to turn around to discover who it was. Even so, her heart skipped a beat in confirmation at the sight of the man in the five-caped greatcoat who was wearing his curly beaver centered on his head, not tilted rakishly, in the style favored by her fiancé.

"Could I take you wherever you're going?"

Since he was clogging the street's traffic with his curricle, it seemed the thing to do to hurry over and be handed up.

"Now where to?" He smiled down at her as he flicked his reins.

"To Smith's shop." She smiled back.

"You'll have to tell me where that is. I'm a stranger to Bath."

"Oh, my goodness, we've passed it!" She'd been just two doors away when he'd picked her up. He glanced back over his shoulder, saw the swinging sign, and laughed. She joined in, though she felt rather foolish.

"Surely your errand can wait, then. I was just going to explore a bit. And I need a guide. What would be a scenic drive?"

"Have you seen Sydney Gardens yet?" she asked, and, when he said no, pointed the way to Pulteney Street.

"You haven't told me, Major Forbes," she said as they crossed the shop-lined Florentine-style bridge, "just why you've come to Bath."

"For the same reason everyone comes, I collect."

"Surely not for a course of the waters. I'll not believe it."

"Why not? The Pump Room is certainly popular. The stuff must be good for something."

"For gout and rheumatism, perhaps, though I'm not convinced of it entirely. But no one your age comes to Bath for the waters. Indeed, according to Aunt Louisa, no one who is not at least an octogenarian comes here at all."

"No? Are you trying to tell me it won't cure my limp?" he teased her. "Well, I am dished. I'd set my heart on it. Still," he added casually, "you did say that your fiancé is similarly afflicted. And if it has not cured him—well, there's no use hoping. Oh, by the by, since you've pointed out that he and I resemble each other, I trust he's not an octogenarian."

"Hardly," she said, laughing. "Oh, I see what you mean. But he came to visit our Aunt Louisa."

"And met you? Fortunate fellow. Just goes to show, I expect, that it pays to be familial. I must make a note of that."

The look he gave her was so intense that she quickly launched into a catalogue of the treats that would have been in store for him in Sydney Gardens if only he'd chosen to come in the summertime. Why, on gala nights there were music, singing, transparences, fireworks, illuminations, all sorts of delights. Vauxhall in London could boast of little more, she assured him as he drove his rig through the pleasure garden entryway.

When she pointed out the labyrinth just beyond the carriage drive, he insisted upon stopping to explore it.

"At your own peril," she said with a laugh. "I've been in it once before and must warn you that I became hopelessly lost."

"Well, obviously you got out. How did you manage?"

"I'm ashamed to say that Aunt Louisa and I simply stood and shouted till our friend Sir George Carstairs came and rescued us. It pains me to say so, but men as a rule do seem better at directions than we women. I hope now for both our sakes that I don't generalize. Are you good at finding your way through mazes, Major Forbes?"

"I was used to think so," he replied a little grimly. "Now I'm not quite as sure."

"Well, that's not exactly reassuring." Lady Venetia paused at the opening, trying unsuccessfully to remember which path she'd taken before between the tall, obscuring hedges. "But since I already know I'm hopeless and your navigational ability is merely in doubt, you make the decision. Which way—left or right?"

"Left," he said without hesitation, and took her hand.

"Goodness, that was decisive." She smiled up at him, her cheeks pink from the nippy air, her eyes sparkling. He thought she looked enchanting. "No one would suspect that you had no idea where you're going. I hesitate to ask it, but is that the secret of being a good army officer?"

"Giving commands when you've no idea whether or not you've made the right decision? Perhaps. But in this instance I've no reason at all to hesitate."

"You mean you are actually that confident of finding your way?"

"No, I mean I don't actually care whether we get out or not."

Even so, he did manage to guide them, by the expedient of trial and error, through the spiraling half mile of dead ends and open passageways, to the center of the labyrinth. And once that objective had been realized, it seemed appropriate to celebrate the achievement with a triumphant hug. And once they'd experienced that much intimacy, there seemed no hope of avoiding the kiss that followed and left them both quite devastated.

Lady Venetia gazed up into Major Forbes's face, and the look was stricken. "Please forgive me," she whispered. "I'm entirely to blame. I should never have come here with you. Whatever could I have been thinking of? Oh, what a dreadful coil this is."

Gareth Wincanton could not trust himself to speak. It would not do for him to tell the lady he was falling in love with that the coil she spoke of so feelingly was far, far worse than she could possibly imagine.

Chapter
Fourteen

MISS AMABEL FAWNHOPE'S FIRST ACT UPON ARRIVING IN Bath was to visit backstage at the Theatre Royal. It came to her as a bitter disappointment to discover that Nicky was not one of the company there. Indeed, nobody had seen or heard of him. This news had been almost too much to bear, for it made her realize that she was not half so much in pursuit of Gareth Wincanton as in need of the solace Nicky alone could give.

Shame on him, anyway! He could have let her know his change of plans. But how like him. It would never even occur to him that she might worry. Amabel accepted the theory of several of the company personnel that he'd most likely gone to Cheltenham. The touring company there had just lost a romantic lead. Nicky, no doubt, had gotten wind of it.

Her colleagues were sorry for her disappointment, but from the theater's point of view, Miss Fawnhope could not have shown up at a more opportune time. "Providential" was the only word for her unexpected appearance. For the young actress playing Jessica was suffering from the grippe and had lost her voice. Could Amabel not fill the role just for tonight?

Since she'd played the part many times before, it would have been unthinkable for her to refuse. Besides, what difference would one evening make? Perhaps it was just as well that she'd be occupied, for now that she'd run pell-mell to Bath, she was not at all sure what action she should take. She had been

269

relying solely on Nicky's guidance. Now she'd have to think the whole thing through herself.

The counterfeit Major Wincanton had run out of excuses for avoiding the Theatre Royal. So when Sir George Carstairs asked Lady Stoke and her niece and nephew to be his guests for *The Merchant of Venice*, Nicky joined the others in accepting the invitation with every appearance of delight. Then at the first opportunity he hurried off to Beauford Square to inspect the playbill. He breathed a sigh of relief when he did not recognize any of the cast names. Mr. Powell's company had, it seemed, continued on their tour. It should be reasonably safe now for Nicky to attend the performance. No need for a new flare-up of the old war wound.

Still, it was not a festive party that entered the theater box that evening. Venetia had been preoccupied throughout dinner. Also she'd appeared a trifle pale. "Wan" was the word Lady Stoke had used when wondering whether Venetia might be sickening for something. Nicky, after weighing the perils of appearing in public against the awkwardness of being left alone with his fiancée, had finally chosen the more gentlemanly course. He'd offered to forgo the evening's treat and stay at home with her. But Lady Venetia had reassured them both that her health was excellent.

Even so, for whatever reason, after they'd been seated in the box Sir George had engaged for them, she retained the same listless manner and showed not the slightest interest in quizzing the company as her aunt was busy doing while punctuating her perusal with running comments on this one's jewels and that one's gown.

Nicky, too, was scanning the audience intently, prepared to flee if he saw anyone he knew. He breathed a silent sigh of relief when the only familiar faces he spotted belonged to Lord Piggot-Jones and Mr. St. Leger, who were in a box directly opposite. The only thing he need fear from those two was that his companions might notice that the pair constantly kept their quizzing glasses trained upon their box. Nicky aimed a ferocious scowl across the void that stretched above the occupants

270

of the pit. The two Londoners took the hint and directed their gazes elsewhere.

But when the curtain went up, the professional side of Nicky's nature took over and he became oblivious to everything except the drama taking place onstage. He studied the actors intently, watching bits of business, observing individual techniques for character development. He was especially intent upon the actor playing Shylock and grudgingly acknowledged the genius of Edmund Kean's revolutionary interpretation of that role.

Lady Venetia was also contemplating the art of acting. Not so much as demonstrated upon this stage—she remained for the most part oblivious to the action there—it was the actor's world in general she wondered about, and whether or not Major Nicholas Forbes was connected with that world.

He had denied it vehemently, of course. And she felt almost disloyal in doubting that denial, for Venetia was fairly certain at this point that she was in love with him. But there was no getting around the fact that Major Forbes was a man of mystery.

For one thing, he'd never bothered to explain just how it was that Mr. Powell had come to know him. At this point Venetia took herself in hand. How absurd it was for her to think that actors had no acquaintances outside their own profession. But still, there was no denying that Nicholas Forbes revealed very, very little about himself. Apart from his military career, that is. About that he was quite expansive. Could an actor become an officer? Highly unlikely. But she did wish that his life in England were not such a closed book to her. A sprinkling of polite applause as two new characters took the stage drew Venetia's attention back to the drama unfolding there.

Nicky's had never wavered. He was sitting on the edge of his seat, with his elbows resting on the box rail, when Amabel made her entrance. So absorbed had he become in the dramatic action that this lovely Jessica was merely Shylock's daughter until she spoke. For a moment he froze in horror, unable to believe the testimony of his eyes and ears. Then an instinct for self-preservation took control. He began to quietly inch his chair backward until he was screened by Lady Venetia, who came out of her reverie long enough to glance curiously his way. "May take a nap," he whispered by way of explanation. From his pallor, she wondered if he was feeling pain.

As the play progressed, Nicky gradually relaxed. He was certain now that Amabel had not seen him. If she had, it would be just like her to come dashing around to their box during the interval and stage a family reunion. What the devil was she doing in Bath, anyhow?

The answer, upon reflection, was obvious. Chasing Wincanton, of course. She'd read the *Gazette* announcement. Well, he'd have to see her first thing tomorrow morning and clue her in on his new identity. Nicky flinched as he imagined her reaction. But he couldn't risk doing nothing. The little busybody was bound to manage somehow to let his particular cat out of the bag. He sat back in the shadows and peered over Lady Venetia's shoulder, once more caught up in the action on the stage. God, but Bella was beautiful! And damn good, too. He felt a surge of pride as his eyes followed her.

Amabel's performance was actually a far greater tour de force than Nicholas realized. For she had seen him. And even as she spoke her lines, a part of her attention was fixed upon Sir George Carstairs's box, which she observed from the corner of her eye at every opportunity.

Miss Fawnhope was accustomed to holding her audience spellbound. It had therefore been an affront to her artistry when she'd become aware that a member of that audience was beating a retreat. The fact that she'd managed to hide the shock of discovery when her eyes, still in character, had traveled in that direction was a tribute to the stern discipline of her art. And the fact that she was able to keep the box under surveillance without revealing that she did so was a second testimonial.

After her initial identification of the gentleman, whose red hair alone was now visible, Amabel had paid little attention to him. Having finally located Gareth Wincanton was enough. It was his fiancée who now claimed all her interest. By the time Amabel made her final exit she had memorized Lady Venetia's every feature.

As soon as the curtain came down, Nicky rushed his party out of the theater. When Lady Stoke protested this unseemly haste, his excuse was to get a jump on the other patrons and avoid the crush. But since Sir George's coachman had not felt the same compunction and was well back in the long line of carriages queued to pick up their owners, they were forced to stand around for several minutes with Nicky glancing repeatedly and surreptitiously over his shoulder.

It was a close thing. He was handing the ladies inside the carriage when he heard a voice trill, "Oh, Major Wincanton!"

The little gudgeon had mistaken him! Well, she wouldn't do so for long, and he couldn't rely on tipping her the wink. Nicky gave Sir George a quick shove that almost landed him in Louisa's lap, then hissed "Spring 'em!" at the driver as he leaped into the coach himself.

This order was impossible to execute, due to the crush of traffic, but they did begin to move away at a pace sufficient to halt Miss Fawnhope in her tracks.

" 'Pon my soul, I believe that little actress was hailing you," Sir George observed, looking back in her direction through his quizzing glass.

"How odd." Lady Stoke craned her neck to see. "Do you know her, Win?"

"Never saw her before in my life," Nicky observed virtuously. "Couldn't've been me she was after. You must've mistaken the matter, sir."

"Oh, to be sure, I must have." Sir George Carstairs, man of the world, awoke suddenly to the fact that he'd been most tactless and tried to rectify his gaffe. "Come to think of it, I do believe that 'Will Canton' was the name she shouted. 'Will Canton' sounds much like Wincanton, don't you know. Some chap in the carriage just behind us, I've no doubt."

"Hmmm" was Lady Stoke's reaction.

Lady Venetia, though, made no comment at all. She'd missed the entire episode. Her thoughts were clearly elsewhere.

Chapter
Fifteen

DESPITE HIS RESOLVE TO SEE AMABEL EARLY NEXT MORN-ing, Nicky Forbes slept late.

The actress and Lady Venetia did not. They both were up be-times, and both appeared in the Pump Room at eleven o'clock.

Miss Fawnhope's objective was to consult the guest list and see if Major Wincanton had entered his direction. Lady Vene-tia, who had announced her intention of going for a walk, had been entrusted to carry a message there for Lady Stoke.

Venetia was seated at a table with its recipient, a dowager who sipped mineral water while holding her nose, when she grew aware that she was under scrutiny. It took her a moment to realize that the lovely young lady staring at her was the ac-tress who had played the part of Jessica the night before.

As Venetia took her leave of her aunt's friend and crossed the room, the actress accosted her. "Lady Venetia Lowther, I believe?" Amabel inquired.

Venetia, puzzled but polite, acknowledged her identity.

"My name is Miss Fawnhope." Amabel's accents were aris-tocratic to a fault. "There is something I think I should tell you."

Just why Venetia was suddenly afraid that the actress's busi-ness had to do with Nicholas Forbes defied all reason. No one knew of that association except her and Nicholas. At least they did not unless Nicholas had told them. This much she was certain of: whatever the beauty wished to confide was bound to be unpleasant.

As the two faced each other across a table that commanded a view of the patrons clustered around the pump, Amabel was beginning to lose some of her self-assurance. Ever since she'd read of Major Wincanton's betrothal, she'd had but one thought in mind—to pay him back for his shabby treatment. Revenge, as she'd pictured it, would be sweet indeed. The problem was that while it would be one thing to grind Wincanton into the dust, exacting vengeance upon this polite young lady, with her troubled eyes, was not the same thing at all. Still, what other course was available? Amabel scotched her scruples and came directly to the point.

"You and I, Lady Venetia, have something in common, it seems. Major Wincanton."

"Gareth?" Venetia was unaware that she sounded relieved. "I'm sorry, but I can't recall that he has mentioned you."

"It ain't—isn't likely that he has. It would not be 'gentlemanly.' And before all else, Gareth's a gentleman." Amabel was warming to her work now, her anger rekindling. "He would not consider it at all the thing to tell his fiancée that while he was offering her marriage he was offering a carte blanche to me."

Venetia was too stunned to speak. Her face drained of color. Amabel felt a pang of sympathy, which she quickly suppressed. "I—I don't believe you," Lady Venetia finally managed to say.

Amabel shrugged and rose, anxious to put the interview to an end. Things were not going at all the way she'd imagined. Damn Wincanton, anyhow. Why was it always the females who did the suffering? "You don't have to believe me unless you wish to." Her voice was pitying. "I just thought you ought to know."

She'd taken several steps away when Lady Venetia called after her, "Wait, Miss Fawnhope. There's something I'd like to ask you." As Amabel turned inquiringly, Venetia lowered her voice. "You're in the theater. Have you ever heard of an actor called Nicholas Forbes?"

"Nicholas Forbes? Why, yes, of course. I should say I have! Don't tell me that you actually know Nicky!"

"Oh, no. I don't know him. I don't actually know him at all. The name just came up recently, and I was curious. Just curious, that's all. Thank you for enlightening me."

Amabel was at a loss to understand why this puzzling conversation seemed to have upset her ladyship even more than the news of her fiancé's infidelity had.

Major Gareth Wincanton thought it might possibly have been the worst moment of his life. After strolling across the street from the White Hart, he had looked in on the Pump Room, where his eyes riveted upon Lady Venetia Lowther and Miss Amabel Fawnhope deep in conversation. For an instant he had stood immobilized. But military tactician that he was, he soon rallied his forces to beat a hasty, if inglorious, retreat.

Once safely out of the line of sight of the two females who, in entirely different ways, had turned his life upside-down, he broke into a cold and clammy sweat. Together, they were bound to bring about his total ruin. Every instinct told him to lose no time in racing back to his rooms, packing his boxes, and haring off to London. But like some doomed classical tragic figure, Wincanton seemed incapable of avoiding the inexorable unfolding of his fate.

Instead, he stood lurking in the Abbey churchyard, watching the Pump Room door. As Miss Fawnhope made her exit and hurried off in the direction of the theater, he stepped behind a pillar of the colonnade. But when Lady Venetia emerged, some minutes later, the major took one look at her stricken face and promptly lost his self-preservation instinct. He squared his shoulders, set his jaw, left off skulking, and went to intercept her.

As for Venetia, she found nothing strange at all in the fact that Nicholas Forbes had suddenly materialized, taken her elbow, and was guiding her toward the Abbey grounds. They climbed the steps leading to the terrace, then went to stand by a stone wall and stare sightlessly at the Avon. He gave her a few minutes to compose herself before he asked huskily, "Can you tell me about it?"

"I shouldn't. You'll think I'm making far too much of the whole business." She spoke so softly that he was forced to stoop to hear it. "Everyone did before. A lady is supposed to overlook that sort of thing. Indeed, not even to know it. But I don't think I could ever learn to share my husband. Especially"—her voice was bitter—"always knowing that I was second choice. I'm proud, you see."

"You could never be second choice."

"You think not?" Her smile was self-mocking. "Then you'll be amazed to learn that I only have to become promised to someone to discover he keeps a harem."

At that point they were joined by a group of sightseers exploring the Abbey and its grounds. "Let's go," he said. They walked down the steps in a silence that persisted until they reached the Orange Grove. "I don't see any oranges anywhere." He glanced pointedly at the trees, trying to lighten her mood a bit.

"It's named for the Prince of Orange, not the fruit." She managed a wan smile as he led her to a bench that faced the promenade.

"You'll have to explain the 'harem' remark," he said, prodding gently.

She was under better control now. But she pulled a handkerchief from her reticule, dabbed at her eyes to discourage any tears that might lurk there, then twisted the tiny square of linen with nervous fingers. "Well, I was rather indulging in hyperbole," she admitted. "There's no such thing as a one-woman harem, is there? But the lowering truth is, I've been promised in marriage twice, and in both instances it's been my bad luck to discover that my fiancé is in love with someone else."

"You mean there was someone else before Ni—before Major Wincanton?"

Venetia, fortunately, was too steeped in misery to notice the slip. "Oh, yes. I was betrothed to someone I knew in Spain. We were considered the 'perfect couple.' Only he had fixed his interest elsewhere." Wincanton listened with increasing foreboding as she went on to describe the shock and revulsion she'd felt upon learning that the gentleman she was supposed to marry had already established an out-of-wedlock household.

"But surely he would have given up his mistress."

"Oh, he said as much. Though I've every reason to believe he loved her. But then you'd be amazed at the sacrifices one is willing to make for a fortune. I was not so heartless as to demand it of him, however. You see, I'd also discovered that his mistress was *enceinte*. I could hardly condone abandoning an expectant mother. Though to give him credit, I never thought for an instant that he would."

"Oh, my God," Wincanton groaned. He waited for a group of strollers to pass and then observed, "But surely yours is a case of 'once burned, twice shy,' is it not? I can't believe that your Major Wincanton has that sort of arrangement."

"Indeed, he hasn't." She laughed bitterly. "But not from want of trying. You see, I've just had a very enlightening interview with a Miss Amabel Fawnhope, who told me that while Major Wincanton was pursuing me with a view toward matrimony, he was offering her a most generous carte blanche."

"That sounds a bit improbable," he observed weakly. "I mean to say, when could he have found the time?"

"You think she's lying, then?" She clutched the straw and then abandoned it. "Well, I do not. Not for a moment. As to how he managed, she didn't say. Perhaps he wrote after our betrothal was announced. Anyway, 'how' has nothing to say in the matter. For I'm sure she told the truth. Also, I'm sure it's Miss Fawnhope he really wants. What gentleman would not? She's a diamond of the first water. I doubt I've seen a more bewitching creature."

"You could not have looked in your glass, then."

"That's gallant of you, Nicholas. But it's also fustian. I've no illusions. I simply have to resign myself to the fact that among females of my class, marriages of convenience are the rule and not the exception—and that gentlemen fall in love with women of quite another stamp."

"Now, that really *is* fustian," he said savagely. "You should not jump to such daft conclusions. My God, you haven't even given Wincanton the chance to defend himself. Most likely he doesn't love this woman at all."

"You wouldn't say that if you'd seen her."

"Oh, wouldn't I? Well, for the sake of argument, let's admit that she's all you say. 'Bewitching' was the term you used, was it not? But you surely must know, Venetia, that a man can desire a woman without having his heart involved. It's not much of a testimonial for my sex, I'll grant you, but there it is. Could you not give your major the benefit of the doubt?"

"Oh, but I do." She took a deep, shuddering breath, trying to hold back the tears that were threatening to flow. "Not in the way you mean, perhaps, but you'd be amazed at how much more sympathetic I am with Gareth than I ever was with Fletcher, my first fiancé. You see, Nicholas, I've no trouble at all now in seeing how it can so easily happen—to fall in love with the wrong sort of person entirely, I mean."

He was at a total loss now, with no idea what to say. "That's most broad-minded of you," he ventured.

"I know. I can scarcely believe it of myself. Why, I've even developed a certain appreciation for the institution of carte blanche. What a pity it is that ladies haven't the opportunity to make the same sort of arrangements that gentlemen do. But now I am being absurd." The tears suddenly spilled over.

Wincanton took her in his arms. "Don't cry, Venetia. Please don't cry, my darling. This can all be straightened out. I'm sure of it. I'd stake my life that Wincanton doesn't really love that actress."

"Oh, but it's not Gareth that I'm crying for. How could you even think so? It's not his deception that's destroyed me. It's yours. Oh, Nicholas, why did you have to lie to me? Why could you not simply have admitted from the start that you're an actor? If I had known, why, then—perhaps, just possibly— I could have walked away before I came to love you."

Chapter Sixteen

NICKY WENT FIRST TO THE THEATER TO DISCOVER AMAbel's direction. Then, as he sauntered the short distance to her Queen Square lodging house, he wasn't overly concerned that he had overslept. Bella was not noted for early rising at any time, and after a performance it was her habit to lie in bed till noon. He was therefore amazed to learn from a rather starchy landlady named Mrs. Massey that Miss Fawnhope had gone out. "As to where she's gone," the woman replied to Nicky's probing, "I really couldn't say."

It took considerable persuasion on his part, laced with considerable more charm, for the landlady to finally allow Nicky to come inside and wait. She did not as a rule rent to theatrical people, she'd explained, but since her previous tenant had left unexpectedly and Miss Fawnhope was only temporary, she had made this one exception. But the inference was clear. There'd be no "goings-on" within her premises. It was only when Nicky explained that he was Miss Fawnhope's brother that he gained access to a small and shabby parlor. Mrs. Massey's sniff had made it clear that while she didn't accept this spurious kinship for a moment, it would do for any neighbors who might be peeping through the curtains across the way.

The waiting seemed interminable. It had come to him as a relief the night before, albeit an awkward one, when Amabel had shouted "Wincanton" after him, instead of "Nicky." But now he wondered if she could have gone looking for the major this morning and been told she'd find that gentleman at Lansdown Circle. Just as his anxiety reached alarming heights, the front door opened and he heard her footsteps in the hall.

Amabel glanced into the parlor, then went rigid. But her initial hostile look turned quickly to astonishment and then delight. "Nicky! I thought you were Wincanton!" She rushed across the room and flung herself into his arms. "Oh, Nicky, Nicky darling, I'm so glad to see you." She reached up to peck him on the cheek. The caress was intercepted by his quicker lips. The intensity and duration of the ensuing kiss would have certainly cast considerable doubt on his fraternal status if the landlady had happened to be watching.

"Oh, Nicky," Amabel said rather breathlessly when he finally released her, "you're a sight for sore eyes. You really are. But wherever have you sprung from? I thought you must be in Cheltenham."

"No, I've been here all along, Bella. But it's a complicated story. And I think you'd best sit down to hear it."

They shared Mrs. Massey's unyielding sofa as Nicky poured out the story of the wager and of all the ensuing complications that bit of drunken folly had brought on.

Amabel was a good listener. She gasped aloud occasionally, her lovely eyes grew even wider, but she did not speak till he was finished.

"Let me see if I have this straight, then. Gareth is not really engaged to Lady Venetia. You are."

"In a manner of speaking, that's right. Though, of course, when she learns—"

She clapped a hand across his mouth. "Oh, please, don't say a word yet. My head is spinning. Let's see, now. Lady Venetia became betrothed to Major Gareth Wincanton, who is really you. And now Major Wincanton has come to town, pretending to be Nicholas Forbes."

"Well, that was not actually his intention. To pose as me, I mean. Venetia simply jumped to that conclusion when she met him, because she knew through a chance meeting we had with Mr. Powell—he was playing Claudius here, you know, but now his troupe's moved on to Nottingham. Anyhow, he said he mistook me for someone else, so she knew that there was a cove loose somewhere who looked like me; ergo, she—"

"Nicky!" Amabel's tone was almost a shriek. "Will you stop it? I don't think I can bear any more. It's all too utterly improbable. Like one of those dreadful comedies of William Shakespeare where everybody is really somebody else."

"Well, at least Wincanton and I are the same sex," Nicky said defensively. "But forget my tangle for a while and tell me why you're here. Not that I can't guess. You saw the notice in the *Gazette*. Am I right?"

"Yes, I came to have it out with Gareth." She looked quite ferocious.

"Did you mind so terribly much, Bella? That he was going to be married, I mean."

"Mind? I was furious. Do you know what kind of offer he made *me*, Nicky? Two thousand pounds a year and a house. That's the kind of offer he made me!"

This time *his* eyes widened. He gave a long, low whistle. "Two thousand pounds plus a house? So what did you tell him, Bella?"

"Why, to go to the devil, of course. *I'm* not good enough for a marriage offer, Nicky." Her eyes filled with tears; whether of hurt or rage, he'd no notion.

"I know I've asked before, but did you love him, Bella?"

"Oh, how should I know? I suppose I did. Well, perhaps I didn't. But I wanted him to propose marriage. That I am sure of."

"Well, if you didn't love the man, the devil with him." He put a brotherly arm around her, and she snuggled up against his shoulder. "I know I shouldn't say it, Bella, but I'm glad about the way it all turned out. My reason tells me you've probably been a fool, but there it is. I'm still glad you didn't accept Wincanton's offer of carte blanche."

"The carte blanche!" Amabel sat up suddenly and turned a horrified gaze upon him. "I had forgotten! The carte blanche! Oh, my heavens! I've really loosed the cat among the pigeons!"

"What are you ranting about now, for God's sake, Bella?"

"Oh, Nicky, I've done the most dreadful thing," she wailed.

"I've just told Lady Venetia that at the same time you were pursuing her with marriage in mind, you were planning to live a life of sin with me."

Lady Stoke was waiting to waylay Nicky on his return to the Crescent. She appeared much agitated. "Something dreadful's happened to Venetia" were her first words. "I've never seen her in such a state. She's locked in her room and won't open the door to me. You see if you can discover what the matter is, Win dear."

But when he tapped softly on Venetia's door, a muffled voice replied, "Please go away."

"It's me, Venetia. We need to talk."

"Not now."

"Yes, now. I know what's bothering you, and I can explain. Do you wish me to do it from out here for everyone to hear?" He looked pointedly at the upstairs maid, who turned brick-red and began vigorously polishing the table she was poised over.

The key turned in the lock. Nicky opened it and went inside while Venetia once more threw herself, facedown, upon her bed. He pulled up a chair, for all the world like an attending physician, and reached for her hand. She quickly jerked it away.

"Be reasonable, Venetia. We can't talk like this. Please, look at me."

He was almost sorry he'd insisted, for when she did sit up and prop herself against the pillows, her face was tear-stained and puffy-eyed, altogether quite pathetically heartwrenching.

"I don't know where to begin." He would not have been half so conscience-stricken if he were guilty merely of the thing she believed he was. "I know that Bella—Miss Fawnhope, I mean to say—has talked to you. But what I'm afraid of is that you're taking it the wrong way entirely, looking at the situation in the worst possible light, that is."

Nicky ran his fingers through his hair in desperation, unconsciously making a hash of its artful Titus arrangement. He was acutely conscious though of the hash he was making of the conversation. But how the deuce to proceed? Above all things,

283

he wanted Lady Venetia to call off their betrothal, but he certainly didn't wish to crush her in the process. Just when she'd finally recovered from the blow of discovering that one fiancé had a mistress of long standing, she'd been planted a leveler a second time. How *used* she must be feeling. Of a sudden his concern took precedence over his instinct for survival.

"You mustn't get the wrong idea," he floundered on, "the way you did with that other cove you were engaged to. You seemed to come away from that business thinking that the only possible reason any man would marry you is for your fortune." He held up a hand to forestall any comment she might make. "Please, hear me out. This ain't easy, you see, since I'm in the wrong of it. I just want you to know that I agree it's right and proper you should break off our engagement. If I were you, I'd do it in a flash. What's not right and proper is for you to keep clinging to the notion that you ain't up to snuff where the opposite sex is concerned. What I mean to say is, you're one of the most desirable females I've ever met."

There was no doubting his sincerity. Venetia's eyes were fixed upon his face. She scarcely breathed.

"That was the problem, don't you see. Not the other way around." He suddenly grew inspired. "I haven't played you false. It was Amabel—Miss Fawnhope—I betrayed. Our attachment was of long standing, you see, and the last thing I'd intended was to get involved with any other female. But then you and I got caught in the storm that day. And then you slipped. And there I was, holding you. Well, you know what happened. God's truth, I couldn't help myself. But I am sorry, sorrier than I can ever manage to express, that I've put you through all this. I know it must be something of a trial, having to keep calling engagements off. But you mustn't let it sour you on romance. The right man will come along for you. I'm sure of it. You know what they always say—third time lucky."

There was a long, pregnant silence. Nicky squirmed uneasily in his chair as Venetia continued to study him. She applied the sodden handkerchief she'd been twisting to her nose and then blew vigorously. The action seemed to bring resolve.

"Do you plan to marry her?" she asked.

"Bella, you mean?"

"I mean Miss Fawnhope. She's the mistress under discussion, isn't she? Tell me. Are there others?"

"Of course not." He was stung.

"Well, then. Do you plan to marry her?"

Nicky was having trouble keeping his personae straight. He had to remind himself that he was Major Gareth Wincanton, toffee-nosed snob. "N-no. I don't think I can do that. Wouldn't be the thing. An actress, don't you know."

Tears welled once more into her eyes, much to his consternation. "Yes, I can see that marriage under those circumstances is quite unthinkable." She took a deep, shuddery breath. "Well, then, that's that. There's no need to break off our engagement."

"Oh, I say! You can't be serious!"

Venetia interpreted Nicky's expression as amazement at her broad-mindedness. It would have been nearer to the mark to say he was aghast.

"Oh, I'm quite serious. If you don't intend to marry the woman you love, there's no reason you shouldn't marry me. It will be a splendid match in the eyes of the world. It will please our families. And we should deal quite well together."

"Oh, no, we wouldn't. What I mean to say is, you mustn't. Damn it all, Venetia, you have to break off our engagement. You can't have that sort of marriage. You were right in the first place when you booted out that other cove. You deserve much better."

"No"—she sighed deeply—"that's just what I don't deserve." Her resolve stiffened. "You've been open with me, Gareth. Now it's my turn to be honest. You see, I've come to understand just what it means to fall in love with someone entirely unsuitable."

"You have?" He looked skeptical.

"Oh, yes. It's true. And it's quite ironic, really. You're in love with an actress. I've fallen in love with an actor. So now you can see why I should make you the perfect wife." She laughed shakily. "I doubt that many couples have quite so much in common."

"You—Lady Venetia Lowther—a viscount's daughter—in love with an actor?" His jaw dropped. "I'll not believe it."

"And why not?" she countered. "You, Major Gareth Wincanton, grandson of an earl, in love with an actress? What's sauce for the gander, you know."

"But who? When? Why?" he sputtered. "My word, surely not Mr. Powell! I know he's elegant—could pass for a toff any day—does, in fact—typecast in all those king-duke-knight roles. But he's old enough to be your father."

"Of course it's not Mr. Powell. Don't be absurd. I don't even know him."

"Well, who, then?"

She sighed deeply. "Does it matter?"

"Of course it matters!"

"Well, if you must know. You may remember my mentioning that I'd met your look-alike. Well, I've seen him a few times since then. And I'd simply assumed he was a gentleman, you see. But then, well, just today—from your Miss Fawnhope, to be exact—I've discovered that he's an *actor*." The term *highwayman* would have sounded less distasteful.

Nicky stared transfixed, convinced his ears had just deceived him. "Now, let me get this straight." He spoke slowly, deliberately. "You're telling me that you've actually fallen in love with Major—I mean to say, with an *actor* named Nicholas Forbes?"

Her face flamed. "Well, I collect he actually is a major. I didn't think to ask Miss Fawnhope about—" She did not conclude her sentence. Her listener was doubled up with laughter.

"I really can't see why you find the situation so amusing," she said icily when he'd somewhat recovered and was wiping his streaming eyes. "I certainly did not develop a case of the whoops when I learned of your attachment to Miss Fawnhope."

"No, no. You mustn't take offense. You don't understand." His shoulders began to shake again, but under the influence of her glare he managed a tolerable state of sobriety. "It's just that here you are, enacting this Cheltenham tragedy about loving an actor— By the by, you wouldn't consider actually marrying

286

one, would you? No? Well, I always thought as much. Love doesn't conquer all, now, does it, and the cove who thought that one up must've had maggots on the brain.

"I'm sorry. I realize I'm straying from the point a bit. But what I'm getting at is, there's no need to put yourself into such a taking. It's quite all right for you to be in love with him. For he ain't the actor, you see. I am— Oh, my God!"

Nicholas slapped his forehead, appalled at what he'd just let slip. "I've sunk the wager." He groaned piteously, then slumped down in his armchair, his head leaning for support against the carved top rail. "What a chivalrous imbecile I've turned out to be," he muttered hoarsely. "Don Quixote couldn't begin to touch me for mutton-headedness."

Venetia, on the other hand, had lost the last vestige of her earlier lethargy and had no tolerance for his. She came leaping out of bed to stand over him and barely restrained herself from seizing his shoulders and giving him a shake. "What do you mean Nicholas isn't the actor, you are?"

"Nothing. Nothing at all. Just got carried away there for a minute. Pay no attention to my ravings. It's been a trying day."

But Venetia's brain was racing, piecing together peculiar bits of conversation and certain odd behaviors that at the time she'd dismissed as merely eccentric. Now she pounced on the obvious conclusion. "You *are* Nicholas Forbes, aren't you, Win? Just like the man in Molland's pastry shop said you were. He had it right all along. You're Nicholas Forbes, the actor!" Venetia fairly crowed in the triumph of discovery.

"No need to shout it to the housetops," he protested in a whisper that he hoped would set the tone. "But yes, you're right, of course. I'm Forbes."

She sat back down on the edge of the bed, feeling suddenly a bit weak-kneed as the full implication of his admission struck her. "Then who—?"

"Major Gareth Wincanton, who else?" came the bitter answer.

"But I don't understand." The fact that she was whispering had more to do with failing breath than his example.

"I know you don't." He sighed. "I'm about to explain it to you."

And for the second time that day, he launched into a recital of the harebrained wager, this time tactfully skirting around the real reason for Wincanton's reluctance to leave town. It was a story that didn't improve much with the telling. It seemed to lack that certain edifying moral example that always makes a tale well worth repeating. But it held his audience. No doubt of that. Lady Venetia hung on his every word.

"So it was all just a drunken bet, then," she summed up at its conclusion.

"That's right. And I've just lost it."

He slumped in dejected silence, with closed eyes, trying to think of some way he might possibly pay off the wager. Bella could be good for a touch. No! The devil with that idea. He'd just have to run for it. That's what gentlemen did when their debts piled up: took a packet out of Dover for the Continent. Lived in exile.

Nicky cut short these morbid thoughts. After all, what did it matter? He squared his shoulders. It was a splendid thing that he'd just done. He'd always been a soft touch when it came to women's tears. A pretty woman's, anyhow. Why count the personal cost? He'd made Venetia happy. He opened his eyes wide then, wishing to imprint Venetia's glow of happiness upon his memory, to call it back to mind during the bleak days of his exile abroad. But Lady Venetia was not glowing. She looked, in fact, like a storm about to break.

"Oh, I say." Nicky could not help sounding a bit aggrieved at this improper response to his chivalric self-destruction. "I don't think you quite get the picture yet, Lady Venetia. You're in love with the right cove after all. There's absolutely no social barrier between you and your *amour propre*. Things couldn't be jollier."

"Oh, no?" she said between clenched teeth. "Well, if that's your opinion, you can't be thinking properly. Hasn't it occurred to you that if *you're* Nicholas Forbes and *he's* Major Gareth Wincanton, then *he's* the one who made the offer of carte blanche to that—that—actress? You may think the situation's jolly, but I say that history's odious habit of repeating itself has gone entirely too far this time!"

Chapter Seventeen

"BOTHERATION!" WAS LADY STOKE'S REACTION TO THE butler's announcement that her carriage was waiting. "Send it away, Hope. No, wait. I can't do that. Lady Mansfield would never forgive me if I left her one short at cards. Come ride with me, Win—oh, *Nicholas,* I should say, though I vow I'll never get used to the matter. Do come along, m'dear. We don't have time to waste, and I wish to tell you what's best to be done."

Nicky's opinion of Lady Stoke had always been high. Even so, it had soared in the past half hour. She had listened to his confession, made at Lady Venetia's insistence, with a breathless interest that was totally devoid of disapproval. "I vow it's better than a play," she'd pronounced at the conclusion of his recital. "And though I was completely taken in, I must say I'm not at all surprised."

Nicky had long since ceased trying to follow her ladyship's forays into the realm of logic. "You're not?" he asked.

"Not in the least. I remember thinking it was a miracle that any member of the Wincanton family could have your looks and charm."

Nicky tried to look modest and did not succeed.

"And then there were things about you that, well . . . did

not seem quite right. Can't put me finger on anything specific, but as I recall now, certain things that you did and said surprised me."

"Not quite the gentleman, I collect."

"No, that wasn't it." Her ladyship was quick to restore Nicky's pride of performance. "Come to think of it, you may have been a bit too much the gentleman. Still, that's merely hindsight, I expect. Wait—now I know what it was that seemed a bit off target. You're too likable by half. And Wincanton as a boy always kept himself to himself. I just concluded that the war had changed him. But then, I doubt that being shot at would make a person more agreeable. At least, I never heard of it."

Now, as they emerged from the house, Nicky saw Jocko Hodges standing in the street by the horses, while Lady Stoke's coachman waited in the driver's seat. His heart sank. "I think we should wait to finish our discussion," he whispered as he handed her ladyship into the barouche while the tiger ran around to take his place as postilion in the rumble.

"Nonsense!" her ladyship replied in her usual carrying tones. "We haven't time to waste. That's why I wanted you to ride with me, remember? The thing is, I wished to speak to you about the wager."

With effort Nicky repressed a groan. Experience had taught him it would do no good for him to try to point out the proximity of the tiger. As far as Lady Stoke was concerned, servants possessed no ears. Nicholas knew better. He could actually hear Jocko's snap to attention.

"What I wish to say is this. Just because you've told Venetia and me who you really are, there's no need to make confession a habit. I'll speak to her as soon as I get home. I'm positive that once she's cooled down a bit she'll see your side of the thing. After all, you're out of work and need the money. My only regret is that Wincanton himself won't be losing a bundle. He should get his comeuppance for playing such a shabby trick on me." Her eyes flashed with indignation. "Well, anyway, I don't see why you should be the one to suffer. So I'm confident that

290

I can persuade Venetia to continue our charade for two days longer. By then your time will be up and you can collect your little nest egg. Yes, by heaven, the more I think of it, the more I'm convinced that there's absolutely no need for you to tell those scoundrels you've been found out. Well, what do you say?"

"Oh, I couldn't agree more, your ladyship," Nicky replied hollowly. "There's absolutely no need for me to say anything at all."

Behind them, the tiger cleared his throat significantly.

Two hours later Mr. Nicholas Forbes entered the portals of the White Hart in compliance with a summons he'd received from Mr. Bertram St. Leger and Owen, Lord Piggot-Jones. A casual observer would have thought he hadn't a care in the world. He was dapperly dressed, in a coat of cerulean blue adorned with large brass buttons. Biscuit pantaloons hugged his well-shaped thighs and calves. His Hessians shone with champagne blacking; their golden tassles added to the gleam. He wore his curly-brimmed beaver at a cocky angle that exposed one side of his fiery hair. Heads turned admiringly as he proceeded up the stairs.

Even as he raised his hand to knock on Wincanton's door, it opened. A servant ushered him into the room, then silently departed. Four empty chairs were placed in a semicircle before the fireplace. St. Leger, Piggot-Jones, and Wincanton were standing with their backs to the glowing coals, a solemn tribunal, staring his way. The Sprig nodded coolly, and Nicky tipped his hat in answer, then laid it, along with his soft kid gloves and silver-handled stick, upon a Pembroke table by the door. He and Gareth Wincanton deliberately avoided each other's eyes.

He took the chair that St. Leger gestured toward, stretched out his legs, and crossed them, trying to appear nonchalant for the benefit of the gentry coves while at the same time attempting to dispel a growing feeling that he was being court-martialed—an eventuality he'd always considered a distinct possibility during his army days. That notion retreated a bit when St. Leger thrust a brandy in his hand. He doubted the army would be that considerate.

"We asked you here to explain yourself." Lord Piggot-Jones threw down the gauntlet as the others took their seats.

Nicky sampled his cognac deliberately, then shrugged. "There's nothing to explain. I made a good run of it, but the jig's up now. They know who I really am."

"They know because you told them!" the Sprig accused, his voice rising in indignation. "Wincanton's tiger heard you admit it. Of all the unprincipled, underhanded, unsporting—But then, what could you expect?" he finished bitterly. "It all comes of punting with a Cit. Should've known you'd have no proper notion of correct behavior."

"Well, then, that's that." Nicky smiled pleasantly at his hosts and set his glass on the candle stand near his elbow. "Seems there's no more to be said. I'll be on my way."

"The devil you will!" The Sprig jumped up to plant himself between Nicky and the door. The action seemed rather ill-advised, since Nicky topped him by at least six inches. "By God, you owe us an explanation."

"By God, I owe you nothing."

"I wouldn't go quite so far as that, old man," Piggot-Jones observed. "As a matter of fact, you owe me a thousand pounds."

"Well, I for one ain't too sure of that." The Sprig glared at his lordship, taking up an argument that had raged before Nicky's arrival. "I still say it's all Wincanton's doing. For I'll bet a monkey he's the one that caused Nicky here to have to blow the gab. Wincanton violated the terms of our wager by coming to Bath, and that's a fact. And I'm blessed if I'm going to pay up till I find out what's what.

"So look here, Nicky, old man, come down off your high ropes and be reasonable." His tone had shifted to cajolery. "If there was a good reason for you doing what you did, I think you should say so. You ain't in no better position than I am to cough up all that blunt."

"The difference is, he's no intention of paying up," Piggot-

Jones observed as he breathed on his quizzing glass and then polished it.

"That was a knavish thing to say." Major Wincanton made his first contribution to the conversation, and Piggot-Jones quailed before his stare. "You owe Forbes an apology."

"Sorry, old man. Don't know what came over me." His lordship smiled weakly in the actor's direction.

Nicky, who had been stung by Piggot-Jones's words despite their accuracy, nodded his way stiffly.

"Oh, do sit back down, Nicky," the Sprig implored, "and let's talk this thing out like gentlemen." He colored then as Nicky gave him a speaking look.

The actor did resume his chair, however, for upon sober reflection he was of the Sprig's frame of mind—it would be far better to nullify the wager than to decamp for the Continent. He started to sip his brandy, then set it down, perhaps remembering the folly of drinking too deep in his present company.

The Sprig assumed the role of barrister. "Now, Nicky, all I ask is that you tell us *why* you told Lady Venetia Lowther that you ain't Wincanton here."

There was a protracted pause while Nicky concentrated on the question. "Oh, lord, who knows," he finally said, sighing. He had already spent considerable time pondering that same conundrum without giving himself any satisfactory answer. So what hope had he of satisfying the Sprig? "Maybe I was just getting stale in the role. It does happen that way sometimes, you know." He squirmed a bit as St. Leger looked murderous. "Oh, the devil with it, then. I don't really know why. I collect it may have happened because I never could stand to see a female cry. Don't ask me to explain why that should be. For all of 'em are able to turn on their fountains at the slightest excuse. And it works with me every time. And, of course, the young and pretty ones are the worst when it comes to oversetting a chap. And the ones like Lady Venetia, who ain't usually prone to that sort of thing, really get under my skin. So I guess that's as close to a reason I can come up with for telling her who I really am. She was unhappy, and I wanted to make her feel

293

better. It didn't work," he concluded with more than a trace of bitterness. "But I wasn't to know that, was I?"

For the first time, Gareth Wincanton was looking fully at his impersonator. He studied Nicky's face intently while the actor contemplated the untouched liquid in his glass. The room was silent.

"Well, for God's sake, man." The Sprig was finally forced to act as prompter. "You've got to go on and tell us why Lady Venetia was crying and why the deuce knowing who you really are would make her stop it."

"No. I've not got to tell you anything." Nicky gave him a level look. "I may only be a Cit, but I don't discuss a lady's private affairs."

"But dammit, we've got to know if it had anything at all to do with Wincanton showing up here in Bath, and I still say it's bound to have. She must have thought about it and figured out what's what. Or somebody else saw him and told her who he was. That's likely, too. But one way or another, his being here is bound to have tipped the scales. And all I need is a little proof of that. Then I say the wager's null and void. And I'll take it up with the membership at Brooks' if I have to before I pay!"

"St. Leger, that's enough!" Major Gareth Wincanton, late of His Majesty's Household Brigade, was accustomed to instilling the fear of God into his army subalterns. It worked on civilians, too. The Sprig subsided. "The devil take your wager. I'm sick of hearing of it. You've made your point. I should never have come to Bath. More than that, I should never have agreed to the impersonation. But what's done's done. I'll pay off the damned bet. But on one condition—that you give me your solemn word, St. Leger, never to mention this business to anyone again, especially me."

"Oh, but I say!" Lord Piggot-Jones yelped in protest, leaping to his feet. "You can't do that. I won. Fair and square."

"Oh, stow it, Owen. I mean to pay you off, as well. Same conditions: forget that all this happened." Wincanton strode over to the writing table, found pen, ink, and paper, and scratched vigorously while the three men stared in silence. "Here." He thrust three sheets of paper into their hands. "Just present these to my banker. Now then, I trust we can consider this whole shoddy episode at an end."

St. Leger and Piggot-Jones glanced at their notes. Their eyes widened, and they quickly pocketed them. Nicky frowned down at his long enough to see that the major had actually increased the amount he would have won. A smile slowly lighted up his countenance, culminating in an impish grin. Then, while Wincanton watched with narrowed eyes, Nicholas Forbes, impoverished actor, ripped the paper in two with a broad, dramatic flourish. After that, unsatisfied with this piece of business, he went on to shred the sections into minute pieces and fling them in the air.

"Damned generous of you, but I'm afraid I can't take your blunt, old boy." He looked Wincanton steadily in the eye. "Don't seem right to take payment for playing such a shabby trick on two lovely ladies. Besides, I couldn't accept money for the best hospitality of my life. Not quite the thing, don't you know." His grin grew wider as the other dropped his gaze.

Nicholas Forbes clapped his stylish beaver perilously near one eyebrow and picked up his cane and gloves. As he paused in the doorway to break his exit, his bow was mocking. "Good day, *gentlemen*."

Edmund Kean, star of Drury Lane, could not have touched the irony Nicky packed into his final word.

Chapter Eighteen

NICKY EXITED THE WHITE HART, STILL LIMPING. THEN, AS it occurred to him that the encumbering bit of characterization was no longer needed, he stepped out jauntily, swinging his cane in an exaggerated rhythm with his steps. He even whistled a stirring marching tune.

His glow lasted all the way down Milsom to George Street before a reaction set in. The whistling slowed down, then trailed off altogether. His cane ceased to swing and rested in his arm crook. His step faltered. Before he knew it, he'd resumed his limp. Finally, he berated himself for a damned, quixotic fool.

What had come over him, anyhow? He had used to be so levelheaded, so accustomed to looking out for his own best interests. And now in the past two days he, a penniless, unemployed actor, had whistled a small fortune down the wind, not once but twice!

He could forgive himself the confession to Venetia. He had owed her that failed attempt to make amends. His eyes were tender as he recalled the feeling of her lips and the softness of her body that rainy day on the Paladian Bridge. But to tear up Wincanton's note! That was the height of folly. And why? All for a gesture. Just for the pleasure of watching that arrogant aristocrat for once in his life look disconcerted. He chuckled softly at the memory. Well, it had been worth something, at that. But not, by God, one thousand pounds. The chuckle ended in a curse.

Nicky had reached the Circus when Wincanton overtook him in his hired curricle. "Get in, Forbes. We have to talk."

And perhaps it was the discipline the army had instilled that caused Nicky to shrug and do so. Or perhaps he viewed the meeting as an opportunity to confess that on second thought he was now prepared to accept his share of the major's money. But the other didn't give Nicky time to sort this out. He flicked his reins and came right to the point.

"I think you'd best tell me why Venetia was crying before you made your confession. That is, if it had anything to do with me."

Nicky saw no reason not to pour out the whole story. After all, there was a kind of inevitability about the situation. It was always the toff who got the girl.

At the conclusion of the narrative, the major seemed to mull the matter over. Then, "That was a damned decent thing you did, Forbes," he said. Even Nicholas, who had at least a glimmer, could not fully imagine just what it cost Wincanton to make that admission.

"Well, that's as may be," the actor answered. "The thing is, you're by no means out of the suds. Oh, Lady Venetia loves you right enough. But she's sorted out that you—not me—were the one that offered Amabel carte blanche. That didn't exactly send her into raptures, you know.

"By the by, I think you'd better let me out here," he said just before they came in sight of the Crescent. "I don't like the notion of us being seen together. Lady Stoke's been damned decent, but no sense rubbing salt in the wound, I'd say."

"I agree." Wincanton pulled up the horses. Then, just as Nicky was about to say he'd changed his mind about taking the blunt, Wincanton said, "I'll not insult you again, Forbes, by offering you money. But I do want you to know I think you've behaved well through all of this, and I must say I'm sorry for my part in the whole, shameful affair."

Nicky sighed inwardly for the lost fortune as he jumped down from the rig. "Consider it forgotten." He managed to sound magnanimous. "Oh, but there is one other thing, Wincanton." He reached for a horse's bridle just as the other started to flick the reins. "About my . . . *sister*. I want you to know that if you ever come sniffing around Amabel again, it'll be bellows to mend with you, and no mistake. And you can take that promissory note to *my* banker."

Wincanton haughtily stared back at him for a moment. Then, to both his own surprise and Nicky's amazement, his face relaxed into a grin. "I don't happen to think you could mill me down in a million years, Forbes. But maybe it's just as well you'll never get the chance to try. I wouldn't wish to risk discovering that you're the better man. For I'll admit now that I've underestimated you all along.

"As for Amabel—you've no cause to worry. I plan to marry soon and be a good and faithful husband. So I doubt that you and I will be seeing each other again, which is just as well, given the mess we've made of things. But then perhaps it's a fitting punishment that we'll each always be just a little in love with the other's woman. Am I not right?" He looked quizzically at Nicky, who refused to rise to the bait but reddened nonetheless. "Well, there it is, then. Anyhow—actor—I wish you luck."

Wincanton cracked his whip, then turned his team in the road with a skill that brought a stab of envy to the other's breast. Nicky stood and watched as his erstwhile double dashed away down Lansdown Hill.

Wincanton champed at the bit for the next two hours, a time frame he'd arbitrarily chosen as sufficient for Nicholas to take leave of Lansdown Crescent. An inordinate amount of that time was spent upon the major's toilette. Perhaps it was the memory of the actor's bang-up-to-the-nines appearance that made him depart from his usual indifference to that sort of thing and discard five cravats before the waterfall arrangement that he strove for achieved perfection.

He arrived at Lady Stoke's front door, arrayed elegantly, if rather staidly (he regretted the bottle-green coat he'd given Forbes), in dark blue superfine and dove-gray trousers. When the butler opened the door in response to his knock, stared at him, and then looked puzzled, Wincanton was at a momentary loss as to how best to announce himself. Just as he'd feared, his "Major Wincanton to see Lady Venetia" caused Hope's jaw to drop. After that, it required a foot placed swiftly in the door to prevent its being slammed shut right in his face.

"It's all right, Hope. You may admit the major."

Lady Stoke, who'd been positioned at a window, had anticipated this sort of contretemps and thus hurried from her chamber, though not quite in time to forestall it. Now she stood mid-stairway, surveying her true nephew. "Well, it's easy enough to see how the impersonation business came about. Although I do believe the other one's . . . a bit taller."

"Better-looking, I collect, was what you meant to say." Wincanton handed his tall black hat to the bemused butler and moved toward her. "How are you, Aunt Louisa?"

Her eyebrows broke all previous records for elevation. "Your concern for my health comes tardily, Nephew. So you will understand if I ain't too touched by it. In fact, I'll tell you straight out, if I had anything to say in the matter, you'd be cut from my late husband's will."

"I can't say I blame you." He glanced back at the butler, who seemed rooted. "Could we go somewhere and have a private word?"

"Several. We'll have 'em in my bedchamber. Hope, you can go inform Lady Venetia that the other Major Wincanton has come calling."

Lady Stoke glanced back over her shoulder as her nephew followed. "My word, you even limp! I must say that Win— Oh, for heaven's sake, I can never remember that boy's real name!"

"Nicholas Forbes. Though I'm certain," he added dryly, "you'd have called him 'Nicky.' "

She chuckled as she motioned him to a chair in her cheerful, cluttered chamber and chose one opposite it for herself. "The actor's got your nose out of joint, then, has he? Well, I don't wonder at it. You're going to have a prodigious lot to live up to. Now then," she commanded, "let's hear your version of this farce."

Lady Stoke nodded with satisfaction when he'd concluded.

"Well, that's pretty well the same tale the other one told. With the same omissions, I daresay. Neither one of you has said just why you were so dead set on staying in London. Oh, I realize no one ever wants to visit relatives—especially in Bath—but to go to those lengths to avoid it? There was a female in it somewhere or I'm a Dutchman. But never mind that now. The question is, what do you intend to do about Venetia?"

"Marry her. If she'll have me."

She nodded wisely. "But you ain't too sure she will, now, are you? Well, good enough for you, I'd say. It's high time one of you Wincantons learned to eat humble pie." She stood up. "But I won't keep you any longer. Her room's third on the left down this hall. And in spite of the shabby trick you played on me, I wish you well." She giggled suddenly. "Do you know, this has all been better than a play. I don't know when I've been so diverted."

Wincanton walked over and kissed her on the cheek, astonishing himself for the second time that day. "You really are a sport, you know."

"Well, now"—she beamed—"that's more like it. You may have picked up a thing or two from the actor at that. But don't dawdle here, lad, practicing charm on me. Get on with your wooing." She gave him a push toward the door.

"Oh, I almost forgot." Wincanton reached in his coat and drew out a sheaf of bank notes. "I meant to ask if you'd do me a favor, Aunt Louisa. Well, not for me so much as for the 'charming actor.' Could you see to it that Forbes gets the money he would have collected if he'd won the bet? He threw the blunt back in my face when I offered to pay him earlier. But I expect he's had second thoughts by now. So if you don't mind, just let him believe it's from you. That'll save his pride."

Lady Stoke closed the bedchamber door rather noisily behind her nephew, counted a slow ten, then reopened it a tiny crack. Her ear was at that opening when Wincanton knocked on Lady Venetia's door. She heard a muffled "Who is it?" followed by a clearer "Go away! I don't wish to see you—ever," then winced for the destruction of her door as she heard a well-placed kick splinter the paneling. "Oh, well, it's a small price to pay to be rid of a companion," she told herself philosophically as she resumed her seat and picked up her neglected tambouring.

"Oh, it's you." Lady Venetia, reclining on a japanned couch, looked up with a stormy stare from the book she pretended to have been reading. "One never knows just whom the name Wincanton will produce. The only thing I am sure of is that I do not wish to see anyone of that name ever again. Now, will you please leave?"

He closed the damaged door to the extent of its capability and limped toward her. "No, I'll not go, Venetia, till I've said what I've come to say." He stood looking down at her, his heart in his eyes and misery etched upon his face. "I've never regretted anything so much as this deception I've been a party to. But despicable as that action was, if it causes me to lose you, all I can say is that the punishment far, far outweighs the crime. I love you, Venetia. I want to marry you. More than I've ever wanted anything in my entire life."

In spite of her hurt, her anger, her humiliation, his intensity was having its effect. But she was by no means ready to hoist the white flag of surrender yet. "Oh?" she answered coldly. "More than *anything*? Would that include two thousand pounds per annum and a house near Drury Lane? Those, I believe, are the terms of your arrangement with Miss Fawnhope."

"Oh, God," he groaned, and sat down on the couch at her feet. "I *have* no arrangement with Miss Fawnhope. Oh, I admit I made the offer. But that was before I met you, dammit. You're all I want. And I know now that you're all I ever wanted."

Lady Venetia was finding these words, coupled with his look of abject misery, immensely satisfactory. Still, she could not resist replying, "Your feelings do you credit, sir. Especially in light of the fact that Miss Fawnhope turned your offer down. Perhaps you are growing accustomed to rejection, Major Wincanton."

"The devil I am!" he retorted as he took her in her arms. "I'd better warn you now, Venetia. I've always gotten whatever I really wanted."

And as he kissed her hungrily, she faced the fact that in no way was she prepared to ruin his perfect record.

Chapter Nineteen

IT WAS TIME HE BROKE THE HABIT OF BEHAVING LIKE A TOFF, Nicky Forbes told himself as he glumly watched the waiter set out the supper that he'd ordered. He could ill afford the gesture of a private parlor in the White Hart. But then, he'd had no choice if he hoped to see Amabel alone. She did not have the status of a private dressing room at the Theatre Royal, and the old dragon she roomed with was not about to let a male— brother or no—into her nunnery at this hour of the night. And so he'd brought her to the hotel to say their good-byes.

"Don't look so Friday-faced, Nicky dear," Amabel said as the door closed behind the waiter and she helped herself liberally to asparagus and prawns. "I'll settle up the bill."

He looked offended. "You'll do nothing of the kind. I asked you here."

"Come off it, Nicky. It's me, not Lady Venetia. So now, tell me. What's this all about?"

"Do I have to have a reason now to see you, Bella?"

Damn, but he was testy. Though why the devil he should be taking it out on her was beyond him. "No, look, I'm sorry. You're right. There is a reason I asked you here. I'm leaving Bath tomorrow morning." He glanced at the clock on the mantel. The hands had moved past midnight. "This morning, I should say. I just wanted to say good-bye, that's all."

"Oh, Nicky, so soon? I had thought you had till—" She put down her fork and stared in consternation. "Oh, no! You've lost the bet, haven't you? They've found you out. And it's my fault. I know it is. I never should have cornered Lady Venetia that way. But I had no way of knowing— Oh, Nicky, how much did you lose? I'll help you pay."

His eyes misted just a bit, and he looked at her gratefully. She really was a brick! "That's damned decent of you, Bella. But it ain't necessary. The swells called the wager off. Since Wincanton came haring down here and muddied the waters, they didn't think the thing was fair." He'd concluded it was prudent not to mention it was his confession to Venetia that had really undone him. And he certainly was not going to let her know that he'd thrown Wincanton's money back in his teeth. Lord, Bella would screech the White Hart down around his ears if she knew that.

"Well, that's certainly a relief." Amabel picked her fork back up and attacked a prawn. "At least you're no worse off than you were," she added philosophically.

No worse off than he was? Nicky mulled the words over in his mind as he crumbled a roll to bits. He wished he could be quite sure of that.

Amabel watched him anxiously. "You didn't fall in love with Lady Venetia, did you, Nicky? I know you were betrothed, but I had thought it was to be just one of those marriage-of-convenience things. Oh, lord, Nicky, don't tell me your heart was engaged. I don't think I can bear it if you've been hurt by it all."

"No," he replied slowly, "I didn't fall in love with her. Oh, it wouldn't've been all that hard to do, you understand, but I didn't. Not as myself, at any rate. But there's something I have to tell you, Bella. Wincanton did. Fall in love with Lady Venetia, I mean. I am sorry."

He watched with horror as tears welled up into her eyes. "Oh, lord, Bella, I don't think I can bear it if *you've* been hurt by it all," he quoted as he handed one of Wincanton's fine linen handkerchiefs across the table.

She dabbed her eyes, streaking its snowy whiteness with leftover makeup, and gave Nicky a shaky smile. "We're really a pair, aren't we, Nicky dear?"

"Did you love him, Bella?" Why he kept asking that same question was beyond him. Perhaps he didn't believe the answers she'd made before.

"N-no. I don't suppose I ever really did. But oh, I wanted to marry him. I wanted it more than I've ever wanted anything in my life. I wanted to be a lady, Nicky. To live in a fine house. At a fine address. And be looked up to. That's what I wanted, Nicky. And Gareth could have given it to me. I wanted to be one of *them*."

"Did you, love?" He reached across the table and took her hand. "Well, I suppose the brotherly thing to do would be to say I'm sorry. But I ain't a bit of it. You see, I've had a taste of being one of them. And I won't say I didn't like a lot of it. Being waited on hand and foot, for instance. And being looked up to for nothing at all except for being wellborn. But when it comes right down to it, the business was beginning to get old. I was starting to get restless. I wanted to do something, not just be somebody, don't you know."

"I know you're lying in your teeth"—she smiled—"but I guess I have to admire your attitude. So what is it you plan to do, Nicky darling?"

"Oh, go to Cheltenham. Try to get on there. And if that don't work out, then it's on to Bristol. At least there's one thing I've learned from all this, Bella." There was pride in his voice. "And it's that I'm an actor. In spite of the nincompoop critics and Edmund Kean, I know it now. I played a marvelous toff, Bella. By George, I fooled the lot of 'em!"

"Bravo!" She disengaged her hand to lift her wineglass in salute.

"And do you know what I really want to do, Bella?" The words came tumbling out. "I decided it all back there when I thought I actually was going to win that curst bet and would have the capital. God knows how long it will take me now, but

I still mean to do it. I want to form my own company, Bella. Be an actor-manager. Shape my own destiny for a change, not be dependent on the whims of prima donnas like Kean—or on other managers. Besides"—he grinned—"I want to pocket the lion's share of the admission charges."

Amabel's eyes were glowing. "Oh, Nicky, how marvelous! Let's do it!"

"I beg your pardon?" He stared blankly at her.

"I said, let's do it. Now. This very minute. Why, we'd have no trouble at all getting together a first-rate company. And with me for leading lady," she added modestly, "you'd pack the house every night. Oh, Nicky! Our own company! I'd like it above all things."

"I don't know what's in that wine you're drinking, Bella, but I'd like a little more of it." He poured a generous amount of champagne into his glass. "You must've missed a bit of what I've been telling you. I didn't win the wager."

"Oh, I heard all that." She airily waved his financial problems away. "I'm quite prepared, however, to back our little venture."

"You!" He looked scornful. "I know Drury Lane has paid you rather well. And maybe you'll pick up a nice piece of change for your work here. But what I'm talking about will take real capital."

She tossed her head. "I know that. And I'm good for it."

"The devil you say. Where did you get your hands on that kind of blunt?"

"From Lord Desmond Keating's father."

"Bella, you didn't!"

"Of course I didn't." She glared. "You, of all people, should know better. What I did do, however, was to accept a bribe. No need to tell me, Nicky"—she set her jaw stubbornly—"that it wasn't the thing to do."

Such a preachment had not occurred to him. "How much?" he asked.

"A thousand pounds if I'd break off with his precious son, which, if he had but known it, I'd planned to do for nothing. But then I decided that the old goat owed me something for ripping my character to shreds. Why, he spent the better part of an hour raving on about how I was dragging his heir to ruin! How I wasn't good enough to be their parlormaid, let alone marry into their family. Well, coming on the heels of Wincanton's carte blanche offer, it was the outside of enough. So I let the old behemoth pay up."

"Good for you, Bella," he crowed.

"Amabel," she corrected him automatically. "So you see, Nicky, you can start your company right away. With me as your partner."

Controlling partner, he thought wryly. Bella was a born bear leader, and with her putting up the blunt—

She seemed to read his mind. "Oh, I promise I'll leave the business end entirely up to you. But I do wish to have a say in the artistic management. What plays to do, the casting—that sort of thing."

"Done!" A huge grin split his handsome face. Well, what the hell. It might not have been the dream the way he'd dreamed it, but it did have this advantage over the original version: it kept Bella by his side.

"There is one thing, though." Her eyes were downcast, her voice so low he had to strain to hear it. "I am quite determined, in spite of recent disappointments, to marry. No offense, Nicky dear, but I do not wish to lead the kind of life your mother led."

"I see." He really didn't, actually, for in retrospect his mother struck him as the happiest-natured person he'd ever known. But then, Amabel was different, always had been. "You ain't still thinking of marrying a toff, are you? Seems to me you might be a lot happier with some rich mill owner. He wouldn't be half so condescending."

"I don't want a mill owner."

"Oh, well, then"—he shrugged—"it's your life, Bella."

"It's you I mean to marry."

His jaw collided with his shirt points. "Me!"

"Yes, you. I've done a lot of thinking, Nicky, and I've come to accept the fact that you're the only man I've ever truly loved or ever will. I had thought I could make do with Wincanton. He always did remind me of you, you know. But now I realize that it would never have done for me. It's you I want, Nicky. And I've been trying to think of a way I could have you and the kind of life I'd like to lead as well. And you've hit on it. Our company. We can make our own fortune. Oh, Nicky, dearest, don't look so stunned. It will be the very thing."

By George, it could be, at that! Here he'd been lusting after Bella for donkey's years, but since she was so determined to marry above her station, the idea of their becoming leg-shackled had never occurred to him.

She watched his expression slowly change from dazed incredulity to a tenuous acceptance of the notion. "Oh, Nicky, you goose!" She jumped up and ran around the table to throw herself into his arms. His expression switched instantly to lecherous.

"Bella, you've got a vicious cruel streak in your nature," he protested some minutes later when she pulled away from him. "No need to be so missish, love. We're betrothed, in case you've somehow forgotten."

"I've not forgotten. And I don't intend to consummate my marriage here on the floor of the White Hart."

"The couch, then?" he asked hopefully.

"No, Nicky dearest." She was on her feet and tidying her hair before the convex glass that adorned the wall, and her eyes grew misty. "Oh, Nicky, I've dreamed of a proper wedding, with a white lace dress, and flowers in my hair. I want to be married at St. Paul's. And I want the world to come. Do you mind all that too much, Nicky dear?"

He walked up behind her and wrapped her in his arms. The glass reflected the tender look he gave her and held it for a moment like a portrait enclosed by a gilt wood frame. "No, I don't mind. We'll say our vows perched on the dome if that's what you want, Bella. For all I want is to be with you always and to try to make you happy."

The words had no sooner left his mouth than he realized to his amazement that they were true.

Its passengers were about to board the London coach next morning when the clatter of hooves and the sound of a speeding carriage caused the heads in the queue to turn. " 'Old up there, guv'nor!" came a shout, and Nicky groaned as he recognized Lady Stoke's barouche with Jocko Hodges, dressed in spanking-new livery, holding the reins. "Hey, actor! I've a parcel for you. But you'd best come get it, for I can't leave me cattle." The tiger grinned impudently as his horses champed at their bits, impatient at being forced to stand stock-still again just as they'd hit their stride.

Nicky cursed under his breath but walked over to the equipage, Amabel trailing curiously behind.

The tiger's eyes grew wide at the sight of the gorgeous actress dressed in a modish mauve pelisse and bonnet. He whistled appreciatively. "You are the one for landing on your feet, I must say, guv."

"You show a little respect for my fiancée." Nicky's expression evidently betrayed his impulse to jerk Jocko off the seat and shake him like a rag, for the tiger hastened to say, "No offense meant, guv. But lor', the lady's a treat to look at, and there's a fact." Amabel dimpled up at him, and his grin returned.

"You said you have something for me." Nicky spoke impatiently. "Well, then, what is it?"

"It's a parcel from me employer, Lady Stoke. Thought you'd be interested to know I've quit me old employer. His Major Wincanton performance fell short of yours, you see, guv. Too dull by half, he was."

"What you mean is that he sacked you." Nicky caught the brown paper parcel Jocko tossed him.

"Our parting was by way of a mutual agreement," the other retorted. "I've no desire to return to Lunnon. I find more scope for me particular talents here in Bath. But that's all by the by. Anyhow, Lady Stoke says to tell you she misses you already and wishes you to have this parting gift. Be seeing you, guv. Ma'am." He tipped his hat saucily to Amabel, then sprang the horses.

"What an odd little man," she observed, but Nicky was too stunned to hear her. He was leafing through the packet of bank notes in his hand. "A thousand pounds," he breathed. "Louisa has sent me a thousand pounds!" His share of the bet! She'd actually made good his share of the bet! He broke into a radiant smile as it dawned upon him that he could now match Bella's capital in their new venture. She was a darling girl, of course, but it was just as well that they'd not begin their married life with her having the upper hand.

Amabel's eyes were big as cartwheels. "Lady Stoke made you a present of a thousand pounds?" she gasped as he retied the bundle and tucked it in his pocket. "Whatever for?" Her expression changed suddenly to outraged shock. "Nicholas! Surely not! That old lady! You wouldn't have! Or would you?"

"Hurry, Bella. They're about to leave." He took her hand and broke into a run.

But after he'd tossed her up onto the roof seat of the crowded coach and climbed up beside her, she reopened the subject. "Aren't you going to explain just why Lady Stoke sent you all that money?" she asked him.

"No, I don't think I am, Bella my love." He grinned. "For it wouldn't be at all the thing to my way of thinking. Not quite *gentlemanly*, you see."

On sale now!

She is determined to reclaim her cherished family
estate at any cost. . . .

THE ROMANCE

The Fifth Volume of
THE DAUGHTERS OF
MANNERLING
by Marion Chesney

After seeing four of her sisters marry for love rather
than to reclaim their home, Belinda Beverley is certain that she can woo and wed the foppish Lord St.
Clair, the current holder of the estate. And her plan
seems to be working until the dashing Lord Gyre
enters the picture and decides he wants the lovely
Belinda all for himself. . . .

Published by Fawcett Books.
Available in bookstores everywhere.

Take a walk on the wild side with . . .

SUGAR ANNE
by Jan Hudson

A furious, feisty, and ferociously determined Sugar Anne has just learned that her husband has skipped town with her silver, her jewelry, the town floozy, and the money he has swindled from investors in a new railroad line. Suspected of duplicity in her husband's crime and mad enough to spit nails, Sugar Anne sets off in hot pursuit of him while being pursued herself by Webb McQuillan, a dashing Texas Ranger. As this twosome embarks on a wild chase through the South, a forbidden passion begins to grow. Entangled in a web of deceit and betrayal, can this love survive a zany and treacherous treasure hunt that might just put the lawman and his suspect on opposite sides of the law?

Now on sale!

ANGEL
IN MARBLE

by beloved *New York Times* bestselling author

Elaine Coffman

Tibbie Buchanan was a heavenly beauty with a
dark past. Once she'd loved a man who'd ruined
her. Now a gifted healer and herbalist, she swore
she'd never surrender to passion again. Then Nick
Mackinnon swept into town. Orphaned at an early
age, Nick had made a fortune in shipbuilding, but
now he wanted to build a better life for himself.
The moment he set eyes on the ravishing Tibbie, he
vowed he would have her heart and soul. But, ever
mindful of her painful past, Tibbie would flee from
love and the man who ached to free her. . . .

Published by Fawcett Books.
Available wherever books are sold.

All the romance, intrigue, and passion
you have come to expect from

ELAINE COFFMAN

Look for all these titles wherever books are sold.

ESCAPE NOT MY LOVE
A U.S. Deputy Marshal never encountered a prisoner he could
not tame until a beautiful schoolteacher crossed his path and led
him on a wild chase from the deserts of the Southwest to the gen-
teel drawing rooms of Savannah. Ruled by a fierce passion, this
lawmaker will learn important lessons about the redeeming
power of love.

HEAVEN KNOWS
An impish young girl leaves her home on Nantucket and returns
years later a beautiful and accomplished young woman. When
she catches the eye of the most eligible bachelor on the island,
their passions flare. Then an ugly betrayal threatens to destroy a
love they thought would last forever. . . .

IF YOU LOVE ME
A young woman torn from her birth family and raised as an
Indian captive . . . A dashing young Englishman bent on adventure and throwing off the obligations of his age-old title . . . A
chance encounter will alter their lives forever, but fate will tear
them apart. Can their love flourish despite his foolish choices and
her deeply held feelings of betrayal?

SO THIS IS LOVE
Out of desperation, a widow alone in the world with three children to raise agrees to marry a man she has never met. The man,
a California timber baron, wants to create a dynasty, and he
thinks he does not want love until his new bride turns his world
upside down. . . .

A TIME FOR ROSES
When a Russian orphan adrift in Regency England encounters a
troubled English nobleman, passions and wits ignite. Their tur-
bulent romance is the talk of the town, but secrets and intrigue
threaten to capsize this stormy love affair.

Published by Fawcett Books.